OPERALAND

Ian Strasfogel

Musico Press
New York

ISBN 978-1-09832-308-0 eBook 978-1-09832-309-7

PROLOGUE

Roderick

Naturally, I detested being in Calgary, and for *Madame Butterfly*, of all things, but Covent Garden had canceled my next production, I needed the money, and it was only three weeks of my time.

Only. The production landed me squarely in the frozen core of the Canadian winter. Mind-numbing blizzards howled down the blank Calgary sidewalks, forcing everyone to take cover in the heated walkways that linked the downtown office buildings in a stiff embrace of steel and glass.

If you're an opera director like myself and merely doing a show to shore up shaky finances, then all you're really looking for is ease of execution. You're not planning to make history; you're not challenging the sainted legacies of Stanislavsky or Giorgio Strehler; all you want is to fatten your bank account and catch up on your sleep. I barely slept a wink in Calgary.

It began harmlessly enough. I was changing planes in Toronto when I saw a telltale blue score clutched under the arm of an overweight gentleman lining up for my flight. *Lord, don't let him be my leading man, that seductive devil Pinkerton.* Needless to say, that's precisely who he was.

Despite my misgivings, I waved my score at the unsexy little man, and disguised my forebodings with some well-worn politesse. "Do we have a match?" I asked.

He took one look at my score and exclaimed, "Whaddya know, Joe!"

Naturally, I was startled. "And who, may I ask, is Joe?"

"It's just an expression, no big deal." He extended his pudgy hand. "Hi, Richie Verdun, pleased to meet you. What part are you singing?"

I explained I was his director, Roderick Cranbrook.

"Oops, sorry, guess I should have known, but I'm pretty new at this game."

An understatement, if ever there was one. When the company had warned me that my Pinkerton would be a newcomer, I assumed they meant some smart young lad fresh out of Juilliard. In point of fact, the man flying with me to Calgary had never been to Juilliard, indeed, he'd barely heard of it. He evidently had been selling cars in the vast wasteland of the American Midwest and somehow or other convinced the good people of Calgary that he was the Pinkerton of their dreams. How or why, I'll never understand. Singers normally start working professionally in their twenties, mid-thirties at the very latest. Here was Richard, well into middle age, coming straight out of nowhere to make his operatic debut as nothing less than the leading tenor in *Madame Butterfly*. I'd never heard of anything remotely comparable.

His chances weren't good. Opera is a special culture. Mastering it takes time, a great deal of time, especially for tenors, who usually are slower to develop than the others. It didn't help that Richard looked impossibly out of place, traveling to his first engagement as a leading tenor clad in strip-mall attire, baggy chino pants, ill-fitting lumberjack shirt, a floppy brown parka that clashed with his jaunty blue baseball cap. True, it was 1983, and men's fashion back then was often timid or stodgy. But the poor fellow seemed blissfully unaware that opera's all about magic, elegance, eloquence. It's the antithesis of ordinary, the polar opposite of drab.

Not that he was vulgar, mind you. He was actually quite agreeable, charming even, in that hapless, harmless American manner that seems to beg incessantly for your affection. I'm British and normally cannot abide such fraudulent nonsense. We all know Americans are just as cutthroat and self-serving as anyone else, possibly even more so, but Richard seemed decent enough underneath all that cultural camouflage, genuinely modest and unthreatening. Almost absurdly eager to please.

When we met at the airport, he was quite anxious about rehearsals. Atypically for me, I felt touched by his insecurity and resolved to feed him an oversized helping of mush: *he shouldn't worry; he'd have a wonderful time; it was just a gathering of friends; Puccini was our god, we all strove to serve him.*

After hearing my little sales pitch, Richard moved in so close that his round, balding head very nearly touched mine. "Roderick, are you shitting me?" He looked like a crazed court jester, Rigoletto's wayward younger brother.

"Richard, I assure you I'm not *shitting you*, as you so charmingly put it. I am just trying in my no doubt inadequate way to put you at your ease. We're all in this together."

"Well, good, I'll give it all I got."

He'd have to give plenty. His Butterfly, Polyna Ostrovsky, was an unrelenting trial. Her husband, Egon Kleinhaus, was hardly less so and he would be in the pit, molding, or, more likely, distorting the performance. Big houses wouldn't hire him – he had none of his wife's considerable ability – but provincial theaters had no choice. If they wanted *La Polyna*, Egon came *mit.* All in all, a less charming, more difficult couple would be hard to find, even in the contentious little world of opera.

I'll never forget the look on Polyna's face when Richard ambled into that first rehearsal, smiling his weak little smile. She turned to me and asked, *sotto voce*, "Is that the janitor? Just kidding, *mon cher.*" I had explained in advance that Richard was *sui generis.* His voice was exceptional – everyone was excited about his future – but those of us who had the benefit of experience would have to be patient and help him along a bit. She professed the greatest willingness to be of service. "*Caro* Roderick, when have I ever refused anyone help?" I smiled politely and changed the subject.

As Richard plodded towards us, Polyna's voice glittered through the gloom of the rehearsal room. "*Eccolo, il grande amore della mia vita.*"

"Sorry?" This produced considerable tittering at the outer edges of the room. Our leading tenor clearly had no Italian at all.

That was the least of his problems. As the long day wore on, it soon became clear that Richard was an absolute, abject beginner, greener than grass, greener than limes, greener than broccoli. The simple instructions "stage right" and "stage left" confused him utterly. I would constantly remind him that stage right referred to the audience's left, regardless of where he might be. He would nod eagerly and then troop off in the wrong direction. He had no concept of natural, relaxed acting. Indeed, his crude posturing hardly qualified as acting at all. As for his basic stage deportment, he slouched about like a browbeaten family retainer or a hapless bystander who had stumbled onto the scene, except for sudden bursts of oddly robotic strutting, as if some mechanical being had taken command of his tubby little body.

His singing, on the other hand, was healthy and in tune. It didn't have a trace of the Italianate warmth and beauty Puccini's music really requires, but it certainly was hearty, so hearty that it sometimes obliterated Polyna's lovely but febrile sound. She didn't find this amusing, so in no time her husband, he of the long baton and short temper, was barking at Richard to sing more softly. This Richard couldn't, or wouldn't, do, which greatly increased the exasperation of the Ostrovsky-Kleinhaus axis. For my part, I felt that while Richard may have been inartistic at times – almost cloddish – he had a clear vocal presence and in opera that certainly counts for something.

Clear voiced or not, Richard was profoundly unready for an important debut. Everyone at that dismal first rehearsal was painfully aware of it, except for dear dim Richard himself. He ignored or didn't catch the increasingly exasperated grimaces people kept flashing in my direction. Instead, he played the earnest schoolboy, eager to learn, willing to change, grateful for any chance to repeat a difficult passage, amazed by our kind indulgence of his many deficiencies.

As the rehearsal finally shuddered to its end, Egon took me aside and said, "This tenor is utterly impossible."

"He's raw. He's untrained. I'll give him some private coaching."

"This will not help."

"I'm rather clever, you know. I think I can reduce some of his more grievous excesses."

"And the missed entrances, the lack of subtlety? What can you do about that?"

"I rather thought that was your department, Egon."

"*Na ja*, but this man is so unmusical he doesn't even keep the tempo." Neither did Egon, but I chose not to mention it.

"Come, come, it's just a first rehearsal. Give him a chance; he'll improve."

"Never in a million years, never in all eternity."

"*Lieber Egon*, where's your native optimism?"

"I don't have any. I'm Viennese." I may not have liked his awkward conducting, but I did rather enjoy his curdled sense of humor. I repeated that we really had to give the poor man a proper chance. Egon looked skeptical and Polyna, who had been hanging on our every word, started to wax poetic about her last *Butterfly* in Brussels where she was partnered by a gorgeous young Mexican, Jorge Alvarado, six feet tall, not yet thirty, with a voice as warm as the Neapolitan sun. "That's all well and good, *cara*," I said. "But it's only our first rehearsal."

"Another one like this and we're going," she replied.

"Going, as in canceling, leaving the show? What about your contracts?"

"We didn't sign on for amateur night. I can't be expected to rehearse myself to death just to humor some shoe salesman."

"Cars, actually. He sells cars."

"That's even worse. He pollutes that way the atmosphere," said Egon. "He has absolutely no place in opera."

"Egon, we really have got to be patient."

"*Warum*?"

"Signed contracts for one thing. Besides, Richard did seem to get a bit better near the end of rehearsal."

"Better doesn't always mean good," replied Polyna.

"If you really feel that way, you should speak to management now, while there's still time to find a replacement."

"*Ach*, that idiot Jennings, he doesn't understand anything." Egon had a point. Roger Jennings was hired as director of the Calgary Opera because he had helped a local grain storage company turn a profit. The board of trustees in their infinite wisdom thought he might do the same for the opera. They were soon disabused of that notion and stuck with a mediocre manager. "I worry that we bring this up with Jennings," said Egon. "He finds us someone worse."

"That's a real possibility, alas."

"So, what do we do?" asked Polyna.

"How about this? We'll focus on act two for the next few days, which doesn't require the tenor, while I give Richard some intensive private coaching. Who knows? Maybe magic will strike."

"Or maybe not," said Polyna.

The prospect of private sessions with Richard filled me with dread. How on earth was I going to turn a bumbling middle-aged man into even a faint approximation of Puccini's young lover?

Richard resisted me every step of the way, not because he was arrogant or bloody minded, but because he was totally untrained. He had taken only singing and music lessons, not acting, not stage movement. And acting, easy as it might appear to the uninitiated, is a complex, evanescent discipline. It can't be mastered overnight. I tried to convince Richard that acting was basically reacting, that all an actor really had to do was lose himself in the given situation and respond naturally to it, but that was beyond him. He kept reverting to posing and posturing. I longed – ached – for a brief instant of credible, lifelike behavior. In vain, alas, utterly in vain.

Into my slough of despond, there did flicker a few feeble beams of light. Richard took rather well to practical tips. He could follow clear and simple instructions, as long as they stayed far away from such intangibles as "credible, lifelike behavior." I got him to stop singing into the wings. He learned to angle himself so he seemed to be addressing his partner while projecting out to the public. He even abandoned those bewildering outbursts of robotic activity. After three days of hard work, he seemed a bit less raw and out of place. Was he an ardent young lover? Was he a convincing Pinkerton? Far from it.

I had arranged to stage Richard's third act aria on his return to regular rehearsals so as to keep Richard and Polyna apart a bit longer. While my cunning little plan avoided direct interaction with the dreaded diva herself, her husband was on hand and in excellent form. Within a short time, Richard's musical insecurities brought everything to a standstill.

"*Nein, nein, nein.* You are always coming in late."

"Maestro, sorry, but I couldn't see my cue."

"Just count and come in automatic."

"I did."

"Then you count wrong. Come, we try again."

Yet once more Richard struggled to master his (very simple) entrance. Once more he failed. Once more Egon did what he does best.

"*Nein, nein, nein*! I have of this enough." With that, he slammed down his score and shot me a dark look. "I wait for you outside." The air in the rehearsal room grew noticeably thicker as he stamped out and slammed the door.

I put the company on break and followed Egon into the hallway. He was quite literally shaking with rage. "I tell you this man is impossible."

"Maybe it would help if you gave him clearer cues."

"I give him the cues. He does not look."

"The last few times you didn't give him anything."

"What is the use? He looks but does not see. I go now to this Roger fellow. I have of the tenor enough. You come with me?"

"I have no alternative." Despite my earnest instructions, Richard remained raw and unfocused. I wasn't running an opera training program; I was staging *Madame Butterfly*. Enough! *Basta con questa pasta*!

Roger Jennings nervously greeted us at his door and ushered us into an unpretentious little office, as plain and bleak as the prairies. There was nothing on the walls to indicate he ran an opera company, no pictures of singers or composers, just some snapshots of the broad rolling farmlands of central Canada.

"I gather you've been having some problems with the tenor."

"That's rather an understatement," I said.

"I don't get it. He gave me a great audition. He sang the hell outta his aria."

"Just now we rehearse it. He comes in wrong every time. He is total impossible."

"I'm sorry to hear it."

"Not as sorry as we are," I said. Roger looked away and started toying with some pencils on his desk.

"There is here really a problem," said Egon.

"A very serious one," I added.

"But we have already the solution."

"We do?" I asked. Evidently Egon and La Polyna had not been idle these past few days.

"*Jawohl.* This wonderful Mexican tenor Jorge Alvarado has sung Pinkerton many times already in Spain and Italy. He is free for the performances."

"What about rehearsals?" I asked. I had been down that dark road before. A lead is indisposed and a replacement rushes in to save the show, thereby destroying the director's conception, since there isn't time for adequate rehearsal.

"*Nein, nein*, I think of you, Roderick, very carefully. He can be here the beginning of next week." That would give us two full weeks together – more than time enough. I'd heard nice things about Signor Alvarado and not just from the Ostrovsky-Kleinhaus mafia. It seemed our problem was solved.

"Well, I don't know," said Roger. "It sounds like a pretty expensive proposition." What else do managers ever say?

"This you decide for yourself," said Egon, "But Madame Ostrovsky and I will not work with this nincompoop. If you do not replace him, we pack our bags and go home."

"But you signed your contracts."

"Sorry, we do not come to Calgary to make a joke."

I must say I was rather impressed. It's true they had signed contracts, but opera isn't a business. It's art, or something rather like it.

Trapped in his seat of power, Roger struggled with Egon's threat. A new Butterfly, especially one of Polyna's stature, would be extremely difficult to find at this late date.

Egon kept admirably calm as Roger squirmed. "Here are the contacts for Alvarado's agent," he said. "This Verdun is a nice fellow, but Puccini comes first."

Roger still said nothing. Clearly, he'd never faced this sort of crisis before. Another beginner. Lord, would we ever get this show on stage?

Finally, Roger spoke. "What'll I tell my board?" The only relationship that ever really matters to a manager, especially in North America, is the one with his employers. Forget Puccini. Forget Mozart. The board must be indulged at all costs.

"Tell them the tenor is indisposed. We make a brilliant replacement," said Egon.

"But he's not sick at all." Good lord, didn't the man know anything?

"Roger, it's the graceful way out," I explained. "It's the best way for everyone to save face."

"While I wind up spending thousands of extra dollars."

"You want to save money, go to the supermarket," Egon snarled.

"Well, let me think about it."

"No. 'If it were done when 'tis done, then 'twere well it were done quickly.'" Roger obviously didn't get the allusion. "It's now or never. Time to decide. We've got artists downstairs waiting to rehearse. I won't playact with them. Neither will Egon."

"*Jawohl*," said Egon, "We cannot wait with this. It is too important."

"What if I have trouble with Alvarado's agent? Once those guys hear you're in a jam, they screw you."

"Then we'll find someone else," I said.

"Whoever we get, he won't have a big voice like Richard." Roger seemed genuinely sorry to be losing him.

There was another sizable pause as Roger grappled further with the problem. He desperately wanted it to go away, but we wouldn't let it, not for one second. Once again, I wondered why so many spineless types end up as opera managers.

"All right," said Roger, "I'll call Alvarado's manager. He's in Madrid, so I won't be able to get to him till tomorrow."

"But Richard must be told today," I noted. "Right this very minute."

"Roderick, I've got a million things to do."

"So do I, or we won't have a production at all." I sensed that Roger needed extra encouragement, so I turned to Egon and said, "Why don't you tell the cast we'll reconvene around two, while I settle things up here with Roger?"

"Thank you, Roger. You will not regret this," Egon said.

Once Egon had left, Roger got wobbly. "You really think I should do this?"

"Yes. It's in the best interest of the show."

"If you say so. But you've got to be the guy who breaks it to him."

"Now, see here, I didn't hire him. You did."

"But you're so good with people. He won't even realize he's been sacked."

"Sorry, but I couldn't possibly."

Roger locked eyes with me in a sudden, startling demonstration of will power. "This is a deal breaker. If you want this guy out, you lower the boom yourself."

"Now, just a second. Egon's unhappier with Richard than I am. Have him do it."

"Not on your life. He'll say something stupid and get us into all kinds of trouble."

"Who's to say I won't?"

Roger's gaze hardened. His eyes blazed with force and determination. "No more dithering. Just go out and do it." Well, well, what a surprise. If Roger Jennings really wanted something, his spine could be ringed round with steel.

I found our tenor in the rehearsal room, compulsively pounding out the section of his aria that had proved so problematic. His powerful voice rang out repeatedly, in tune and on time. Why couldn't he have done it when it really mattered?

Richard looked up as I neared him. "That's right, isn't it?"

"It is."

"That's how I learned it. That's how I've always done it, but Egon keeps speeding up on me."

"He does?"

"You bet. His hands flop around like a giant Mixmaster and, before I know it, he's changed tempo."

"Surely not."

"Look, I'm the poor sucker dealing with him and I tell you he keeps hopping around like a..." Richard stopped and studied me a bit. "Hey, what's wrong? Is something eating you?"

"Richard, we've got to talk."

"No problem. Sit down. Take a load off." We settled ourselves at a rickety table littered with half-empty water bottles and stray rehearsal schedules. I wanted to start, but found it curiously difficult. There was this round gentleman, at least ten years my senior, lolling on his chair, absurdly ignorant of the blow that would shortly flatten him. I'd fired people before. I was acquainted with the awkward formalities, but Richard's innocence – or blindness, or complete and utter stupidity – robbed me of speech. As I struggled to find the right way to broach the matter, Richard leaned forward and asked, "What's the matter, man? Cat got your tongue?"

"Well, actually, Egon and I have been..."

Richard, fool that he was, plunged into the Stygian depths. "God, that guy. I try my best, but he just hollers and howls at me. It drives me totally bananas. I mean, it's not his fault he's German, but still..."

"Actually, he's from Vienna."

"You know what I mean. He gets upset over nothing and wastes our valuable time."

"Richard, the conductor is always right."

"Except when he's wrong."

"Egon's certainly not wrong in your case."

"What the hell does that mean?"

"It pains me to say this, but I'm afraid we're going to have to replace you."

"Replace me?"

"You can't be all that surprised," I said. "Things haven't been going well. You're upset. Egon's upset. I'm upset. It's best for everyone."

His face was frozen in shock. Surely, he must have sensed the catastrophe lurking round the corner.

"Now look, it's really not as bad as all that," I continued. "We're determined to handle it in a considerate and forbearing manner, so as not to harm your chances elsewhere. We'll just tell everyone you've taken ill. The cold up here is a perennial problem. No one will question it. You'll receive your full fee, go back home and work with your teacher, and then, with any luck at all, you can start out again on a more promising, less problematic path." Pale, drained of color, his face retained its hurt, astonished expression.

"Polyna," he finally said. "She's always had it in for me."

"It's got nothing to do with her."

"Oh, come on, just because I'm not part of your tight arty group, you think I don't know what's what? This is her work. It's got her sweaty fingerprints all over it."

"Blaming others doesn't strike me as very helpful."

"What is? Packing my bags? Clearing outta here, tail between my legs?"

"That's not how I'd characterize it."

He wagged his head from side to side. "You really let me down, man. I thought you were on my side. I thought you really cared."

"I do care, but I care even more about the show. We're obliged to give the public the best *Butterfly* we can."

"Fair or unfair. Right or wrong."

"Richard, be reasonable; you're just starting out."

"Yeah, but I'm no spring chicken."

"Whatever your age, it's simply too early for you to be doing something this exposed. It's wrong for you and wrong for the show."

"Why didn't you warn me? Why didn't you just say my ass was on the line?"

"I tried, but you never..."

"*It's nice. It's getting better. You can do it.* That's all I ever got from you, sweet talk, la la land. You never once told me the truth."

"Sorry, I rather thought I had."

"Right, sure." He turned away. His shoulders drooped; his head hung down. It was a painful minute or so before he asked in a pale, plaintive voice, "You got kids, Roderick?"

"I'd have thought my sexual orientation would have been clear to you by now."

"Doesn't stop a guy from having kids. We had a nice married fella out on the lot with two teenage boys. At age forty-five, he saw some young dude cruising down the street and that was it."

"Sorry, but I fail to see the point."

"Kids are the point, kids. They look up to you all their lives. You're their Dad, their hero, their star, then, wham!"

"Good lord, man, it's nowhere as drastic as that."

"The hell it isn't. I finally get to the majors and lose the whole damn game."

"You haven't lost a thing."

"My kids' respect, their belief."

"Don't exaggerate, Richard; you aren't going to lose anything at all."

When he spoke again, it was in his earlier, more plaintive tone, which seemed in curious contrast to his almost brutal singing. "Carol, she's my oldest, you know what she did when she heard I got this job? She went and bought herself a ticket to fly out here for the premiere. She's just started living on her own and every penny counts but her old man's dreams mean so much to her that she just had to make the sacrifice. The boys are busy with school and my wife Kit hates flying, so the only one coming out is Carol. Or was. Sure hope she can cash in that ticket." He slumped back in his chair.

"Well if there's really a problem, I'll see if the company will cover it."

"It's not about the money!" We shared a tense few moments before his anger subsided. "Sorry, just feeling kinda emotional."

It was at exactly this moment that Polyna danced – no, twirled – into the rehearsal room. "My mistake," she said, "I was looking for a place to vocalize."

"Give us a few minutes," I said. "We're just finishing up."

"Of course, *caro*, of course. Sorry to interrupt." And with that, she duly danced her way out again, barely disguising her delight at seeing Richard downcast before me.

After another prolonged silence, Richard started in again, even more quietly than before. "You know why I did all this, why I went through hell and high water to train and condition myself so I could finally make it in Operaland? My kids. They believed in me. They sat me down and convinced me to give up my job and take the plunge. They went, 'You worked like a dog year after year selling cars. Do something you want, something you really love. Go out there and be a star tenor.'"

"You mean to tell me this whole thing was your children's idea?'

"And my wife too, of course. They're behind me, man, one hundred percent, and now you're asking me to go back home, tail between my legs, and hand them some crap about getting sick. How can I do that? How can you ask me to piss away my dreams after all their love and encouragement?" How small and sad he looked at that moment. How defenseless. Finally, a new mood came over him. He stiffened up and raised his gaze until he was staring straight at me. "My family's right, you know. I *can* sing. Give me one more chance and I promise I'll give you one hell of a Pinkerton, I really and truly will."

I rather doubted it, but he'd gotten through to me somehow, that curious fireplug of a man. Despite my seeming rationality, I do work in the opera. I've got this soft spot, this Dickensian weakness for sob stories and tearjerkers. I was staging Puccini, for heaven's sake! And so, against my better judgment and with considerable wariness, I became Richard's advocate.

Roger Jennings was delighted. He was spared the tedium of hiring a replacement (and paying an extra fee) and avoided the indignity of explaining everything to his board. Egon and La Polyna were less amused. Much as I suspected, however, they weren't really ready to give up their handsome double fee. Instead, they did their best to make rehearsals extremely tiresome, with numerous demands from *la Diva* and the occasional choleric outburst from the *Kapellmeister*.

Opening night belonged to Polyna, of course; *Madame Butterfly* is always the exclusive property of its leading lady. As for Richard, well, he sounded healthy and didn't bumble about as much as I had feared he would. Luckily for him, the public in Calgary proved extremely tolerant. No one laughed or threw rotten tomatoes. Even the press was fairly kind. It certainly didn't count as "one hell of a Pinkerton," but it wasn't disastrous either.

As the bows drew to a close, Richard jogged over and engulfed me in a sweaty bear hug. Like most neophytes, he still was in the throes of opening night nerves. "I hope I didn't mess up too bad. I kinda got lost in that final exit."

"I doubt anyone noticed," I said and attempted to extricate myself.

He was unwilling to let me go. "Man, I really gotta thank you for getting me through it."

"Nonsense," I replied. "You were the one who was out there. Keep working that way and all will be well." In fact, his case was so unlikely, his talents so idiosyncratic, I couldn't possibly predict with any certainty what the larger operatic community might make of him. All I felt at that moment was relief. Somehow or other, we got through it. I could collect my fee and go home.

My thoughts were interrupted by a sudden shout from Richard: "Carol!" He set me free and rushed over to embrace a tall, gangling young woman who seemed stunned by all the backstage clamor and confusion. He dragged her over. "This is the girl I've been telling you about," he said, "Carol, my oldest."

We shared some pleasantries and shook hands. I was startled by her damp palms and uncertain air, not to mention her unfortunate attire – a polyester pantsuit in a dangerously electric cerise. "Now, you be nice to her, Roderick; she's my biggest supporter."

"Oh, Daddy, come on." At that moment, Richard was waylaid by an exuberant trustee and I was left to chat with her on my own. I asked how she liked seeing her father on stage.

"Oh, it was great. I'm just so proud of him."

"I can imagine."

"Can I tell you a little secret?"

"By all means."

"I never really saw an opera before."

"You're a lucky woman." Carol seemed shocked. "Just being clever, my dear. Pay no heed."

"Daddy told me you helped him a lot."

"One does what one can."

"No, no," she said, "You were really great, him being so inexperienced and all."

"It was my pleasure."

"Can I ask a silly question?"

"Ask away."

"Daddy's pretty good at this, isn't he?"

I was a model of tact and discretion. "Yes, he most certainly is."

"Do you think he's going to get famous?"

"Is that important?"

"To him it is. He always wants to be best at everything. He'd get sore at my brothers if they beat him in just about anything."

"What about you?"

"I'm the girl in the family. I didn't have to shoot hoops with him. I guess I was kinda lucky, huh?" There was a small pause while we studied each other from opposite sides of the moon. "But you still haven't told me if you think Daddy is going to become famous."

"I've really no idea. These things normally take quite a bit of time. If he does get famous, he'll have you flying all over the globe." I've no idea why I chose something so trivial; I must have wanted in some small way to impress her.

"He will?"

"That's what opera singers do. They fly from country to country to make their careers."

"Gosh, I don't know how often I could take off from work. I was pretty lucky my boss let me fly out here." Our conversation soon dwindled to a close. I felt terribly embarrassed for the poor girl, mixing so uneasily with the cognoscenti. She really had no idea of the life her father sought for himself.

I wondered if Richard did either.

PART ONE

LEAVING GRAYSTONE

CHAPTER ONE

Richie

The first thing you gotta understand is I've been singing, really singing, ever since I was a toddler. I was a leading pint-sized interpreter of such all-time greats as *The wheels on the bus* and *Baa, baa, black sheep* and *Here we go round the mulberry bush.* I'd belt them out at the top of my tiny lungs any time, any place–at the dinner table, in bed, in the grocery store, the mall, the playground, on the toilet. I just loved the physical pleasure of making all that sound. And getting lots of attention didn't hurt either. By the time I reached sixth grade, I was so loud, they gave me Curly, the lead in the annual school musical, a cut-down version of *Oklahoma!*. I started off the show with a rousing boy soprano version of *Oh, what a beautiful mornin'* (my man voice hadn't kicked in yet). By the time I scampered out for my final bow, it was clear I had scored a triumph. Everyone stood and cheered and totally turned my head.

See, it's all about Vitamin A. Applause. Once we hear the roars and shouts of the crowd, there's no turning back. It's like it's hard-wired, this need for public approval. We want everyone on the planet to like us, love us, worship us. It's just how we humans are. Deal with it.

Oklahoma! was the standout of my boy soprano days. I retired from singing during puberty, when everything went topsy-turvy: I'd be Cinderella one minute, Prince Charming the next. Once things settled down and I sounded like a proper grownup, I auditioned for Doc Williams, the director of our local church choir. It only took a few bars for him to welcome me with open arms. Don't be too impressed. I was a tenor and the few guys in the section were so old and weary, all they could do was wheeze.

A few months after I graduate high school–August, 1959, if you're really curious–Doc Williams gives me a big solo to sing at the end of service, the *Panis Angelicus*, a beautiful tune, short but intense, which he transposed into baritone territory so I could nail the high notes. When the performance comes around, I'm really feeling my oats and, boy, do I make those high Gs shine. After the service, as everyone files out, I see Kit heading straight for me like a vision, a real-life mirage.

You gotta understand I had a giant crush on that girl ever since she walked, no, floated into my ninth-grade math class, looking like Ava Gardner's kid sister–short but shapely, with luxurious black hair and tender gray-blue eyes that changed color, depending on the light or her mood. I drove myself crazy (and her, too, no doubt) trying to get her attention, but she just wasn't interested. She was dating this hotshot Franklin, a super-smart eleventh grader and captain of the math team. I took the hint and turned my attention elsewhere.

In our junior year, Kit's mom got a terrible cancer. Her dad had died years earlier, so it was up to Kit, young though she was, to deal with the crisis. She spent her last two years of high school studying as best she could, while taking care of her mom and working part time to help with the finances. Her mom died the spring of senior year. All us kids went to the funeral. It was a somber affair, it really shook us up. My heart ached for Kit, who seemed so forlorn, so utterly alone.

To make matters worse, her mom's medical expenses had gobbled up all the family's money, so Kit couldn't go to U Mich like everyone expected. The last weeks of school were terrible for her. She wandered through classes like a ghost.

Now, three or four months later, here she is again, heading straight for me, looking more beautiful, more soft and delicious than ever. I'm so blind-sided by the sight of her, so upside down and inside out, I just stand there, dumbstruck.

She flashes me her sunrise smile and goes, "Richie Verdun, how wonderful to see you. Your singing today quite literally took my breath away." That's how she always speaks, in complete and balanced sentences. If only I could.

She's standing right in front of me, waiting for some sort of response, but I'm completely tongue tied. There's this tumult inside me, this wildfire deep in my gut. Finally, after what must have been six million years of ridiculous infantile silence, I mutter, "Gee, Kit, thanks."

"Do you know who wrote your solo?"

"What solo?"

"The one you just sang, the *Panis Angelicus.*"

She's looking at me with such sweetness in her eyes, standing right across from me, shining, glowing in the noontime sun, I forget what she just asked, forget everything I ever knew. We're stuck with another long silence as my heart hammers and stammers and I feel like a total fool.

"I don't know, some guy?"

Rather than calling it quits, rather than getting the hell away before she's forced to spend another minute with the class dunce, Kit stays right where she is and smiles.

"Richie, you've got the music clutched to your chest. Who composed it?"

"Oops, sorry." I read her the guy's name, as best I can. "Seizure Frank" is what comes out.

"Richie, sorry, but that doesn't sound quite right. César Franck was a French composer, wasn't he? You make him sound so American."

Normally, I don't take well to criticism. In this case, Kit's little dig has the opposite effect. It frees me up, I'm back to my normal self. I go, "Hell, honey, we're in America. Suck it up."

"César Franck wasn't American, and besides, I'm not your honey."

I give her my *here comes a joke* look, where I pull the weirdest, craziest face I can. "You may not be my honey now, but you sure as hell will be."

Brilliant move, right? What a wordsmith, what a wit. The bad news is she just laughs and beats it outta there. The good news is that in no time at all, we're seeing each other, crazy mad in love, scheming and dreaming, and before you know it, we're teenage newlyweds with one, then two, then three little kids and a million things on our plate.

Yet, even then, in those early days of building our life together, when we were insanely busy and scraping for every single buck, I continued to take singing seriously. Every week I studied the music for the next Sunday service using my trusty little pitch pipe. (I don't have perfect pitch and don't read music well and there was no way in hell we could afford a piano.) Doc Williams called me his old reliable because I refused to stroll into rehearsals unprepared and make a fool of myself. Most everyone else would sight read hymns sounding like cats in heat and never even blink an eye. Not me. I really cared, especially when it came to my solos. I'd have them pretty much ready for rehearsal, almost memorized. (I could pick up things in those days much faster than I do now, which is a nuisance since they keep throwing so much new stuff at me to learn.)

Anyway, even back then I didn't want to come off like a jerk and Doc Williams really appreciated that and his praise meant something. I mean, he'd gone to U Mich for a masters in choral conducting and knew what the hell was what. I liked that he valued me and after a while the rest of the gang stopped their kidding and complaining: "Lighten up. Richie. You're making us all look bad." They *were* bad, total amateurs, and they shouldn't have taken advantage of good old Doc, wasting the poor man's time like they did, but it was just Graystone, Michigan, a tiny place in the middle of nowhere special, and they really didn't get it.

But I did. To me it was music. It was singing. It was my voice. And that meant every morning without fail I'd do my vocalises, a full set of arpeggios going up as high as I could, which didn't win me any friends at home, let me tell you. Okay, Kit was pretty supportive, but Jesus, the kids, they'd growl and howl like I was some kind of threat to their sanity. It was *my* sanity I worried about, especially with all their shenanigans, them being young kids and all. Usually it was Timmy, the middle one. He was always on my case about one thing or another. Carol, the oldest, was pretty much the quiet type, always reading books like her mom, always thinking things over before she opened her mouth.

Things got better for Kit and me after I got a job as a salesman on Frank's lot, so I only was working days and we finally could start affording things. We moved into our house, bought a second car, took proper vacations. Kit was still pretty much a homebody because Billy came along as a big surprise to all of us, which meant she had to spend another bunch of years back home with him. She worried all she'd ever be was a professional mom, but she just soldiered on and never once complained about all the insane things the kids made her do, like scolding and praising and cleaning and cooking and ferrying them all over the damn place.

Anyway, right at the end of that period, Billy was maybe six or seven, Doc Williams comes to me after service and says there's someone he wants me to meet and takes me over to this tall, and I mean way taller than me, carrot-haired woman in a tight black skirt and smart gray jacket which makes her look unlike anyone else in church, actually unlike anyone else in the whole town of Graystone. It was like she just stepped out of one of those old black and white Hollywood movies, you know, the ones where everyone is rich and clever and fascinating and lives in New York in a fancy penthouse. Anyway, as we're going over to her, Doc explains that Elizabeth Fanning had been his voice instructor at U Mich but recently moved to Graystone. "She's a terrific teacher and I'm sure she can help you, especially with your top." I'm thinking *who needs helping, everything's okay*, but he's got this *don't mess up, it's for your own good* look, so I just hold my tongue and wait to see what happens.

Doc and I stand right in front of this glamorous creature and all she does is take my hand and give it a good swift shake. (She's got one helluva grip.) That's it. No smile. No special look. I mean, I've heard of cool, but this is ridiculous. Doc asks her what she thinks of my singing and she looks straight at him, not me, and says, "If Mr. Verdun is interested, I'd be interested too." And I'm asking myself, interested in what, an affair, a trip to Paris, a heated swimming pool? Sure, I know what the whole thing's about, but she's so removed from it all, so aloof, it makes me completely nuts. Before I can put in my two cents and cut through all this crap, I hear her say to Doc, "Make sure he has my number." And she's gone. Whoosh. Just like that.

Doc starts making excuses for her. "Sorry, she can be abrupt sometimes."

"Abrupt? She acted like I don't even exist."

"Trust me, she knows you exist. And I really think you should take her up on her offer."

"She made an offer?"

"In her own cryptic way. All you have to do is give her a call."

"Maybe I don't want to."

"Look, she's a fantastic teacher, the best of the best. She basically retired once she got married, so it's a big honor she's willing to work with you. She really was impressed."

"I'm not impressed with her."

"You should be. She's a great teacher and you need her help. You don't have a top. You can't do fast passage work. You can't sing pianissimo. You tire easily. You can't sustain a line."

"I'm the best singer you got and you know it."

"You impress people and get compliments and you should. But your voice doesn't resonate. It lacks that tenor ping. That's what Elizabeth can give you."

"What the hell is a ping?"

"You know perfectly well. Pavarotti has it, Corelli has it, Tucker." He stares at me. "You have heard those men, right?"

"We got kids, remember? You know how busy we get. Kit hears the opera Saturdays but I'm out working on the lot. By the time I get home the opera's over and the kids are freaking out."

"You seriously mean to tell me you still haven't heard a fully trained tenor voice? We've been talking about it for ages."

"What can I say? I'm a busy guy."

"How busy are you right now?"

"I promised little Billy I'd toss him some easy ones."

"That doesn't sound so urgent. He can wait."

He's got me firmly by the arm now, which is not what I'd expect from our calm and correct choir director. In no time at all the two of us are marching to his tiny cottage a block or two away, and when I say tiny, I mean tiny, two bedrooms upstairs, kitchen, living room downstairs. If you eat too much, you can't squeeze in the door, but he gets it from the church rent free and the commute is nice and easy. Anyway, we march into his living room, which always looks like a tornado just landed. He's got all these books and scores and records spilling off the bookcases onto the chairs and sofa, assuming there really is one. I think I once saw it when he and his wife straightened up for an after-church reception, but I could be mistaken.

"Sit yourself down," he goes.

I give him my *here comes a joke* look. "Where?"

"Richard, for once in your life get serious!" he shouts and that's really odd, because Doc Williams never once raised his voice at me, not in all the years I've been in his chorus.

"Take it easy, man, I was just kidding around."

He throws his hands up, way up, like he's reached the absolute end of his patience. "All right, all right, have it your way. The eternal teenager, everything nice and easy, nothing worked for, nothing believed in. Second best can pass the test, so why make an effort over anything?"

Naturally this pisses me off. "Now wait a second. I work like a dog for you. Stop giving me the ass."

"Stop acting like one."

"I love you too, sweetheart." By now, we're both so fed up, so frustrated and angry we're facing off in Doc's living room like a pair of teenagers spoiling for a fight.

Doc's the first to back down. "Sorry, but I just can't understand why you refuse to develop your talents."

"They're developed already."

"Richard, you don't even have an A flat."

"I do too, most days."

"That's not good enough. There's lots of wonderful music I can't give you because of your technical limitations."

"Wow, what a shame."

"Look, Elizabeth is offering you something important. It's the chance of a lifetime."

"For your pal to make some cash." The moment I say it I know I've gone too far. His smile vanishes.

"That's it. I give up." He walks past me, squeezes past actually, opens the front door and goes out to stand on the stoop. It's spring outside, a really nice fresh day with light wind, a bright blue sky and the amazing scent of things growing after months and months of darkness and bitter cold.

"Just for the record, Miss Fanning's comfortably off. She's not doing it for the money. Well, I guess I've wasted enough of your time. If I've hurt your feelings in any way, I'm truly sorry. You know how much you mean to me and the chorus. You're a cherished part of this community."

This really startles me, knocks me upside the head. Here's this very smart, very devoted musician who seems to live his life entirely in scores and records, someone just about as different from me as possible, who's got this interest in me, this belief that almost scares me. I mean, I sing because I can and I like to and that's that. But he's coming from some other place entirely.

As I'm dealing with this, or at least trying to, Doc steps back into the house and gestures towards the street. "I envy you, Richard. You'll have a lovely walk in this beautiful weather while I'm forced to stay here studying scores." It's clearly time to go, but I don't. Doc seems puzzled I don't take his cue. Frankly, I'm puzzled too. "Well, on your way now, mustn't keep little Billy waiting."

Then I surprise myself. "You said you had something important for me. What is it?"

"Oh, just a singer I thought you should hear. Franco Corelli. He was the Met's leading tenor."

"Was he any good?"

"No, he was just about the worst singer I ever heard, worse even than you." I laugh at his feeble joke, mainly to encourage him. "Are you saying you'd like to hear his record?"

"Sure man, why the hell not."

"What about your son? Isn't he expecting you?"

"Nah, let the little bastard wait."

"Well, all right then, all I have to do is find it." Good luck with that. I settle myself down on a brown plaid pillow in the corner of the sofa, the only part of it I actually can see, the rest is covered with all those scores and books he loves so much. I honestly can't imagine Doc doing anything around the house other than studying those scores or listening to LPs. It's as if he never wanted to live like a normal human being.

All the while I'm thinking this, he's pawing through these piles and piles of records till he finally pulls out this dusty LP single with a very handsome Italian guy, real matinee idol material, staring at me from the cover.

"That guy's an opera singer?" Doc just shakes his head, gives me about the fiftieth dirty look of the day and pushes aside more junk to get over to his battered old record player.

And then Franco Corelli sings.

God, how that Franco Corelli sings. It seems impossible any man could sound like that, so rich and strong and fiery, like there's this energy inside him, this force that goes on and on. And as the song continues and gets higher and higher, Corelli's right up there with the music, blazing through the sky, and I'm wondering how any one person could make such an impact from a simple plastic disc, like the LP itself somehow dissolves into pure force, pure power and, okay, I'll say it even if it sounds way out there, pure beauty. Yes, that's what I'm hearing here, pure male gorgeousness. Not that pretty-pretty fag sound you get from those boy bands the teenage girls go for. No, something every guy wants, something big and heroic and grand, and as he's singing, something's growing inside me, this desire, this hunger, this almost angry determination to be there with him, do this with him, because all of a sudden a guy I never heard of, never even knew existed, has suddenly zoomed into my life and set it on fire with this insane insatiable urge to sing like him, live like him, *be* him.

Okay, okay, that's totally impossible. I'm no idiot, I know that, but still the moment I hear his incredible voice I want to at least try to do what he does. Because I can, I know I can. Not as well as him, of course – no one can be *that* good, and hell, I know I can't go up as high as he does, probably never will, but I've got this power, this strength, this man force inside me that I always felt, always enjoyed, but never really got into, never really explored. Now, thanks to this man and his song, I'm inspired. I'm intent. I realize how much I always liked reaching deep down inside me and bringing out this punchy, powerful sound. I want more of it now, want to push and extend and develop what's buried inside me. I want to grab hold of my gift and make something of it, do something with it, because I can, I really and truly can. And in some new way, I *must.*

I want my voice to go out there and grab people, throttle them, conquer them, smash them, make them my fucking slaves. I know it's completely mad, but that's what I feel, that's what's going on deep down inside me during the – what? – maybe three minutes of his song, and that's new for me and very odd, because the last place I usually want to be is inside myself, examining myself, life being so much fun, so delightfully distracting. But when I hear Franco Corelli belt out that old Neapolitan song, I take a look deep down inside myself and realize that it isn't just bullshit or flattery when folks come up to me after church and thank me for singing so great. They mean it. I give them something, maybe not something physical, maybe not something they can weigh or measure, but something they can *feel.* It lifts them out of themselves, out of their tiny trivial lives, and sends them into a universe of blazing, brazen sound.

The song suddenly ends. I say *I gotta go* and rush out the door before Doc can even ask what's up. I run as fast as my pudgy legs can take me over to my car and drive like a demon back home, all fired up, with this incredible ridiculous urge, and I blast through the door, and Kit's standing in the hallway with this *where the hell were you?* look. She goes, "Little Billy gave up on you and went off to play with a friend." But I don't care, I take her in my arms, squeeze her, crush her, big and hot and crazy, give her this giant knockout kiss and before she can say anything about the kids or where I've been or what's going on, she's in my arms and I'm carrying her upstairs into the bedroom, our private stronghold, so what if the kids are outside? When we're done, when we're finally finished and panting and sweating and smiling and giggling like little kids lost in the amazement of each other, the total miracle, she finally goes, "What on earth was that all about?"

And then, full of love and delight and endless, ridiculous possibility, I tell her.

CHAPTER TWO

Elizabeth

Of course, you want me to discuss Richard Verdun. Everyone does. You want to know how I of all people came to be his primary teacher, the true architect of his current success. And you want to know how our whole collaboration turned into this giant fiasco, a rupture so messy and unpleasant that even now years later, it causes me unspeakable pain, while he, much to his discredit, pretends we never worked together at all. But facts are facts. I absolutely was the person, the one and only person, who lifted him out of his hobbyist mentality and gave him a fully functional technique, which has served him extremely well down to the present day. It's important to state this. I'm a singing teacher. I need to attract good students, and Richard is far and away the best-known member of my studio, even if he hasn't been part of it for ages.

It all started in earnest when, after five years of irregular lessons with me, and very little hard work, Richard finally listened to what I had been telling him and rolled up the sleeves of his absurdly unstylish lumberjack shirt, exposing his powerful well-muscled forearms. Those manly forearms really shouldn't have mattered, of course, but I have to confess they did. That brief hint of his deep power, his true virility, stirred me up so much that in the end I ruined everything. My hopes and longings grew and grew until finally one day, poof, *finito.*

The vast bulk of our work before then, nearly five years' worth, was fitful, erratic and irritating. At least it was to me. I was the professional, he the clueless amateur. He approached our work with an almost bizarre lightheartedness, as if the last thing on earth he wanted was to make the deep and absolutely essential commitment of time and energy to properly support his voice. He complained constantly that I was being too hard on him, too fussy. He'd say, "Come on, you know I sound better than anyone else in the whole damn chorus," as if that was some sort of accomplishment. I've heard of low standards, but his were subterranean.

I had moved to the tiny and demoralizing town of Graystone, Michigan, not long after marrying Ed, my one and only experiment in the dubious institution of marriage. The poor man had just bought the life insurance agency there and needed to know the town. I didn't want to know it at all, of course. Ann Arbor had been bad enough after my thrilling but all too brief years of striving in New York, but Graystone – god, what was it? Two movie houses and some mildly pleasant people who didn't know or do much of anything. Oh, yes, it also contained Doc Williams, my former pupil at the University of Michigan, who acted as midwife to my arrangement with Richard Verdun. "I think he's really got something. I think you'll be intrigued," he said.

Intrigued? I was bewildered.

Richard Verdun was a curious-looking fellow, not fat so much as relentlessly pudgy, and short, like all too many tenors, alas. In high heels I could easily peer down at his growing bald spot.

On the other hand, there was nothing flimsy about him. The fellow was solid, sturdy like one of those open bed trucks he sold to area farmers. This isn't a trivial point. Tenors are all too often hothouse flowers that wilt and wither away. Richard Verdun was built to last. As for his voice, well, in those early days he was little more than a run-of-the-mill church singer with no top, no flexibility and no endurance. He did, however, have a certain steel in his voice, a compelling insistent power that made my ears perk up, virtually forced them to take notice. How to contain this power, how to tame it. That was the challenge. It very nearly was the ruin of me.

In any case, in he came for his first lesson, this baby truck of a man, stomping through the carpeted hallways of our home.

"Good afternoon, Mister Verdun. I'll keep it short and to the point. You're here because I'm convinced your voice has potential, but it's going to take considerable time and effort on your part. Can you commit to it?"

"I'll commit to anything to get me a high C."

"I'm not so sure you have one."

"Then how am I gonna sound like Franco Corelli?"

"You never will."

"Gee, great, just what I wanted to hear."

"Mister Verdun, with patience and good training, there's only one person you'll ever sound like and that's yourself." My perfectly obvious comment seemed to startle him. I wondered if I'd ever met anyone so staggeringly naive. "We're going to develop *your* voice, *your* sound. Anything else would be disastrous."

"But Franco Corelli's my hero. He's why I'm doing this in the first place."

"That's all well and good. But it makes no difference. You're tethered to the voice inside you. And I can bring it to the fore. The good news is there's a clear technique to singing well, an actual practical strategy. The bad news is it takes hard work."

"How much hard work? As you probably noticed, I'm not twenty-two any more."

"Neither am I."

"Sorry, that's not much of an answer."

"It will take the time it takes, Mister Verdun."

And so we began. I was relentless with Richard in those early days, perhaps a bit too relentless. I refused to let him get away with anything in the hope that my severe truth-telling would lead to a swift breakthrough. No such luck. He was too stubborn, perhaps, or just too dumb. I've really no idea what his problem was, but he made little improvement during our all-too-infrequent lessons. He claimed he did his exercises. He swore he understood what I was saying. But if he did, then why did nothing change, why was he still singing flat and why, oh why, did he keep whining? Every time I pointed out a mistake he winced as though he'd been slapped. Why couldn't he take it like a man? Why was he so bound up in his hurt feelings and slighted pride? The whole point was to learn how to sing.

Madame Raitzin, my old teacher, would have never put up with it. She'd have shown him the door in the first ten minutes. She couldn't tolerate the American worship of niceness *ueber alles.* She told it like it was. She was blunt to the point of savagery. You either collapsed under her onslaught or sprang into action and accomplished things. Her lessons made it clear that singing isn't for sissies. You've got to be tough and resilient. You must struggle, and struggle hard, to shake off lazy habits and find your true voice and sing like a genuine singer. Richard so far was unwilling or unable to do any of this. His approach was happy-go-lucky Midwestern, easygoing verging on the sloppy. He acted like just another blinkered amateur, eager to lap up a few compliments, but unwilling to make a true effort. All this had the unpleasant side effect of bringing back dark memories of my Ann Arbor days, where I was known as *Madama Negativa,* because I had the audacity to speak truth to incompetence.

Why then did I continue with him? Why didn't I just give up? The hard cold steel deep at the core of his voice, the vigor, the virility that cut in as he reached the *passaggio,* the treacherous bridge between the voice's center and its exultant high, it was so distinctive in Richard's instrument, so stirring, so strong, I had to pry it out of him, had to get it functioning. If only he'd shape up, if only he'd listen, if only he weren't such a baby, if only, if only...

To make matters worse, we rarely worked together more than once or twice a month. Richard put in long hours at the "lot," as he called it, a rather threadbare Chevrolet dealership at the far edge of town where Ed bought his new sedan each year, mainly to help shore it up. My husband had a part interest in the business, as he had in many unsuspected nooks and crannies of that little town. One day he surprised me by saying that he was one of Richard's most loyal customers.

"I wish he were loyal to me," I said.

"Why do you say that?"

"His lessons are going nowhere. He acts like a total amateur."

"That's only because he is," remarked my clever husband.

Things remained dire with Richard until I laid down the law. "Now see here, we've been at this for over two years and where on earth are we?"

"Right here in your lovely living room."

I could have strangled him. "I'm being serious. We've come to the end of the road. You haven't been making any progress."

"Course I have. Just two months ago I nailed the high G."

"Then lost it a mere two weeks later."

"I was getting over a cold."

"It hasn't come back in our lessons."

"Maybe, but I got it last Sunday in the shower, cross my fingers and hope to die."

"No jokes please. You miss your lessons, make feeble excuses and treat this entire process like a joke. Well, it isn't, Richard. The art of bel canto can't be attained by amateur dabbling."

"I'm doing the best I can, really. I'm sorry I missed all those lessons and, yeah, I guess I sometimes cheat on the exercises, but it's not because I don't want to do them, I just don't have any time. Look, Miss Fanning, you don't got kids, you don't really know what a big deal it is, how they fill up your days so fast with so much stuff, they get you coming and going. I mean, my kids are busy with a million different activities, Carol and her cheerleading, Timmy with wrestling and now Billy's going out for the little league baseball team, which has practice almost every afternoon."

"How nice they're all so athletic." He failed to note my sarcasm.

"Yeah, it is pretty great, but it's a lot of driving back and forth. Carol's the only one with a license, so it's me and Kit who do most of it and then I gotta make a living down at the lot and things aren't so great there. Frank's on our case because we're not moving units fast enough, which means I gotta put in more hours hustling cars and once I get home, there's all kinds of squabbles between the two boys I gotta referee."

"So what. Our work here has nothing to do with raising a family or earning a living or fulfilling the all-American dream. It's about art. Devote yourself to it or give up."

Suddenly, so suddenly I thought I'd worked some black magic, it was as if a man didn't face me any more, but an eight-year-old boy. Richard's swagger deserted him. He slumped on the sofa in my music room, a picture of abject misery. How could I upset him like that? How could I cause such discomfort? He was well meaning, after all, undereducated, of course, naive, certainly, but basically sweet and hardworking, if not on behalf of his singing, then surely in support of his family.

"All right, Richard, I'll give you one last chance, but only one."

"Sure, anything you say."

"First and foremost, you've got to come here regularly, no more missed sessions, no more phony excuses. Week in, week out, I want to see and hear you working on the proper technique."

"Fine, no problem."

"Richard, it's been a problem from the moment we met."

"Not any more. I'm a changed character, completely reformed. Promise." There was no grin this time, no sly boyish smirk, only a tentative little smile, a very dear one, I must confess. I began to feel reassured.

"Good. Now that you've completely reformed, you can see me twice a week."

"Twice?"

"Absolutely. I've got to be sure you work properly."

"You know I do, Miss Fanning."

"But not properly. I've got to get you in here more often, check your work more thoroughly. Otherwise, you simply won't get there."

"Where's that? The Met?" He was grinning again, looking for all the world like a sitcom character awaiting the next wave of canned laughter.

"Singing properly is serious business, life and death, yet you treat it like some kind of joke. We can't stagger on this way any more. We must take a more stringent approach. You've got to come over here at least twice a week, fully prepared, fully committed to the fine art of singing."

"Look, Miss Fanning, I really do want to sing properly, you know I do." Actually, I didn't know. I merely hoped it might be the case. "The fact is I'm really feeling the pinch budget-wise and now you're asking me to take more lessons. Sorry, but I just can't afford it." Along with his sloppy work habits Richard also had an unfortunate obsession with money, how little he made, how much things cost. I hated that sort of crude American materialism, everything reduced to mere dollars and cents. I remember how at our very first lesson he complained about my fee, forty dollars, a paltry sum, half the going rate in New York, and asked if I could give him some "wiggle room." I found his comment inelegant, to say the very least, and no doubt should simply have said that my price was my price, take it or leave it, but he was charming in a rough sort of way and his voice was so promising that, very much against my better judgment, I reduced my fee to the absurdly low rate of thirty dollars. I distinctly remember warning him at the time that he mustn't let this bargain-basement price – that's what I called it because that's what it most certainly was – lead him to undervalue what I would be giving him. He flashed me this earnest-schoolboy, cross-my-heart, hope-to-die look and assured me that never would be the case. In no time at all, of course, it was.

This time I was ready. I told him I'd accept a far lower fee, money wasn't really the point, he just needed to work, and work hard, not only in my studio but also back home, where I expected him to do his exercises faithfully, day after day, week after week, no matter how busy or tired or distracted by his family he might be. Needless to say, it was the low fee which attracted him.

"You mean to say you'll teach me for, like, fifteen bucks a pop?"

"Even less, if you're truly feeling the pinch."

"Wow, I guess I gotta do it. I never say no to a bargain."

Things were indeed different for a while. Since I was seeing Richard twice a week, I really could tell when he was working and when he wasn't. Whenever I'd catch him loafing I'd pounce and assign another exercise and, lo and behold, rather than protesting, he'd nod earnestly, swear he'd attend to it and bit by bit, lesson by lesson, he improved. He had better breath control, steadier pitch, more even passage work. The G was soon established, even the G sharp. But this blissfully constructive period didn't last long.

One Sunday, a lovely June day, I was waiting for Richard in my music room when I realized he was late. Extremely late. Outrageously late. There had been no phone call, no message of any sort. I knew he wasn't sick. He just had sung in church, fairly well, I must say, which added insult to injury. What was going on? We had come to our new understanding a mere three months before, yet once again I was faced with his truancy. How dare he behave like this? How dare he let me down?

I roared into action. I called his home, but no one answered. No doubt I should have stopped right there, crossed him off the list and looked for another protégé (not that I was likely to find one in that provincial wasteland) but I was out for blood. I drove, virtually flew, over to his house like an avenging angel.

Despite all the time Richard and I had been working together, I'd never visited his house. I would occasionally exchange a few words after church with Kit, Richard's wife, a startlingly attractive young woman who usually had her hands full controlling her squirmy children. Other than that, I really had no idea of who these people were or how they lived.

I reached their small shabby house in record time. It lay in a working-class area of small lots and simple two-story units, each as bland as the next. As I roared up to the curb, there was Kit, down on all fours, tending to some faltering pansies. She was startled to see me. No doubt she sensed something was seriously wrong. When I told her that her husband had missed an important lesson, she offered to call the car lot, since she assumed they must have had an emergency there. The only emergency I was aware of was Richard's blatant affront to me and the seriousness of our work, but I didn't bring it up. His poor wife was only trying to help. I thanked her for her offer and followed her into the house.

Their cramped living room had clearly been held hostage by hordes of rampaging children. Toys, school books, athletic equipment, shirts, socks and underwear littered every available surface. There was little hint of adult habitation, only a few pieces of battered furniture. How could the woman live like this? Didn't it drive her mad? Evidently not. She sailed through the unholy mess without comment or apology, impervious to the chaos in which she lived. As we came to a small passageway just outside the kitchen, Kit opened a door to a tiny room which must have once served as a pantry. The small windowless space was lined with bookshelves; books rose like sacred tablets all the way to the ceiling.

"I come here to escape the kids," she said. "Not that I succeed for long. They use all sorts of excuses to interrupt. Once they're off at school, it's much easier. I can slip in here and lose myself for hours. I'm pretty much addicted to reading."

Who could have ever imagined that Richard's house would have a room as calm as this one? I briefly wondered if he ever made use of it. It seemed most unlikely; the titles were much too serious. Here were Austen and Dickens, Steinbeck and Salinger, Heller and Cheever, works of quality, not the trivial trash, the Jacqueline Susann and Leon Uris, I usually found cluttering the marble coffee tables of Ed's banker friends.

She observed me checking the titles. "I've got the complete Dickens," she explained, "the complete Conrad, the complete Willa Cather and, of course, my beloved Jane Austen. She's my absolute favorite, I never tire of her."

"Who does?"

"You're a fan too? Don't you just love her wit? The elegance of her style?"

"I also love students who come to their lessons promptly."

"Oh, sorry, I forgot. I'll get right to it." She went to call the lot but returned a short while later to say no one there had seen him. "I'm sure he won't be long. Would you like to stay here and wait?" I nodded tersely. "My boys will be coming home soon. Maybe they can tell us something."

"Or maybe not."

"I hope you're not too angry with him."

"How angry is too angry?" I said, attempting a smile.

"I'm sure it just slipped his mind. Richie's a Graystone boy, you know, a small-town kid, easy come, easy go. He's not really used to big-city attitudes."

"Such as showing up on time or having the courtesy to call when you realize you're going to be late?" I said, rather more sharply than I'd intended.

"You mustn't take it personally. I'll go out on an errand and ask him to make sure the boys do their homework, and he'll absolutely agree, and when I get back, all three of them are stretched out on the sofa sipping sodas and watching wrestling on TV. When Richie flashes his smile at me and explains he simply forgot, I guess I just accept it. That's the sort of person he is." She suddenly seemed aware that we had been standing in a room with only one chair. "It's awfully cramped in here. Why don't we go out front?"

She led me back to the catastrophe that was her living room and pushed a tattered chair in my direction. I settled myself into it cautiously, while she perched on a corner of their severely abused sofa. "You know, I see you all the time in church, but we never seem to talk. My fault surely, not yours. I'm always chasing after the boys. Even in church it's all I can do to keep them from tearing the place down. Anyway, I just wanted to say how grateful I am to you for coming into Richard's life. It's making a big difference."

"Not as big as I hoped."

"I'm sorry he's gotten you so upset."

"What do you expect? He misses his lesson with no call, no explanation. It's totally unacceptable." A glum silence settled over us, but it wasn't all that long before she was talking again.

"You know, this may sound strange, but you've become a role model for me."

"I have? How on earth could that be?"

"You've done so much with your life. A distinguished teacher of singing, who performed in such famous opera houses."

"They weren't especially famous and there weren't all that many."

"Oh, I'm sorry."

"Don't be. It was something I had to do and so I did it."

"That's exactly how I feel." She must have noticed how startled I was, because she quickly added, "I mean, I've been taking courses at M.S.U. for some time now, working towards a masters in English literature. I've got a lot of catching up to do, but I absolutely love it. Once I get that degree, I'm going to find a job that has something to do with books. The kids will be old enough and Richie totally approves."

"Well, at least he's supportive of *you*."

She breezed right past my little jab. "I wish I could have laid the groundwork earlier, but Richie and I got started so fast with all this..." She gestured vaguely at the mess that engulfed her. "But, you know, on Saturdays, when Richie's working the lot and I'm ferrying the kids here, there and everywhere, I try to catch the Met broadcasts as often as I can. They truly brighten my week..."

She then launched into a little rhapsody about the magic of the human voice and reminded me of the opera lovers who'd come backstage after I sang in Albany, say, or some other minor venue. They'd natter on about how splendid I was, how brilliant and unforgettable, and I'd believe the sweet dears, because how could I not? I was hooked on curtain calls, addicted to applause, and then I'd go back to New York, proud and happy with myself, and take a lesson with Madame Raitzin and she'd say I sang like a pig. I'd be utterly dejected, because I knew she must be right, everything I was doing was wrong, and then I'd remember those dear sweet people in Albany who thought I was so wonderful and all I wanted was to escape my teacher and her impossibly high standards and go back to Albany and bask in its easy applause. And so it went for years and years, yes and no, up and down, positive, negative, until I had enough of the whole ridiculous game and wound up in the middle of nowhere married to a businessman who paid all the bills.

My grim ruminations were cut short by the penetrating wails only a small boy could produce. As Kit rose to deal with the problem, the two contending forces came whirling into view. It was an unequal contest. The taller older boy had clamped his brother's head under his left armpit and was shouting "Give up? Give up?" while the younger one responded with ear-shattering screams. Their frantic struggle seemed not to faze Kit in the least. She waded right into the thick of battle, grabbed her older son, extricated his smaller brother and forced the combatants to settle down on opposite ends of the sofa.

She stood between them, arms crossed over her chest in stern disapproval. "I expect an apology, Timothy. You're older than he is and much bigger."

Grudgingly, the big boy murmured, "I'm sorry, Billy." Then he glowered at the carpet. "This is Miss Fanning," his mother explained, "Daddy's voice teacher." He continued his sulk and refused to look at me. "Timothy, what did I say about manners?"

Without looking up, he held out his hand in my direction. "Hello."

"Hello, Miss Fanning."

"Hello, Miss Fanning." I took his hand and shook it. It felt like a dead fish.

"Miss Fanning came over to see Daddy. Do you happen to know where he is?"

"Fishing."

Did I hear correctly? Fishing? Not a medical emergency or major business crisis, but *fishing*?!

Even his mother seemed startled. She asked if he really was sure. "Yeah. He came running in here with Frank right after church, got changed real fast and was gone."

The thought that Richard's truancy was due to a fishing expedition was truly beyond the pale. My anger transformed into a white-hot resolve to track the man down to the ends of the earth if need be, and put him permanently in his place. You do not toy with Elizabeth Fanning. No, never, *giammai.*

I asked where he might be, trying my best not to sound too infuriated. Kit explained that Richard's favorite spot was at the end of Prescott Road, where a short trail led down to the river. I thanked her profusely and sprinted towards my car. Considerably alarmed, she followed after me, warning that the trail would wreak havoc on my shoes. Fair enough, I thought, I'll wreak havoc on my tenor.

I often said to Ed that I don't do nature. I'm a city girl through and through. I may walk in parks but I don't hike trails. Nonetheless, there I was on that dismal day jumping out of my car in my best Sunday pumps (patent leather, no less, one-and-a half-inch heels) onto the muddy brambly trail at the end of Prescott Road. After a few minutes of sloshing about in search of the stream, briskly striding past trees and bushes and a welter of weeds (or were they actually flowers, don't ask me, I'm no expert), I heard the rush of water and, much heartened, picked up my pace until I came to a rough clearing where, to my surprise, I found my husband Ed bent over a large metal box filled with the hooks and lures of the avid fisherman. He rose to embrace me. I stiffened at the touch of his muddy, fishy hands.

"Sweetheart, how great, what brings you here?"

"I might ask the same of you."

"I'm fishing with Frank and Richie."

"Richard was supposed to be at our house, remember?" Ed looked genuinely puzzled. "Don't you notice anything? Every Sunday Richard has his lesson."

"I didn't realize."

"Indeed you didn't. Where is he?"

"Is he in big trouble?"

"No, of course not, I'm perfectly delighted he ditched me to go fishing with the boys."

"Come on, it can't be that bad."

"Are you going to tell me where he is, or do I have to hike another five miles to find him?"

"He's just over there, right by the shore." He turned and shouted in that general direction. "Hey, Richie, I gotta little surprise for you."

"Sure as hell hope it's a nice one." Richard's voice soared over the water, carefree and blithe. Needless to say, this only increased my fury.

"Go get him, darling. Good luck." Ed made a flamboyant gesture towards the stream, a sort of servant's scrape and bow. I swept past him, still contending with the tempest inside me, and squished along the trail until I saw two compact stubby figures, one casting from shore and the other, Richard, up to his thighs in the frothing water. The moment he saw me coming he abruptly faced away, as if to vanish from the scene.

Frank, the fellow on the shore, was an out-of-shape entrepreneur who owed the survival of his car dealership to a recent infusion of cash from my husband. When they were in the thick of negotiations, Ed insisted I give dinner to him. It was the first and last time we ever socialized. "Oh, hi, Elizabeth, you and Richie having problems?"

"You might say that."

"Go easy on him, okay? He's the best salesman I got."

"So bloody what." As Frank retreated up the trail, Richard slowly, grudgingly splashed his way towards me. He looked for all the world like a waterlogged muskrat.

"Look, I know you're angry, but Frank's my boss. He asks me at church to go fishing. How the hell can I say no?"

"Without even calling me? Without making even the slightest attempt to explain?"

"Your husband said he was going home to change. I figured he'd let you know."

"Don't blame Ed. This is entirely your fault. Face it like a man." Richard seemed flummoxed by this, whether hurt or shocked, I didn't know and didn't care. "Respect, that's all we poor humans seek and I never get it from you, quite au contraire."

"Okay, maybe I was dumb to think Ed would tell you, but I really had to come out here. Your husband's my boss's boss. I couldn't just not go."

"You most certainly could."

"I gotta stay tight with these guys. I can't insult them."

"So you happily insult me. I give you lessons virtually for nothing and you couldn't care less. You just play at being a singer. You never really work."

Richard reddened alarmingly. "I fucking work my ass off."

"Kindly watch your language," I said (quite calmly, I'm happy to say) and started the long trek back to my car. I hadn't taken more than a few steps when I heard applause and shouts of bravo. I looked to my right and saw Frank and my husband huddled behind some bushes giggling like schoolboys. They had heard everything. "Laugh all you like. I wash my hands of him."

"Better use lots of soap," Frank said. I tried using my stare of death, but Frank was too busy laughing to notice. Let those overaged infants have their fun. I've done my duty and said my say. *Basta con questa pasta. Finì!* As I got to my car, I looked down and saw my ravaged shoes, casualties of this preposterous excursion. I hurled them into the woods and drove like a madwoman back home.

Once inside, I poured myself a very strong, very dry martini. As it blazed down my throat, I wondered all over again how it had come to this, how I had let an infantile amateur disrespect me and mock the art I cherished. My thoughts were slashed to ribbons by the chiming of the front door bell. I could barely bring myself to answer, but in the end I did, and there was Richard, facing me head on, his cheeks flushed, almost flaming, whether in shame or fury I couldn't tell.

"Look, look, I know I royally screwed up," he said, "but you can't just stop my lessons."

"I most certainly can." I started back towards the music room. Richard thundered along right behind me.

"Don't go, Miss Fanning, don't go. You gotta give me a chance. Just listen to me, listen, please..." I was on the threshold of the music room and about to slam the door when Richard unleashed a big broad high A flat, perfectly placed, perfectly projected. I froze in my tracks. He'd never done it before, never managed that note without cracking or wobbling or going flat. He kept holding it. The note broadened and shone. I was astounded by its sheer physical impact, its vibrant thrusting force. When he finally cut it off, it was as if a magnificent gilded hero had suddenly left the room.

"Sing it again. Prove it wasn't mere luck." He strode over to the piano, played an A flat chord, sang the note again and held it even longer. It was every bit as good, maybe even better, a bit more forward, a bit more intense. "Yes, not bad," I said. "Now you just have to practice it over and over until it's second nature, so that no matter how tired or distracted or uncomfortable you might be, you can always hit the note perfectly every single time."

Talent is a trap. A deadly drug. It ensnares you with promise and possibility, entrances you with dreams and before you know it, you've given up everything, your pride, your reason, your self-respect. A mere five minutes ago I despaired of the man. Now, I was back in his thrall.

We resumed our work and surged through the following months with Richard working tirelessly, never once protesting or procrastinating. No matter how often he failed, he'd try again, harder than ever. I now focused on his top extension because without it a tenor is nothing. Richard's voice is naturally dark and weighty. He needed to unleash his so-called money notes. Over time, very much time, he did indeed do just that. His progress was so convincing, I felt he could tackle a major new challenge.

For some time Richard's chorus master had wanted him to sing the *Ingemisco* from Verdi's *Requiem.* I had always felt it was too hard for him, too high. (It requires a shining B flat.) Now at last he had the tools to master it. We worked all through the long harsh Michigan winter and it was bliss, pure bliss, what I was put on this earth to do and he too, he too. He finally was so secure in his technique, so rock solid and grounded, that every lesson really and truly was a celebration of him, of me, of music. Richard's *Ingemisco* gradually emerged. It wasn't the gentlest version I ever heard, or the most touching, but it was stirring. When he hit the final high note, really hit it with no fudging or faking, he was no longer a good healthy church singer, but a genuine tenor with a full fervent voice and the technique to back it up. It wasn't completely in place, of course, the scales remained uneven, some notes hovered flat, but he was getting there. That wild dream I had that I might someday make a true singer out of him seemed entirely, almost amazingly possible. With each new lesson I became more and more certain, more and more convinced. I'd found a genuine tenor, created it, shaped it, empowered it. I was Pygmalion and Richard my unlikely Galatea, my living masterpiece.

I remember so well our last lesson, a few weeks before Easter. The snow had just melted and struggling crocuses somehow or other found the strength to force their way up through the sea of mud and rejoice. The sun was out that day, blazingly bright. There was even birdsong. Were the robins back already? Had winter gone by that fast? Ed was off on another of his interminable "business trips" and Richard tramped into the music room, his face a bouquet of smiles.

"Come on, honey, let's do it. I'm truly loaded for bear."

"It's Verdi, Richard, not a hunt."

"Yeah, yeah, but Doc has the first read through next week. I gotta do the whole piece today, no stops, no corrections, nail the sucker cold." He was right. He had never sung through the whole piece from beginning to end. Everyone in the choir had good reason to wonder whether their buddy Richie could actually get through it. After warming him up, I gave him his opening C, off he went, and, yes, the piece was there, solid, almost severe, incredibly male and insistent, yet, amazingly, when the key change came, when the suppliant pleads for mercy, Richard sang softly, really softly, with no loss of body or heart and it was genuinely sweet and soulful. I looked up at him from the keyboard as he sang and saw the faint dew of tears on his cheeks. Was he really crying, that solid, stolid man child? Yes, he was. He didn't stop, he didn't look away, he sang through his tears nobly, valiantly. Then I realized I was weeping too.

We just looked at one another, stared in dazed wonderment. And then, I hardly know how to say this, how to believe this, but it had to happen and it did. We kissed. We kissed with the fury and passion of Tristan and Isolde, those mad lost lovers, kissed with an onrush of heat and conviction and yearning, one for the other, now and forever, and not two days later, only a very short while before Richard would sing the Verdi in church, when my great accomplishment, my genius for teaching would finally be clear to one and all, he sent me a letter – no phone call, no courtesy visit, just a letter, if you can imagine it – a brief cold letter, which I quote in its entirety.

"Dear Miss Fanning, just so you know, I won't be taking any more lessons with you. Please leave me and my family alone. Thank you, Richard Verdun."

Just like that, he was out of my work, my life forever. No matter, my studio in New York is doing quite nicely, thank you, though, to be completely honest, I still haven't found a student to rival him.

CHAPTER THREE

Richie

You figure you find a voice teacher and your voice gets better or it doesn't. End of story. With Elizabeth Fanning it was way different. A grand opera which took me totally by surprise. Me, Richie Verdun, who's used to surprises.

As soon as I started working with her, I realized she was not the type of person you'd normally run across in Graystone, Michigan. She was very New York City, and not in a good way. She was extremely professional, extremely cut and dried, extremely sure of her own opinions and she had about ninety million of them. But so what? I was there to develop my voice, not marry her. Most of the time I basically accepted her hard-ass behavior, her tough, warts-and-all, take-it-or-leave-it criticism. I assumed all voice teachers were like that, you know, nuts, but normal nuts. Once things turned upside down and we got to the crazy part, I thought otherwise. Better late than never.

The crazy part started with that amazing first run through of the *Ingemisco,* as I'm singing my heart out, sounding like a god, and seeing the world through a mist of tears and I look over at Elizabeth, and she's weeping too, and the tears keep flowing and the music keeps soaring, until I come to the killer high B flat that ends the whole piece, and I grab it and hold it and bloom it, and then it's over.

I feel pretty fantastic, of course, especially about the final B flat, so it's only natural I walk over to my teacher, sitting there at the piano, and give her a big hug, even lift her up in the air, which is no easy thing. I mean, she's, like, two inches taller than me and pretty substantial. Nonetheless I get her up there, and, well, before I can even think or say anything, she lets out a kinda animal shout and grabs my hair and pulls my head right against hers and gives me this deep French kiss. It's incredibly embarrassing and stupid and awkward, but Elizabeth just pulls back, smiling at me, glowing, like she won the World Series or something, so I say, "Elizabeth, Miss Fanning, look, I'm a happily married man" or something equally original. I just know I have to get out of there, pronto. And I do. I whiz back home in my car and walk in the door, hardly have time to take off my jacket and give little Billy a hug, when the phone rings, and it's her saying *she understands, she's an artist too, she'll take care of it, don't worry*, and, me, not wanting to spend one more second on this crazy weirdo nonsense, I say thanks and hang up, thinking, of course, that's that.

But it's not, as I discover the next day when I get home from work and Billy and Timmy are tearing into each other like usual and Kit isn't there to stop it. I wade right in and pry the jerks apart, and once they're settled down, I ask them where's Mom, and they say they don't know, which is weird, since she's always with them at home after school. I go into our bedroom, figuring she's taking a nap, but no one's there. Next, I try the reading room, Kit's little library. She always wants me to knock before bursting in, she needs a little warning, a little transition time to get herself back down to earth after reading one of her books.

"Kit?" I go. "Kit?" No sound from her, nothing. I open the door a crack and there she is, sitting in the chair reading some Jane Austen. I can tell it's Jane Austen because she has this big old gray volume with all the lady's novels, which she reads again and again to comfort herself when things get a bit much, whereas with me, I'd just have another beer. Anyway, the moment I see that book, I know something's up.

"Kit," I go, "everything okay?" No answer, which means, of course, it's not. "Is something wrong? I came back early from work, so you can't be mad about that." Still nothing. She turns a page and keeps reading. Uh oh. "Was it something I said? Or one of the boys? I know it can't be Carol, since she's beyond perfect, at least in your eyes." Not even this seems to get a rise out of her. In fact, this deep freeze is the worst I've ever seen, and if I don't do something fast, I'll be standing there forever, so I put my mug right up in hers and make a giant grimace, which I know she doesn't like, but I need her to react.

"Richard!" she shouts. She only calls me that when she's mad.

"Look, I don't mean to disturb you, but I know something's wrong. Could you please tell me what?"

She looks at me like she can't believe I'm putting on this innocent act.

"I had an interesting visit from your singing teacher today."

"Miss Fanning?"

"Yes, though she says you're on a first-name basis now, so you surely must mean *Elizabeth.* I gather you've been having a remarkable time together – making art, opening up new vistas, her exact words, 'new vistas.' Exactly what sort of vistas do you two have in mind?" She looks straight at me like she's expecting some sort of answer, but I'm still at a total loss. "I'm a grown up, Richard," she continues. "I can take anything as long as I know what it is. So tell me, what have you two clever people got hidden up your sleeves? Spell it out for me, please."

"Kit, what the hell are you driving at?"

"Your teacher – at least I thought she was your teacher, now I'm not so sure – came here today after lunch, stood right over there in the doorway wearing this oh-so-superior expression, and said she just wanted to prepare me for something that really would be for the best. I naturally asked her what she was alluding to and she replied in this insultingly smug and self-satisfied way, 'Oh, that's not for me to explain. I leave it all to your husband.'" Kit crosses her arms now and stares at me like I'm some kind of enemy alien that snuck into her home while her back was turned and murdered all her kids.

"Kit, there's nothing to explain at all. Zip. Nada."

She looks me square in the eyes and asks in a very low, very tight voice, "Are you having an affair with her?"

The idea is so wild, so completely off the charts, so out-of-the-ball-park impossible, that I laugh. I roar. I whoop and holler until the kids come running to the door and knock and ask if everything's okay. I tell them nothing's wrong, then check to make sure they're gone before I continue with my wife. "Honey, you know that's totally crazy. Never, ever in a million years would I have sex with her. Or anyone else for that matter, only you. You know that."

"Do I?"

"After all this time you sure as hell should. You're my lady, Kit, always were, always will be. End of story."

"Not according to her. She said that now you're becoming a real singer, things have to change, big things, painful things, but necessary to the development of an artist, another very important, very fancy concept for her, '*the development of an ahr-tist.*'"

"Honey, I don't know about this artist crap, but I do know I'm just the lady's student. I see her twice a week and that's it."

"And you're really not fucking her?" Kit never used that word out loud until now and says it with such anger, such hurt, it makes me feel like the bottom of every barrel in town. After a pause, a really long pause, I explain very patiently, very calmly, how I need the lady for my voice and absolutely nothing else, because I basically can't stand her. I go on in this vein until Kit settles down and buys the story I'm selling and thank god she does, because it's the truth. I promise my love I'll call Miss Fanning in the morning and lay down the law: lessons are for singing only. Kit's totally relieved and reassured and that night, once the kids are safely out of the way, we do what we do best, and I'm feeling great and she's feeling great, but then, next morning, a million things come up, mainly with the kids, and I get distracted and forget to make the crucial phone call.

Anyway, later that day, I'm working the lot and getting kinda excited about the rehearsal coming up, when I'll show the other singers how I can nail the *Ingemisco.* It's a Tuesday afternoon, warm and sunny. Frank had just advertised some specials, so there's lots of people sniffing around and suddenly there's also Ed, Elizabeth's hubby, which is pretty unusual, since he doesn't show up at the lot much. He's standing at the entrance, looking tense and unhappy, which I find kinda odd since we got so many customers on hand. Being friendly and a little bit curious, I go over to him to see what's up and before I even say hi, he grabs me by the elbow and leads me out back, and as we're walking, I notice my elbow's shaking from side to side, and it isn't me, it's Ed, he's a nervous wreck. We finally get to the back alley. He lets my elbow go and before I can say anything, he takes a big swipe at me, bam, just like that. Fortunately, the guy's way old, over sixty for sure, and I'm able to fend it off. When I see he's about to go after me again, using his head like a battering ram, I spring into action, clamp him in a bear hug and we're waltzing around like a pair of drunk college kids until his age does him in and he finally simmers down.

"Ed, Ed, come on, take it easy. What's the problem here?"

"You."

"Me?" He tries to break my hold, but I'm still in control. I may be overweight, *pleasingly plump*, I call it, but I'm still pretty fit.

"Let me go, god damn it, let go!"

"No more punches, Ed, okay? I gotta preserve my manly beauty." I give him my *that's a joke* grin, hoping he'll realize there's no hard feelings, but his lips stay tight and thin.

"You've got one hell of a nerve," he says. "You pretend you're my buddy and all the time you're balling my wife."

"Not true."

"Bullshit. Let me go!" Suddenly, I remember who I got this bear hug on, Ed, my boss's boss, mister money bags himself. I'm trying to get Frank to give me more sales time on the floor and one bad word from this guy and my chances will melt faster than a snowball in hell.

"Okay, man, I'll lay off, but no more rough stuff. I don't want to get my hair mussed." I give him another smile, which also has no effect. He's still mad as hell, but I gotta let him go – I'm stuck in a lose-lose situation.

Ed takes a few steps away, dusts himself off and glares over at me. "You know, all I have to do is snap my fingers and Frank fires your sorry ass."

"Why would he? I'm the best salesman he's got."

"You're fucking my wife."

"Ed, I'm not, I'm not. I swear to god I'm not."

"Bullshit, man, she confessed. Just minutes ago she told me you two are in love."

"Ed, I'm married. I got kids. I only love my wife."

"That's not what Elizabeth said."

"Trust me. I don't play around, never did, never will, and I really don't love your wife." In fact, I hate her for making all these problems for me, but I keep that to myself.

"I'm not making this up, Rich. Lizzie said you two were going to run off and start a new life together in New York."

I'm dying to point out that no one's running anywhere with her, she's way too old and crazy, but instead I just say, "Ed, I love my life in Graystone. I'm staying right where I am."

We lapse into this deep uneasy silence, squinting and staring at each other like two overweight cowboys in a wild west movie, wondering what comes next, when suddenly, like bam, totally out of the blue, I laugh and I mean really laugh, a super big, super long belly laugh, *har, har, har.* I don't know why it happens, but it does.

"Stop laughing," he says. I nod and try to hold it in, but it keeps on bubbling up. "I told you to stop that laughing."

"I'm trying, man, I really am." It's not that easy. The whole idea of me and Elizabeth being some kinda hot couple is beyond ridiculous, a scene from a terrible TV sitcom. It's even worse because Ed doesn't realize how nuts the whole thing is. "Sorry, Ed, but what she's been telling you is pure fiction. This romance you're so worried about, this so-called love affair between her and me, it never happened and never will. She made it all up, she really did. No offense, but she's way out there in la la land. Open your eyes, man. Face the facts."

At first there's nothing from him, no words, no movement, just stiff strained silence. Then I sense a shift in the atmosphere, a little relaxation, like somehow or other a brand-new thought is finally worming its way through all the curves and folds of his not very big, not very functional brain. He asks me in a faint, wounded voice, "Rich, are you actually trying to tell me she made the whole thing up?"

Hello, what took you so long? I think, but what I say is: "I totally respect you, man. You're my boss's boss, a big shot in the community. Everyone looks up to you and so do I. I'd never play around with your wife. I'm not that kinda guy. And, yeah, now that you ask, of course she made it up." As I say this, Ed's anger and suspicion dribbles away, until all that's left is the worn-out look of an old, unhappy man.

CHAPTER FOUR

Kit

"But he never reads!"

That's what my friends said when Richie Verdun and I started dating. I hung out in high school with the whiz kids, the *brainiacs* who later forged lives as lawyers, professors and doctors. None of them could believe that feisty young Catherine, a devotee of Jane Austen, could be attracted to the class chatterbox, a self-declared non-reader who had no interest in making the honor roll.

"What do you guys talk about?" my friends would ask. "He never even opened *Pride and Prejudice.*"

It made no difference. When tragedy struck, when the worst of the worst happened to me, Richie offered a strong and loving hand. Though he seemed uninterested in science or philosophy or the arts, it was thrilling for the shell-shocked young woman I was to connect with a man who was pure joy, pure masculine energy. At a very dark time, he led me to a roomful of light.

Please don't misunderstand. Despite his generous heart and stirring voice and thrilling sex drive and inspiring commitment to life, my beloved husband could, and frequently did, drive me completely mad.

One splendid Saturday in June, for instance, I arrived home in an excellent mood. After getting a double masters in English literature and library science from M.S.U. I had begun talks with the local school board about starting a library in our high school. The board expected me to find the funding for it, and I had just returned from an exhilarating chat with Doc Williams about a foundation in Detroit which he thought might be willing to help.

Opening the door, I called for Richie and the kids. There was no response, but I could hear muffled shouts and thumps coming from somewhere upstairs. Obviously, Richie and the boys were having one of their weekend roughhouse sessions. I soon realized that the combat wasn't being held in one of the boys' rooms, as usual, but in ours. This was an absolute no-no. After Timmy shattered my reading lamp during a vigorous bout with his young brother, Richie and I laid down the law. No fighting in the parental bedroom. Ever.

When I opened our door, there was Richie, grappling on the floor with our older son Timmy as Billy looked on, a cheering section of one. The room was ravaged. The mattress had been pulled off our bed to serve as a wrestling mat. Pillows and sheets were scattered everywhere.

Timmy, a high school wrestling star, had somehow or other forced Richie, his bigger and much heavier rival, onto his back. His strong young legs snaked around his father's left leg, while his arms clamped down on the other. He seemed to be prying his father apart.

I held back in the doorway as Richie lay pinned, with his legs spread impossibly wide and his rear end tilted up, facing me. Not only was it undignified (to say the least), but it looked as if our young son might be causing him some serious damage.

"Give up, Dad?" Timmy shouted. "Give up?"

"No, never," said Richie, obviously in considerable distress.

"You can do it, Dad. Push him off," said Billy, never a great fan of his older, stronger brother.

Richie kept writhing about, while his son hung on, his muscles taut with aggression. "Face it, Dad, you're split."

"No."

Timmy's lips twisted in a snarl. "Come on, motherfucker, give!"

I had to intervene. "Timothy, that's enough! Let him go!"

"Aw, Ma," said Billy, "lighten up. They're just having a little fun."

"It's not fun, it looks excruciating."

"Sure as hell hope so," chuckled Timmy.

"Get off your father this instant!"

"Okay, okay," Timmy grumbled, "don't have yourself a cow." He reluctantly released the hold and unwound himself.

Once freed, Richie unleashed a fierce battle cry, tackled his son from behind, flopped his full weight onto him and stretched him out flat on the floor.

"Howdya like them apples?"

"You'd better say uncle, Timmy," Billy said, happy to see his brother in distress.

"It's uncle time, son. No way in hell you're getting free."

Timmy simmered in silence, thrashing this way and that under his father's substantial bulk.

"Richie, let go!" I shouted.

"Come on, kid, where's that magic word?"

"Never!" replied Timmy. His father levered his broad frame forward, putting even more pressure on his son.

"What's gotten into you two? Stop!" I shouted.

"Come on, son, it won't kill you. Say the word."

"Asshole?"

"Guess again," replied Richie. "It starts with a *u*."

"You suck."

"Try again. I'm not letting go till you say it."

Timmy unleashed a litany of mockery. "Dickhead. Scumbag. Fuckface."

That was it. I marched over to the dresser and grabbed a big crystal vase filled with peonies I'd just cut from our garden, then ran over to the combatants and doused them, as if they were battling dogs.

My husband slowly rolled off his son and lay flat on the carpet, panting heavily. Mission accomplished.

"Billy," he gasped, "get your father and brother some towels."

"What's gotten into you?" I repeated. "Wrestling in our bedroom? And the *language* you used, Timmy..."

"It's a just dumb guy thing, hon," Richie said. "He doesn't mean anything by it." He noticed Billy was still standing in the doorway, fascinated. "We're waiting for those towels, son."

As Billy ran off, I turned back and surveyed the wreckage of my room: the mattress off the bed, soggy sheets and pillows, and peonies scattered all over the floor.

"It sure is a shame about those flowers," said Richie, sounding abashed.

"It's a shame you don't act your age."

"Wow, Dad," said Timmy. "You're really in trouble with your wife."

"That's enough," I said. "You're in trouble, too."

"Why? Dad challenged me to a match and we had one."

"That wasn't a challenge, son. I just said you couldn't split me. A simple statement of fact."

"But I did. I peeled you like a fucking banana."

"Only because you cheated," interjected Billy, arriving with the towels.

Timmy spun on him furiously. "You're such a fucking liar."

"And you're a cheater."

"I am not!"

"You sure as shit are!"

I had to shout again. "Out! Both of you! Out!"

"But, Ma--"

I clapped my hands sharply. "The groceries are in the car. Bring them into the kitchen. I don't want to see either of you for a good long while, understood?" They rose grudgingly and started to leave. "Not so fast. Put the mattress back. Toss the flowers in the trash. Drape the sheets over the bannister to dry."

To my relief and amazement, the boys did as they were told, then hurried off to unload the car.

I looked over at Richie. He still was flat on his back. He hadn't moved since the end of the fight, not even to grab a towel. "How are you doing?" I asked.

"Never better."

"That's what you always say. Any chance you might be in denial?"

"Denial is a river in Egypt."

I smiled in spite of myself. "You're incorrigible."

He smiled back. "And sweaty. And sexy..."

"Don't get ahead of yourself, big boy.'

"Big boys do it the best."

Irritated though I was with Richie and all his shenanigans, seeing him pin our strong young son had fired me up.

"Are you really up for it?" I asked.

"You know me, hon."

"You're sure?"

He reached up to me. "Come on, sweets. I just pinned a high school wrestling champ."

"By jumping him from behind," I noted.

"Served him right, the little smart-ass."

I laughed. I always had a soft spot for Richie's swagger. With considerable caution I eased myself onto him and covered his damp body with mine. I loved the feel of his generous full flesh, the rough mineral scent of his sweat.

"You certainly do know how to take care of yourself."

"I'll take care of you, too."

"Mmm, that would be lovely..."

I snuggled into him more deeply and kissed him on the mouth. "Any sore spots? Any need for Kit's special massage?"

"Yeah, maybe..."

I reached down and started stroking. Suddenly, with a sharp intake of breath, he heaved himself upright. He looked paler than ever. Beads of perspiration glistened at his temples.

"What's wrong? Are you in pain?"

Dead silence.

"Timmy really did hurt you, didn't he?"

"Of course not. I'm fine."

He was so clearly the opposite I had to laugh.

"Stop laughing at me!" I stopped. A dry tight silence enfolded us. "You think I'm a loser, don't you? You think I'm just a jerk."

"Richie, really, I haven't the—"

"Why don't you get outta here? Leave me alone."

"But, Richie, I'm just trying to—"

"I said get outta here! Leave me the fuck alone!"

CHAPTER FIVE

Richie

There I am on the bed, still damp from the dousing Kit gave me, my muscles on fire from the thrashing I got from my son in a wrestling match I never should have fought, and I'm thinking *what's going on here? what just happened?* I mean, sure, Timmy's a real good high school wrestler, but I've got eighty or ninety pounds on him, I always could whip his ass. But this time as we squared off, I suddenly noticed that he was taller than I was. When we put our hands on each other's biceps, I realized his were big as grapefruits. When did that happen? A minute later he traps my legs and pries them apart in a banana split, a hold only jerks get caught in. It's beyond humiliating, your butt is high in the air for everyone to snicker at, and, boy, does it ever hurt, your legs are in two different time zones. True, when Kit storms in, I get my revenge and sucker Timmy into a schoolboy pin, but I gotta face facts, he whipped my sorry ass. And then, to make things worse, I take it all out on Kit and treat her like shit, which makes *me* feel like shit. Which is also the way I've been feeling at work these days. Things were great when I started, absolutely terrific; my boss Frank took me on when I was basically still a kid, and bit by bit, as I discovered I could sell cars like a champ and really enjoyed doing it, I became his secret weapon, his best-selling employee. We got so close he even gave me a twelve percent commission, which was more than anyone else. He kept it off the books, of course. It was our little secret, our own special deal. Hell, when he went through his nasty, and I mean let-it-all-hang-out, guts, balls nasty divorce from Cindy, Kit and I let him sleep over on our couch, not once but many times.

Anyway, you know how things go. That was then, this is now. I guess the big divorce settlement (in Cindy's favor, of course, Frank was a skirt chaser from the get-go) is what did it. He needed more cash, he had to restructure his business and when he did, my best buddy Frank was replaced by his greedy money-grubbing twin, who takes me aside one day and tells me our sweetheart deal is over. The special commission I earned as his all-star best seller five years running, not to mention steadfast friend, is now a nonstarter. He shoves me back to the measly ten percent I used to get and I can't do much about it. I certainly can't leave Graystone. Billy and Timmy are still in high school and Kit's trying to start a library over at their school. They've got every sport under the sun, but no library, which drives Kit totally bonkers. So I have to stay put and support my family and take it on the nose like a man.

Then it gets worse. Frank fires some of his best people, like that really great guy Hector, the night cleaner, and brings in some half-ass company to replace him with lazy lowlifes who drink on the job and leave the place dirtier than ever, but the price is right so Frank doesn't care. Then he hires kids who do what he says and take tiny commissions, only seven percent, if you can believe it, seven, and they accept it. There's a recession on, a job's a job, so the place is full of new faces, untested but cheap, and sales stay stuck in the basement.

One of the new guys actually has some talent, Willie Margashack, a conceited shit with this high school football hero *ain't I terrific* look. Somehow or other, he's always in my face about how many cars he sold, how he set a new company record for first year sales, how he'll beat my all-time record, just give him a few years. In no time, Frank's giving him the full ten percent commission, way ahead of the other new guys, which is all the jerk needs. He's out on the lot crowing to everyone how Frank truly loves him, how he's the best thing since sliced bread, which makes me and my pals, the few older guys still working the lot, groan and cover our ears. Willie doesn't notice. He just keeps bragging and boasting until it really starts getting to me.

It finally blows up when a buyer comes in one Friday afternoon and I can tell right away he's a Corvette type, so I show him the new model and give him the pitch, but he gets sticker shock and settles on a Malibu. Fine, no problem. He'll see me the next day to close, but then on Saturday Kit's off with Timmy at a match, when Billy gets a terrible toothache. It turns out he needs a wisdom tooth extracted and I have to call in sick. When I come in Sunday, the girl behind the desk says Willie made the sale for me yesterday and I figure, great, good news, I started the sale, he finished it, we share the commission fifty-fifty. Two days later, Frank calls me into his office and to my amazement this smart-ass punk is sitting right next to him, with this shit-eating grin on his face and Frank goes, "Now look, Richie, I think there's some misunderstanding about commissions between you and young Willie here." *Young Willie,* Frank's new golden boy.

"No misunderstanding at all," I say. "We share fifty-fifty, same as always."

"Not this time. He's entitled to more. He switched the guy up from a Malibu to a Corvette."

"Hell, I showed that guy Corvettes the moment he came in. He said they were way too expensive."

"I guess our friend got him to reconsider." He pats Willie's thick shoulder like he's his pet poodle, and, needless to say, I'm pissed. "So, here's what we're doing. You each get your five percent commission, Richie for the Malibu, Willie for the Corvette."

I can't believe what I'm hearing. "Now hang on, that's not fair. I arranged the deal and got the guy set up."

"For a Malibu," says Willie, "a lousy no-frills Malibu."

By now I'm so angry I'm ready to rip his ears off. "Shut the fuck up. You think you're so clever going behind my back to the boss. It's my damn sale and you know it." With this, Willie boy stomps towards me and Frank tells him to cool down and go back on the floor. Once the kid's gone, I say, "What is it with you and that guy?"

"Come on, it's totally fair. He's getting the commission he deserves. And you'll still get two or three hundred bucks."

"But Willie gets far more."

"He deserves it."

"For fuck's sake, I've been with you almost twenty years, five times best seller, and you're cutting me off at the knees."

I look at the smug bastard sitting there at his stupid desk like he's some big shot and I'm just this nobody, and this heat comes over me, this savage fury. I go, "You know, you're a prick, Franko. You really and truly are." Suddenly, he's up on his feet and marches over to me so tight, so close we nearly butt heads, and I realize maybe I went too far.

"Listen, Verdun, that kid's got a great future here. And you're not our top seller any more." He walks over to the door, opens it and says, "Now go out and make me some money."

Years later, I got to sing the Drum Major in *Wozzeck*, hardest damn part I ever learned, pitches all over the place, but once I got it, I had it forever. And the good news is it's short. I get full fee and beat up the baritone big time. How often does a tenor do that? Anyway, the reason I bring it up is the opera's all about this sad sack soldier, Wozzeck, whose life hits rock bottom. His wife's a whore, his kid's a retard, his bosses are nuts and just when you figure things couldn't get worse, he picks a fight with his wife's current boyfriend, me, the Drum Major, who's way bigger and stronger than he is. After I pound him into the sidewalk, he turns his bloody mug to the audience and goes, "One thing after another." That's what this period felt like, one big shit pile after another. And the beating I just got from my big guy Timmy's the biggest shit pile of all. I feel so bad about this, so old and useless, I start splashing around in my own personal black lagoon – me, the happiest, easiest guy you could ever hope to meet.

Salvation comes from a totally unexpected direction. Doc Williams asks if I'd like to sing two arias at this concert he's organizing to raise a few bucks for a new church organ.

"Who'd pay to hear me sing?" I ask. That's how low I was, how dark and down.

"Lots of people."

"No way. They'd pay for me to shut up."

"Who cares, as long as they buy tickets. Anyway, you're wrong, people love your singing. I hear compliments all the time."

"I don't."

"Get a hearing aid."

At this point I'm still part of the great unwashed, a performance virgin. I don't know opera from okra. There was that *Oklahoma!* back in sixth grade, but I was a boy soprano then, that doesn't really count. In fact, to tell the truth, when Doc Williams sweet-talked me into doing his little concert, I'd never even sung through an entire aria. I heard them, of course, liked them, even sang along with my favorite recordings in a half-assed kind of way, but Elizabeth never gave me one to study, put them strictly off limits. She said I wasn't ready, they were all way too difficult. She was the back-to-basics type, you know, scales and arpeggios up the wazoo, until you get so sick and tired of all that technical shit, you're ready to quit singing, except you can't, because you're actually starting to sound good.

Which means I was pretty scared by Doc Williams' proposition. I really bought into Elizabeth's line that arias were a giant challenge. I figured you had to be an incredible musician and linguist and philosopher and historian and god knows what else, none of which I was or ever could be, to perform them, so I got all tied up in knots about them, had this giant block, which was completely absurd. I did the *Ingemisco*, right? – and did it damn well. That's an opera aria you happen to sing in church. Doc kept mentioning stuff like that, how I already sang much harder pieces in church, like the Verdi or the *Panis Angelicus*, how we'd have such fun working together, how I was so much more talented than I gave myself credit for, how even Elizabeth thought I had the goods, how everyone loved the sound of my voice, how I was such an incredibly sexy good-looking guy (all right, maybe he didn't go that far). Anyway, in the end he won me over and thank god he did, cause if I hadn't done that little concert, I wouldn't be where I am now, and that's the absolute truth.

We choose one Puccini and one Verdi, not real imaginative, but, hey, we're new at the game. I'd start off with *Ah, la paterno mano,* a slow sad number from Verdi's *Macbeth,* mainly because Doc loves it, thinks it's noble and beautiful and not all that hard. It doesn't go into the upper stratosphere, there's no high C, thank god, which I never had and never will, and I figure if Doc thinks I can do it, why the hell not? The other aria's my choice, a total no-brainer: *Nessun dorma* from *Turandot.* My hero Corelli sings it like a god and I want to be godlike too, so I tell Doc we're doing it, and he looks at me strangely, like *are you really sure?,* and I say *sure as shitting,* or some other elegant remark, and he smiles and says, "Whatever you say, Richard, you're the star."

That's the kind of guy he is, totally supportive, totally in sync, funny, friendly, frank, the anti-Elizabeth. Doc always starts a session by saying how great I sound, how well it's going, and then, when he's got me feeling I'm the king of all tenors, he slips in a zinger, like maybe I could sing it softer, or louder, or faster, but by that time I'm so encouraged by all his positivity, so optimistic and confident, I don't mind the criticism, I just go back and try again until, note by note, phrase by phrase, everything starts sounding better. I find I really like the process, the gradual puzzling out of music, the slow and steady adjustment of every single detail. I keep working with Doc like a man obsessed and gradually my mood changes. I'm not angry and frustrated any more, I can finally pull the plug on my little black lagoon and let it start draining away.

I'll be singing in this big reception hall tacked on to the back of the church, which they mainly use for parties and church socials. They set up a row of platforms across the back wall for concerts and such, so everyone has a good view of the stage. I mean, what's the point of performing if the folks can't even see you? It's an early October night, but the air's still got some heat to it. The turnout's surprisingly good, the church folk seem excited as they hustle up and down the aisles, setting up folding chairs to accommodate the extra crowd. The atmosphere's festive, everyone's cheery and out for a good time, friends greet friends like they're at the county fair, but they're not, it's a concert, a genuine concert, not like they have here in Frankfurt, perhaps, where people feel it's such an honor to listen to great music, they hardly even breathe, it's much more relaxed than that and, frankly, much more my taste.

Don't get the wrong idea, Doc's programmed real music, but he blends the easy and the tough. He starts with a violinist from the Detroit Symphony, who plays some fast flashy solos with half a million notes which seem to please the crowd, then there's a pianist who's faculty at Ann Arbor playing Beethoven's *Moonlight Sonata.* It turns out most of the people know the main tune, so they go *ahh* when they hear it, but seem disappointed when the music turns in another direction. A jazz band from Grand Rapids ends the first half with a medley of show tunes which everyone loves, of course, except Doc, who gives me this look that says *I try to give them quality, but guess what they really like best.*

We waltz out to start the second half and it's like, whoa, there's lots of people out there. Backstage I kind of forget how full the hall is, and suddenly there they all are, waiting to hear me sing. I don't see my family, which is probably just as well, but I do see that smart-ass Willie Margashack with his hot young wife. I figure he's here to see me fail, but even with him, even with all those people out there, I'm not really nervous. Hell, I'd gone over the songs week after week, played them a million times on my Walkman, what could possibly go wrong?

Plenty. Doc settles in at the piano and begins the Verdi. It's a pretty heavy piece about the murder of this poor guy's family and I'm holding back so I don't get off track. The night before at the dress rehearsal, Doc got all over me for not being expressive enough, so we did it again and I really let go and got all emotional and suddenly had this vision of my two boys lying in pools of blood and it made me so upset I had to stop singing. "Maybe that's a bit *too* expressive," went Doc. Anyway, I take it real easy on the Verdi this time and don't get too far out there. That's probably why the response at the end is like, *thank you, okay, but so what?* Over the years I've learned that you can't play it safe. Audiences want fighters, heroes, conquerors.

The lousy applause doesn't spook me. No, the moment Doc plays the intro to the Puccini, I think *great, good news, I get a do-over.* I sail right into it, I don't even think or feel very much, I just *sing,* till I get to the final *vincerò,* when I really go whole hog and give it all I've got, and then it's over. There's a weird pause before I hear the rat, tat, tat of hundreds of hands clapping, quietly at first, then growing and growing, so I make a little bow, and then another.

I remember Doc, gesture to him, and he gets up from the piano and bows too, and the clapping continues, louder now. Doc joins me and grabs my hand, and we take another bow, and as we're bowing, he whispers, "See, they really like you", and now there's a new sound, like wild elephants trampling around backstage. I look over and see some musicians in the wings giving me the thumbs up and stomping on the floor and I'm thinking, *holy shit, they're professionals.* Then I face front again and the public starts getting up, first one, then three, then ten, till most everyone's on their feet, and it's like I'm suddenly back in sixth grade, the pint-sized Curly soaking up the applause, getting high on Vitamin A and I suddenly realize I really could get used to this.

I bow and bow like a wind-up doll, till Doc leans over and says, "Let's not overdo it," so I shake his hand like crazy, because I'm not leaving till I show the world how grateful I am to him for getting me through this. He's a complete and absolute champ. Once I'm offstage, I'm zapped, totally depleted. I drag my dazed ass over to a rickety little chair and collapse on it and spend the rest of the concert in a state of suspended animation, like *did this actually happen? did I actually do that?*

When the concert's over, I stumble into the entry hall to greet the public and accept their congratulations, wondering all the time how come so many people, friends and strangers alike, are coming up to me and saying how great my singing is, and looking like they really mean it.

After the crowd thins out, the family finally appears, Carol first, who gives me a chaste little hug and a peck on the cheek, as if she doesn't really know how to deal with it, then Billy, who doesn't say a word and stares at the floor. Kit arrives in a cloud of rosy perfume. She croons in my ear, "Darling, that was just beautiful," and I say, "You're beautiful," and we lock on a big one, and out of the corner of my eye I see Billy and Carol cringing, like god forbid anyone should know they're actually related to those two sex perverts.

After a good long drink at Kit's magic well, I go to get my coat and Timmy comes out of the shadows. We've pretty much been avoiding each other since we had our little bout. When we do meet around the house, he keeps flashing me these arrogant stares, like *I whipped your sorry ass*, and when I ask him what's up, he goes, "Want a banana split?"

"Well, son, what did you think?" Silence, long pause.

"It was okay."

"Okay? Your father was fantastic." God bless Kit, she's always on my side, always.

"I guess."

"Timothy, the entire town stood up and cheered your father. How can you possibly talk that way?"

"Okay, okay, get off my case."

"It's all right, hon. I'll handle it." I give her a gentle shove and she steps aside, giving us a little space. "You know, I'm pretty sad we're not talking any more. I really miss those chats we used to have... Son, did you hear me?"

"What's there to chat about?"

"I don't know, school, life, girls..." I flash him my *here comes a joke* look. "Banana splits."

He gives me a little smile. "I thought you didn't like them."

"Man, anything you dish out I can take, because it's from my kid, my son, my big guy, central to my life, a giant part of it..." I'm suddenly all emotional, which is embarrassing as hell, but I feel what I feel, I can't lie. "In that first song, the slow one, the one I didn't do so well, I actually was thinking of you."

"You were? Why?"

"It's about a father whose kid was just killed."

"You saying you want to kill me?" I can't tell if he means it as a joke or not.

"Timmy, get a grip, of course not."

"Then, what?"

I won't give up on this, I can't. "When I was rehearsing with Doc last night, I had this image of something awful happening to you and, well, you got your license now, your own car. Take care of yourself, don't do anything stupid."

He gets this impish grin on his face. "Like getting trapped in a banana split?"

"You sure as hell won't be trapping me. I'm retiring from the local wrestling scene."

"Yeah, just as well, you're a better singer than wrestler, way better."

"You're saying you liked it tonight? You liked your dad's singing?"

Finally, after what seems like two or three centuries, he goes, "Dad, why are you even asking? You know you sounded fantastic."

I hug him so close, so tight I nearly crack his young ribs. After a few seconds, I feel his back muscles tense up, like *who is this crazy guy?* But I don't let go, I can't, not for a good long while.

I barely sleep that night, my eyes keep popping open while I rehash all that success, all that whooping and hollering, but it gets me overexcited and tomorrow's a regular workday. I keep telling myself to let go of the concert and sleep, but it's hard to do. Once or twice I manage to get the right rhythm going, but just as I'm rounding the bend, I bounce wide awake and relive all over again that amazing ovation. And so it goes, hour after hour, till the first rays of the rising sun slap me in the face and make it official: No sleep for you, bud, get up and face the day. Time to go out and sell some cars and make more money for Frank, so he can build himself a second swimming pool.

As I pull into the lot, two of the guys start applauding, meaning it as a joke, of course. I park the car, get out and give them a comedy bow, to show I don't take this stuff seriously. But, it's applause, man. Everybody loves applause.

I'm walking towards the office, when who do I bump into but Willie Margashack, the boss's new pet poodle. Usually he's sneering at me or pretending I don't exist, but this time he's all smiles, like he's just swooning at my magnificent presence. Naturally, I'm wondering what drug he's on. "Hey, Richie, my wife's in love with you."

"She's got real good taste."

"No, seriously, she totally flipped last night. I mean, I'm not into that sort of stuff, but she thinks you're the greatest ever."

"Well, whaddya know, I'll deliver my thanks to her in person, but only when you're not around."

"That'll be the day." He gives me this bright smile, like nothing bad ever happened between us. "By the way, no hard feelings, eh?"

"About what?"

"The Corvette, remember? Truth is, I'd gladly split the difference on that commission, except Marilou's expecting and we're tight on cash." I guess I must look stunned, because I really am. "No bullshit, man, it's the truth."

Without thinking, I shoot out my hand to him just like that. "No hard feelings here, either." And we shake. At that very moment, Frank comes out, sees us shaking hands and goes ballistic. "Cut the smooching, girls. There's customers on the lot. Go out and make me some money." We give him the hairy eyeball, like we're on the same side now, staff against management-- another important first-- and take our time getting back to the grind.

For the next few days I'm the man of the hour, everyone's hero. The climax comes Sunday after services when I'm surrounded by, like, twenty people who heard me at that little concert. They're all completely amazed by how wonderfully I sang. And I totally suck it up. How can I not? Worship me all you like.

Whatever goes up must come down, splat, all over the pavement. That's what happens the next day, Monday, when reality kicks in and everyone, even me, even the kids, even my darling Kit, goes back to their normal routine. It's a giant letdown. I know it sounds ridiculous, but I hurt so much from this crazy feeling of being suddenly forgotten that I begin to wish the whole thing never happened. It's like my singing counted for nothing, *less* than nothing, so why the hell bother in the first place?

Fortunately, good old Doc Williams notices. He takes me aside after Wednesday rehearsal and asks me over to his house for a pick-me-up.

I'm sitting on one of the broken-down chairs in his mishmash living room as he pours me some whisky. The Scotch is totally amazing, liquid smoke. It slides down sharp and clean.

"Richard," he goes, "I've got a proposition for you."

"Sorry, man, I don't swing that way." He shoots me this scowl, like *when the hell will you grow up?*

"I'll pretend I didn't hear that. Anyway, here's my proposition. We do a full concert this spring, just you and me, an hour or so of music. You sing some new arias along with a few songs and maybe I'll challenge myself and play a Mozart or Haydn sonata, so you won't have to perform every single second. We'd rehearse once or twice a week and schedule it around Easter, which gives us almost six months to put the whole thing together. Does that appeal? Could you do it?"

Crazy. I was so down at that point, so low, it never once occurred to me that Doc would ever want to work with me again. "You really mean it? You're actually willing to mix it up with me again?"

"Of course, why else would I suggest it?"

"Because you're a masochist?" As soon as I say it, he winces.

"Richard, the only thing I really have problems with is your humor."

"Oops, sorry. I'll try to control myself."

"Please, I'd be most appreciative... So, it's agreed then, Verdun and Williams, back by popular demand?"

"You bet."

"One other thing. I think you should get paid this time."

"Paid. Really?" This is an evening of big surprises.

I think about his tiny house, how simply he and Marcia live compared to us. "But what about you, Doc? Couldn't we at least share fifty-fifty?"

"Frankly, we're talking about very little money, a few hundred dollars at most. I think it's best you have it."

I really don't know how to handle his generosity. "Doc, that's real nice, and I very much appreciate it, but why are you doing this?"

He shakes his head slowly from side to side like he can't believe I don't know and gives me the typical Doc look, very intense, very serious.

"Richard, can I ask something personal?"

"As long as it's not about my advanced sex techniques. That's between me and Kit." As soon as I say this, I remember what he just said. "Sorry, it's the whiskey."

"I certainly hope so. You know, Marcia's a big fan of yours. She's always loved your voice."

"Really?" I'm startled. I never felt Doc's wife took any interest in me at all.

"After our little concert she asked me the same thing I've often asked myself. What's holding Richard back? Why doesn't he just do it?"

"Do what?"

"Turn professional. You could. You sing at a very high level." Another shocker. Sure, people always said nice things, but this is totally different. "Why is it so hard for you to accept that you sing well? Because you do, Richard, you absolutely do."

"That's nice, I'm flattered, but you're talking about something young guys do. I'm getting up there, Doc. I'm no kid."

"Age has very little to do with it. Your voice is strong and fresh. You really have a chance for a career."

"What kind of career?"

"Well, I'm no astrologer, I'm just telling you the material's there. Shortly before Miss Fanning left Graystone, do you know what she told me?"

"I'm the hottest guy on earth?"

He snaps at me, barks like a rabid dog. "This is serious, Richard."

"Sorry."

"Elizabeth said, and she never, ever said this sort of thing unless she really and truly meant it, 'This man could be an important Wagnerian tenor. Why is he wasting his life in a place like this?' You've got a special gift. Go out and give it a try."

"Doc, how can I possibly go off to some awful place like New York and mix it up with people I don't know in a scene I don't understand, spending thousands of dollars on food and housing and coaches and teachers, when I'll probably wind up broke?"

"Luciano Pavarotti isn't broke. He makes a fortune, especially when he sings those outdoor concerts."

"He's one in a billion. Nothing to do with me."

"That's what you think."

"Doc, please, I'm nuts but not that nuts. An occasional recital, a few solos here and there, fine, no problem. I love to sing. I'll do it. But dragging my sorry ass all over hell and gone hoping people might actually want to hear a pudgy middle-aged car salesman play operatic tenor? Forget it. Never gonna happen."

After that, all we can basically do is shake hands and say goodbye. My head still ringing with whiskey, I lurch my way back home.

You know how it is when something's up, but you're not quite sure what. There's a plot brewing and it's all about you, but nobody's talking. That's exactly what I stumble into over the next few months. For example, I'm over at Doc's working on our spring recital. We're running through *Vesti la giubba*, which I really love, it fits me like a glove and isn't long or real high, which is always a plus, when the phone rings. Doc answers but moves away so I can't overhear. The cord's pretty short and my hearing's pretty sharp, so even though he's hunched over the receiver, I distinctly hear him say Kit's name.

Once he hangs up, I ask if he was talking to Kit. His big moon face gets blotched with red. "Lord, no, Richard. Why would I be speaking with her?"

"I don't know. You tell me."

"It was Marcia, actually. She was talking about your wife. She bumped into her at the mall."

"Kit never goes to the mall. It's one of her pet peeves."

More blushing. "Well, maybe Marcia got it wrong. Maybe I misunderstood."

And that's it. He buttons up tight and I take the hint. There's just no point in pursuing it.

This also is the year our dear boss Frank gets the genius idea of hiring two new salesmen, who happen to be his new wife's kid brothers. Not that nepotism has anything to do with it. Obviously, if you put more salesmen on the floor of a small car dealership, everyone winds up with fewer sales. Seeing as how this brilliant innovation comes just around Christmas, when all of us are counting on earning some extra cash, the slick new move isn't popular. A bunch of the guys choose me and Willie–yeah, like we're a team now–to go to management and complain. We march into the front office and lay it out for Ed and Frank and they basically say, *don't worry, everything will be fine, there's plenty of sales to go around.*

Completely outraged by their bullshit, I go home and tell Kit what creeps they are, what assholes. She listens like a trouper, but it's not long before her eyes glaze over. Finally, after going on and on for what must have been six complete *Ring* cycles, I give the poor lady a chance. "Well, you know what they say, don't get angry, get even."

"How about I strangle Frank with Ed's necktie? That way, Ed gets stuck with the rap and I kill two birds with one stone."

"Very funny. Richie, trust me, you'll get past this. Be bold, be assertive. That's all you need to do."

"Assertive about what?"

She smiles at me, just smiles, no comments, no hints, no help, nothing. I try to get something more out of her, I charm and coax and press, but nothing works.

It's a real busy period for me--end of the year, everything's hectic. There's Thanksgiving, of course, with all the madness that whips up. There's also Carol's birthday, with mine right after. Wrestling season starts, I gotta watch Timmy's matches. Then, there's this giant clearance sale out at the lot, which usually creates lots of extra business, though this year, it's pretty much a bust. As an extra added attraction, it turns out Billy needs lots of expensive dental work he could have avoided if he listened to his Dad and brushed his teeth once in a while, but what the hell does Dad know?

I somehow or other manage to keep it together until we arrive at the big event, my birthday-- December fifteenth, in case you'd like to send a present. A week or so before, I tell Kit I'm calling Papa Giovanni's to make reservations same as always. That's how we celebrate, go over to this great pizza joint in Irvington, order two or three giant ones and three Greek salads, wash it down with lots of coke and beer, a delightful night out and not all that expensive. But Kit wants to do it herself this year, which is odd because she's been so busy. But then, I get it, the coin finally drops. She's planning a surprise party for me. Doc's in on it too. That's why she's been calling him so often. It also pretty much explains the weird looks the kids have been giving me. Fine, no problem, I'm always ready to party.

The night arrives, the family gathers, but there's no sudden knocks on the door, no shouts of "Surprise, surprise!" It's just us chickens. The meal's fantastic, of course, Kit at her very best, a big slab of roast beef cooked medium, exactly how I like it, with roast potatoes, creamed spinach and this amazing tomato stew with eggplant and zucchini she found in some fancy French cookbook. But all the time I'm thinking, it doesn't feel right, there's gotta be something more.

Kit goes off to the kitchen and the kids are joking around, going, "Gosh, I wonder what she's doing in there" and nonsense like that, until Kit shouts, "Okay, kids, ready," and Timmy turns off the lights and she returns with the cake. You have to understand Kit's really dressed up for the occasion with this long sleeve grey number she picked up in Detroit so she could look professional when she's meeting with foundations. Anyway, she comes towards me looking like my own personal movie star, holding the cake with lots of candles, not the full forty-two, that would melt the icing, and even though the boys are singing happy birthday totally out of tune, like it's some kinda joke, I'm still feeling great as my sweet beauty drifts towards me, glowing in the candlelight, holding this beautiful cake she made all by herself, my favorite, chocolate with mocha butter cream. I bend down to blow out the candles and see *Opera Star* written in big chocolate letters. I don't really think about it, I just blow out the candles and cut up the cake, which is utterly delicious and disappears in no time.

After it's gone, I sit back, totally stuffed, totally satisfied, until Carol says, "Daddy, we want you to have a happy birthday, and a happy every day, and do something you really love."

Timmy's next. "Yeah, like you keep complaining about your job and the customers and your creep of a boss. That's not right."

There's a little pause. "Billy, go on," Carol says, "it's your turn."

"I forgot."

"Forgot what?" I ask.

"Our little presentation," says Kit. "We only went over it once."

"Presentation?"

"Darling, you've worked year in, year out, always for us, our future, our well-being, so that we could always have what we needed. And we do. Now it's your turn. Take a few years off and see if you can actually make it as a professional singer. Go to New York, do what you have to, but give it a genuine try. We think you can, Doc thinks you can, and we all think you'd be much happier doing something you truly love. And if you're happier, we're happier. Don't worry about money, we'll be fine. The house is paid up. Carol starts working this spring, she'll be totally self-sufficient. I'll be working too. Yes, my job just got approved, the grant for the library came through. Isn't that wonderful?"

Instead of answering, I get all teary eyed, which is pretty damn embarrassing, especially in front of the kids, but there's nothing I can do, I'm totally overwhelmed.

It's ages before I get back to normal. "Great news," I go. "Kit finally gets to pay all the bills."

CHAPTER SIX

Rigby

Richie Verdun appeared at Maestro's door one blustery February afternoon, thickly swaddled in L.L. Bean winter gear like a voyager from a distant planet. And his was indeed distant–a tiny town somewhere in the wilds of middle Michigan. He beamed and gave a cheery wave.

"Hello, hello, Verdun's the name. Singing's my game."

"Hello, welcome." We made an amusing contrast, I thought– trendy *moi*, looking, I hoped, like a cool young New Yorker in my standard uniform of tight-fitting jeans and short-sleeved white linen shirt, and he, bundled up against the bitter cold like the abominable snowman's shorter younger brother.

He looked me up and down. "Aren't you freezing? You're not even wearing socks."

"Maestro's apartment is terribly overheated."

"You sure you're not making a fashion statement?"

I had to smile. "Guilty as charged..." When I offered him my hand, his firm enthusiastic grip painfully reminded me I needed to join a gym.

Of course, I couldn't afford one and probably never would. Artistic poverty, *la vie de Bohème*, was the fate I'd chosen. My parents back in Covington, Kentucky, couldn't believe that that their only child preferred opera and ballet to fishing and hunting, that I'd rather practice Bach on our out-of-tune upright piano than watch game shows on TV with them.

Thanks to a small bequest from a bachelor uncle, I was able to escape to New York, where I enrolled at the Manhattan School of Music. I majored in classical piano, until my primary teacher, with considerable lack of tact, and, alas, considerable accuracy, said to me, "*Dahrlink*, you're extremely musical, but you'll never make it as a soloist." I was despondent for about ten minutes, then changed my major to collaborative piano and focused, quite happily, on accompaniment. To tell the truth, I never much wanted to be a famed virtuoso, I just wanted to *be* in music, *live* in music any way I could.

But my uncle's bequest ran out. I worked odd jobs and played countless auditions for singers almost as broke as I was. Finally, mercifully, a fellow pianist who looked after a distinguished old opera coach told me he was moving and asked if I'd like his job. Would I!

The work wasn't difficult. I'd prepare Maestro's meals, take him out for the occasional walk and make sure he took his pills. In return, I could stay rent free in one of his spare bedrooms and make use of his splendid old Steinway. I soon discovered that the man I was taking care of was a musical marvel. He had come to the Met from Italy as a very young man, when Caruso was still singing there, when Gatti-Casazza was its brilliant manager. His long years of collaboration with some of the greatest names in opera had given him a profound understanding of the repertoire. So what if Maestro could be difficult, so what if his apartment was gloomy and his kitchen absurdly small, I was directly connected through him to opera's glorious past.

One of my duties was to arrange the rental of his spare bedroom. A friend of a friend had told me about a Midwestern choir director whose star tenor, Richard Verdun, was heading east for auditions.

The man himself now stood before me, exuding an openness and amiability one doesn't usually experience in the catty world of opera. "I'm so pleased to finally meet you. I'm Maestro Borgianni's assistant, Rigby Converse."

"Any relation to the sneaker folks?"

"If only. I'm just a poor starving musician. The neighborhood is teeming with them."

"I guess that's good news."

"Not if you're looking for a loan."

He laughed with disconcerting exuberance. "Good one, son. So, any idea when I can meet the Maestro?"

"Actually, he's under the weather at present and keeping pretty much to his room."

"Sorry to hear it."

"Don't worry. He'll be back on his feet very soon."

"By the way, that's some doorman you got. I didn't understand a word he was saying."

"Join the club. He favors a medieval variant of ancient outer Slobovian."

"Guess I'd better brush up on it."

"It won't help... Heavens, sorry, I've left you standing in the corridor. Come in, come in. May I offer some help with your bags?"

"Nah, thanks, I can handle it..." He hauled his large and clearly very heavy suitcases into the foyer and was stopped short by the large portrait of Puccini that faced the front door.

"Wow, impressive. Who's the big shot?"

I was startled, to say the least. How could a singer not recognize the greatest Italian composer of the twentieth century? "I'm sorry about the funereal lighting," I said, "but Maestro hates anything brighter than a sixty-watt bulb."

"Lucky us."

"Lucky us indeed. He provides us with the cheapest housing on the Upper West Side."

"Three hundred bucks a month is cheap?"

"Welcome to New York, Richard."

"Richie, please, no needed for formality."

"Richie, then. I'm happy to report that while your room may be overpriced, it's also quite large, at least by New York standards."

"Glad to hear it. A big guy like me needs all the space he can get." Richie may have been somewhat overweight, but he was compact and reasonably fit. There were countless singers, many of them quite famous, who were far heavier. "So," he said, referring to the portrait of Puccini, "who's that big shot again?"

"Puccini." He looked as befuddled as I was. "It's a stunning portrait, no? Boldini made it just after the premiere of *La Rondine.* Maestro picked it up in a Roman flea market decades ago."

"That was some lucky pick. It's gotta be worth a bundle."

"Yes, probably. It's never been reproduced. It's very much a hidden treasure."

"He sure looks like a big shot, doesn't he, with that cape flung over his shoulders. He's got that *I'm hot and you're not* look."

"Yes, well, he did write *La Boheme...* Come, I'll show you to your room."

As we walked down the hallway, I realized to my surprise that despite his youthful voice and vigorous demeanor, our boarder was a good fifteen or twenty years older than me. I also sensed that he wasn't thrilled by the general dinginess of Maestro's apartment. Personally, I ignored all that and reveled in its magnificent history. It was, as Maestro insisted on calling it, *un tempio dell'arte.*

CHAPTER SEVEN

Richie

I gotta be honest, I'm a country guy and hate New York's honking, bonking lifestyle, but you gotta live and train there if you want to make it in Operaland. Good old Doc Williams lines up a place for me in the apartment of an old-time opera coach who rents out his spare room to aspiring young (and not so young) singers. The rent strikes me as ridiculous. I mean, you can lease a brand-new home in Graystone for what this guy charges for a single room. Still, I've got no alternative. I pounce on it, sight unseen, and hope that I made the right decision.

I get there in early February, 1982. Maestro's building is one of those pre-war apartment houses on West End Avenue, tall and tottering and in urgent need of repair. As I stagger into the lobby (my bags weigh a ton, thanks to all the opera scores I packed), I notice some of the paint's peeling off the walls, revealing an earlier color scheme which clashes with the current one. Also, the tile mosaic floor, all leaves and flowers, has big chunks missing, so it looks like a jigsaw puzzle the kids were too lazy to finish.

Fortunately, the day I arrive the elevator's relatively functional. (I discover later that it's on its last legs and breaks down repeatedly.) It makes weird grunts and groans with an occasional anguished squeal but it gets me to Maestro's floor. I plop my bags down in front and ring his doorbell. I'm welcomed by a tall, thin, soft-faced fellow, more kid than guy, who wears wire-rim glasses like my old aunt Sarah.

This turns out to be Rigby Converse, Maestro's assistant, who leads me right to my room. As I drag my bags after him down the long dim hallway, the walls are covered, and I mean floor-to-ceiling covered, with giant posters announcing performances at the Metropolitan Opera, not from this year or last year (that would make some sense) but from 1935, say, or 1942, or 1951. Why? What the hell for? By then, I did know the standard repertoire, *Aida, Carmen, Tosca* and such like. From recordings, of course – I still hadn't seen a single live opera performance. But up there on the wall are works I never even knew existed, like *Fidelio* or *Der Fliegende Hollaender*, which I came across much later. As for the singers, well, I did know Jussi Bjoerling by then, also Richard Tucker, but the others were total strangers.

When we get to my room, it's just like the hallway, dark and dingy, only it's not posters this time, it's photographs, a grand reunion of ancient opera stars. There's no Corelli, no Pavarotti, nobody I ever saw on a record jacket or magazine cover. The whole room is crammed to overflowing with unknown old-timers in puffy wigs and dumpy headgear. It's like I entered the graveyard of opera, its final resting place. It's pretty unnerving, not to mention completely bizarre.

"Wow, I sure as hell won't be lonely tonight."

"Amazingly enough, Maestro and his wife worked with virtually all the singers you see here. They were active in the Italian wing of the Metropolitan Opera from as early as 1918 to the late 1960s. That's why Maestro calls this place *un tempio dell'arte.*"

"Say what?"

Rigby doesn't answer my question, he just goes, "By the way, the closet on the left is off limits. Maestro uses it for storage. Please take the one on the right."

After he leaves, I haul my bags onto this twin-sized bed jammed in a corner next to a lopsided chest of drawers. I pull out the many scores Doc said I had to bring because serious singers only work with scores, not anthologies. No doubt they do, but the damn things weigh a ton and take up lots of space. I put my music on top of the chest in four big piles and toss my clothes in the drawers. It doesn't take long. I mean, how many shirts does a guy need? I've got four. They're perma-press, easy to wash, quick to dry. Then there's underpants and undershirts, ten of each, six pairs of socks, blue and brown, to go with my slacks and the brown checked jacket I bought last week at Myers Men's Shop in Detroit, because Kit said I had to dress up for auditions.

I take my slacks over to the closets and the first one I open is crammed to the gills with cocktail dresses and gowns, like you'd see in an old-time Hollywood movie. I immediately realize I've opened the closet Rigby said was reserved for Maestro's storage. Hat boxes are stacked on the upper shelf, one on top of the other right up to the ceiling. The inside panel of the door crawls with so many high-heeled shoes in so many different colors their owner must have gone out partying every night of the year, back in the 1940s and 50s, when there was all that high-class night life in New York City. As I'm taking all this in, I realize that the faint sour smell I noticed in the hallway is much stronger here. It's gotta be coming from the clothes.

The closet next to it is mine, of course, and completely empty, so I hang up my things and head out to the kitchen, which, no surprise, is pockmarked and dingy like the rest of the place, with the added attraction of big oil stains above the stove, like no one ever cleans it, which makes me think, okay, that's it, the joint's a total dump. I'll find another place and leave by the end of the month.

Just as I'm about to give Rigby the bad news, he throws me a curve ball. He's standing by the beat-up old stove and says, "Come, Richie, sit. I'm making us lunch."

"Thanks," I go, "that's real nice, but you don't need to bother."

"It's no bother. I've made enough *pesto* for a week."

"*Pesto*?"

"You know, *pesto alla Genovese?*"

"Honestly, spaghetti and meatballs is as far as we go in Graystone, Michigan."

I settle myself down at a rickety table while he forks out some spaghetti from a colander and twirls it onto a plate. He flashes me a giant grin as if to say, *here's the star attraction*, and starts drizzling this green glop all over that perfectly nice plate of spaghetti. Even though I'm incredibly hungry, I have to say it doesn't really tempt me and that's unusual, because I love to eat and it's way past my feeding time, but the spaghetti's got this dark green weirdness all over it, spinach, no doubt, and I hate spinach.

I take a deep breath, say a silent prayer and grab my fork, but Rigby stops me in mid-stab. "Wait, I forgot two crucial ingredients." He takes out this sand-colored cheese, grates it all over the spaghetti, then scatters around some tiny brown nuts. "Okay, now it's ready. *La cena* è *pronto*." I give him a puzzled look. "*Traviata*, act three, remember?" I don't, but give him a firm confident nod, so he won't think I'm a total idiot. "The basil's greenhouse grown, hydroponic, nearly as good as in Italy."

"Glad to hear it." I realize I can't avoid tasting the stuff any more. I twirl up a bite, pop it inside, start chewing and... it's amazing, the warm pasta, the garlicky sauce, the sweet nutty cheese, the little bits of peanuts, or whatever the hell they are. The green stuff isn't spinach at all, it's something richer and deeper, that comes together inside my mouth like my own private personal food festival.

The dish spins things around for me. I decide I really like and trust the guy who made it.

"Rigby, my man, just between me and thee, those old dresses stink up my room like crazy. Any chance we can deep six 'em?"

"Everyone asks that question, and, frankly, I'd love to toss them out, but Maestro won't have it. He's devoted to his wife. He needs her clothes with him."

"But she's dead, right?"

"Fifteen years, maybe even more." I guess I must look shocked. "No, no, it's not like that. It's sad, it's sweet. You'll understand when you finally meet him. Maestro adored his wife, still adores her. Her memory keeps him calm. As for the stench, a few air fresheners will clear it up. I'll see to it later."

"High-powered ones, extra heavy duty."

"Don't worry, they'll work. Our last tenant said she barely noticed the odor at all."

"Yeah, her nose fell off." He gets this startled look. "Not to be rude, my friend, but hanging on to those tattered old rags is bizarre."

Suddenly he's all fired up. "So what? Opera's bizarre. Life's bizarre. I'm bizarre and probably you are too. I mean, no offense, but life isn't just plain Jane vanilla, you know, especially the world of opera." I'm dumbfounded by his sudden spurt of passion. "Sorry, I don't mean to lecture you, but there's just so much blindness out there, so much narrow-minded ignorance, so much cruelty and intolerance and..." He calms down a bit, then continues, "Look, I wish he'd get rid of those clothes too, but it's Maestro's home and we have to play by his rules."

"Or pack our bags and leave?"

"I certainly hope you're not planning to do that. Anyone who likes my *pesto alla Genovese* as much as you do has to be an exceptionally deep and perceptive human being."

"Who says I like it?"

He sprouts a timid smile. "There's still some left. Could I tempt you?"

"You actually need to ask?"

What happens next really startles me. The spaghetti's in a colander right there in the sink, the sauce on the counter next to it. Put one on top of the other and it's done. Not if you're Rigby Converse. He takes a pot, puts it on to boil and when the water finally bubbles, he plunges in the spaghetti, sloshes it around for ten seconds, tops, dumps it through the colander and plops it onto my plate. True, the pasta's steaming hot now, but the guy went through this giant song and dance just to make sure my second helping was exactly like the first. I find that incredible. Also, completely insane.

Anyway, I'm in pasta heaven again, slurping up Rigby's superb *pesto,* when he asks, "So, what are your plans? What's your next engagement?"

I can't bring myself to tell him the sorry truth.

"Well, now you ask," I say, airily, "it looks like I'll probably be doing Calaf at the Met."

"Goodness gracious, bravo, good for you! I really had no idea we were hosting a Met artist. *Turandot's* not in the repertoire this year. What season are you singing it?"

"I'm not really sure."

"Wait, you're singing Calaf at the Met, but you can't even tell me the dates? I must say that's extremely unusual."

"Richie Verdun's unusual."

"He most certainly is." And then he stares at me so razor sharp I know the jig is up.

"Okay, okay, sorry, I misspoke. When I said I'm singing at the Met, the truth is I'd love to, I deserve to, but, as a matter of fact, I'm not."

"I pretty much assumed you weren't." Then he goes quiet. There's this long embarrassing silence.

When he speaks again, he's not angry or snooty, like, *what sort of an asshole are you?* No, he just says in his low delicate voice, "You know, it happens pretty often that my colleagues come back from exciting engagements elsewhere, and they ask what I've been doing, and all I've done is helped Maestro around the house, or given some young singers a few random coachings, and when I tell them this, when it's clear I can't come close to matching the brilliant prestigious things they've just returned from, it's not a pleasant feeling. At such times, I feel I'm not even in the profession."

"But you are, at least, way more than I am." As I say it, he gets this wistful look and my heart goes out to him, *whoosh,* just like that.

"It's a real problem. There's so little work in opera and so many people seeking it."

"But Maestro's this world-famous coach."

"Years ago, when he was on the staff at the Met. He hasn't worked there in ages. He's basically out of the operatic loop."

"Not as far out as I am."

"You surely must have something. Don't you work with regional companies?"

"I'd sure as hell like to, but nobody knows me. I'm just starting out."

"Starting out? At your age?" It hits me like a slap in the face. "Sorry, I don't mean to be rude, but most of the people auditioning today are ten to fifteen years your junior. Forgive me for saying it so baldly, but that's just the way things are."

"Age should have nothing to do with it. Either you can sing or you can't."

"Young and cheap, that's what they're looking for, not gentlemen of a certain age."

"At least you think I'm a gentleman."

"I know you are. You asked for seconds of my *pesto.*"

After Rigby goes out to buy some heavy-duty air fresheners (they really do work), he asks me to sing for him. I'm pretty excited about this, since he's probably got lots of connections out there in Operaland. He waits for me in the living room alongside this giant piano. It's set up like a sacred altar with all the furniture facing it, so you know this is where the action is, this is what really counts. The room itself is loaded with memorabilia like all the others, along with some new touches- music manuscripts, conductor batons, autographed programs, costume sketches, beat-up stage jewelry, more or less anything that's got something to do with opera, especially ones by Puccini, who I soon find out is Maestro's resident god, not Verdi, who's too old-fashioned for him, and certainly not Wagner, who, horror of horrors, wasn't even Italian. In fact, Rigby calls Maestro's place *Villa Verismo,* in honor of good old Giacomo.

I tell Rigby I'll sing *Turandot* first. He nods but doesn't move. "Aren't you gonna get your score?"

"There's no need."

"Really? I'm impressed."

"Don't be. I've played it a lot the past month."

Boy, does he ever play it. The moment he sits down at the Steinway and gives me the first bars I know he's a good pianist, better than good, great. It's like singing with a full orchestra. Not to say anything against Doc Williams, he's the guy who inspired me to go out there and do it in the first place and I'll always be grateful, but as a pianist, well, he's got his weak spots. He misses notes, plays wrong chords and keeps choosing weird tempos at the worst possible times. Rigby's got this great instinct for singers and singing. He'll sense you're having trouble before you notice it yourself and speed up or slow down to make things easier. Believe me, that's a gift.

I finish the aria and know it went well, how could it not, with Rigby making magic at the keyboard. I wait for the compliments, but he just asks, "What else do you have?"

"*Vesti la giubba.*"

"I'm afraid I'll need my anthology for that. People don't sing it as often as they used to." He picks up the book and starts flipping through it, looking for the aria, while I start feeling strange. I know I sang *Turandot* well, but Rigby hasn't said anything. It's a tough minute or two, me standing there like an overgrown kid waiting for praise and him not even noticing how hungry I am for it. When he finally finds the music and starts playing, I sing *Vesti la giubba* more determined than ever to impress him.

After I finish, he looks up at me from the piano and doesn't say a word. There's this bizarre silence. "Come on, man, I can take it. Fire away."

Rigby keeps staring, then sighs and finally says in that soft gentle way of his, "Forgive me, Richie, I don't like saying this, but you sound like, well… a bull in a china shop."

CHAPTER EIGHT

Rigby

I'll never forget the shock on Richie's face as I lowered the boom. Even though my first instinct is always to spare people's feelings, his situation was dire. He had to be shaken out of his provincial bad habits. Fast.

He was furious. "A bull in a china shop? I'm that bad? Come on, man, get a grip."

"You need to get one yourself. You've got to tone it down. You're giving too much voice."

"People need to hear me."

"They'll hear you better when you shape your phrases and keep your voice in line. Right now, everything's too grand and unrelenting."

"Opera *is* grand. The Met needs gigantic voices."

"It also needs artistry, musicality, emotion."

"You're saying I don't have that?"

"You don't have enough."

Richie reflected a bit, then grimly walked over to shake my hand. "Rigby, you're a helluva nice guy, a fantastic cook and an all-time, all-star pianist. But I'm obviously not good enough. I'll never measure up."

He turned and started to leave.

It was my turn to lose it. "Where the hell are you going? It's just criticism. It's for your own damn good!"

He stopped and huddled mournfully in the doorway. "Yeah, you're right... I just want so much for this to work. And I started so incredibly late."

"That's neither here nor there. The important thing is work. With work comes improvement. And after that, who knows?"

"You're right. I'm an idiot. Sorry man, I apologize. I acted like a fool." He ventured a few steps closer to me. "So, what's the verdict? What did you actually think?"

"Warts and all?"

"I'm rough. I'm tough. I can handle it."

"You weren't so tough a short while ago."

"I get passionate. I take things to heart."

"Maybe you should take them a little less to heart," I said. "Maybe you should just listen and learn."

"Okay, teach, I'm listening."

I gestured for Richie to sit on Maestro's throne-like chair facing the piano, while I sat back down on the piano bench.

"First and foremost, you're a real operatic tenor."

"You mean it? You're saying I'm not crazy to be doing this?"

"No, not at all. You've got a big powerful instrument, a *vocione,* as the Italians say. There aren't that many around."

"So I can land that contract at the Met?"

"Let's stay serious, okay? To be totally frank, your voice is most impressive, a true *spinto,* very suited to Canio or Calaf and probably even heavier roles than that. You sang both numbers well, but they're not right yet, and, frankly, I wouldn't audition with either one. At least, not at the moment."

"Man, come on, I'm not twenty-five. I haven't much—"

"You only get one chance with these people. You've got to give them your best."

"That was my best."

"Yes, no doubt, but you can do better. The *Nessun dorma* basically works. It's too bombastic, of course, it needs some toning down, but the main problem is your Italian. Everyone in opera expects correct pronunciation, especially in Italian. If it's not there, you're out the door. The good news is the rules of Italian pronunciation are extremely clear. Anyone can master them. All you need to do is clean out your vowels, enunciate your consonants and place them far forward in your mouth. You'll get the hang of it, millions of others have."

"You didn't mention *Vesti la giubba.* How did that come across?"

"Well, frankly, I'm curious, do you know what happens in the opera?"

"I suppose I could make a wild guess, but, honestly, I spent so much time preparing it, I never had a chance to read the story."

"You really did that? Learned the aria, but never bothered listening to the whole opera or reading a summary of the plot?"

"What can I say? I'm a busy guy."

"Well, busy or not, you've got to know the libretto. Operas tell stories through song. That's what the art form is. You've got the notes, you've got the general gist, but not the character, the urgency of the whole situation. And that's what *Vesti la giubba* needs. It's barely three minutes long and a human tragedy. A man is destroyed by his wife's infidelity. In the actual opera Canio kills his wife." Richie was shocked by this, genuinely astounded. "Yes, it's a human tragedy and that's what you've got to suggest. If you sing it like you just did, impresarios will never engage you, never in a million years."

"Thanks for the good news."

"I'm dead serious. You've got to dig into the material far more deeply, you've got to be completely involved. And you should be involved, you *must.*

Music requires your absolute devotion. You must commit to it heart and soul. That's what Maria Callas did. That's why she's an immortal."

I took a deep breath and went on. "Opera isn't really a profession. Sure, some people make a pretty nice living at it but in reality, it's a madness, an obsession, a quest. No sane person would ever embark on it. The odds are against you. The pay is laughable. The stakes are absurdly high. And it's incredibly hard work and often incredibly frustrating. But I can assure you, Richie, from my own brief experience, there's no greater joy, no greater honor than devoting your life to opera, without any thought of ovations or fees or fame. It truly is its own reward."

As I finished my crazed cri de coeur, I realized to my profound embarrassment that Richie Verdun was staring at me in disbelief. I couldn't blame him.

And then -this is why I've become so devoted to him, so entirely in his thrall- he rushed over to me, arms spread wide and trapped me in a titanic bear hug. He lifted me high off the piano bench and squeezed with all his might.

After he set me down, he placed both hands on my shoulders and stared at me intently. "Rigby, my man, you just said something I always felt, but never could really say."

"Yes, well, a life in music isn't something one chooses, it chooses you. And we poor struggling musicians have to deal with the consequences as best we can."

" *We* musicians? You're including me?"

I smiled and shrugged. "What do you think?"

We stood there a bit longer, opera's odd couple, relishing the closeness of the moment, the unexpected intimacy.

"So, what comes next?" he asked, at last. "Sounds like I got a lot of work ahead of me."

"Maybe, maybe not. First and foremost, you need to get your audition arias in shape. You have to find a first-rate coach."

"I think I just found him."

CHAPTER NINE

Richie

I'm not going to show up ignorant and unprepared for my first coaching session with Rigby, so I run over to that opera shop they got tucked in a corner of the Metropolitan Opera and stock up on tapes and librettos of the arias I'm singing. I listen to the complete *Pagliacci,* not once but twice, and discover Canio's a natural born killer, which means I was doing it much too politely. When Rigby and I meet, I tell him I want to work on *Vesti la giubba* first, so I can pump more bite into it.

"No, that's premature. What you need above all are the basics, proper rhythm, intonation and pronunciation."

"I thought you wanted me to do all that acting type stuff."

"First things first. We'll concentrate on the sacred trinity of rhythm, intonation and pronunciation. R.I.P."

Operaland's teeming with self-appointed experts, teachers, coaches, conductors, directors, colleagues, impresarios, agents, managers, prompters, wardrobe assistants, piccolo players, you name it, and every single one of them's got all sorts of suggestions for all sorts of occasions and mostly it's whatever fool thing happens to be in their head at the moment. Rigby's signature R.I.P. is different from the usual Operaland nonsense. It really and truly works. In fact, if there's one single takeaway from my whole crazy story, it's this. Master the basics. Get your singing clear, clean and confident, so when you're finally out there on stage singing your heart out and dodging bullets from a million different directions, you've got something you always can fall back on. R.I.P.

Rigby and I are halfway through our first session. I'm struggling with the F sharp in the middle of the Canio aria and keep blasting it out over and over to get it really in tune. After one of the blasts, I hear someone say in a hoarse, wavery voice, "*Ma bravo, un tenore di forza.*" I look up and there's Maestro Borgianni, a ragged old scarecrow hunched over his walker at the far end of the room. Even though I've been in the apartment three or four days now, this is my first look at him – he pretty much stayed locked up in his bedroom. He's extremely old, Rigby thinks he's way up in the eighties, a skinny stringy type, very short, two or three inches shorter than me, and pretty much always bent over, so he looks even shorter. He's like an old photograph come to life, the black and white kind on thick slabs of paper, studio portraits of grandpa and grandma standing stiffly side by side fifty, sixty years ago, which is when he must have bought the clothes he's wearing, a stained white shirt and floppy, baggy brown trousers that must have fit him once upon a time. He's got this bright red scarf twisted round his neck, turns out it's his favorite item, he wears it all the time. I guess it makes him feel bohemian and artistic. It's gives him a renegade look, like he's the Pirate King of opera.

Rigby gets up from the piano bench. "Maestro, this is our new boarder, Richie Verdun."

"Richie, what sort name that?" His actual words. Even though he's lived in New York for over fifty years, his English is still pretty much his own personal invention.

"Richie's my nickname, Maestro, most people call me that. My birth certificate says Richard."

"Oh, Riccardo." He thinks this over a bit, then shoves his walker a step or two nearer and studies me again, more closely this time. "*Tenore*, what age you have?"

Just what I need to hear. "Actually, I just turned seventeen. Pretty impressive for a teenager, no?"

Maestro B doesn't have much of a funny bone. "Why you make now joke?"

Rigby isn't amused either. "Don't tease him, Richie. He asked a serious question and deserves a serious answer."

"Sorry, Maestro, just having a little fun. I turned forty-two last December."

"Is true?" He looks over at Rigby, who confirms the amazing fact. "Sound very much like young man, fresh."

"That's good news, right?"

He doesn't answer, just pushes his walker further into the room. You're supposed to push those things gently, but he bears down hard and gets tangled up in one of the throw rugs. He jiggles his walker this way and that, trying to get free. I go over to help, but he shrugs me off, says he can do it himself (at least, I think that's what he says, his accent makes everything a guessing game). Finally, he lifts the whole walker up, shakes off the rug, then slams it back down to give it a good lesson, and makes his way towards me. "*Permesso?*"

Rigby translates for me. "He's wondering if he could listen a bit."

"Of course. It would be an honor."

There's a big old armchair facing the piano about six feet away. Maestro lets go of the walker and, like a Frankenstein monster with herky-jerky movements, staggers over till he's directly in front of the chair and collapses, bam, right into it. It's scary in a way, but also incredibly impressive. The guy may be riding on empty but, boy, has he got guts.

He sits there and listens intently while Rigby and I go back to work. We're trying to sort out the speed-up, or *accelerando*, before the aria's climax. We repeat it a few times so I can get my breathing right and clean up my vowels, which are much too American. It'll be ages before either Rigby or Maestro signs off on my Italian diction, but these days when I sing gigs in Italy, people often come up to me after the show gabbling away, convinced I speak Italian since my diction's so good. Hard work, my friends, lots of long expensive hours with Rigby, Maestro B and many, many others. Anyway, as Rigby and I keep repeating the passage, Maestro starts squirming, he's obviously very annoyed, until he finally can't contain himself any more. He heaves himself out of his chair, his cheeks flushed bright red, and goes, "*No, no, cretini,* too fast, *piu adagio!*"

To make sure we get the point, he lurches over to his walker, grabs the handles, uses it as a kind of lectern, launching into a monologue in Italian. He's yakking away a mile a minute, when his pants start sliding down. Let me tell you, this is not a pretty sight. I start seeing all sorts of things I don't want to, his not very clean boxers, his bulging belly, his knobby banged-up knees. Strangely, he doesn't notice what happened, even though by now his pants are bunched around his calves, god help him if he takes a step, which he fortunately doesn't, he's much too busy lecturing. Rigby listens respectfully, says *si* or *no,* like everything's completely normal, not once pointing out that Maestro's lost his pants, until, suddenly, without saying a word or making a sound, he slips behind the old guy, hoists his trousers back up and cinches the belt tight. He even zips up the fly without meddling with Maestro's valuables, the sign of a world-class dresser. Rigby's back on his piano bench in no time and Maestro's none the wiser. He finally runs out of steam and ends his grand aria. "*Ebbene, giovanotto, chiaro?*"

It turns out Maestro's insisting that Leoncavallo, the composer of *Pagliacci,* always felt singers speed up too much before the final *ridi, Pagliaccio,* and ruin its impact. Maestro B's teacher at the Turin Conservatory knew Leoncavallo personally, so there's a direct link between Maestro and the master himself and Rigby has to respect that. Sure enough, when Maestro finally plops back in his chair and I sing it again, Rigby does slow it down and Maestro's in total bliss.

Maestro's outburst seems to have worn him out. His cheeks return to their usual ashy color and bit by bit his eyelids flutter and before you know it, he's taking a snooze, without snoring, thank god, while Rigby and I keep working. When my hour's over, I ask Rigby if I have to pay Maestro for his comments.

"Oh no, it's my session, not his. He just got carried away. Mind you, it only happens when he thinks someone's talented. He's very picky about who he gives advice to."

"Wow, I'm honored." I look over at the sleeping grandpa. "I guess I'll thank him later."

"Do it now. He won't mind."

I walk over and give him a light tap on the shoulder. He sits straight up like he got an electric shock. "Sorry, Maestro, I just wanted to thank you for listening to me."

"*Non fa niente, tenore.* I tell you now some more."

"Really? I don't want to tire you out."

He gives an impatient gesture for me to come and sit near him. "*Anche tu,* Rigby, *vieni qui.*" We scare up some chairs and fan out in front of him, like we're sitting at the feet of the master. He's very pleased by this: it's not just me who likes an audience.

"Is a very long road you have, *tenore,* very hard, but important, eh? *Importantissimo.* They come to you starving, *il pubblico,* they want so much, need so much and in their little lives is nothing, *niente, un deserto,* and so with the opera you must be *grande* for them, *immenso.* You must give to them like the most great, most generous person and fill their empty souls with something *magnifico.*"

"Magnificent," whispers Rigby, worried I'm not getting it, though the funny thing is I am.

Maestro B takes his right hand, the one that doesn't tremble so much, and gives my shoulder a good strong shake. "Riccardo, I just now hear you." *Ear* is how it sounds, he never says a proper h. "You have this power, eh? *Questo potere* and is no *piccolino* – no little nobody, who run after the diva, saying is now serving dinner. No, *sei primo uomo.* You real man, first man, carry on your back the opera, strong, strong like ox – but then suddenly, *paff! No, no,* must always be *primo uomo*, every *momento*, every *minuto*, not suddenly turn into *un piccolino*, like Rigby here, *un finocchio, un fegatino.*"

Rigby looks offended, and I figure Maestro said something nasty, so I go, "Hey, easy, Maestro, Rigby's my main man and one hell of a piano player."

"For opera you need giant figure, *un eroe, un campione.* So, what you want to be? Little *niente*, little *comprimario*, or big hero everyone remember forever?"

"Gee, that's a tough one. Let me give it some thought."

"You not hero? You not want?" His cheeks turn scary red again.

Rigby rushes to my defense. "Of course, he wants to be a hero, every man does. He was only making a little joke."

Maestro shakes his head violently back and forth, his red scarf flapping like a tattered flag on the battlefield. "No time for joke, eh? Complete serious!" He can't keep his rant going for long. He pauses, takes a few deep breaths and sags back against his chair. "Know where you are, Verdun? Know what this place is? *Un tempio dell'arte...*"

"A temple of art," Rigby translates, though, honestly, I get it right away.

"And no joke, no *stupidità*, only serious, only devotion night and day to what the great masters make and we small people, we *piccolini*, try as hard we can to bring alive, keep alive, the glorious flame of genius."

"Well, we'll certainly try, Maestro, but in the meantime Richie and I still have lots to do on *Vesti la giubba.*"

This isn't what Maestro wants to hear. His tiny eyes get that *don't fuck with me* look. "*Questo tenore* not serious, not understand temple of art."

"He will, Maestro. Give him time."

"No, *tenore* must be strong, *potentissimo!*"

"He's not weak at all. Far from it. If you just give him some time, he'll..."

"*Basta, silenzio! Va via, fegatino, va via!*" He gives one of those Amneris type gestures, *get out of my palace and never come back.*

Strangely enough, Rigby does what Maestro wants and leaves. As for me, I'm fascinated. We don't have folk like this in Graystone, Michigan.

"*Vieni qui, tenore.*" The old man obviously wants me to get closer, so I go over and kneel right by his beat-up old chair. He studies me closely, his coal-black eyes, Svengali eyes, I call them, are crawling all over me. "*Senti, tenore,* I hear something in *la tua voce* and it make me very much worried."

"Am I doing something wrong?"

"No, you do just fine. But the others, they make problem. They hear *una voce* like you got and eat it right up, *paff.*" He mimes slurping down a forkful of pasta.

"You think the guys in opera are gonna ruin my voice? Maestro, I won't let them."

"*Tenore,* just you wait. They give you sweet words and good money and excellent contract and whisper in ear like *Satana lui stesso, 'Senti,* Signor Verdun, Wagner...'" He whispers the name, draws it out like the last temptation of Christ. "Wagner. You perfect for Wagner, *un tenore drammatico.* It make you very famous." His cheeks get all red again, he wags his finger furiously. "*Ma no,* Verdun, *non si fa!* Wagner no good for you. It completely kill the voice."

"It does?"

"*Assolutamente.* It ruin you *presto, prestissimo.*" A lot of singers I've bumped into have said something similar, but this guy takes it to an entirely new level. "*E la musica di questo* Wagner, what is it? No beauty, *no melodia, niente, niente di niente.*"

At this point, I still haven't heard a Wagner opera, though I have listened to a few famous excerpts. I mean, sure, I like the *Ride of the Valkyries,* everyone does, but that's for orchestra, not singers. When he writes for the voice, look out, baby, Wagner doesn't mess around. "Funny you should say that," I go. "I don't like his stuff either."

He grabs my shirt and reels me in until I'm staring straight into those hard little eyes. "*Attenzione,* eh? *attenzione.* Always protect *la gola, la tua voce.* Voice is everything for singer, everything. What else you got on earth?" Then, like the high priest of Operaland, he kisses his hand and presses it to my forehead, like it's a blessing, like he just gave me the best advice of my career. And who knows? Maybe he did.

It's April. I've been pounding notes with Rigby for over two months and pounding the pavements looking for work. No luck so far. It seems you only get engagements if you have an agent and you only get an agent if you have engagements. In other words, they screw you coming and going. I try to keep positive by concentrating on the concert I'm singing next month with Doc. Finally, one fine spring day, the man himself calls. After the usual *blah blah* about how sorry he is that he never seems to be free on the few weekends I've been back in Graystone and I say it doesn't much matter, since I'm so busy with Kit and the kids, Doc finally comes to the point.

"Richard, I'm afraid the church won't able to present our concert next month."

"What?!"

"I know, I'm disappointed too. When I proposed the date I hadn't realized it's the weekend of the volunteer fire department supper. We can't compete with that. We'll never attract a crowd."

"Come on, we're giant stars. We'll pack it to the rafters."

"The church seems to think otherwise. We have to wait till the fall." I can't believe how disappointed I am. I really wanted to show the folks back home how much I've improved. "Frankly, for my part," he continues, "I need more time for the Mozart anyway, the rondo is beyond treacherous. The postponement comes as a great relief."

"Yeah, I guess it's just as well. It'll give me more time for auditions."

"Yes, you must be busy with them. How are they going?"

"Great, really exciting. I'm up for Luigi in *Il Tabarro.*"

"Really? That sounds wonderful."

"I know, it's terrific. Even though it's a small company, all the reviewers cover it." As a matter of fact, I'm not up for the part at all. I was just one of twenty-seven lunks who showed up to audition. I haven't heard from them yet, so who can really say?

"Well, I'm sure you'll do splendidly. You know I only wish you the best."

"I know, Doc, thanks."

I briefly consider suicide, then console myself by hunting through this book Rigby gave me, an enormous catalogue of opera companies, symphony orchestras, agents, competitions, foundations, conservatories, you name it, they got it. It's about the millionth time I check through it. I want to be sure I'm leaving no stone unturned. I gotta follow through on even the remotest possibilities, since, to be perfectly honest, I've come to realize that my chances of making it are minuscule.

To start with, no foundation gives money to singers my age. We're too damn old. Oh, there is one, but it's for Wagnerian tenors and I'm absolutely not doing that after the lecture Maestro B. gave me. As for finding an agent, I'm a car salesman, right? I'll call anyone for anything any time. Day in, day out, I'm on the horn to all the agencies in New York, asking if I could sing for them, and what happens? *Send us a resume. Tell us where you've been singing. We're not adding new people to the roster. We only hear singers in the fall.* In other words, I get not one single audition, not one shred of interest, nada, nothing, nix. I have a bit more luck with opera companies, but only the small ones, not the Met or City Opera. It turns out that the little guys, bless their impoverished souls, are willing to consider novices like me. That's how I got to audition for that *Tabarro.* Which is something, I guess, a tiny start. But of what, and headed where?

In the midst of all these cheery goings on, midway through the month of May, when everything's blooming and beautiful and I'm stuck in my own personal December, I'm sitting in the kitchen sipping my morning coffee, getting the energy going, when I hear the front door open and after a pause, the soft thud of a body collapsing. Maestro's been pretty wobbly lately, so I rush out, but when I get to the entryway, I find Rigby, his clothes torn and dirty, down on all fours on the carpet.

"It's nothing, Richie. I'm okay." He turns towards me and I see there's a shiner over his left eye and streaks of blood across his cheek. Someone obviously beat him up, though why a hothouse type like him would get in a fight is beyond me.

"That eye looks pretty bad. Maybe we should go to the emergency room."

"I just told you I'm okay."

"Don't fuck around, man. It's your eye."

"Thanks, but my vision's perfectly normal."

By this point I'm kneeling beside him, checking the damage up close and personal. There's only the normal scrapes and bruises that come from a barroom brawl, nothing life threatening, so Doctor Verdun's reassured. I reach under Rigby's armpits and haul him to his feet. He's amazingly light. Doesn't he ever eat? "How's your head, man? Any pain, any throbbing?"

"No, I'm just fine." He leans against the wall and looks at me warily.

"Would you like to tell me what happened?"

"No."

"At least let me get you cleaned up, you look pretty unappetizing." I head into the kitchen and he follows, keeping close to the walls in case he gets dizzy.

Just as we reach the kitchen he puts on the brakes. "Is Maestro in there?"

"No, he's back in his room, taking a nap."

"You're sure?"

"Absolutely."

"Good. I really don't want him to see this."

"Well, lots of luck. That eye's gonna be black and blue for quite some time."

He slumps into a kitchen chair, while I go over to the sink and wet a towel with warm water. I go back to him and start dabbing at his cheek, trying not to press too hard. He takes it like a trooper, an occasional wince or two but nothing dramatic. I go to the frig, toss some ice in a plastic bag, cover it with another towel and hand it to him. "This should help with the swelling." He puts the pack on his face, thanks me and sits there, looking away.

"Rigby, I know you'd rather not talk about it, but I understand, a guy's got his needs. No big deal."

He's surprised, but all he says is, "Just don't tell Maestro, okay?"

"Why would I?"

"I don't know, just don't." Poor fella, he's such a sorry sight, with his spindly legs and toothpick arms, he must be hopeless in a fight. "I should have known better, but he seemed nice, you know, dark and beefy, just how I like them. But this morning, when I got up to go..." Next thing I know the poor kid's crying, sobbing his fool heart out, until suddenly, somehow, he's in my arms and I'm holding him close, like I did with Billy when he lost his first fight and felt completely destroyed.

"It's okay, guy. You'll learn from this. You'll be more careful."

"It's like I'm a magnet for them. They sniff me out."

"I can't say I blame them. You're quite a catch."

He gives a bitter laugh. "Maestro gets so judgmental, you know, so high and mighty."

"I thought you were pretty much family with him, an honorary nephew or something."

"Once in a while, maybe, but not when I need it most."

"Ah, he's just from another age."

"And his daughter's no better."

"The one who lives on Long Island?"

"Yes, she didn't even visit when he went to the hospital. I begged her to, but, oh, no, I'm the enemy."

"Enemy? You do absolutely everything for him. You even pull up his pants and zip up his fly."

He grins for a moment, then turns dark again. "As if he even cares."

"Look, if Maestro makes you so uncomfortable, leave, stay somewhere else."

"I live rent free, the piano's mine to use. I can coach whoever I want whenever I want. And crazy as he is, Maestro's great to talk to, especially when it comes to Italian opera."

"Just not when it comes to you."

"Yes, he's an idiot on that particular subject."

"Man, look, I can see how it makes financial sense to stay here, but maybe your folks could help you find..."

"What folks?"

His anguish gets to me, but before I can say anything, I hear the clomp and swoosh of Maestro's walker coming down the hallway. Before you know it, he's at the kitchen door. He sees us two at the table and in three seconds flat, his coal-black eyes zero in on Rigby's shiner. He slam-bams his walker right over to us and bends down till his face is only inches away from Rigby's.

"What I tell you, *fegatino?* What I warn?"

Here comes one of those moments where you just gotta trust me because, *mondo bizarro* though it is, it really and truly happens. Maestro reaches down and clutches his own balls like he's milking them for all they're worth and with the grip he's got on them, they won't be worth much for long. His entire face gets red, not just his cheeks, but absolutely every part of it. It's like I gotta call the fire department before he spontaneously combusts.

He yells at Rigby, howls. "*COGLIONI, FINOCCHIO, COGLIONI!* Ox in field fuck cow. That what god want. That what god say. Ox fuck cow. Only cow. Not ox. Ox never fuck ox. *GIAMMAI!* Is wrong. Is terrible. Is sick. Understand, *fegatino*? You break god's word! YOU FUCK TOO MUCH THE MEN!" He finally runs out of steam, thank god, releases his jewels and his face goes back to its normal chalk color.

I'm so stunned by this, I just stand there, thinking, *wow, these Italians are some crazy motherfuckers.* Rigby's shattered face brings me back to reality.

I spring into action. "Hey, Maestro, go easy. Give the poor guy a break."

The old man braces himself on the walker and swings his angry mug my way. "Why you speak, *tenore*? What you know? My daughter say get rid of him, boy too difficult, not real man."

"Come on—"

"*Tenore*, you know nothing. *Niente*."

"I know he's a great guy."

"No! Make trouble and do stupid thing."

"Not stupid," says Rigby.

"What you say, *fegatino?*" Maestro swings around and lasers his eyes back on Rigby. "Next time police come, bring you home like criminal. That why my daughter warn me, say *giudizio, babbo, attenzione*."

"Who cares what she says?" goes Rigby. "She treats you like shit."

"What you say?"

"Nothing, Maestro."

"What you say, Rigby? Speak, *finocchio*, speak."

"Don't call me that!" This pretty much shuts everyone up. I realize I gotta act.

"Whoa, guys, halt, stop. I don't know anything about your daughter, Maestro, but if you're talking about what happened to Rigby, that big shiner, I did it. I'm the guy who beat him up." They're both pretty astonished, but that doesn't stop me. "We had a little fight just fifteen, twenty minutes ago. Right, Rigby? Right?" Rigby covers up his amazement as best he can. "See, Rigby knows I got this martial arts experience and like most guys, he's competitive, so we staged a little show and tell."

"What?"

"Rigby and me were having a friendly little discussion about my kung fu moves and I show him my East Cloud, West Tiger routine." Here I give a truly pathetic imitation of a Bruce Lee movie. "See, I do the East Cloud, West Tiger and Rigby wants to try it and he does the move and kinda miscalculates and smashes me into the door. Now, it really hurts, I'm pretty goddam angry, so I give him the Double Dragon."

"Double Dragon?"

"Yeah, Maestro, two dragons. It's much more effective than one." I fake another move for him. "Boom, bam, bash, upside the head! He goes down, wham! Right, Rigby?"

"What?" Maestro asks again.

"What can I say, Maestro, I don't know my own strength. He zigged when I zagged and the rest is history."

"*Istory?*"

"Frankly, I think our young friend needs a little lie down after that. Why don't you go back to your room, pal, take a nice nap and heal?"

"Aye, aye, sir." Rigby skedaddles out of there and Maestro watches him go in dull bewilderment. After a few beats, he turns back around and it's like he sees me for the very first time. He hunches over his walker, his eyes scan me carefully, while he considers an astonishing new idea.

"No, *tenore, non* è *possibile*," he goes. "You *finocchio* too?"

Once we've cleared up that little misunderstanding, I help Maestro back to his room and contemplate my next move. Remember that *Tabarro* I mentioned? It's been four weeks and I still haven't heard, so I decide to give them a call. This young gal with a high society voice goes, "We don't discuss such matters on the telephone."

"Sorry, but you said you'd be in touch."

"Only if we want to engage you."

"Well, do you?"

There's frost in her voice now, contempt. "We haven't called you, have we?"

"No."

"Then the answer's pretty clear."

"Not to me. I mean, come on, why the hell can't you people have the common decency to just..." That's when she hangs up. She's way too important to take abuse from a no-name tenor who's not even good enough to sing *Il*

Tabarro for the Queens Metropolitan Opera, with piano, mind you, no orchestra, using tacky rented costumes and sets of cardboard and masking tape in a beat-up high-school auditorium before an audience of twenty-two nobodies for fifty bucks a pop. I stumble back to my crappy little room and slip into a deep, miserable sleep.

It must be hours later when Rigby busts in and awakens me. He's smiling broadly, even though his shiner is blooming up around his eye. "First, and most importantly," he goes, "you're a champ, Richie. You saved my derriere with Maestro today and I'm eternally grateful."

"Well, let's see what the old man says tonight."

"It'll be as if nothing happened. That's how he is, a sudden storm and it's over."

"Glad to hear it."

"You'll be even gladder when you hear this."

"I will? What happened?"

"I play rather often for an agent named Erich Hirschmann, a refugee gentleman of a certain age with an unspectacular list of third tier singers, except for the baritone Brent Cavendish."

"Isn't he's doing something at the Met?"

"He's doing something everywhere. The commissions on his fees keep Erich in business and allow him to represent others, most of whom don't work much, which is neither here nor there, except that today I played a rather dispiriting set of auditions for him and had to troop back to his small seedy office so he could write me my check. As soon as I entered, he received a phone call that went on and on, and I couldn't help overhearing that some regional company was looking for a singer, and Erich listened and nodded, listened and nodded, listened and nodded."

"Man, could you speed it up?"

"No. This is how *you* tell a story, Richie. You deserve a dose of your own medicine." Rigby seems totally changed, upbeat and confident. It's hard to believe he was writhing on the carpet just hours ago. "So anyway, after staying on the line for a good three or four minutes, Erich said he was sorry, he didn't have anyone for them, and hung up. He picked up his pen and started to write my check, when for no reason other than idle curiosity, I asked him what the phone call was about. I wasn't so sure he'd tell me – after all, I'm not on his staff, partly because he doesn't have one, it's truly a tiny agency, but also because Erich couldn't possibly consider me a friend. I'm half his age to begin with, born here, not over there, and anyway..."

Rigby's really pushing it. "Come on, man. Cut to the fucking chase."

"You always string out your stories, Richie... Anyway, as I was saying, Erich Hirschmann told me that the Calgary Opera was desperately looking for a Pinkerton for performances next February and they were auditioning here next week. I told Erich I happened to know someone who'd be perfect, and he asked me who, and I said he just got into town, but he's worked with Maestro and me and we're both deeply impressed. Erich pointed out they only want someone who's sung the role on stage, *ein eingesungener Pinkerton*, as he so charmingly put it, and, shameless fellow that I am, I told a white lie and claimed that you sang the role some years back in Grand Rapids."

"I almost sold cars in Grand Rapids."

"Close enough, right? Herr Hirschmann wasn't very eager to accept my recommendation, so I reminded him how the mezzo I brought him last year now sings leading roles at City Opera, and he pointed out that the bass I pushed the year before has found no work at all, and I said basses are always a problem, but my man's a genuine leading tenor, and we went back and forth, until Erich, great continental that he is, heaved a deep sigh and said, '*Ach*, you Americans, always so enthusiastic.' He called the Calgary Opera right on the spot and set up an audition for you this coming Tuesday."

Guess who got the part.

PART TWO

A PROFESSIONAL OPERA SINGER?

CHAPTER ONE

Richie

Wow, you think, *great, you finally broke through, you made your debut with a respected company. You're making a major splash.*

Wrong. First off, I still don't have management. Sure, Erich Hirschmann put me up for the Pinkerton and negotiated the contract (and took his ten percent, plus expenses). But it was basically a tryout. He wanted to see how well I did before putting me on his list. I'm pretty optimistic it'll happen, seeing as how the folks at Calgary Opera want to invite me back. Agents always like it when their artists get return engagements. But that's tomorrow's business. Today, I just got off a seven-hour flight from Canada.

I open the front door to Maestro's apartment, but no one's in. I figure he and Rigby are out on their afternoon walk. As I bring in my bags, I start getting the feeling that something's off, but I can't say what. Maybe the hallway's got fewer posters, or a new coat of paint, but what do I know? I'm a singer, not an interior decorator.

I open the door to my room, and this I do notice. It's been replastered and repainted and it gleams, it shines. As I put down my bags and take it all in, I'm stunned. Most of those funny old-time photos of opera stars that Maestro loved are gone. What sort of magic did Rigby use to get the old guy to give them up? I open his wife's closet and it's completely cleared out, there's not a single shoe or hat box left. I rush back to the entryway, where I first got a twinge that something was off and, sure enough, Maestro's prize possession, the giant portrait of Puccini, is also missing in action.

Just as I'm wondering where it went, I hear a key twist in the lock. I turn around and there's Maestro hunched low over his walker with two ladies helping him. No Rigby in sight. Maestro's focusing on the ground, so he doesn't really notice me.

"Maestro, hello, it's me, Richie, I'm back from Calgary."

He doesn't respond. Instead, the tall lady on his right comes over and shakes my hand. "Good afternoon. You must be Mister Verdun. I'm Renata Sanderson, Maestro's daughter."

This pretty much trips and flips me, but I try to keep my cool. "Hi, pleased to meet you."

"And this is his caregiver, Angelique."

"Hello to you too."

"Hello sir, welcome back." Angelique has dark cocoa skin and sounds like a cello. She's in a neat white nurse's uniform, very fresh, very tidy, and wears this intense perfume, from gardenias, I think, or roses, which sweetens the air, almost overwhelms it. It's a shock to see Maestro with a nurse. I ask the daughter where Rigby is.

"Mister Converse? He moved, actually. I'm living here now, which makes us roommates, or apartment mates, whatever's the right term."

"Roommates is fine by me."

She smiles and I smile back. She's a tall, fine-looking woman, more or less my age. The only odd thing is she's wearing men's clothing, gray slacks, a tight-fitting black sports jacket like you'd buy off the rack at a men's shop, except it slides nice and tight over her curves. I learn later that she's office manager for a law firm downtown and this is more or less the regulation outfit for her job.

Maestro still hasn't said anything. His daughter taps his shoulder and he twists around to face her. "Mister Verdun's returned, *babbo.* Isn't that lovely?" He keeps staring at her like he's under a spell until Angelique gently turns his head in my direction. He scans my face but doesn't react. "You mustn't be concerned. He had a little stroke, but he's coming back. Aren't you, *babbo*?"

"*Si, si.*" There finally seems to be a faint flicker of recognition. His forehead knits up, he hunches forward and squints to see me better. "*Tenore?*"

"Yep, it's me, Maestro. I just came back from singing Pinkerton in Calgary. It really went great out there, especially the aria." I wait for a response, but don't get one.

"He's been going through a difficult patch, but he's making progress, I'm happy to say." Maestro keeps staring at me like he's really and truly puzzled. Renata realizes I'm taking it hard. She says in a low voice, "I think we should discuss things in private, don't you?"

"Sure, of course."

"Angelique, please, it's time for father's tea."

"Come on, dearie, let's go into the kitchen." The nurse tries to get his walker going but it's stuck, so I go over to give them a hand.

The moment I do, Maestro says in this faint, whispery voice, "Aria go okay?"

I thought he hadn't been following at all. "Hell, yeah, especially on closing night. I really nailed the final *ah, son vile.*"

"Not take too fast?"

"Well, Maestro had some pretty weird notions but I held my own."

"Bravo, *tenore.* Always hold, always fight. What Maestro you got?"

"Egon Kleinhaus. Ever hear of him?"

"*Un tedesco* conduct Puccini?"

"Sorry, what's a *tedesco*?"

"A German," his daughter explains. "They're not father's favorite people."

"Or mine either. Especially this Egon guy. He had a nasty temper and a downbeat like a wet noodle."

"*Si, si, sono sempre così.*"

"Angelique, Father really must get his tea."

She nods and starts leading Maestro away, when he asks, "*Ma dove il mio caro* Rigby?"

"Sorry?" I'm still hopeless when it comes to Italian.

"My father's been asking after Mister Converse for quite some time and I've no idea where he is. He left abruptly, and rather unpleasantly. There seems to be no forwarding address."

I instantly think of Erich Hirschmann. "I can get one."

"Fine, please tell me later. Angelique, be sure Maestro gets his two red pills."

"Yes, Ma'am," she says and guides him towards the kitchen.

"Angelique, what do I always tell you?"

"Sorry?"

"His red scarf. It's on the floor. Pick it up. Put it back on him."

"Of course, Ma'am, sorry." She scoops it up and ties it around Maestro's neck. I wish I could say it has its usual effect, you know, turns him into this cool hip guy, but it just makes him seem older than ever. Angelique leads him down the hallway, a shapely young woman helping a battered old man. It's a distressing sight.

"Mister Verdun, our little talk?"

"Oh, sorry."

"Father can be quite difficult if he doesn't have his red scarf."

"I know, it makes him feel artistic."

"Actually, this is the first time I've heard him discuss anything even remotely artistic since he came back from the hospital."

"Wow, I'm flattered."

She flashes me this *let's not go overboard* look as we enter the living room. "I'm afraid I haven't touched anything here yet. Poor *babbo* was living in such chaos and uncleanliness I decided to make the bedrooms my first priority."

"You did a great job. How did you ever convince him to discard those old clothes?"

"You mean, mother's things? I did it while he was in the hospital. He hasn't noticed yet and that's all to the good. I trust you understand."

"I promise I won't say a word."

"Thanks so much, Mister Verdun."

"Can I ask you a question? What happened to the painting of Puccini?"

"Oh, that old thing. I sent it out for restoration."

"Doesn't Maestro miss it? He always used to say, 'Be careful, *tenore*, Puccini watching.'"

"He did, really? How sweet."

She gestures vaguely and tells me to take a seat. I pull up one of those old-fashioned wood chairs with stained upholstery while she settles down on the piano bench.

"Of course, it was just a matter of time. *Babbo's* over eighty and he's been heavily medicated for years. Shortly after you left, I learned that father had passed out while taking a walk. Unfortunately, I was out of town, stuck at an endless conference. It was days before I could get to the hospital and when I did, the prognosis wasn't good. I felt it wasn't fair to expect Mister Converse to deal with Maestro's new condition. He's not medically trained and, of course, he's not family. I gather you and he are friends."

"Yeah, we're pretty close. I do all my coaching with him."

"I'm afraid he's very put out with me. If you find him, and I assume you can, please tell him I bear him no ill will. If I get his new address, I'll be happy to forward his mail. But frankly, it's *babbo* I'm most concerned about, *babbo* must always come first. As you can imagine, his care is quite expensive.

Angelique requires a living wage and fixing up the apartment wasn't cheap either..." At this point my radar starts blipping and blaring. You don't sell cars for nearly twenty years without knowing when something's gonna cost you. "Honestly, I was completely shocked when I learned what Mister Converse had been charging for your room. Much as I'd like you to stay on, I've got to charge a more realistic price."

"What's your idea of realistic?"

"Four hundred fifty dollars a month."

"Yikes, that's a fifty percent increase."

"I can assure you the new rent's in line with prices up and down the avenue."

"Maybe I need to find another avenue."

"Maybe you do. Now, if you'll excuse me, I've a million things to attend to." And that was that.

I used to think agents were these slick types with sexy secretaries and fancy offices with electric typewriters and nice thick carpets and classy modern furniture and signed photos on the wall from all kinds of famous people. Not Erich Hirschmann. His agency is just him and no one else, not even a part-time assistant. He's got this tiny trap of an office not far from Carnegie Hall, which must have been a maid's room at one time, or a large storage closet. It's maybe ten feet by twelve and crammed with banged-up metal filing cabinets and battered bookcases holding cardboard boxes and stacks of papers, artist contracts, I guess, or business letters, or resumes, or old takeout menus. A rickety old spinet is jammed against the wall and loaded down with more filing boxes and magazines and opera programs. There's a scratched-up wooden desk that looks like he found it on the street, with two metal folding chairs facing it. His clients sit on them while he lounges in a brand-new brown leather recliner, the one fancy item he's got and pretty much state of the art. I guess he's willing to spend money for his own comfort but not for anyone else. It's hard to believe this junk heap is the office of the guy who represents Brent Cavendish, one of the biggest opera stars out there, but it is.

Anyway, junky or not, messy or not, Erich runs the agency that got me my first job. You work with what you have.

I sit myself down on one of those metal chairs and go, "Look, before we even get started, do you happen to know how I can get in touch with Rigby Converse? He moved out while I was away."

He gives me a crooked grin. "He probably had enough of you."

"Look, it's really urgent. I'd be most grateful. I'll even give you your check."

"That is not funny. We all must be paid for our work." In addition to the usual agent's ten percent, Erich charges extra for expenses, in my case, two hundred bucks for phone calls and mailings, though who he called and what he mailed is pretty much a mystery. A few months later, when money becomes a huge issue for me, devastating actually, I'll regret that surcharge, but now all I want is a career. I hand him his check, that's three hundred eighty dollars I'll never see again. He tosses it into the mess spilling out of his desk drawer. If a guy ever needed a secretary or a cleaning lady, it's him. But he'd rather save the money.

"I gave you your check. Can I please have Rigby's contact?"

"*Mein Gott,* the things I must do for my singers." Erich starts rifling through a big pile of papers at the far side of his desk. He finds a head shot and hands it to me. "Here. She always is working with him. She probably knows where he is." As I'm copying down her number, Erich asks, "So, you bring with you the review?"

"You mean, of *Madame Butterfly?*"

"You sang maybe a different opera?" He takes the clipping from me with this sarcastic smile on his face. He obviously can tell I'm not happy with it, and suddenly, without asking or warning me, starts reading it aloud. "'After singing a dull and unromantic love duet, the American tenor Richard Verdun somewhat redeemed himself with a thunderous rendition of his third act aria.

While his phrasing and stage deportment left much to be desired, there is steel in his voice and considerable carrying power. All in all, he was hardly Puccini's elegant cad and certainly no equal to the impassioned Madame Ostrovsky.'" He looks over at me, beaming, like he just told an excellent joke. "But why do you make such a face?"

"It's a shitty review, one big insult."

"Of course, he dislikes this and that, but you can make of it good use."

"Yeah, and never work again."

"Nonsense. Everyone wants a tenor with *steel in his voice and carrying power.*"

"You mean, just leave out the other stuff?"

"Why not? It's what the gentleman wrote."

"But he basically couldn't stand me. It'd be cheating."

"Everyone cheats in this world. Why not you?" That superior grin of his is getting on my nerves, but I really need an agent. "So, tell me, how did you like being on stage? It was your first time, no?"

"You know what they say, the first time's the best. I absolutely loved it." An outright lie. Actually, my first time on stage completely blindsides me, it's this weird out-of-body experience. I'm singing and moving around, performing Pinkerton like I'm supposed to, but I'm also watching myself doing it, like I'm living a real-life dream. Rehearsals don't prepare me for this. When I rehearsed, the work lights were on, there were stops and starts, I was focused on a million tiny details, like the door slides *how*, I've got to stand *where*, the conductor wants *what*. Once the lights go down, I'm suddenly aware how big the opera house is, how incredibly far back I am from the public with the giant gash of the orchestra pit separating us. I don't really see the paying customers. I can glimpse a few vague shapes here and there, but it's like they jumped into a giant black sack and vanished.

Another strange thing, it's quiet on stage. You'd think the exact opposite, there would be all kinds of clatter with the orchestra blasting full out and your colleagues wailing away, but, no, most of the sound goes right past you into the big dark catcher's mitt of the auditorium, the end result being that each and every one of us winds up in our own little world, focusing like crazy on what it is we gotta do, which in my case means *give more support here, ease up the breathing there, beef up the double d's, spit out the final t, look at the girl like you love her, look at the guy like you hate him, be sad, be happy,* etcetera and so forth. It's my first time out, remember? I gotta pay close attention so I don't disgrace myself. Nowadays, I'm more experienced. I don't have to be so cautious. Still, you gotta be in control out there. If you aren't, you really can get in deep shit. As the following episode proves.

My Butterfly in Calgary is Polyna Ostrovsky, a real piece of work, who did everything she could to annoy me. She even tried undermining me with the company director, fat lot of good it did her. Anyway, we're at that moment in the act one love duet when Butterfly begs Pinkerton to treat her well. (Lots of luck with that, honey, he's just in it for the sex.) The violin plays this incredibly tender melody and Polyna, a forty-year-old creep who in real life is the exact opposite of the sweet and loving Madame Butterfly, is really *on* tonight, really inspired. She's not playing her role, she's living it, *being* it. The spell she casts over me is so great that there's no Richie any more, there's no Polyna, just this sixteen-year-old geisha girl kneeling before me, who kisses my hand and steals my heart and makes me miss my cue.

Yes, thanks to Polyna's brilliant performance, I blow the simplest entrance in the whole damn opera. I never had trouble with it before, no one does, it's nursery school easy, but that night I'm so distracted by her, so *touched,* I enter a beat late. Now, honestly, this isn't a big deal. No one out front notices, I leap back in real fast, but the conductor is Polyna's husband and no friend of mine. He pounces on it and starts thumping his chest, like *follow me, asshole, I'm the boss.*

Just as I'm remembering all this, Erich says, "By the way, I heard from one of your friends, Egon Kleinhaus."

What is this guy, a mind reader? "I wouldn't exactly call him a friend."

"Oh, but you should. A singer always must make friends with the conductor."

"Not that guy. It wasn't possible."

"Then you won't be surprised to hear the feeling's mutual. He says I send him a terrible singer. You completely drown out his wife."

"Sorry, the lady totally deserved it."

"Yes, maybe, everyone says she is difficult."

"And that's on her good days."

"I also know Roderick Cranbrook."

"Boy, it's like you got spies everywhere."

"This is a difficult profession. I have to know what's what. This Cranbrook fellow thinks you are nowhere so bad as Egon says."

"Gee, thanks."

"He is British, you know, a man of understatement. The only singers he really likes are from his country and usually also from his bed, which means, of course, they are male with rather thin voices, but very elegant, you know, very decorative."

"I don't know about any of that. All I know is the guy really helped me." Erich smiles and arches an eyebrow. "Not that way, man, come on."

"I like you, Herr Verdun, you are really quite amusing."

"And I've got a terrific high B flat."

"Not according to Egon Kleinhaus."

"According to Rigby Converse, according to Roderick Cranbrook, according to Roger Jennings."

"Even him? The head of Calgary Opera?"

"Absolutely. He really liked me. He said he wanted me back. So, whaddya say, will you put me on your list?"

Complete silence. I watch as my agent, or potential agent, or lifelong enemy, puzzles things out. It takes quite a while. "Very well, here is what I suggest. I send you to auditions, not as a Hirschmann artist, but as a Hirschmann prospect, a Hirschmann hopeful. The companies accept this, they still will hear you. In a few months we meet again and I make my decision, yes or no."

"Hey, wait a minute, I just made a successful debut."

"*Rather* successful, *somewhat* successful."

"Gee, thanks for your support."

"You want another agency? You know where is the door."

"No, no, don't take it that way. I just mean I'm a leading tenor. There aren't so many around."

"There are more than you could imagine. Everyone thinks he can sing." This really gets me. I slump back into my seat. "*Komm*, why so serious? You actually have a very good chance if you sing at your auditions some Wagner. Everyone is looking for a Heldentenor and no one seems to find one."

I flash this image of old Maestro B wagging his finger at me, warning me to protect my voice. "Sorry, I'm not that kind of singer."

"Oh, but you are. And Mister Converse agrees."

"That's the first I've heard of it."

"Then you obviously have not listened."

"Look, Mister Hirschmann, I totally respect you and I hear what you say loud and clear, but to be perfectly honest, I really want a shot at the French and Italian repertoire. That's what I love, that's what I do best and it's also way easier on the voice."

"Well, the artist is always right, unless, of course, he is wrong. I do what I can for you and then we see how it goes."

As soon as I leave Erich's office, I contact Rigby's friend. She tells me he just moved to Manhattan Avenue, but doesn't have a phone. I take down his address and go over there.

The street he lives on is different from West End Avenue, even though it's only a few blocks away. In the madness of the city, the totally wacky way it organizes and reorganizes itself, his street's as edgy and lowlife as West End is safe and middle class. As I get to his block, I see that Rigby's building is a beat-up five-story tenement with black fire escapes crisscrossing the front like oversized iron shoelaces.

I go up the crumbling front steps and ring Rigby's buzzer. After what seems like ages, there's a click, then static, then the delicate faint voice of the man himself. "Hello?"

"Rigby, my man, it's me, Richie."

"Richie, you're actually back?"

"Sure as hell am. Can I come up?"

"My place is a mess."

"So what? Just buzz me in." He does and I enter the hallway, which is a whole 'nother kettle of banana fish. I mean, Maestro's building is no great shakes, but this is totally ridiculous. There's this intense dog stink, like everyone in the building let their pooch have a field day in the lobby. The plaster's cracked, the paint's flaking off, some of the mailboxes have their doors wide open, like they've just been burgled. As if the place doesn't have problems enough, some kid has scrawled Matt 82 all over the stairwell. Thanks so much, Matt, and fuck you too.

I'm halfway up the stairs when I bump into Rigby coming down. I'm thrilled to see him and give a big hug. "Hey, man, how's it going?"

"Okay."

"Just okay? What's it like up there?"

"Not too inspiring."

"Can I take a little peek?"

"I actually thought we'd go out for coffee."

"Only for a second? Please, I'm really curious." I really need to see how my friend's doing, so I sort of force him to change direction and take me upstairs. When we reach his apartment, he shoots me an anxious look. "Don't worry," I go, "I'm not from *House Beautiful.*"

Reluctantly, he opens the door and stands to one side. It's a small shabby space, as empty as Maestro's was full. There's hardly any furniture, just a single metal folding bed, some boxes here and there, and a small kitchen table with two wooden chairs next to a small refrigerator and tiny gas stove. That's it, nothing else, absolute bare bones.

He can tell I'm pretty appalled. "I'll get some furniture eventually."

"How about right now?"

"What do I use for money?"

"You gotta have something saved up."

"Don't be so sure."

I look around and realize he doesn't have a piano. "How are we gonna coach if there's no piano?"

"How about changing the subject?"

"It's your livelihood, man. A piano's essential."

"Don't you think I bloody know it?" It's one of the few times I've seen Rigby lose his cool.

We head downstairs, and it's a relief to get out into the fresh air, if you're crazy enough to call what they got in New York fresh air. We walk over to this neighborhood diner while I rattle off my adventures in Calgary with Polyna and Egon and the whole merry crew. He listens, but he's not really with it, he's stewing in his own goulash. I run out of steam by the time we enter the diner, so we're both quiet as we sit in one of the fake red leather booths and examine the menu, not that it's worth examining. Even after we order and our coffee and bagels arrive, we're still not talking. I finally hit on a way to get going again.

"Look, Rigby, about that piano, we can meet at Maestro's and have our sessions there."

"Don't be ridiculous. She'd never allow it."

"Renata? Of course she would. She's pretty reasonable."

"Not about me."

"Come on, she feels bad about making you move out. She even asked for your address so she could forward your mail."

"What a thoughtful, caring woman."

"Look, I'm sorry you don't live there any more and Maestro misses you too, but he's very sick. He needs to be with his family."

"Renata couldn't care less about Maestro. All she wants is his money."

I remember how quick she was to hike my rent. "Yeah, maybe you have a point."

"Of course I do. The lady's only in it for the cash. Listen, Maestro collapsed while we were walking on Riverside Drive a few weeks ago. The ambulance got there fast, thank god, but it really was a close call. I tried right away to find Renata, she was at a meeting somewhere. I told her it was serious, but she only appeared a week or so later and when she did, she barely greeted her father or me, just rushed off to talk with his doctors. Once their conference was done, she took me aside, thanked me for my help and said she'd take over."

"Take over?"

"Yes. No notice, no explanation, nothing. I told her I felt very close to her father and wanted to stay involved. She said, and this is an exact quote, 'No doubt, but it's just not possible.' It turned out that Maestro had given her power of attorney years ago, when they were on better terms, which meant I had no legal standing. I was – and am – totally irrelevant. I left the hospital and dragged myself back home. The very next morning a messenger arrived with a letter from Renata's lawyer, claiming I'd been living there illegally the past three years. I had never signed a document or contract with Maestro. I never needed to. It was always understood I'd take care of him and stay in my room rent free. I gave him total friendship and total devotion, not to mention free home health care, while Renata lived her life and never once showed any interest. Now that he's reaching the end, she sends me away without even a thank you. The fucking bitch..."

He's facing me now, grim and earnest. "The next day I went to see him at the hospital. The nurse on duty told me his room was off limits, I pushed past her and marched right in. There was Renata staring at me in astonishment. 'How dare you send me that letter!' I yelled. 'It's a fucking outrage!' Then I noticed that there was a whole team of doctors surrounding Maestro's bed. They were looking at me like I was some kind of lunatic, which, of course, I was. I mumbled an idiot excuse and ran out of the hospital back to the apartment and not long after, the doorman was on the house phone, saying the movers had come to pick up the pictures. I asked him which pictures and he proceeded to speak his usual impenetrable gobbledygook, so I told him to send them up. Definitely a big mistake. I opened the door and found these four hulks standing there, these four horsemen of the apocalypse. They said they came to pack up the Puccini portrait and lots of the autographed photos and take them to the Dwyer Auction House."

"Auction house? Renata said the painting was being restored."

"So she can sell it. She's auctioning everything next month. She'll make a small fortune."

"But she said..."

"That woman will say anything and everything to suit her own purposes... Of course, I did my best to talk the movers out of it, but they had consignment papers signed by Renata, which they claimed were legal, so I just stood there, gaping in disbelief, as they took down all the pictures and laid waste to the apartment and raped Maestro's past. Once the loot was hauled off, the place felt so naked, so desolate, I couldn't stay there another moment. I found this apartment that very same day."

"It sure is some beauty."

"I've got no money!"

He's yelling at me, Rigby, my pal, my buddy, the sweetest softest guy on the planet. Without thinking or considering, I just blurt out, "Listen, I got this genius idea. You're tight on cash, I've got plenty, thanks to the good folks in Calgary. I'll give you the money you need to get set up. You'll buy yourself a piano, second hand, of course, I'm flush but not that flush, get more furniture, maybe even paint the walls and live like a human being."

"Richie, you can't possibly do that."

"I sure as hell can. I got a thousand spare bucks, maybe even more. Pay me back when you can."

"That may be never."

"Come on, you're young, you're talented, no problem."

"No, really, I can't take your money. You need it too." He's right on that one, but I don't listen. I'm on a mission to haul him out of the mud and set him back on the path. After a few days of pleading, I finally get him to stop his noble act and borrow my money and buy whatever he needs. And I'm a thousand bucks poorer.

Maestro always takes this long siesta after lunch, leaving Angelique to twiddle her thumbs, so I say to her one day, "How's about getting yourself some fresh air while Maestro takes his nap? I'll be in the living room learning my scores and if he needs anything, I'll handle it."

A little frown crinkles her smooth broad brow. "Miss Renata won't like it."

"But you would, wouldn't you? Everything's blooming outside. There's buds on the trees, birds building nests, daffodils popping up, not to mention crocuses."

"Oh, Mister Richard," she says dreamily, "you do tempt me."

"That's the whole idea."

Two days later, once Renata's off to work, Angelique takes a stroll in the park while Rigby slips in for a visit. I greet him at the door and lead him to Maestro's room. Renata's pretty much left it alone. I guess she figured he'd holler too much if she tried to redecorate, so it's as dingy and dusty as ever, opera's graveyard.

Maestro's stretched out flat on his back, fully dressed, on top of the covers, legs spread wide, his bare feet flopping to the side. The shades are drawn. Everything's hushed and quiet. Every now and again, he lets out a huge wheezy snore that rattles the room and jangles my nerves. Rigby and I creep forward till we reach the end of his bed. I give him a gentle nudge and go, "Hi, it's me, Richie. I brought you a big surprise." He pops his eyes open one by one, cranks his head around and gives me this *don't disturb the sleeping dragon* look. "Sorry about your nap, Maestro. It's me, Richie Verdun, remember? The guy you call *tenore.*" There's still no response. I poke my face right into his. "It's me, see? Richie, Richie Verdun."

Another pause, then a frown, a squint and finally, his paper-thin voice. "*Tenore?*"

"Yeah, of course, it's me. I got a nice surprise for you. Look who just dropped by." I gesture for Rigby to get where Maestro can see him. "It's Rigby, Rigby Converse, remember? The pianist, your assistant. He really missed you."

I step back so Rigby can take the spotlight. "*Caro maestro,*" he goes and grabs the old guy's hands in this really intense *io t'amo* way you use in Italian opera. Maestro's startled by Rigby's passion, but that doesn't mean he actually knows him, he's still got this blank stare. Rigby isn't discouraged, he starts speaking Italian a mile a minute, but Maestro's face stays twisted in a question mark until Rigby finally gives up. It's like he just buried his favorite grandpa.

"Sorry, man, I guess we chose the wrong day." Right as I say it, the front door slams. Figuring it's Angelique back from her stroll, I rush into the hall and find Renata.

"Er, Renata, hi, everything okay?"

"Not really. I've got this blinding headache. I couldn't stay at work a minute longer."

"Gee, I'm sorry to hear it." You bet I am, with Rigby stuck in Maestro's bedroom. "Can I get you something, an aspirin, an Advil, a hot young lover?" She flashes me this look, like *how can you joke at a time like this, when life as we know it has ended.*

"Where's Angelique?"

"Actually, she's taking a little break."

"She's here to look after my father, not take breaks."

"My fault. It was so pretty out I thought she could take a little stroll. I figured if anything happened with Maestro, I'd run in and handle it."

"Angelique's a professional. She's trained to deal with victims of stroke."

"But nothing's gonna happen if I..."

Suddenly, we hear this loud click. Renata rushes into the hallway, snaps on the light and there's Rigby, creeping like a thief out of Maestro's bedroom. It's an oddball moment, like in those Rossini comedies, when the action suddenly stops and everyone sings about how surprised they are. We're surprised all right, but it's no comic opera.

Renata puts on her frostiest, most upper-class voice. "Mister Converse, you know you're not welcome here. I won't have strangers wandering into my home."

"I'm no stranger!"

That does it. Everyone goes ape shit. Rigby unleashes this giant diatribe, and I mean giant, calling her a heartless bitch who never loved her dad and only cares about money and has no soul and no heart, and as he attacks her, she slams right back, calling him a sick sissy boy who's hooked on rough trade, who lived off her dad and stole all his cash, which, of course, is untrue, but who cares about truth when clawing each other raw. As they wail and flail away, I see that my little brainstorm of bringing Maestro and Rigby back together was the stupidest stunt I ever dreamed up, and I've dreamed up some doozies, and just as I'm thinking this, just as I realize I'm a moron for creating this huge mess, who stomps in but Maestro himself, totally wide awake, totally his old self, slapping his walker in front of him like a flyswatter. "*BASTA, CRETINI, SILENZIO!*"

Everyone shuts up. All eyes are on Maestro as he pushes himself up from his walker till he's standing taller than you'd ever think possible for someone who had a stroke. He frowns and wriggles his middle finger at Rigby, slowly, impressively, like the scarlet princess summoning her slave boy. "*Fegatino,*" he goes, "*vieni qui.*" Rigby's amazed, the old guy hadn't a clue who he was just minutes ago and now he's back, wilder and wackier than ever. The kid hustles over and gives Maestro a hug. Maestro hugs him back and pretty soon they're having a giant hug-in, until Renata can't take it any more. "Fine, *babbo,* enough. Mister Converse has to go."

Maestro just glares at her. "No, *giammai. E il mio figlio.*"

"No, father, he's not your child. You only have me." Maestro ignores her and goes back to hugging Rigby and she suddenly gets this stricken look, like the kid in the playground no one ever plays with. I see the hurt and rejection on her face and remember how she once told me that her dad never forgave her for not going into music, for choosing *la vita stupida*, as he called it, and while Rigby's my great pal, it just seems wrong for Maestro's daughter to be left out in the cold like that, so I walk over to Rigby and tap him on the shoulder and, straight-up guy that he is, he understands and pries himself free and slips out the door, leaving Maestro hunched over his walker, older and lonelier than ever. I try to cheer him up and say his young friend will be back, but, of course, it's a hollow lie.

I'm still huddling with Maestro when Renata says, "Mr. Verdun, I'm afraid I can't let you stay here any more. Kindly leave by the end of the month."

It isn't long before Erich Hirschmann summons me for a major meeting.

"You tell me you are learning Don Jose with young Mister Converse, so I contact your friend Mister Jennings in Calgary and suggest you sing it there. They schedule *Carmen* in 1985."

"Wow, great idea. What did Jennings say?"

"He says you do for him a very nice Pinkerton, but your voice is too heavy for Don Jose. I tell him Jose is a much heavier role than Pinkerton, even Jon Vickers sings it. My words make no impression, he wants a lyric voice, even though it is wrong. Why is this man running an opera house?"

"Beats me." I'm shocked and disappointed. I sang like a champ in Calgary. On closing night Jennings took me aside and said he wanted me back. Not this time, I guess. And probably never.

Erich has other news as well. "I am afraid I also have not very good reports about the auditions you sing. Only one company offers a contract."

More depressing news, but I accentuate the positive. "Great. Which one is it?"

"The New York City Opera."

"Wow, fantastic, that's the best of the whole lot. What's their offer?"

"It's for one and a half years from now, the 1984 fall season, a six-week contract for Gastone in *Traviata* and Borsa in *Rigoletto.*"

"Who the hell are they?"

"No one knows, not even me. For this, they pay you $300 a week for six weeks and no air fare from Detroit. They say you now live in New York."

"Yeah, I guess that's kinda true." I do the math in my head. The money's pathetic.

"I must be honest with you, Mister Verdun, I pay my secretary better."

"You don't have a secretary."

"Of course, no one accepts such a ridiculous salary. The good news is that you sing with City Opera. Miss Sills believes in your voice."

"But gives me a shit contract. Pardon my French, but she does. Once I pay all my living costs, I'll basically be singing for free."

"But you have the honor of singing in New York City." It suddenly hits me and hits me hard. I spent thousands of dollars and thousands of hours busting my hump trying to make it in Operaland and I'm still nowhere. I aced those auditions and all I wind up with is a shit contract at City Opera. "Cheer up, my friend. Miss Sills did not become a star in one short week. It takes her very much time."

"Which I don't really have."

"True. You are not young."

"Thanks for reminding me."

"Well, what do I tell the lady? You agree to her offer or not?"

"I know this is gonna sound crazy, but I really can't be the third guy on the left." Was I really turning down the New York City Opera?

Erich looks strangely impressed. "Fine, I tell them this."

"Fine? It's not a mistake?"

"You are the artist. If you cannot do it, you cannot..."

"But you'll still put me on your list, won't you?"

"With all the problems you have, what would be the point?" A grim silence settles in Erich's tiny office. Every last folder in the room, every program and contract, head shot and press release droops with it, sags with it, collapses. "Of course, there is one way to solve this problem, but it requires a different approach."

"How different?"

"Listen and decide for yourself. You audition the last two months for the best American opera companies, but nothing comes of it. Why? What goes wrong? True, you sometimes make a poor impression, but every singer before the public has one time or another made a poor impression, maybe even worse. So, what then is the problem? You are looking in the wrong place. Here in America we have very few opera companies which do very few productions. Every year their auditions are besieged by more and more talented young artists. And even a few older ones..." Here he gives me a wise-guy grin. "Europe is quite different, especially Germany and Austria. There you find lots of year-round companies that are looking for singers, especially those with big voices, and yours is certainly big. It's not my first choice for Mozart, but for Wagner it does very well." I'm about to give him my anti-Wagner speech, when he goes, "I know, I know, you prefer not to sing him. You have your silly ideas. Still, the simple fact is you have one piece of luck. You are a tenor. Before them the whole world bows down."

"It's not bowing down to me."

"For the moment. You haven't auditioned in Europe. No one knows your work there. Every year I arrange for a few select singers to go over and audition at the very best European theaters. I do not promise a contract, of course. That would be ridiculous, but at least you would be trying in a place where opera is a way of life with many, many companies and an acceptable rate of pay. This is the only way I can continue with you. You must try your luck in Europe or we shake hands now and say goodbye."

"Wait, wait, you really think I should pull up stakes and move to Germany?"

"Assuming you are lucky enough to find a position there."

"But I'm American. I want to sing here."

"So do many others, but there isn't enough work. You recently auditioned for seventeen different opera companies and only one wanted you."

"Yeah, and a fat lot of good it did me."

"So, what is then the problem? Why not try something new?"

"I got a family here, my boy's still in school."

"They also have schools in Germany."

"But they speak German over there."

"Really, they speak German in Germany. Who knew?"

"Sorry, I didn't mean it like that. It's just... your idea's really mind boggling."

"Yes, we come to a fork in the road."

"And I don't know which way to turn."

"I tell you a little story. In my early twenties I was assistant to Dr. Hugo Stern of *Konzertagentur* Stern in Berlin. One day I walk into the boss's office and in his place is his associate Christian Meyer, a man I never even notice before, who tells me he has just bought the agency and my services are no longer needed. Just like that. It is 1934. Dr. Stern is not the first or the last Jew who sells his business in the middle of the night and leaves Germany and, of course, I realize I also must vanish very fast and I do.

"I will not bore you with my ten-year odyssey to reach America. You only must know that I made this vow, this solemn promise never to forgive those fucking Germans, who kill my family and send me into exile. I never go back there. I make in America a new life. I somehow or other start my own agency here, but it is very hard. Many days in a row I eat the canned spaghetti. Anyway, after a few years of beating my head bloody trying to find my people work, what do I discover? There are very many opera houses opening back up in Germany and there are very few singers."

"Why not?"

"*Mein Gott*, there was war, remember? A terrible war which *they* cause and every misery, every suffering they have they totally, absolutely deserve... In any case, Germany has very few male singers left, also not that many women, so how can they now make opera? I realize here in America are many good young artists eager to work and suddenly, I have this dilemma. Do I stick with my principles and follow my vow and have nothing to do with those awful Germans who ruin my life, and win the Nobel Prize for personal integrity? Or do I get for my clients the work they need and live in the world as it is?"

"You're saying you went back there?"

"Of course. Sometimes in life we must do things we think we never do."

"I'm used to that. Last year I was out on the lot, selling cars."

"Then why do you not take advantage?"

"Because I don't know how much it costs."

"Very little indeed, considering what you get, first-class contacts with first-class theaters who take you very serious. For setting this up, I charge a one-time fee of three thousand dollars, payable in advance. In addition, you pay for the trip itself, another two thousand at most. The whole thing is maybe five thousand dollars, very little money for such an enormous chance."

Whoa, wait, five thousand dollars? My year in New York has already cost me a fortune, what with crazy high rents and endless coachings and plane trips back home and the thousand I just gave Rigby. How the hell do I find five grand?

"Mister Verdun, I'm waiting for your reply."

"You know, I'd really love to, but it costs way too much. Maybe I can do it next year."

"By then you are a hundred and twelve."

Wow, what a comic. "All kidding aside, I just..."

"I do not kid. I am total serious. Act quick or do not act at all."

"Look, I'm really short of cash. Could you offer me some sort of payment plan?"

"Sorry, I am not a bank."

"In that case, maybe you could do me a special favor, seeing as how we're such great buddies and all..." I give him a big smile and hope for the best. "Is there maybe a chance you could offer me a discount?"

"Is there maybe a chance you could let me sleep with your wife?"

"That's not funny."

"Neither is your suggestion, dear boy."

That does it. "I'm not your fucking boy! I may be new to this game, but at least I'm not a crook!"

His face turns red as ketchup. "Who are you calling the crook?"

"You, you greedy son of a bitch, you! You charge three thousand bucks for a few lousy phone calls, three thousand bucks! That's highway robbery, out-and-out fraud. You ought to be fucking ashamed."

His face is white now. Frozen. "That's quite enough, Herr Verdun. There is the door."

CHAPTER TWO

Kit

We'd begun our separation – professional relocation would probably be a better term – in 1982. Money was tight. We could only afford to be together one weekend in four, so Richard usually booked his flight home the last Friday of every month and returned to New York the following Monday. Yet there he was coming up the walk two days early on a fine Wednesday afternoon.

"Can't a guy just want to be with his family?" he said when I asked if everything was okay. Then he gave me his *here comes a joke* look, a look I'd seen a thousand times and always enjoyed, silly though it was. "I was figuring if I showed up early, I could get some extra action."

The strange thing was he didn't seem interested. There was no urgency in his voice, no trace of sexiness. "Seriously, Richard, is something wrong? Did anything bad happen?"

"No, everything's great."

"Your agent really didn't hear from any of those companies?"

"No."

"That's odd. They're taking a very long time."

"Nothing happens fast in opera."

"It makes no sense. It's nearly the end of the season."

"What do you know about it? Why would you even care?"

I was shocked at his sudden vehemence. "I do care and I should. I just find it strange you haven't heard anything from all those companies."

"The hell with those companies. Who needs 'em?"

"You do. Where else are you going to sing?"

He faced me in utter exasperation. "Don't you get it, Kit? I'm a flop. I'm leaving New York the end of this month and moving back home. The return of the family failure."

I was so stunned by the complete reversal of all he'd done, all *we'd* done, I hardly knew how or where to begin. Richard had just made a successful debut, sung lots of important auditions and inspired the whole family, when suddenly he was giving it all up. How could he? How dare he? I had to do something, say something, but what? "Richard, sorry, but this can't be what you want. You tell the kids all the time to go out and fight for their dreams."

"Look, I came pretty close, but the odds are against me and the cost is horrendous. And after all that expense and effort, all I got was one lousy gig in Calgary."

"It wasn't lousy. Carol said the public went wild."

"For the soprano, not me." His voice was fading away, I barely could hear him.

"Darling, sorry, but I can't believe any of this. It doesn't sound right."

"They're doing a *Carmen* out in Calgary, okay? They need a Don Jose. I spent over a grand coaching it with Rigby. It's a perfect part for me, right up my alley. But they don't want me. They won't ask me back."

"Well, it's their loss."

"It's *mine*. I don't have any work."

"But you've hardly even begun." Richard was always the family optimist, his outlook always so bright. I was the one with doubts. "Darling, be patient. You've barely given it a year. As for the money, I'm getting a raise at the library, we'll be okay."

"Great, now I can sponge off you, like some kinda leech."

"That's just ridiculous."

"Come on, I'm a guy. I'm supposed to support my family."

"Lord, it's not the Middle Ages. Women work, women earn. And why not."

"Good for them. I still feel like shit."

"You shouldn't. You did all the big things, all the difficult things. You even paid for my degree. I'm just returning the favor. Why can't you simply accept it?"

"Because it hurts, Kit, it really hurts." He looked so beaten at the moment, so desolate, my heart ached for him. "And those auditions Erich sent me to? I had – what? – fifteen or twenty over the past month. I paid Rigby a fortune to prepare for them. All I got was two nothing roles at City Opera."

"City Opera? That's marvelous."

"Not if you sing lousy parts."

"Still, it's a wonderful company. I'm glad you got in."

"I'm glad you're glad. I turned them down." Another bewildering move from the man I thought I knew. "The offer sucked. I'd be losing money to sing with them."

"But it's the New York City Opera."

"The New York *Shitty* Opera."

"What does Erich Hirschmann say?"

"About what?"

"Everything. Your prospects, your future. What's he going to do?"

"Nothing."

"But he's your agent."

"Not any more. He kicked me off his list." I stared at him in mute dismay. "He wanted me to go over to Europe on this big audition tour, but it's a giant gamble and it costs an arm and a leg, five or six thousand bucks."

"We could manage it."

"Kit, please, the whole thing's finished. When Hirschmann said he'd charge three thousand just to set it up, I yelled and screamed and called him a rip-off artist, so he threw me out the door. A little while later, I realized what I'd done and called to apologize. The moment he heard my voice, he hung up. He's had it with me. I'm toast."

I wish I could say I reassured him at that point, but frankly, I was so shocked by what he'd done, so amazed at his stupidity, I just sat there, dumbly staring at him. "I came close, Kit, incredibly close..." I reached over and pulled him towards me. He snuggled a bit, but didn't embrace. I held him and felt his breath go in and out, slowly, mournfully. "What can I say? Your Richie's a dumb fuck. And I want it so bad, I really and truly do."

"Then keep trying."

A few days later I was in New York walking down a tight hallway of opaque glass doorways, hunting for suite 706. When I finally reached it, I had a sudden attack of nerves. What was I doing here? Could I actually help at all? Only the other day I had an appointment with a far more important person than Erich Hirschmann and greatly enjoyed it. He was a powerful philanthropist, Ray Solomon, much sought after by all sorts of Michigan nonprofits, yet I never once felt nervous or on edge with him. We both loved books, cared about kids and had a wonderfully productive meeting. This was entirely different. All I really knew about Richard's agent was his name and address. I had no idea what sort of person he was or what strategy I should use. I took a deep breath, wished myself luck and entered.

His "suite" was every bit the wreck Richard had told me it was, much more aging bachelor's pad than office. Studying a large sheaf of papers, the great man himself was ensconced on the one decent piece of furniture in the room, a leather reclining chair of startling modernist design. He was physically unprepossessing, pudgy and on the short side, his thinning hair dyed a harsh and unnatural brownish black. He reminded me of Melville's Bartleby, the morose obstructionist clerk who "would prefer not to."

Clearly puzzled by my sudden appearance, he pointed vaguely in the direction of the hallway and said, in a harsh German accent, "The ladies' room is that way."

"I'm actually here to see you," I said. "I promise it won't take long."

"Promises, promises. Always they give me promises." He leaned forward and studied me a bit more. "You are not a singer, by any chance?"

"Oh heavens, no."

"Good. There are far too many in this world. They make for me only problems." I couldn't help thinking they also made him money. "You would not believe how many walk in here, hoping I put them on my list."

"Well, of course, you're a major agent."

"Not so major as you think."

"You're being much too modest. Everyone knows you're extremely important."

"From your mouth to god's ear, Madame. So, what can I do for you? Why are you here?"

I closed the door behind me. "Actually, it's not about me, sir, it's my husband."

He was suddenly on his guard. "And who might this husband be?"

"One of your singers."

"*Ach,* singers, the curse of my existence... Does this singer have a name?"

"Yes, Richard Verdun. I'm his wife, Catherine." A storm cloud scudded briefly across his brow. "I just wanted you to know that Richard is very sorry he offended you."

"Do not concern yourself. It is all quite settled. He no longer is on my list."

"But he wants to be. He should be."

"So, why doesn't he come here himself? Why does he send you as messenger?"

"I came here on my own. He doesn't even know I'm here."

"How do you think he feels when he finds out? He is a man after all, he has his pride." It was a good point. I'd been uneasy about it from the start. "You know, it really is not nice to sneak around him like that."

"I didn't exactly sneak."

"Of course, you did. You go behind his back and treat him like a three-year-old...." He leaned forward on his desk, laced his hands under his chin and studied me as if I were an exotic object, a delicate hothouse flower or delusional housewife. "Most curious. Even though you are American, you follow your husband *all' Italiana.*"

"What's that?"

"Most of the wives of the Italian singers follow their husbands everywhere, stick with them day and night, even in the rehearsal rooms, even the bathrooms. That way they stay in line."

"You know very well Richard doesn't need that sort of policing."

"Doesn't he?" He almost leered as he said it. Lord, did he have nerve.

"You've got the wrong idea. I know him inside out. He'd never behave like that."

"I see, your husband is a man of virtue," he sneered.

"He's also a very good singer."

"Who calls his agent a thief, or *ganaf,* as they say in Yiddish. We Jews do not like to hear such things. It gets us very much upset. "

"Look, you have every right to be angry, but I hope you can get past it. You know what they say about the quality of mercy."

"There is no mercy in the opera."

"Mr. Hirschmann, you've got plenty of compassion. You found him when he was no one and got him his first job."

"His *only* one."

"But there'll be many more. He's first-rate material. He'll make you a fortune."

He smirked and settled back in his chair. "You know, there is an opera, *Alceste*, it is not very popular. They did it maybe twenty, thirty years ago as a vehicle for the great Kirsten Flagstad. I am one of the five people who actually saw it. This opera tells of a wife, Alceste, whose husband, the king, is about to die. The gods take pity and decree that this much-loved man will be spared if someone will die in his place. Everyone refuses, of course. Who willingly gives up his own life? But Alceste loves her husband so much she becomes the substitute cadaver and goes down to the underworld so her husband might live – a symbol of female loyalty."

"I'm not a queen and not a symbol and don't plan on dying any time soon."

"Yes, but this heartwarming image of the good wife giving up everything to save her beloved man is all well and good in an opera hundreds of years old, but not here, not today. It may be unfashionable to say it in this age of so-called women's lib, but a woman's place is at home and not in the office of her husband's agent, sorry, *former* agent. You waste my time with this. Good day."

"NOT SO FAST!" The words shot out of my mouth. The old man was shocked and frankly, so was I. "I didn't take the bus all the way from Michigan just to be dismissed like that."

"A bus? You mean to tell me you come all this way in a bus? That is most uncomfortable. Why not go by plane?"

Erich Hirschmann was the last person on earth I'd ever discuss my fear of flying with. "Flying's much too expensive."

"Ah, yes, money problems." He gestured morosely at his cramped working space. "You cannot believe the rent they charge me."

"Take Richard back. His fees can help with the rent."

There was an excruciatingly long pause before Hirschmann spoke again. "How do I know he won't insult me again?"

"I won't let him."

He regarded me steadily, like a dealer assessing a new painting. "Well, he is a tenor. Maybe it can work."

"Oh, it will, I'm sure of it."

"One can be sure of nothing in the opera. The odds of a career are against him."

"The odds are against us all. And still we try. It's who and what we are," I said with considerable, perhaps excessive, passion. "He has it in him to be a big success, he really and truly does. Just give him one more chance."

He seemed lost in deep thought, making complex, almost anguished calculations that I was too naive and untutored to comprehend. Finally, he gave a deep sigh, as if his deliberations had completely exhausted him. "You are quite impossible, Mrs. Verdun, you make it quite difficult to resist."

That was it, the moment I hoped for. I grabbed both his hands and shook them repeatedly, compulsively. I was flooded by a warm wave of relief. "Oh, thank you, Mr. Hirschmann, thank you."

"I take your husband back on one condition and I am not so sure you will like it."

My anxiety came flooding back. "What's the condition?"

"No one talks to Erich Hirschmann like your husband did, no one. But Richard Verdun insults me to my face like I am a crook, a fake, a liar. I do not allow this. I cannot. My fee is now five thousand dollars."

Shocked doesn't begin to describe my reaction. I was stung, stunned, outraged. I suppressed my fury and said in a tight small voice, "Richard told me your fee was three thousand."

"Actions have consequences." He smiled as he said it, smiled as he observed my stifled rage. "The tour is much harder to arrange now. I have to make many more phone calls and mailings and reservations, and all at the very last moment. This is a great deal of extra work, very time consuming. Five thousand dollars barely covers it."

"It's an enormous difference to us. It puts a big strain on our finances."

"It's a strain on *me.* I now have to call again all the *Intendants* and get them to agree to hear your husband, even though he insults me and behaves like an absolute idiot. Five thousand dollars, or the whole thing is off." He put out his hand as if he expected me to give him his fee right then and there in one-dollar bills.

Furious though I was, outraged though I was, I had no choice. "Fine, five thousand dollars. I'll get out my check book."

"You know, you make the right decision." He seemed very pleased with himself, while I stood there fuming. He had kept me standing the entire time. "*Ach, mein Gott,*" he said, "I completely forget my manners." As he set up a folding chair for me, I suddenly was assailed by doubts. Had I given in too soon? Should I have fought for a lower fee? Perplexed, confused, disturbed, I sat down and took out my check book.

"Not quite yet. We make now a little celebration." He opened a desk drawer and to my surprise produced a small bottle of champagne. I've never been much of a drinker. Richard always joked about what a cheap date I was. "I must apologize in advance. It is not properly chilled, I have no room for an ice box here." Just what I needed, a hangover on top of everything else. "It's never too late, or too early, for champagne in the opera, and you had such a hard time last night on the bus, and maybe also today. I drive a hard bargain, *nicht wahr*?" He gave me an ingratiating smile, which irritated me even more. "I cannot imagine how a charming woman like you can endure so many difficulties."

"Oh, I'm tougher than I look."

"Then drink a little champagne. Let your spirits soar." He rummaged in one of the many battered boxes lined up against the wall and fished out two champagne glasses, whose delicacy and elegance contrasted with the grimy chaos of the room. "Don't worry, I keep them always clean." He returned to the desk with the flutes and wrestled off the cork from the champagne. Its hollow pop echoed through the cramped space. He offered me a glass almost as full as his, then stood up to make a little toast. "To all the beautiful women. Even with that ridiculous women's lib and all the silly anger you hold against men, we adore you. You make us your slaves." He clinked my glass and drank. I sipped cautiously. "Very frankly, you deserve Dom Perignon, but I have only Moët, and just the half bottle." He smiled amiably and took another healthy gulp. His dyed hair bewildered me. It kept changing with the light from black to brown to royal blue.

"You know, it does not make me happy, charging the extra money. Maybe I find a way, maybe we find a way. My apartment is nearby, just a few blocks. It is very attractive, very neat, not messy like this place, with Kirchners on the wall, even a nice Max Beckmann. You know the artist Max Beckmann? A great German artist who Hitler drives away and finally ends up in Saint Louis, if you can believe it, Saint Louis. Anyway, he is a hero of my youth and I have this little etching. Also this nice douche, I think you could use it, after that terrible bus ride..." With this, he got up from his chair, wearing the crazed crooked smile of men who think they're being sexy when they're acting like total fools. Poor deluded man, he was twice my age and notably out of shape. As I rose to face him, he seemed unperturbed by the fact that he was two inches shorter than me. "It will be very discreet, Madame, very *luxe...*"

With that, he reached out and grabbed for my arm. I shoved him away with great gusto. He wasn't expecting it, lost his balance and fell back against the desk. As I dashed out the door, I heard a thump and muffled shout, but Erich Hirschmann held no further interest for me. Richard would find another manager.

The elevator was a long time coming. As I waited, I heard him call my name. "Help, Mrs. Verdun, help," he cried, "I need you."

"Too bad." Really, the man was beyond impossible.

"Please. It's serious."

"Nonsense." By then the elevator had arrived and I was about to step in, when he shouted, "I can't see!" That troubled me. The man was elderly, after all.

"What do you mean you can't see?"

"I can't. Please come back." Maybe he really was hurt, brain damage, perhaps. I let the elevator go. Muttering to myself about manipulative senile men, I stomped back into his office and found the agent on all fours at the foot of his desk, frantically hunting for something.

"I can't find my glasses."

"Your glasses? I thought you couldn't see."

"I see nothing without them."

"Find the dumb things yourself." I turned to leave again, when I noticed his spectacles at the base of the door frame. "Here. Take your stupid glasses."

"Thanks. You really save me." He scrabbled over and reached out to take them. As he did, I noticed a big blotch on the front of his shirt.

"You're bleeding."

"*Ach,* it is nothing."

"You don't know that. Let me check."

"You are suddenly now the doctor?"

"My boys keep sending one another to the emergency room. I'm quite well versed." By now he'd put his glasses back on and was sitting on the floor, his back against the desk. He had this flattened look which struck me as completely appropriate. I knelt beside him and checked his left temple, which was still trickling blood. "Put your hand on it and press hard."

"But it hurts." Rather gingerly, he put his hand to his head.

"Harder, or it won't do any good. I'll get some water. Where's the bathroom?"

"The key is in the desk." I ran over to open it and was confronted with a welter of envelopes and ticket stubs and pencils and pens and staples and paper clips. The man lived in total anarchy. Shoving away piles of detritus, I finally spotted a key strung on a lanyard looped through a wooden paddle.

"Left out the door, end of the hall," he croaked.

I wet some paper towels in the bathroom and returned to his office, where I dabbed gingerly at his wound. "How's your head?"

"Embarrassed."

"Any pain, any pulsing or pounding?"

"No, I hit very slight."

"What day of the week is it?"

"*Ach, komm*, don't be stupid."

"What day of the week?"

"This is so idiotic."

"I've got to check. Maybe you have a concussion." When could I finally get out of there? I had a bus to catch, a family to rejoin. How I missed them at that moment. How I longed for Richie and the kids.

"I tell you I am fine."

"So what day is it?"

"Friday, of course."

I held up three fingers. "And how many fingers?"

"Seventy-five."

"Seriously. No jokes."

"All right, all right. Three. I act like a fool and you treat me even worse."

"Because you deserve it. You're sure there's no pain, no throbbing?"

"Of course." He closed his eyes and shook his head from side to side very slowly, very mournfully, as if he was beating the drum for his own funeral. "You know, I did not mean this. I just have a stupid impulse. And, I really respect you, I respect your husband."

"Then charge the proper price, the one you first quoted Richard." He couldn't believe I was challenging him. "You heard me. I've had enough. And so I assure you has he."

He lowered the towel. His wound had stopped bleeding. The atmosphere in the room was hushed, almost reverential. For the first time I felt he was looking at me with something approaching respect. "But you have to see it from my perspective—"

"Three thousand dollars, or I'll make a big fuss. I'm sure there's some sort of agents' association that would be most interested to hear from me."

Was it my imagination, or had he turned a shade or two paler?

"But I have so many extra expenses."

"Three thousand dollars!" He jumped. I actually made the old man jump.

"Mrs. Verdun, you drive a hard bargain."

"I most certainly hope so."

CHAPTER THREE

Richie

You can't say no to a rich guy. When he commands, you obey. Which is why, even though I just got back to Graystone, Kit has to rush off to Detroit to meet this big-shot money man, the guy who funded her high school library. She'll be away Thursday through Saturday, leaving me to deal with Billy on my own, thanks so very much. Nowadays he basically just goes off to school, hangs out with his friends or shuts himself in his room doing god knows what, though I got my suspicions.

The night Kit leaves I sleep as best I can and wake up grumpy, gloomy and unrefreshed. Once Billy's off to school, I moon around the house, asking myself over and over why I fucked everything up. To make matters worse, I get a call from Timmy out in Ann Arbor. It's his freshman year at U Mich and his coach is barking at him because he keeps losing to a guy who's ten pounds lighter. Well, excuse me, but Timmy's gotta stop whining and show what he really can do, so yours truly, whose own hopes and dreams have basically collapsed, is forced to give him the old pep talk and say *he's really got it in him, he almost was state champ last year, he can beat anyone, anytime, anywhere,* etcetera and so forth, until he finally goes, "Great, Dad, thanks for nothing," and, bang, hangs up on me. I'm like, thanks, son, love you too.

I'm in no mood to call my buddies. I can't play the guy game of boasting and bragging and saying how terrific things are, when they're the exact opposite, it's too damn pathetic and embarrassing. Instead, I stay home and stew and rue and think what a bummer it was to have gone to the trouble of learning Don Jose in *Carmen,* paying Rigby mega bucks, only to ruin things with my agent, so there's no way I'll ever have the fun of stabbing that Carmen bitch to death. Yeah, I know, bitter words, brutal words, but that's how miserable I feel. I toss my bummed-out butt into bed and go to sleep early.

I wake up to discover it's Saturday morning, nearly ten o'clock, and I'm achy and fuzzy like I hit the bottle too hard, even though I only had one beer with my burger and soggy frozen fries that I didn't properly thaw. Kit told me a thousand times how to do them properly, but I'm just no chef, they came out like wet plaster. I stumble my worn and weary self down to the kitchen where there's a note on the table from Billy, saying he's out for the day with Wiggins and Beano, whoever the hell they are. I take my coffee into the living room and there to my amazement is Kit, rolled up in a ball on the sofa, business suit, scarf, shoes, stockings and all, like she just came back from a meeting and collapsed, whomp, without undressing. I bend over and kiss her shoulder.

She stirs, sees it's me and shoots up her arms to me, like she wants me down on top of her, right now. It's a big surprise to be welcomed like that, especially after my all recent miseries, and it keeps on getting better. Without saying a word, she pulls me onto her and hugs so tight I can hardly breathe. It takes me about ten seconds to catch on and the shoes, the socks, the clothes go flying and we're at it hot and heavy, especially her, she's leading this time, pulling and pushing me this way and that to places I thought we'd never go, and when I think it's over, she wants it again, which almost never happens. I'm happy to oblige and we're upside, downside, inside and out, till I'm just this panting mass of manhood, whipped and wiped out.

When I finally come back to earth and ask what all the wild stuff was about, she flashes her dimples at me. "What would you say if I told you Erich Hirschmann put you back on his list?"

"I'd say you're smoking some pretty strong weed."

"It's true. He expects you in New York on Monday." I stare at her, slack-jawed. "People change, Richie. Time moves on."

"Not that fast… Anyway, you've been in Detroit with your money guy. Where does Erich come in?"

"Can't you guess?" She looks incredibly pleased with herself, sitting there on the sofa, which is pretty much a mess, the pillows scattered everywhere. She finally takes mercy and gives me a little hint. "I saw your agent."

"But you drove to Detroit to see your..."

"And took the bus and went to New York and tracked down Erich Hirschmann and got him to change his mind."

I'm so astonished by all this, so floored and flummoxed, that all I can do is squeeze out a pitiful little, "You did, really?"

She explains how the bus was her only option, especially since she wanted to surprise Erich early the next morning. "You know, Richard, honestly, you've got to be more careful with him. He's exceptionally touchy, especially about being called greedy."

"Which he a hundred percent is."

"He's over sixty, he's never going to change. He was furious about that rip-off comment you made."

"It *is* a rip-off. He's charging too way much."

"But he's getting you to Europe. He's making your career."

"*I'm* making it, Kit, *me.* The whole thing's highway robbery."

"You've got no alternative. There's simply no other way. Just remember that he's extremely thin-skinned, especially when it comes to money. You mustn't insult him, you mustn't—."

"Stop ordering me around! Stop acting like I'm a total fuckup!!"

The room grows very still. Kit's sitting on the sofa looking so sad and forlorn, that my mood completely flip-flops. Maybe I took things too far. Maybe I should have counted to ten.

It takes her a while to respond. "For god's sake, you've done everything and anything you wanted in New York for one entire year while I stayed home and dealt with the children and paid the bills and started a new job and never once complained. In all that time, all you ever heard from me was, 'Great, Richie, good for you. Go out there and follow your dreams.'"

I take a few steps towards her and go, "Look, hon, I'm sorry I got so hot under the collar. I'm glad you went to see Hirschmann, I really am. It took a lot of guts... Kit, did you hear? I said I'm very grateful..." But she's already out the door, headed for her own private sanctuary.

Monday afternoon, back in New York, I walk into Erich's office, eager to plan my audition tour. "Great to see you, Mister H. I'm so glad it's all been arranged."

He settles back in his fancy chair and stares at me from a million miles away. "It's only arranged if you agree."

"Agree to what?" he gives me this pitying look, like *how can you possibly ask such a stupid question.* It's clearly gonna take longer than expected, so I get one of those nasty metal folding chairs and set myself up at the foot of his desk. "What do you want me to agree to?"

He waves his hand at me like he's batting away a fly. "You know, your wife really made an impression. To come all the way to the city in a Greyhound bus, that takes nerve. She is very loyal, very brave."

"Well, Kit likes you too, Mister H." This isn't strictly true but he doesn't need to know it. "So, tell me, what's the plan?"

"Do not rush me, Herr Verdun."

"Sorry, don't take offense, I thought that—"

"Just answer this one question. Will you dance with the devil? Yes or no?"

"I'm not exactly sure what you mean."

"Well, sometimes, when we're dancing, we do not like the partner we have, but we still have to dance."

"Okay, sure, but what's that gotta do with me?"

"I make clear to you," he goes, clearly annoyed that he has to state the obvious. "Herr Verdun, I expect you to sing a Wagner aria when you audition in Europe."

"You know I don't do that."

"Your dislike of Wagner is very charming, very original, perfect for the dinner party, it makes you an interesting guest. In this office it makes you a fool."

"You know damn well I'm no fool."

"Then sing Wagner. Every company I send you to in Germany, Austria, even France, needs Wagner tenors. I tell them you are a true Heldentenor. They want you to sing for them Wagner."

"Which I told you I won't do."

"Because you play the fool."

I shoot out of my seat and head straight for the door. As my hand grabs the knob, I realize I've been there and done that. It didn't work then, it won't work now, so why even bother? Besides, what will Kit say?

I turn around to face my agent, or tormentor, or executioner, I'm no longer sure which. He's smiling at me, actually smiling, like I'm an amusing circus act. "It is very wise you do not leave, because this time I will not run after you. I have of your curious craziness really enough. Please sit down. We have a serious talk."

After a little pause to let him know I'm doing him a favor, I sit back down on the metal folding chair. "And I don't like being called a fool, either."

"Really?" He smiles his sour smile. "My dear boy, Wagner is your only possibility. Dance with the devil and succeed."

"Look, I know you'll think I'm crazy, but this Wagner stuff..."

"It's not *stuff.* It's art. It's very nice you like Verdi and Puccini. So do I, so does everyone. But people want singers like Domingo and Pavarotti for that. You are not the proper type."

That's a shock. No one's ever said that to me before, not Rigby, not Maestro B, not Elizabeth, absolutely no one. "Sorry, but I really can't believe that."

"You know what this Jennings fellow in Calgary really says? I do not mention because I want to spare you, but being kind is sometimes also cruel. He told me your voice wasn't romantic enough, the ladies don't drop down dead at your feet. That's why he won't ask you back... No more dreams, Mister Verdun, no more illusions. Straight talk, common sense, as we say in Yiddish, *tacheles.* Your voice is heroic, not lyric. Strong, not beautiful. You maybe have a career if you sing Wagner. Otherwise, there really is no point."

"Look, I know you're big on Wagner, and I truly respect that, but you gotta see it from the singer's point of view. His roles are voice breakers. I gotta protect myself."

"*Ach, komm,* who tells you that?"

"Old Maestro Borgianni. He used to work at the Met."

"A thousand years ago with the dinosaurs. And anyway, he is Italian. These people know nothing about Wagner, nothing."

"I heard about this hotshot young tenor who got a contract right out of grad school as Heldentenor with this small German opera house. Once he got over there, he realized he was in way over his head and asked if they'd let him sing some lighter roles, a Verdi, maybe, or a Puccini. They said, no, impossible, they signed him up for Wagner and that's what he had to do, or they'd get him for breach of contract. He caved and sang a few Tristans, a few Lohengrins and wound up destroying his voice."

"He probably never had one."

"No, no, my pal said he sang great until he got into Wagner."

"Who is this person? He repeats to you stupid singer gossip."

"It's fact. Those roles are way too heavy for me."

"You do Calaf, you do Don Jose. They are heavy too."

"Not like Wagner."

"You know nothing of Wagner. You never sing a note of his music."

"Sure, but I know he's really..."

"Enough!" And with that, he gives a giant grunt, pushes himself back from the desk, stomps past me and flings open the door. "Thirty-five years I have this agency, thirty-five, I represent many singers, some of them stubborn, some of them difficult, but of them all the most stubborn and difficult is Richard Verdun. Get out before you make me insane."

Then Rigby walks in. Talk about surprises.

Erich isn't surprised at all. He starts tearing into him too. "*Mein Gott*, you certainly take your time. You arrive so late it all blows up in my face."

"You mean he actually won't do it? Richie, say it ain't so."

"Say what ain't so?"

"You're really not going to sing Wagner?"

"Why should I? It's completely—"

"Enough is enough is enough!" He's no agent, he's a diva. Give him a wig and let him sing Tosca. "I listen to your impossible friend for thirty minutes all by myself because you cannot even get here on time."

"I'm really sorry, I tried my best, but the subway didn't come."

"*Ja, ja*, everyone is always blaming the subway." So much for Rigby. He goes back to reaming me out. "I get a wonderful new idea for you. Everyone's excited, everyone's interested, everyone but you. It's too dangerous. It's too radical. You are frightened of the big bad bear."

"Actually, it's a wolf."

"Enough! You make me total insane." He stalks over to the coat rack and grabs his raincoat. "I go now. To the park."

"What about us?" Rigby asks.

"You do what you want. Just try not to blow up my office." He spins on his heels and leaves, pounding his way down the hall.

"Wow, what's eating that guy?"

"You, Richie, you're making a terrible mistake."

"Come on, man, not you too."

"Yes. Me too..."

"But Maestro made me promise never to sing Wagner. He said it would ruin my voice."

"That was his blind spot. He had no feel for that music at all."

"But it's hard as hell and always lies in the break."

"How do you know? You've never studied it. And just because it lies in the *passaggio* doesn't mean that you can't sing it..." As he says this, he goes over to the upright piano stuck in a corner of the office. It's covered with tottering towers of programs and papers and magazines. "Come on, help me clear it off."

"Why?"

"You'll see." It takes some time to uncover the piano lid, but once it's cleared off, Rigby flips it open. "So, tell me, how many Wagner operas have you actually heard?"

"I don't know, two or three, enough to know I don't like them."

"Have you ever heard *Winterstuerme*?"

"No, what's that?"

"Just about Wagner's most famous tenor aria. You've really never heard it?" I shake my head no and he gives me a woeful look, not to make fun like Erich, not to mock, but to show I missed out on something spectacular. "Let me play it for you. It would fit you like a glove."

"Which I don't want to wear."

"How do you know unless you hear it?" He takes out one of those tenor anthologies from his beat-up old briefcase and gestures for me to join him on the piano bench. I settle myself next to him, it's a pretty tight fit. He flips through the score, hunting for the aria. When he finally finds it, he goes, "I'll need you to turn pages. Just wait till I give you a nod."

I'm the world's worst page turner. I usually puzzle out where I am by following the words. In this case, Rigby's humming the voice part, not singing it, so forget about words. Also, the music's real passionate and he bobs his head so wildly this way and that, I can't tell if he's grooving to the score or giving me a cue to turn the page.

What happens next is hard to explain. The aria's short, barely three minutes. It pretty much stops before it begins, but what music it is, what incredible, mind-boggling sound. The aria's a love song the tenor sings to the soprano after he discovers they're brother and sister. I mean, come on, it's Wagner. Incest is great, have yourself a ball. You'd figure a moment like this when two siblings start going at it would either be yucky or totally hilarious, but the music takes it somewhere else entirely.

I sit there astounded, awestruck, flubbing every cue, while Rigby keeps screaming at me *too soon! too late!* but I don't really care, the score completely grabs me, I'm totally under its spell, and Rigby's feeling it too. Page turn or not, he keeps driving the music harder and harder, closer and closer to the wild urgent sex these crazed siblings need. It's a small room, so everything's amplified, everything's super intense, and I'm pulled further and further into the madness and badness of the whole incredible scene, and I suddenly see clear and sharp as day that Rigby was right, this is for me, it fits me to a T, when the front door bursts open and Erich marches in. The two of us are so out of it by now, so entirely and completely somewhere else, we just stop and stare at him.

"I interrupt something important?"

"Yes, it actually is pretty important. The scales fell from his eyes. Didn't they, Richie?"

Erich turns to me for an explanation, but I'm still tangled up in the music, still trying to understand the strange place it took me to. Finally, I go, "I guess I gotta apologize for all that nonsense about Wagner."

He rushes forward, grabs me by both shoulders and twists me around on the piano bench so I'm facing him. Lo and behold, he's smiling at me, actually smiling, like he really wishes me well, like everything nasty he ever said or did meant nothing, this is our moment, this is all that counts.

Weirdest of all, he runs his hand roughly through what's left of my hair, kinda musses it up, like I used to do to Timmy or Billy on one of those rare sunny days when I didn't want to strangle them. "*Ach*, you tenors," he goes, "what misery you put us through, what craziness... Mister Rigby?"

"Yes, sir."

"You take the *Herr Heldentenor* home and pound his head so full of *Winterstuerme* he sings it perfect even in his sleep."

CHAPTER FOUR

Kit

It was the end of April. Richie had come home from New York for a few weeks of relaxation before setting off on his audition tour. He relaxed a bit too much, I'm afraid. Even though he picked up his scores from time to time and sometimes even listened to his Walkman, I had the impression he was far more interested in being with me and the kids than studying his arias.

One Saturday afternoon, Doc Williams called. "Kit, this isn't easy for me to say and lord knows the last thing I want to do is alarm you or stir up a domestic hornets' nest, but the fact of the matter is Richie's not ready for that audition tour."

My heart plummeted. "He's not?"

"No, emphatically not. He dropped by this morning to go through his arias. It was the first time I heard them and, frankly, I was extremely dismayed."

"He's not singing well?"

"The problem isn't vocal, thank god. His voice is actually stronger and richer than ever, which is obviously all to the good. But, and this is a very big but, his German pronunciation is terrible. He's singing only one German aria, the *Winterstuerme,* and absolutely everyone is going to ask for it. If he sings it for a German or Austrian theater the way he just sang it for me, they'll laugh him off the stage. I mean, *lieblich* is not pronounced *lieblick.* One might think so here in Michigan, but—"

"I hope you told him that."

"I didn't. That's why I'm calling you. I'm quite aware I should have, but you know how eager Richie is for praise, how profoundly *needy.* I couldn't rain on his parade and so, coward that I am, I said everything was fine. I feel guilty about it now, of course."

"Of course," I said, rather coolly. I was starting to have an ugly suspicion about where our talk was leading. "So, what do you think we should do?"

"Well, I'd be perfectly happy to coach him on diction, but German's not my strong point. He needs that man he works with in New York."

"Rigby, you mean?"

"Yes, Richie's extremely taken with him. He should change his plans and fly back to New York as soon as possible and do some serious work. Otherwise, those auditions are doomed."

"Would you be willing to tell him that? He takes your opinion very seriously."

"He respects yours even more."

"Lucky me," I said, "I can hardly wait."

I found Richie on a ladder, removing the basketball hoop from over the garage door. As I marched up to him, he sensed that something was amiss. He left the hoop dangling sideways off its mount and clambered down to face me. "What happened, sweets? Is there some new screw-up at school?"

"No, I just got off the phone with Doc Williams."

"What a coincidence. I was over at his place a few hours ago, running through all my arias. He thinks I'll be giant in Germany."

I steeled myself and began. "Richie, to be perfectly honest, Doc just now told me he had serious reservations about one of the arias you sang, that German one."

"You mean *Winterstuerme*?"

"Yes, he thinks it needs more work."

"That's funny. He told me he thought it was fine."

"I suppose he didn't want to discourage you. And, naturally, neither do I."

"Good," Richie said. "Positive reinforcement. That's the name of the game."

"Which is why Doc thought it would be a good idea to go back to New York and do some more coaching with Rigby."

His whole body jolted, as if a bee had stung him. "I did a shit load already. Rigby and I spent two damn weeks on that aria and it's just three minutes long."

"Even so, Doc says your German's not right. He thinks it needs more attention."

"That's not what he said this morning."

"He's having second thoughts. He thinks you should work more with Rigby."

"But I just saw him!"

"So, see him again. I'm sure he'd be delighted."

"Of course, at thirty bucks an hour."

"Who cares what it costs. Rigby can really help. Don't you want to be heard at your best?"

"Kit, Kit, please. Positive reinforcement. Happy thoughts, encouragement. I don't need you tearing me down."

"I'm not. I'm just being realistic."

"Look, I'm a big boy. I know what I'm doing. My German's perfectly okay. Everything's gonna be fine... Now, if you don't mind, I'll finish taking down that hoop."

With that, he climbed up the ladder, leaving me right back where I started from.

A few days later I returned from a heartening survey of the library work site. Things were moving ahead. Some shelving had been installed, some lighting fixtures mounted. Even a few windows were up and functional. Best of all, the school board had given me the go-ahead to order books. Naturally, Jane Austen's masterworks were at the top of my list. I was excited by the thought of recruiting new converts.

Richie greeted me at the door with a peck on the cheek and an impish grin.

"Hey, hon, sorry, but I gotta head back to New York for some extra coaching." I smiled and said nothing. "Okay, okay, so it took a while. Sue me." I continued to hold my tongue, though lord knows I was tempted to tell my dear husband a thing or two. "I guess yours truly can be pretty difficult, huh?"

"You, Richie? Never."

"You know, Rigby had begged me to stay longer in New York to get *Winterstuerme* one hundred percent correct. Especially the pronunciation. But I missed the family too much..." He stared at the ground morosely for a moment. "Sometimes it's like I'm at war with myself. I worry that when I'm over in Europe, I'll get so homesick for you guys I'll totally screw things up."

"How could that happen? You're a big boy now. You told me so yourself."

"I did, didn't I?"

"Darling, I completely believe in you. So does Doc, Rigby, the kids. Why, even the great Erich Hirschmann believes in Richie Verdun."

"He'd better. He's charging a fortune to set up these auditions."

CHAPTER FIVE

Richie

The last day's the worst. By now I've sung in twelve opera houses, it should have been more, but I got sick midway through and had to cancel a few. I started in Austria, then went over to France and I'm finishing up in Germany, which has more year-round opera houses than any place on earth. At ten in the morning I board this very nice, very sleek train in Bremen where I auditioned the afternoon before, damn well, if I say so myself, and they said so too, though they only offered me a few stray performances the season after next.

Anyway, I'm supposed to change trains in Hannover and arrive in Frankfurt at 2:30, which gives me plenty of time to scoot over to my hotel, get freshened up and be at the theater on time. Only when we reach Hannover, the connecting train's not there. All my others were on time. (It's Germany, after all, the trains are always punctual, except, of course, when they're not, like now, when I need it most.) I sit in the waiting room, studying my scores, having a little snack – okay, not so little, I love the wursts they got here, especially those thin long *Wiener wuerstchens*, which are like our hot dogs back home but with lots more flavor and a wonderful pop when you bite into them. I'm on my third batch, when the train finally appears, an hour and three quarters late. I realize it's gonna be tight, meaning no time to freshen up, just zip to the theater and sing. I also realize I'll have to warm up now, since I won't have time later on. I go into the bathroom and do a few scales and when I come out, people are looking unhappy, like *you're disturbing my peace and quiet.* I give them my sunniest smile and sit back down and try to take in the scenery, then recheck the time, it's just as tight as ever. I zip back to the john to put on my jacket and tie, then back to my seat for another look at my music (I sing the same three arias, I know the stuff cold, but it never hurts to check), then back to the john for another warmup, then more weird looks as I head back to my seat, then more calculations, I'm really cutting it close, then more vocal warmups, more angry stares, etcetera and so forth, until at long, long last I'm at Frankfurt *Hauptbahnhof.*

As we pull in, I discover to my horror it's 4:32, I'm already two minutes late. Unlike many of my colleagues, I don't get the heebie-jeebies before performance, maybe a slight tingle in the tummy or an edgy impatience to go out there, but sick-to-the-stomach nerves? I never get them, it's not the Verdun way. But this time, my heart's pumping like crazy as I jog through the station to the taxi stand out front, my bag and briefcase flapping against my thighs. A cab's right there waiting, thank god. I tell him to take me to the opera.

"*Die Oper?*" he asks.

"*Jawohl.*"

"*Die Alte Oper?*"

"*Ja, ja,*" I go, "*die Oper.*"

"*Die Alte Oper?*"

He's a broken record, he keeps repeating the question. "*Ja, ja, die Oper, die Oper. Schnell, schnell!*" We finally start out and a clock whizzes by, 4:36. I'm six minutes late, as we sweep past new office buildings and well-kept little parks and suddenly arrive at a magnificent old building, tall and broad, with layers and layers of windows and arches and a strip of painted decorations just under the high peaked roof, with a winged horse on top. It's big, it's important, what else can it be but the opera?

Once we arrive, I toss some D marks at the driver and head straight for the *Kuenstler Eingang*, the artist entrance. Pat me on the back, that's a little German I picked up. I'm huffing and puffing as I leap up the stairs, push open the heavy wooden doors and come face to face with a beefy guy reading a newspaper at a large empty desk.

"Excuse me," I go, "the audition?"

"*Verzeihung*?"

Uh, oh. One of those rare Germans who don't speak English. "The audition where they're singing for the opera?"

He obviously doesn't get it. "*Moment*," he says, picks up a phone and dials. The clock over his desk now reads 4:40, my heart trips over itself. I gotta get out there and sing.

An elegant man in a gray suit with a creamy white handkerchief folded into his chest pocket comes out to greet me. "I'm Boris Radkowitz, the house manager. May I help you?"

"Yes, I'm here for the opera auditions."

He gives a weary smile. "Oh dear, you've come to the wrong place."

"Isn't this the opera?"

"Yes, the *Alte Oper*, the old opera. We just do concerts now. We make a special point of calling it the old opera so people will know."

"I didn't." By this point, my heart's down around my ankles.

"That's most unfortunate. The opera's back by the train station. Just ask the driver for *Frankfurt Oper*."

"I already did."

"He must have misunderstood. They very often do. We're quite used to it." He smiles a gentle smile, as if this situation is somehow amusing. "There are cabs outside. Just say *Frankfurt Oper*. I'm sure you'll have no problem."

I rush out to the taxi stand, which, though full of cabs a moment ago, is now completely empty. I run back inside but the manager is gone, there's only the guard, the guy who speaks no English. "Taxi!" I shout. "I need a taxi *schnell, bitte, schnell!*" By some miracle he seems to understand, nods, dials a number, barks something or other into the phone and points to the cab stand outside. I run back out there, but not before I notice it's 4:43. Fortunately, a cab drives up immediately. I throw my bag and briefcase and battered self in, say "*Frankfurt Oper*" and we're off.

But only for a block or two. We're still near the *old* opera, the *wrong* opera, when we get stuck in this immense traffic jam, which makes perfect sense, it's a quarter to five, the end of the business day. "*Schnell, schnell!*" I shout, as if it might help. The driver holds up his hands helplessly, which, of course, is all he can do.

Ten minutes later, we finally arrive at a big modern concrete building, ugly as they come, which I guess is where they do opera now. I run inside, only to discover I'm at the main entrance, when I need the stage door. I rush to the box office window and shout "*Kuenstler Eingang*?" at the startled lady working there. She points outside and to the left and I follow in that general direction and discover it's a very long building with no side door, so after a minute or so of heading that way, I ask a passerby where the backstage entrance is and he sends me back the other way, past the box office, past the main entrance, to the other side of the building, where I finally find what I'm hunting for.

I open the door, flop down my bag and go, "The audition?"

The guy at the desk shakes his head. "All finish." He looks at me like I just broke the law.

"Look, I came all the way from America. Is there someone I can speak to?"

"Sorry. All go home."

"But it's not even five o'clock."

"Opera tonight. Everyone needs to eat." He shovels make-believe food into his mouth to make sure I understand. I understand all right, boy, do I ever. I'm standing by his desk, wondering what to do next, when the guy says, "Mister, Mister, there is Frau Kasel, assistant of the *Herr Intendant.*"

I look up and see a middle-aged woman heading for the door. I rush over to cut her off. "Excuse me, excuse me, miss, do you work for Herr Klauzer?" She stops and nods yes and looks at me in bewilderment. "Ma'am, sorry, I'm Richard Verdun, the tenor. I was scheduled to sing for Herr Klauzer today."

"Yes, we wondered what happened to you."

"My train was very late."

"I'm sorry, but I'm afraid the audition's over."

"But I came all the way from New York."

This gets her attention. "You come from Herr Hirschmann, do you not? We waited twenty minutes for you, then Herr Klauzer had to leave for the airport."

"Is there anyone else I could sing for?"

"No, Herr Klauzer does all the casting himself."

"Can I come back tomorrow?"

"He'll still be at the conference in Lausanne. Then he goes to his family in Sweden."

"But how can I sing for him?

"Well, I can call him Monday and see what he wants to do. I'm sure it can't be before the start of next month."

"But I'm leaving for New York tomorrow."

"Oh, what a shame." She actually seems to mean it. "Maybe you can change your ticket."

"I'm afraid that's not an option." I mean, how the hell can I afford at least ten extra days of food and lodging here, not to mention the penalty for changing my ticket? Even if I do all that, how can I be sure he'll actually hear me? "Isn't there some way I could call him?"

"Unfortunately not. As I say, I can reach him Monday to arrange another audition."

"I'll be back in the States by then." I'm so disappointed and heartsick and sorry for my pathetic self that her next words take me totally by surprise. "Listen, this is a most unfortunate situation. I'd like to make it up to you. Why not come to the opera tonight? We do *Traviata* with a very good cast. I'm sure you'll enjoy it. As our guest, of course. Do say yes."

"Gee, that's awfully nice." And it is, too. It's basically the first good thing that's happened to me since I took the doomed train to Frankfurt.

"The curtain is nineteen hundred thirty. It will be in my name, Frau Kasel. This makes it for the box office simpler."

"Thanks very much. You're awfully kind." I pick up my bag and start to leave.

"You know how to find your hotel?"

"Actually, now you mention it, I don't."

"You're staying where?"

"Hotel Frankfurt Rex."

"It's a bit far. You've got that big bag. Let me call a taxi."

"Nah, thanks, I can manage. Just head me in the right direction." The truth is I've been burning up money here, singing auditions that have led nowhere, well, almost nowhere. I did get two guest performance offers for 1985, that's two years away, but no permanent contracts, no actual living wage. Frankfurt was pretty much my last hope.

"Are you sure you want to walk?" goes Frau Kasel. "It's such a warm day."

"I'm rough, I'm tough. I can handle it."

She gives me the directions, which are pretty straightforward, then looks again at my bag. "Are you really sure? It's at least fifteen minutes by foot. *Komm*, I get you a taxi."

"No, no, thanks, I need the exercise." I wave to her cheerily and set out in the blazing sun. After a few blocks I'm a wreck. It's unusually warm for May, I'm sweating like a pig, my bag weighs a ton and my briefcase isn't much lighter. I start longing for a cab, but they're all taken, it's rush hour. I gotta keep struggling on, watching banker types breeze past me, eager for their first beer after work, while I lug and tug my bulging bag and banged-up briefcase and weary ass and miserable life over to the hotel, one giant block at a time.

My room turns out to be a jail cell – what did I expect for fifty bucks? – boring and blank with tall thin windows looking out on a beat-up garage and a long line of garbage cans. It's not dirty, of course (they don't do dirty in Germany), it's clean and correct, but also drab and depressing, which fits right in with my mood. I can't call Kit, she won't be home yet, and, anyway, all I can tell her is I'm coming back empty-handed. Truth is, I've barely spoken to her. First off, the six-hour time difference drives me completely batty. Second, most of the theaters gave me the brush off – *you're great, we love you, get lost* – so there's nothing much to report. I figure all I can do now is bind up my wounds and give Kit the bad news when she picks me up at the airport tomorrow.

In the meantime, I rip off my sweaty clothes, rush into the shower and blast the hot water. In thirty seconds it turns ice cold. When I splash out of the tub to call the desk and complain, the guy says there's nothing wrong with the water, and when I say there is, he calls me a liar, and when I protest, he hangs up. In short, it's a high-class place, service with a snarl.

By seven P.M., the opera house, the real one, the modern one, the ugly one, is swarming with people, which shows how powerful singers are, we can draw incredible crowds. As I take in all this love for opera, belief in opera, I feel this hunger to be part of it, this raw desire to go out on stage somewhere, anywhere, and sing my fool head off. Then I remember my shit day, the late arrival, the canceled audition, and I don't want to have anything to do with an opera house, not now and maybe not ever again.

Forget *Traviata.* I spin on my heels, push through the crowd, cross the plaza and follow some random street, hunting for a place where I can drown myself in beer.

One of the weird things about Frankfurt is how all the streets look alike, the opposite from New York, where each one's so distinctive it seems to be shouting *look at me!* Here, none of them really stand out, they hide in the shadows and sulk. The street I stumble down is typical of the town, anonymous and forgettable. I pass by low apartment houses, a small hotel, a little grocery store, a men's shop, until I come to a place called Tante Olga. Delicious smells are wafting out through the door, but there's no menu in front, no reviews. I guess anyone who is anyone knows already that the place is really good.

I open the door and enter a giant party. The noise level's high, the restaurant's packed out with a crowd that's well fed, well paid and well past fifty. I start wondering if all this hilarity is really right for me, maybe I should find someplace quiet, but then I notice rows and rows of photographs of what's gotta be opera singers all over the walls. It's like being back at Maestro's, except the singers here aren't old-timers. I even recognize a few.

As I'm studying them, a slim young guy sneaks up behind me, holding a stack of menus. He's wearing a big-sleeved white linen shirt and black leather pants. (What is it with German guys and leather? Don't they know it looks like melted plastic?) He babbles away until I tell him I only speak English and segues with a perfect, "I asked if you have a reservation." When I say no, he looks startled. "You really should have called, sir. All I've got is a table by the kitchen."

"That's all right, as long I can get me some beer."

"This is Germany. We always have beer." He leads me past the pictures and the bustling crowded tables to the far end of the room, a gloomy corner by the kitchen doors, which windmill open and shut whenever the waiters whiz past. He can see I'm not impressed. "I did mention it's near the kitchen."

"I'll take it. Just get me a giant beer."

A few minutes later a waiter appears with the biggest beer I've ever seen. I mean, it's epic, over a foot high, broad as my fist and totally welcome. I guzzle it down as fast as I can. It sloshes around inside me and life starts losing its hard edges.

As I creep into a nice beery haze, I notice a striking couple about ten tables away. I can't see the woman's face, her back is to me, but the little guy's straight in my line of vision and he's the arty type, one of those sensitive fellows who get all gooey listening to Mozart. He's got pale blond hair curling around his shoulders, delicate whitish skin, and a physique that could use some manly exercise. The lady's pretty much his opposite. She's impressively tall, considerably taller than him. Even though her back's to me, I can tell she's well put together, trim and fit. Her reddish hair is flecked with gray, pulled tight in a smart little bun. She's wearing a glamorous black wool suit with collar and sleeves trimmed in red velvet, restrained but chic, like she's from Paris or something.

When they get up, rather than heading for the exit, they start coming my way. I guess there's some picture they want to examine. But, as they advance, I realize with a megawatt jolt that the lady's not from Paris, she's from Graystone, my former teacher, Elizabeth Fanning. The last thing I need is her craziness. I stuff my face inside my jacket like I'm hunting for my wallet and leave it there till I'm certain she's left. When I peek back out, there she is, right beside my table, staring straight at me.

"Richard Verdun, my heavens, small world. What are you doing here?"

"Drinking a beer."

"Yes, so I notice. I was wondering what brings you to Frankfurt."

"I could ask you the same question."

She crinkles up her eyes at me. "Tit for tat, is that what this is? Come now, that little contretemps of ours happened ages ago. As a matter of fact, I'm happy to see you. It's like a family reunion."

"We're not family, Elizabeth."

"Well, we've certainly been through a lot together. More than most, as you very well know." She turns to her companion and says, "This fellow studied with me back in the dark days when I still was living in Michigan. What a struggle it was. He fought me at every turn, but when he finally buckled down, there was no stopping him. He's a full-fledged professional now. He just made his debut in Canada."

"My," her companion goes, "that's really impressive."

"Of course, it was only in Calgary and Pinkerton's not the best role, either for him or tenors generally. Still, a start is a start. Congratulations."

"Thanks," I say, as coolly as possible, while wondering how she found out about Calgary.

"So, Richard, why are you here?"

"The usual reasons."

"There's nothing usual about Frankfurt unless you're a banker. Don't be coy now. Are you performing, auditioning, studying?" She gives me a crooked grin. "Are you working for the CIA?"

"As a matter of fact, I am," I go. "Full time."

We dance our little dance, while the young guy looks on, puzzled. I can't say I blame him. "Oh, sorry, I'm being rude. This is my student, my protégé, actually, Franklin Mulholland. Meet Richard Verdun."

Franklin's very much the fashion type. Everything's high end, the pale gray silk shirt, the blue linen sport jacket, the tight-fitting jeans, the jaunty striped cotton shawl. He offers a floppy hand. "Happy to meet you, sir." He doesn't look happy. Come to think of it, neither do I.

"Young Franklin's a lovely singer, very artistic, a light lyric baritone with an elegant sense of line. You could learn from him."

"Yeah, I bet."

"I'm being serious, Richard."

"So am I."

She looks at me expectantly, like I'm supposed to offer her a seat, but I stay cool and distant and pray she'll take the hint and leave. No such luck. She takes the chair across from me, folds her coat over the back and sits down. "Franklin, stop staring at your watch. The curtain's not till eight. We're going to a concert," she explains, "at the old opera. Funny, isn't it, how they give concerts at the opera?"

"Tell me about it."

"Franklin, you really should sit. We'll be here quite a while." *Not if I can help it*, I think. "Darling, do be a good boy and find yourself a chair."

Franklin gives a sigh and slouches off. As he leaves, she winks at me like a fellow conspirator and mutters, "Fetch, Rover, fetch."

"You've got him well trained."

"I certainly hope so."

"Isn't he a bit young?"

She roars with laughter. "Franklin? He's a darling, but not in that way, heavens, no. He's been knocking around his parents' home for years, homes, actually, one in Bedford, the other on Park Avenue, a third in Palm Beach, you get the idea. He's intelligent, he's musical, he just doesn't have a voice. His parents insisted I take him on, I couldn't say no, they're extremely well connected. Anyway, last month they got the brilliant notion I should set up an audition tour for him, a testing of the European waters, as it were, even though it's wildly premature. I arranged it as best I could. I'm no agent, but I do have my connections. I even got him the chance to sing for Herr Klauzer."

"The guy at the opera? How's that possible?"

"Money talks, Richard. Everyone knows that. After he sang, the *Herr Intendant* was very charming, very correct."

"Meaning?"

She rolls her eyes. "The man is a pro. He knows real singing. Need I say more?"

At this point the maître d' appears, lugging an extra chair, followed by Franklin, spouting German. Elizabeth leans over. "Isn't he just wonderful?" she says. "People here think he's a native."

The maître d' sets down the chair and Franklin slips him a bill, a pretty large one, I suspect, and joins us. "Richard was just telling me what he's doing here."

"Actually, there's not much to tell. I've been traveling around auditioning. This is the final stop."

"How is it going? Any offers yet? Any juicy contracts?"

"I've got a few leads."

"Really? Where?"

"Oh, here and there."

She turns to Franklin. "Richard always has been rather secretive. It's one of his greatest charms. But, enough posturing, Richard – tell me, what did Herr Klauzer say?"

Either the beer's too much for me or I'm more upset than I thought, because somehow or other, without even being aware I'm doing it, I blurt out to my former teacher, the last person on earth I actually want to share this with, how I went to the wrong theater and missed my audition, a perfect example of saying the wrong thing at the wrong time to the wrong person.

"What a shame," she goes. "I'm so very sorry to hear it." She even sounds like she means it. "Did you land any contracts elsewhere?"

"Like I said, I've got some leads."

She sees right through me. "Well, I'm sure things will develop. You've got a fine voice and that's what counts. You'll be heading back to New York, I suppose."

"Yeah, I'm on the plane tomorrow."

"We'll be back next week. Why don't you give me a call? Maybe I could help."

"Help what?"

"Not to blow my own horn, but I've been thriving since my divorce. Ed has been most generous. I now have a studio in New York which is bursting at the seams – forty-three students, many from out of town. I've got some very exciting, very promising artists like young Franklin here, but there's always room for you. I mean it, Richard, forget all that brouhaha from before. I'll find you proper roles and sharpen your languages. Franklin here could fix your German."

That does it. I stand and shoot out my hand. "Thanks for dropping by, Elizabeth."

It's like I didn't do anything – she just carries on. "I know you've had setbacks. I know you've missed your goals and frankly, I'm worried. Whose idea was that Pinkerton anyway? It's totally wrong for you. I mean, really, to go out on stage and sing it for your debut... And then, to get such a terrible review."

"What review?"

"Haven't you seen *Opera World*?" Clearly, I haven't. "Well, I'm sorry to be the bearer of bad tidings, but they sent that awful Stefan Kazinsky out to Calgary and he's just so ruthless, you know. He has no sensitivity, no accountability. Erich Hirschmann's your manager, isn't he? He should have known better. Pinkerton's wrong for you, absolute folly. No wonder Kazinsky hacked you to bits."

That's it, I've had enough. I slam my fists on the table. "Shut up, Elizabeth!" To my amazement, she does. The tables around us grow quiet too. Young Franklin looks troubled. "What's your problem, blondie? Something bothering you?"

"I think you misunderstood," he says, nervously. "Miss Fanning's on your side. She only wants to help."

"Bullshit!" I get up and grab his chair and seesaw it back and forth like I'm trying to rock some sense into him, even though I'm the one who needs it, but at that moment I don't see it, I don't feel it, I just want that asshole gone.

He finally slides off his chair and scurries behind Elizabeth. "Richard, really, you're acting like a child. Don't you understand how..."

"Leave me alone!" It's my best effort yet, a major league bellow that gets everyone's attention.

The maître d' appears. "Is everything all right, sir?"

"No, the lady's bothering me."

"That's utterly ridiculous. We're old friends having a reunion."

"No, we're not."

"Of course we are."

We go on and on until the maître d' says, "Very honestly, I cannot understand what exactly is the problem, but I do think it would be very good for everyone if madame and monsieur continued their discussion outside."

"You heard him, Elizabeth. Time to go."

She gives me a deadly stare. "You think you're clever, Richard, you think you're smart, but you're totally, impossibly lost." She rises from her chair in icy splendor like the diva she is. "Come, Franklin, mustn't be late for the concert." She hands her coat to her protégé and semaphores out her arms so he can help her into it, but he's not up to the challenge, he's shaky after all the fireworks. She gets so annoyed with his fumbling that she grabs the coat from him and puts it on herself, then strides out in cold fury with Franklin following meekly behind.

I turn back to the maître d'. "As you can see, she's no friend of mine."

"I'm sorry to hear it, sir. May I get you something else?"

"Yes, another large beer and a bulletproof vest." This goes over his head, of course. Europeans never seem to get my jokes. "Forget the vest, just bring me more beer. Thank you."

He goes off to place the order. Most of the people nearby seem to have lost interest in me. They're babbling away like before, while I slip back into my black lagoon. I dread what it's gonna feel like when I return to Graystone.

The waiter appears with my beer. "What do you like now to eat?"

"Nothing, thanks."

He shoots me a worried look. "This goes pretty fast to the head."

"I sure as hell hope so."

After a few minutes of serious imbibing, I feel a sudden sharp grip on my shoulder, an icy clamp that startles me out of my boozy state. I look up and see this amazing creature, like some kind of witch goddess, wearing a long emerald green caftan that's cut dangerously low, revealing the start of her sagging breasts. A clunky chunky necklace studded with giant gems hangs around her neck and, as if that weren't enough, she's got rings on her fingers too, equally huge. Even her makeup's extreme. There's a smudge of rouge slanting across her cheeks, her eyebrows are pencil thin and arched way high and her lipstick's so bright you can see it from twenty paces.

"*Guten abend, mein Herr,* I am Frau Olga. This is my restaurant. You disturb my waiters and also my customers. They do not like it when people make scenes."

"Sorry, but the lady started it. I just wanted her to leave me alone." One penciled eyebrow goes up, so I add, "She used to be my teacher."

"Your teacher? You are a little old to be a student."

She drifts over to the chair facing me. As she passes, I get a strong, almost overwhelming blast of lilac perfume. She hunches over the back of the chair watching me quietly. Her eyes are sapphire blue, they've obviously seen a lot and I bet they haven't missed much either. "So, tell me, what do you study?"

"Actually, I'm done studying, I'm an opera singer."

"An opera singer?" She's amazed. She looks at me with a new, almost eerie fascination. "Singers," she goes, "they are my favorite. I go very often in the opera and..." Her eyes narrow a bit. "You are tenor, no? *Hoch dramatisch.*"

"We've been talking for maybe two minutes. How could you possibly tell?"

"The body, the look. Also the speaking voice, so high and clear, *gute Resonanz.* And plenty of support down here, this also helps." She leans forward and taps my belly lightly with her rings, which I find pretty weird – I mean, we barely even met. "I very much admire singers. That is why I put them on my wall."

"There sure are a lot of them."

She looks at me in a teasing sort of way. "There always is room for one more."

"Well, save me a place, I'm really, really good." It just whizzes out of me, I'm almost as startled as she is.

"Maybe you actually are."

"Oh, I am. Trust me."

"But you never even tell me your name."

"Is it important?"

"Of course, Wagner writes a whole opera about it." These days I sing Lohengrin, but at the time I had absolutely no idea what she was talking about. "It is a perfect part for you, *hoch dramatisch,* though maybe even better if you lose a bit the weight." Why is it always open season on my waistline? I'm not fat, just ripe and juicy. "So, what is your name, tenor?"

"The name's Richie Verdun. I'm American, in case you couldn't tell."

"I thought you were maybe Chinese." She smiles and I'm thinking, *wait, did she actually make a joke*? "It must be hard to have such a terrible name."

"What's terrible about Richie?"

"No, Verdun, the battle. So many die for nothing. I was a little girl then, but I still remember the stories, the suffering." I must be giving her blank stares, because she adds, "You have the name and do not know?"

"Frankly, I never met anyone who cared."

"How can you not? It is horrible what happened there, terrible."

This shuts us up for a bit, then she says, "So, you are a tenor, Herr Verdun. Everyone needs a tenor. Tell me, where do you sing? When is your next performance?"

What to say? How to tell her? I slump deeper into my chair and avoid her gaze.

She grabs both my shoulders. Her eyes blaze at me. "I am no idiot, you know. What is the problem?"

Suddenly, the words start flooding out, the beer, I guess, or the fact I know I'll never see the lady again. "To be absolutely honest, I don't have any engagements. Oh, I got some possible little gigs here or there, but nothing solid, nothing significant. And I've got three kids back home, two are still in school. And that costs major money."

"*Ach,* you Americans, money, money, money. You are an artist. You must not give up."

"Who said I will?"

"I hear it in your voice."

"Look, I just had a shitty day. I came here to sing for Herr Klauzer. My train was late and I missed my audition. Now he's gone for ten days and I gotta fly home tomorrow."

"So stay."

"It's way too expensive."

"Money again, always money. You really have no engagements? You are a tenor. How can this be?"

"I started late. I only made my professional debut last February at age forty-three."

"*Wunderbar, erstaunlich.*" She looks at me differently now, like I'm no freak, I'm a once-in-a-lifetime miracle.

"Sorry, but things aren't so *wunderbar*. My career's going nowhere and I'm no longer a kid."

"*Ach*, you are very healthy, very solid. You sing for many years."

"But I gotta get some work, I gotta really sing. I came over for auditions and did really well, but I only was offered guest engagements. And they're just offers, not signed contracts."

"*Mein Gott*, you are so *pessimistisch*. I'm sure you get them."

"Even if I do, a few performances here and there isn't a real career. Frankfurt was my last hope."

Once I say it, I'm back in my black lagoon, glooming and dooming, silently, of course, but Frau Olga's no dope – she sees right through me. "Now listen, stop this nonsense and pull yourself together. I know Herr Klauzer. All the time he comes to my restaurant. He is an important figure, difficult and arrogant, even a bit of a genius. He knows good voices and you tell me you really have one."

I squeak it out as best I can, "Yeah, I do."

"Then stay and sing for the man."

"I can't afford it."

"Forget the money. You say you want to sing. Then sing. Sing your heart out."

"I'm trying."

"Try harder." She's like a football coach, prepare, execute, deliver. Yeah, coach, we know, but when? How? With what?

"Look, I know you mean well, but doing it, making it all come together, especially in Operaland, is hard. I've given it my all."

"Then give it, please, some more."

I don't really have a comeback for that. I just reach for my wallet and say, with an apologetic little blip of a smile, "Gee, Frau Olga, it's getting pretty late. I better pay up and go home."

"Sorry, I am not finished with you."

"What's that supposed to mean?"

"Frau Olga has her plans. *Komm...*"

Without any warning, without even bothering to hear whether I have the slightest interest, she hauls me to my feet and drags me towards the big flight of stairs at the far side of the room. It takes us forever to get there, she's very much in demand. Everyone seems to know her or want to know her. They've all got complaints or compliments or gossip to share and she indulges them, plays them for all she's worth.

We finally arrive at this small table at the base of the stairs where a shriveled-up old guy in a battered three-piece suit, wearing spectacles like an old-time university professor, is huddled over his wurst and sauerkraut, packing it in as best he can. (His hand's kinda shaky and his aim's not too good.) She taps him on the shoulder, he looks up, wipes off his chin with his napkin, and beams at Olga like she's his long-lost love, though, frankly, who'd want him? He's gnarly and all used up. Of course, Olga is too, so maybe they're a perfect match. Anyway, the two lovebirds, or ex-lovebirds, launch into a lively all-German conversation, which I can't understand. The old guy looks my way from time to time. He doesn't seem impressed.

Once we're finally heading up the stairs, I ask who he was. "Otto Greissle, a *souffleur* at the opera. He gives the singers their lines. You probably meet him later."

We finally reach the tiny balcony that overlooks the main floor of the restaurant. She lets go of my hand, and about time too, my skin's raw where her giant rings cut into it, and opens a curtained glass door. "*Meine Schatzkammer.* I spend fifteen years making it."

I'll bet she did.

It glitters and gleams like a walk-in jewel box. There's a long sleek sofa, some broad leather armchairs, and a few brass floor lamps that shoot triangles of light up onto the ceiling. Dozens of bright abstract pictures shine on the walls.

"In the twenties, when I start out, every time I have extra money from acting or modeling I go out and buy this, because it is fresh, it is our art. I soon have some Kokoschka prints, even a little Klee, a Breuer chair, two Gropius lamps. Then the dark times come, this art is not allowed. I store it all away and pretend it does not exist, but when the catastrophe ends and we have no longer war, I go out to the *Flohmaerkte* and discover people are selling these things for very little, they are desperate for cash, and I suddenly have some. Once I open this restaurant I finally have space for my collection. Do you like it?"

To be honest, I don't much care for the stuff. It's too cold and modern, but I don't want to offend her, so I go, "Wow, what can I say? It's amazing."

Frankly, I find it harder to keep my eyes off her jewelry, it's gotta be worth a fortune.

"Can I ask you something?" I say at last. "Are those jewels of yours real?"

She giggles like a schoolgirl. "*Ach,* Herr Verdun! *Theaterschmuck, alles falsch.* I wear this in *Graefin Fritzi,* a boulevard comedy I play in 1955, a silly piece that runs very long and finds me finally a husband."

"What happened to him?"

"We go in different ways. He buys me this restaurant to get himself free."

"That's a pretty big price."

We're interrupted by some knocking at the door. Olga goes to get it and reappears a moment later with her doddering ex-boyfriend. He's short to begin with, but to make matters worse, he's got some sort of back problem so he walks at an angle, like he's folded up over himself. His face is folded too, with deep creases running from the sides of his thick hooked nose to the edge of his jaw. He looks like a human basset hound.

"Otto Greissle, meet Richard Verdun."

"*Ach, der Herr Heldentenor. Eine grosse Ehre.*" He gives me a curt little nod, making it clear he's in no rush to join my fan club.

Taking the hint, I stick out my hand and say, "Well, great to meet you both. Thanks so much, Frau Olga. This place is really spectacular."

She rushes over to block the door. "You think you can just say goodbye and never come back? *Nein, unmoeglich.* You sing now for your supper."

"You mean sing, as in actually *sing*?"

"Of course, I very much want to hear you, also Herr Greissle."

"So, that's what this is all about. Very sneaky."

"But of course. You make me curious. Also him." Otto nods without much enthusiasm.

"Well, it's really flattering, but I'm hardly in shape. I just had a lot of beer."

"It gets you relaxed," says Olga.

"Too relaxed."

I reach for the door again and Madame grabs me in an iron grip. "I am serious. You sing please for me just one aria."

"I didn't bring my music."

"That is no problem." She points at Otto's broad wrinkly forehead. "He is the walking opera house. Whatever you sing he knows."

"Does he know *Winterstuerme*?" The moment I ask, Otto hobbles over to the piano and starts playing. He may miss a few notes here and there, but he makes it sound just as passionate and powerful as my best buddy Rigby, and Otto's playing it by heart.

He stops after a minute or so and says, "You miss long ago your cue."

"Sorry, I was busy listening."

"This man is the heart of the opera," goes Olga. "Wieland Wagner, the grandson, invites him to coach in Bayreuth."

"Only one season," says Otto. "Then they take the other man back."

"But still you get there."

"Not for very long."

"*Ach,* you always do this, talk against yourself."

"Well, it sounds great to me," I interject. "Herr Greissle's a wizard with Wagner."

"*Danke,*" Otto says and gives a little smile.

"No more *Komplimente.* I want to hear you sing."

"Okay, okay, but you gotta understand I haven't vocalized."

"Neither have I," says Otto, smiling. I'm actually starting to like him.

While I position myself next to the piano, Frau Olga drifts over to the sofa and sits down, her caftan fanning out around her. She picks up a throw and wraps herself in it. It's covered with bright squares of different colored fabrics.

"Wow," I go, "that's some shawl you got."

"Anni Albers. I buy last year in auction."

Before I can say anything, Otto begins the piece again. I start singing and discover to my amazement that, despite all the craziness, I'm in excellent voice. Maybe it's the beer, maybe it's the company, all I know is I'm singing great.

Frau Olga's sitting barely ten feet away and totally, incredibly involved. She's mouthing the words and moving with the music and living each line like she's doing Siegmund, not me. You'd think it would be distracting, but in fact it's actually not. It's like in the theater when once in a very rare while you get this special audience, this astonishing collection of strangers that's totally with you from the start and the whole show ignites. After all, an evening of opera isn't just us singers up there on stage, it's the public too, they're part of the show and their input can make the difference between an okay performance and a night you'll never forget. That's what I feel right now with Frau Olga. By some odd magic her love and knowledge of the aria pulls me closer to it than I ever was before. I always was put off by the brother-sister incest, which I find flat-out gross, and then there's the text itself in this old-fashioned German that's so ornate and highfalutin it takes a PhD to decipher it. When I sing it for her now, none of that matters. All I feel is the passion of the scene, its total human honesty.

I stop and there's deep silence, the clatter and chatter downstairs has vanished. It's just us three, caught up in the glow of Wagner's genius. In most of my auditions I sang the aria pretty well, but, to be honest, I was often self-conscious. I knew everyone was sizing me up. That's what auditions are for, of course, to judge you, to see what you can do. This time, though, when I sing for Frau Olga, well, this is gonna sound nuts, but I suddenly feel this genuine gratitude, this affection, all right, I'll say it, because it's what I really felt, this *love* as I look at Frau Olga, sitting like a queen with that shawl in bright blocks of color draped round her shoulders. I know for a fact that not once in all my auditions did I ever make more of the music. This was the absolute best, and it was all thanks to her, the amazing Frau Olga.

The room is hushed. Otto sits on the piano bench, beaming at me, like *whaddya know, you really are a Wagnerian tenor.* Frau Olga gets up and glides towards me, her arms outstretched. She clutches me tight to her lilac-soaked bosom and it's the perfect ending to a miserable soul-crushing day, and then, this is the crazy part, this is the amazing part, it's like everything falls apart or comes together, maybe both at the same time, and I start blubbering away like I haven't done in ages. I try to hold back, of course, but I just can't help myself.

I hold Frau Olga close, my eyes burning with tears, and she's shushing me and soothing me. It's like she almost knew I'd react this way, I somehow or other had to. After a good long while she finally goes, "My dear boy, *mein Bub, das war so schoen.* I had no idea, none."

"Sorry..." The tears are still flooding out of me, they simply refuse to stop.

"Nothing to be sorry, my love. It happens to us all."

"Not to me," I say, wiping away the tears.

"*Ach, mein Bub,*" she goes again, "*mein armes Kind.* How can Frau Olga help?"

My crying has stopped. My eyes are finally dry. I'm back to myself again. I go, "Any idea how I can find this Klauzer guy?

CHAPTER SIX

Sami Tomi

I was only twenty-seven when Reinbert Klauzer offered me the post of *zweiter Kapellmeister* at the Frankfurt Opera. Difficult though he could be, he valued my work and kept pushing me forward. I got chance after chance, *Ballo in Maschera, Rosenkavalier, Così Fan Tutte,* even *Meistersinger* and *Wozzeck.* Within a year he had promoted me to *erster Kapellmeister* and then, the year following, in a sudden, almost shocking development, he crowned me GMD, general music director. I was so scandalously young that some uncharitable souls claimed that like Athena I had sprung full blown from Herr Klauzer's ample brow. Totally absurd, of course. I look nothing like him.

I had been promoted thanks to some terrible rows Reinbert had with the much respected, much admired Herr Wendelin, the company's long-standing music director who made no secret of his detestation of the new and challenging productions Reinbert kept putting on stage. *Too modern,* the old man said, *too iconoclastic, an absolute outrage.* I found them sometimes bad, sometimes terrific, but always intriguing, always worthy of debate and discussion, if not total acceptance. And I was in the majority. The press, the younger intelligentsia flocked to Reinbert's shows. The Klauzer era was born and I was a privileged participant, a willing co-conspirator. Then, suddenly, most unexpectedly, Richard Verdun stumbled onto the scene.

It was 1983, a brilliant bright Saturday in May. I'd just driven my beloved new Mercedes 380 SL from Geneva to Lausanne for a lunchtime meeting with Reinbert. Evidently a complication had arisen with *Carmen*, the opening production of our next season. We could have handled it over the phone, I suppose, but the weather was splendid and I was eager to drive my new car, a lapis blue coupe convertible, whenever and wherever I could. It was the only luxury I'd allowed myself up to that point and I loved it to excess.

I'd been studying scores relentlessly all morning. All I wanted was to break out of my hotel room and zoom along the highway through the fresh glowing air, feeling free and fortunate. The trip was barely twenty minutes, the car flew over the road, it seemed rude to brake too often. I lost myself in motion, and music vanished from my mind.

I felt refreshed as I pulled up in front of one of the sprawling marble-clad villas that faced the glistening lake. It was an impressive Swiss monument to solid nineteenth-century wealth and solid aesthetic values, opulent, but not too opulent, a perfect place for opera impresarios to meet and discuss all those administrative details that were no doubt terribly important, but which I found intolerably dull. The day was staggeringly sweet with spring, it made me happy just to breathe. Turning my back on the enticing lake, I crossed the crisp green lawn towards the grandiose main entrance. No one seemed to be about. I checked my watch. Where had everyone gone?

I pushed open the double front doors and entered a large entryway covered in dark oak paneling. "Hello?" I shouted. "Anyone there?" No answer. Not a soul in sight. I advanced down a narrow hallway past a row of yellowed oil canvases. Stringent Swiss ancestors stared down at me disapprovingly. I reached another door. It had a handwritten sign taped onto it: "ECOD, the European Confederation of Opera Directors." I entered a large airy ballroom with herringbone parquet flooring and tall windows on three sides that overlooked the villa's small but extremely well-manicured garden, which alternated marigolds and petunias in rigid obedient rows. Beyond them, the broad expanse of Lac Leman sparkled in the midday sun. The room held rows and rows of gilded wooden ballroom chairs with files and folders scattered about, remnants, no doubt, of the recent meeting. There was no sign of Reinbert or, indeed, of anyone else.

I'd brought along the study score of the Schoenberg, so I sat myself down in the first row with the lake shining before me and plunged back into the nightmare world of *The Survivor from Warsaw*. I was conducting it that evening with the Orchestre de la Suisse Romande, my first time with them and their first time with the piece. It wasn't long, but it was tricky and the orchestra had a rather spotty record with Schoenberg. M. Ansermet, their founder, had detested his music and published a strange diatribe of a book "proving" that Schoenberg's twelve-tone system was illogical and impossible. Maybe it was, but surely not his music, especially not this brief shattering work which follows a doomed prisoner from the Warsaw ghetto to the extermination camp. As the narrator and countless others are gassed to death, the chorus rises en masse to sing the *Shema Yisrael*, the ancient Hebrew prayer in protest and repudiation, a fierce frightening moment. I immediately follow this shock, this savagery, with the anxious *tremolando* opening of Beethoven's *Ninth Symphony*, turning the whole evening into a kind of spiritual pilgrimage, a struggle out of darkness into light, a voyage from cruelty and murder to joy and brotherhood.

I was completely engrossed, lost to the world around me, conjuring up the shape and feeling of the pause between the end of *The Survivor* and the tentative *tremolandi* of the Beethoven, when I gradually became aware of a cool strong hand on my shoulder. It was Reinbert.

"Why study, my friend? The notes are always the same."

"Yes, but I'm not. And neither is the orchestra." He almost always greeted me with a witticism of some sort, real or imagined, as if my commitment to music was somehow in poor taste. He knew very well that if I wasn't constantly lost in music, planning it, rehearsing it, making it, I'd probably go mad. We shook hands warily. We were close colleagues, "co-conspirators," as I put it, but not personal friends. Reinbert was too much of a loner for that, too much a man of power, and I spent most of my time with scores.

"Where is everyone? I thought I'd come to the wrong villa."

"They bundled into cabs and rushed off to Chez Guillaume Tell. It's got the best fondue in town."

"Weren't you tempted?"

"Not if I have the honor of your august presence." He smiled, whether with pleasure or disapproval I couldn't quite tell. "You know, it's a minor matter. There was no need to drive over here."

"What can I say, I love my car."

"I don't blame you. I'm extremely envious."

"You, Reinbert? Never."

Our conversations often had strange pauses and one settled in here. I waited patiently for him to start up again. "I'm really quite sorry to miss your concert, but duty calls."

"Of course, I totally understand." The opera house in Geneva was doing *Samson* and Madame Romanescu was singing Dalilah. It was a pretty open secret that she was one of Reinbert's numerous lovers.

"How were the rehearsals?"

"A bit unsettled. They're still not sure of the Schoenberg."

He gave me a tight little smile. "I warned you the Genevans were conservative."

"I'm not, Reinbert, and neither are you."

"I couldn't do in Geneva what I do in Frankfurt. It's hopelessly old-fashioned."

"The attempt has got to be made."

"You're a brave lad, Sami Tomi, but you're young."

"It worked in Frankfurt," I said stubbornly. "It's going to work in Geneva."

"*Jawohl, Herr Kapellmeister.*"

It was time to change the subject. "You said we had a *Carmen* problem."

"I've just been asked by my colleague, Herr Rudolf in Munich, to release this Garreth Hill chap so he can sing some Florestans for them."

"But he's our opening night Don Jose."

"Herr Rudolf is quite desperate. He's willing to share costs in a new *Traviata* if I grant him this one favor."

"Horse trading again?"

"Call it what you like. I'm rather tempted. I heard Garreth Hill two years ago and wasn't all that impressed."

"But who do we have for Don Jose?"

"We've always got Herr Kuehn."

"Shouldn't we find someone different? It's a new production."

"As I just told you, I'm not a fan of that Garreth Hill."

"But the stage director urged us to hire him."

"*Hart bleiben.*"

"*Hart bleiben?*"

"Stay tough, my young friend, stay hard in bed or anywhere else for that matter. Don't let them walk all over you."

At that moment I noticed a pudgy middle-aged gentleman making his way towards us. He was a curious apparition. He wore a pale blue windbreaker, too short to completely cover the brown checked sport jacket he wore over tan chino pants. He was much too informally dressed to be an opera administrator. Was he perhaps the building superintendent or a member of his staff?

"Hello," he said in a startlingly resonant voice, "do either of you speak English?"

"I do," I said. Reinbert did as well, of course, but he held a wary silence.

"Great, then maybe you could help me. I'm looking for a Mister Klauzer, the head of the Frankfurt Opera."

"Well, it's funny you should ask..." I began.

Reinbert grabbed my arm and said, "Actually, he's not here."

"He's not? Any idea when he'll be back?"

"He isn't coming back."

The man was as astonished as I was. "He left, really? His secretary said he'd be here today and tomorrow."

"She's mistaken," said Reinbert.

"But where did he go?"

"I haven't the faintest idea."

"Do you?" the man asked, turning to me.

It was quite obvious that Reinbert expected me to keep the game going, so I did. "Sorry, I'm afraid I don't know either."

"Do you happen to know where he's staying?"

"No, neither of us does," said Reinbert. "And now, if you'll excuse us, we're in the midst of a meeting."

"Okay, sure, sorry to interrupt." He took a step or two, then returned. "Here's another quick question. Could you describe him to me? I need to see him but I don't even know how he looks, never even once saw a picture. Pretty dumb, huh?"

"Well," said Reinbert, clearly relishing the game, "he's not the most prepossessing person on earth. He's rather short, dumpy almost, and he's wearing a brown tweed suit." Reinbert was in fact wearing dark blue with a maroon silk scarf casually draped around his neck. He was tall and lean and extremely elegant. "But there's really no point in waiting. He's simply not coming back."

"Yeah, well, maybe he'll change his mind. Thanks for your help." He walked across the room and stationed himself by the door.

"That's why I have Frau Kasel," Reinbert said, studiously keeping his back to the man, "to save me from every self-proclaimed conductor or director or composer or designer or singer or dancer or god knows what who stumbles across my path. Tell me when he leaves."

"I rather doubt he will. Wouldn't it be easier to take a few minutes and find out what he actually wants?"

"*Hart bleiben*, remember? Don't let the bastards push you around."

"He didn't seem like one."

"You're such a sentimentalist. You even weep at the end of *Madame Butterfly*."

"And you just laugh."

"My dear fellow, I've got taste. Now, back to *Carmen*," said Reinbert. "If I release this Hill fellow, we'll give the part to Kuehn and..."

"Aren't you concerned about the director? He expects to be working with Garreth Hill. Don't you think he'll..."

"Just let him try." I rose to leave. "Not so fast. We haven't yet talked about your contract." I sat back down. I had two years left with Frankfurt. Reinbert had dropped numerous hints about renewing. The truth was I'd been getting a wide range of offers lately and found it both encouraging and confusing. Opera house or symphony hall? America or Europe? I looked at my watch. I'd spent longer with him than planned. I had to get back to Francesca.

"Sorry, but I really can't get into it right now."

"Well, don't drag it out too long. There are many young conductors in this world."

"I know, Reinbert, I know." I rose to shake hands.

"I mean it. You may be the flavor of the month, but I'm the man who discovered you, the man who promoted you, even when they told me I was mad."

"Maybe they were right."

"All the more reason for you to stay in Frankfurt."

"Reinbert, you're completely incorrigible."

"No, I'm inexorable. That's much worse." We laughed and shook hands. "*Toi, toi, toi.* Fight the good fight for Arnold Schoenberg."

I turned to go. The room was filling up with opera executives. Our stocky visitor had latched on to one of them, who was pointing in Reinbert's direction. Obviously, the game was up. Rather than leaving, I decided to wait and see how the famous eel of the Frankfurt Opera would wiggle his way out of this particular entanglement. As our visitor crossed over to us, I saw he was smiling. I assumed he'd be furious, I certainly would have been, but, no, he seemed to take it all in stride.

"Mister Klauzer, I'm always happy to meet someone who likes a joke as much as I do. It's a giant pleasure. My name is Richard Verdun." Reinbert was completely caught off guard. Displeasure oozed from every pore of his body. Our guest seemed not to notice. "The thing is, my agent really wants you to hear me. Erich Hirschmann in New York, remember? He thinks I'd be right up your alley. He arranged for me to sing yesterday, but I had a little argument with the German railroad and arrived too late. Your very nice secretary told me you were here, so I jumped on a plane, and hello." At that point he actually gave Reinbert a nervous little wave. I was deeply embarrassed for him.

Reinbert's voice was tight and low. "I distinctly told Frau Kasel that I wasn't to be disturbed."

"I totally understand. I know you're involved in all sorts of important stuff here, but the fact of the matter is I delayed my flight back home so I could sing for you this weekend. I'll pay for everything, of course, the room, the pianist, you name it. I just want you to hear me sing. I'm the tenor of your dreams."

"My dear man, can't you see I'm in the middle of a conference?"

"How about right after? There's a little bar across from my hotel. It's got an upright piano, not too good, but the notes are basically there. Of course, with all your expertise you probably could whip up something much more professional."

"I'm not whipping up anything for anyone. There's nothing I can do."

"I know it's pretty unexpected, me coming after you like this, but I just thought you'd want to get a sample of my work."

Reinbert gave him a poisonous look. I leaned over to the intruder and said, "I really think it's best you go."

He seemed startled to hear me speak – as if I'd been invisible before – then took an envelope from his jacket and handed it to Reinbert. "Well, could you at least take a look at this? It's from one of your staff. It's in German, so I can't really make it out, but I know it's something nice."

Reinbert glanced down at the envelope with distaste. "Kindly spare me."

The poor singer was completely dumbfounded. He brandished the envelope again. His hand was shaking. "But he's really a big fan. He urged me to chase after you."

"Did he?"

"Don't you want to know what he said?" Reinbert kept silent. I'd rarely seen him so tense and irritated, but he didn't yell, he didn't make a scene. Something was holding him back, the other managers perhaps, or maybe it only was me. "How about your friend here taking a look?"

He thrust the letter into my hands. It was from Otto Greissle, the phantom of the opera, we always called him, our trusted *souffleur*, a man of encyclopedic knowledge whom everyone admired, even Reinbert. He kept him on as part-time backstage help even though he was well past retirement age. "Aren't you curious to read Otto's note?"

"Not especially."

"He actually was very impressed," I said. "This fellow has obviously gone to a great deal of trouble to get here."

"Look, I've set up a very clear procedure for auditions. I hear singers only on Fridays at scheduled intervals, not just whenever a fellow manages to catch me out in public. If you really want to sing for me, call my secretary Frau Kasel on Monday and tell her I want you added to the June 14th auditions."

"But I leave for the States on Monday."

"June's the best time of the year. All of Germany's in bloom. I look forward to hearing you then."

"Yeah, sure, thanks." The singer shook hands glumly, then turned and trudged towards the door. We watched him leave in silence.

When he finally had left, I spoke up. "That seemed harsh."

"I can't be hearing singers every five minutes. I'd never get anything done."

"Yes, but still, you could have..."

"*Hart bleiben.* Remember?"

"As you wish, *Herr Intendant.*" I rose, as did he, and we shook hands with a solemn, self-conscious formality.

Walking back towards my car, I saw a familiar shape sitting on a bench facing the lake. Our singer was crumpled over himself quite awkwardly. One part of me thought it might be best to ignore him. My other side was worried–maybe the poor man needed help.

I walked over and asked if he was all right. He straightened himself up and gave me a not very reassuring smile. "Is that Klauzer guy always so mean? He went after me with a fucking sledgehammer. Pardon my French, but he did."

"He's pretty distracted by the conference, you know, he's got a lot on his mind."

"I changed my ticket, flew here from Frankfurt, and what the hell for?"

His face looked wan and dispirited. It tugged at my heart. "Are you staying here in Lausanne?"

"Yeah, I'm in a hotel up near the railroad station."

"I've got a car. I'll drive you there."

"Great, thanks. It takes forever with the bus."

As we made our way to my car, I introduced myself. "I'm Sami Tomi Pekkonen."

"What a mouthful. Do I call you Sammy or Tommy?"

"Both, if possible, though I answer to either one."

"So, what do you do at the opera? Are you Klauzer's assistant?"

"You could say that."

When we reached my car, the singer suddenly became much more animated. "Oh, man, is that your car? I bet all the girls want to ride with you."

"Well, not all."

"Come on, these are the sexiest wheels going, fast and sporty, built to last forever. What chick could possibly resist?" We got inside and he studied the detailing with an almost bewildering intensity. "These guys are fucking geniuses. You know, in an earlier life I sold cars for a living."

"You did, really?"

"Yeah, no shit. Oops, sorry about the cursing—"

"I'll survive. So, you actually sold cars. Why did you give it up?"

"I'm better at singing opera – and I really was good at selling cars." He said it with a calm assurance that startled me. He now seemed totally different from the battered man I just had rescued from a park bench. "Say, would you mind doing me a favor and putting down the top? I gotta see how they engineer it." I started up the motor and the top came down swiftly and soundlessly. My guest watched in rapt wonder. "Wow, smooth as cream. It used to be so complicated on those GM models, with flippers and levers and god knows what else, and then they expected me to go out on the floor and sell them. But this little jobbie... I could move twenty units a day."

I had started the brief drive into town by then. "You mean to say you could actually sell twenty cars in one day?"

"Nah, that's an exaggeration. I guess my all-time record was seven, but that's still pretty damn amazing. A sale takes a lot of time, there's all these forms you gotta fill out and credit reports to get. It's not a *wham, bam, thank you, ma'am* type deal at all."

I was fascinated. Ever since I was a kid, I had obsessed over cars, but up to now I'd never met anyone who actually sold them, except, of course, for the dealer in Frankfurt who got me my Mercedes. My rider was amused, almost startled, by my interest in a profession he had so willingly given up. He very gamely answered my no doubt completely naive questions about working for a small car dealership in the middle of America. Who knew there was so much to it?

In no time at all, we were right by the tall boxy train station in the center of downtown Lausanne. Our surroundings had changed drastically, from the haute bourgeois elegance of the lakeside villas to the dingy factuality of working-class housing. None of the buildings was a public embarrassment – this was Switzerland, after all – but the whole area spoke of limited options and limited ambitions. It was certainly not a neighborhood where leading tenors spend the night. I pulled up in front of the singer's hotel, a squat four-story postwar building whose once white stucco had turned gray and flaky over many long years of neglect and troubled cash flow.

"Well, here we are, Mister Verdun."

"Richie, please. That's what everyone calls me back home."

"Best of luck, Richie, I'm sorry things didn't work out."

He was about to shake my hand when he suddenly was struck by something. "Look, I don't know what it is you do, but you're his assistant, right? You're with him every day."

"Most days."

"Mister Klauzer said I could sing for him in June. That's real nice of him, but I can't just hop on a plane and fly back to Europe like that. Hell, the trip down from Frankfurt damn near broke me, but I had to do it, had to give it my all. And what I'm wondering is, could I maybe at least sing for you? I'll pay for the pianist, I'll pay for the room, anything, just so someone close to Herr Klauzer hears me before I go home."

"I doubt he'll change his mind. He's not the most flexible person."

"Yeah, but you work in his office, you know what makes him tick."

"Up to a point."

He leaned closer. "Come on, pal, you can do it. I promise I'm worth your time. I'm the real McCoy. I really and truly can sing. I know you don't know me from Adam. I know I walked in off the street. But this audition means the world to me. It's a giant deal, a matter of life and death, and that's no exaggeration. So, what I'm asking is, could you be the great guy I already know you are and spare me a little of your time?"

It almost embarrasses me to say that his last comments undid me. I'm Nordic. I usually hold a protective distance from the world, but somehow, this tubby guy with his endearing smile and open manner got to me. I found myself saying, "Well, if you take the train to Geneva and meet me around six at the stage entrance of Victoria Hall, that's their concert hall, I'll see what I can do. Just ask for Maestro Pekkonen."

He was taken aback. "Maestro?"

"Yes, I'm a conductor."

"You? You're younger than my son Timmy."

"I rather doubt it. In any case, get there by six and I'll hear you. I don't know how much I can help. Herr Klauzer does all the vocal casting. One other thing, don't be late. I've got a concert tonight. I only can give you fifteen minutes."

CHAPTER SEVEN

Richie

When we met by the lake, Sami Tomi Pekkonen – or ST, as I call him – was wearing jeans and a short-sleeved shirt, stylish, but very informal, so I figure I'll do likewise. I wear my trusty old chinos and a green and brown checked lumberjack shirt I just got back from the cleaners, so it's nice and fresh looking. I walk into his dressing room at the hall that night and, there he is, looking like a god, fresh shaven and scrubbed till he's shining, wearing the crisply pressed black pants of his tail suit and a super sharp white dress shirt with sapphire studs and a tightly knotted white bow tie. A vest in creamy white silk is cinched tight to his waist, which is almost as thin as a dancer's. There's not a trace of fat on him. Some guys have all the luck.

Of course, clothes aren't really the point, singing is. I gotta grab hold of myself and pull off some serious bel canto. I tell him I'll sing *Winterstuerme.* It wasn't so long ago that I swore I'd never sing it, but by now it's become my go-to aria. The cute young pianist begins and right away I realize she's the real deal, as good as any I've worked with. This is no small thing. The pianist is the ground you stand on, the roots of your tree. It turns out her idea of the song is less stormy and wild than Otto's was back in Frankfurt so I don't need to give as much voice, which makes the aria sweeter somehow, more romantic, and that's okay – it's a love scene, after all (a weird one, for sure, brother seduces sister), but singing the aria is a breeze with this pianist, and I can tell I've got the big man hooked. He's all scrunched up in his chair, totally intent.

"Very interesting," he goes. "Have you ever sung the role on stage?"

"No, sir. But I sure would like to."

"Yes, it would be a good fit."

"Maybe you could tell that to Herr Klauzer." He looks a bit miffed, like I crossed an invisible line, and he's probably right.

"I'd like to hear the Flower Song from *Carmen* next. You have sung the part on stage, haven't you?"

"Sure," I go, "lots of times."

"Where?"

"Oh, you know, smaller companies back home, Kansas City and such like." It's a total lie, of course, but so what? We're a long, long way from Kansas City. I rummage around and find the score and give it to the pianist, who's absolutely gorgeous with dark flowing hair and big luscious lips. "By the way," I tell her, "you really play great."

"*Grazie.* You really sing well," she says in this adorable Italian accent.

She gives me a sunny smile. Her teeth are movie-star perfect, white and even. I smile right back at her. Suddenly, I hear some polite coughing from the other side of the room. "Excuse me. I should have introduced you. Richie Verdun, meet Signorina Francesca Simioni of the Frankfurt Opera."

We shake hands. "Pleased to meet you, ma'am. You can play for me any time."

"*Molto gentile, signor.*"

"*Mille grazie,*" I say, using one of the few Italian expressions I know.

"If you two don't mind, I'd still like to hear the Flower Song." I can't really tell if he's annoyed by our kidding around, he's got this Nordic calm that pretty much hides everything.

She starts the prelude right as I'm thinking this, and when I start singing, it feels out of focus. I guess the flirting got me distracted, and ST's no dope, he notices at once, and I notice he notices, which makes things even worse. I've gotta pull myself together before the aria heads totally south. We're at the point where Jose sings about how he hated Carmen while he was in jail. I try to get into the anger the poor guy's feeling, and believe me, it's about time, Carmen's been toying with him since forever. Anyway, I'm able to latch onto all the frustrations of the day and the aria livens up. It's got more energy, more push – real power.

The maestro seems pleased, but then he throws me this curve ball and asks if I can read through the whole part for him. You heard me, the entire role from beginning to end. Now, I spent the past three months coaching Don Jose with Rigby, so I do know every note, but I never sang it in public, it'll be one helluva challenge.

It goes amazingly well at first. I get through the act one duet with Micaela without any flubs. Then we jump to the duet in act two where Carmen basically destroys his career in the army. Aside from bobbing behind the lovely Francesca once or twice to check the words, I manage just fine. By the middle of the third act I'm thinking, *wow, I really can do this*, until ST suddenly shouts, "Stop, stop!" He jumps out of his chair, marches over to the piano and starts flipping through Francesca's score, while I'm like, *what's the problem? it's going just great.* He finally finds what he's looking for. "Right here where we stopped, Jose sings, *je te tiens, fille damnée.* What's he thinking at this moment? What's he feeling?"

"Isn't he mad at Carmen?"

"Of course, but why, what has she done?" I know there's gotta be some reason but my brain cells go dead. "Have you any idea at all what you're singing?"

"Yeah, sure, sort of."

"Sort of isn't good enough. Look, I like you very much and want to help, but opera tells a story. All you're giving me is notes."

"But good notes, right? I blast 'em right outta there."

"That's irrelevant. What's happening to Don Jose? What's he after?"

I can't answer him. I mean, come on, I know the words and music, I can sing the goddamn part. I'm just not the host of the Metropolitan Opera Quiz, or a university professor, or a music critic. I'm an opera singer, I go on stage and sing.

"Well, to be honest with you, I'm a little shaky on the story."

"Shaky? You performed the part on stage."

"Actually, to totally level with you, I never performed it anywhere."

Who says honesty is the best policy? ST gets this look of icy irritation. "I go to all this trouble, and you tell me a lie?"

I'm so embarrassed my cheeks heat up like a furnace. "I'm really sorry. You've got every right to be upset. I guess I just wanted to impress you."

"I'm not impressed by lying."

"Of course not. I was wrong. I really and truly apologize." When will I learn? When will I start acting like a grownup? "Look, I know this part inside out, it fits me like a glove. Just say what you want and I'll give it to you any way you want, angry, scary, crazy, whatever. Just tell me and I swear I'll do it right."

He doesn't say anything. He's giving me the Finnish freeze-out, when, like some miracle, Francesca pipes up from the piano bench, "Why don't you conduct him, *caro*? Maybe this gives a better idea."

"Perhaps," he says. "You have worked with conductors before, haven't you?"

"Of course, I just did a *Madame Butterfly* in Canada." He doesn't need to know it was my only operatic performance.

"All right then, we'll give it a try. Let's take it from the very same point." He gives the downbeat and everything transforms. It's a mind-blowing, life-changing moment when Sami Tomi Pekkonen conducts me in the last two acts of *Carmen.*

The thing that maybe comes closest to it is the day fireflies showed up in Graystone. They're pretty rare up where I come from. I guess our town's too cold for them or too dry, but one summer, a very nasty one, when Billy and Timmy were both still in grade school, I noticed a few of them lighting up on the lawn as the sun was going down after an extremely hot and muggy day, which is why I guess they were out in the first place. Excited, I called the boys – Carol was away on a sleepover somewhere – and the two little guys came scampering out and shouted like wild men when they saw the spectacle. I told them they could catch some and bring them back inside and then they'd have their own private light source for days, maybe even weeks to come. This really charged them up. Before I knew it, they were racing up and down the street, clutching after fireflies, pretty wildly, I'm afraid. They killed more than a few, but some of the poor things did survive and I put them in a big bell jar which I left in their bedroom so the boys could observe this astonishing phenomenon.

Later that night, I came in to check on them. It was three in the morning. They weren't in their beds. They were wide awake over by the window, staring, hypnotized, at the fireflies. I tiptoed over and went *boo.* They screamed like the devil while I roared with laughter.

"Okay, okay, tone it down, guys. We don't want to wake Mom."

"She should see them too," said Timmy.

"Yeah, Dad, she really should."

The kids were right. The sight was amazing. We looked awestruck at their pulsing yellow-white light, couldn't take our eyes off it. The fireflies would fade a bit, then glow up again in a quiet easy pulse, like human breathing, like the mystery of life itself.

Making music with Sami Tomi Pekkonen is like those fireflies, mesmerizing, mysterious, unforgettable.

He starts working with me right where we stopped in act three, when Jose finally realizes that Carmen's been playing him for a jerk. ST's maybe ten or twelve feet away. He doesn't have a score, he's got it completely memorized. He raises his hands, hones in on me and, this is the crazy part, the part that's so hard to understand, I know right away I'll do whatever he wants, however he wants, no questions asked. Don't ask how this happens or why; I'm no scientist, I just sing. He pulls the music out of you, pries it out, like no one else on earth.

The whole session's a test, of course. He won't take me to Klauzer unless he's sure I can deliver the goods. He changes tempos a lot, goes back and alters the mood of scenes and phrases, turns slow sections into fast and vice versa. Weirdly enough, all this switching around isn't nerve-wracking or scary, it's like we're discovering *Carmen* together, all sorts of *Carmens,* making them up on the spot, and they all make sense somehow, they all totally work. One time it's easygoing and lyrical, the soft side of Don Jose, his clueless dreamer boy quality. Then we repeat the sequence and ST drives the music ahead, it's tense and hard charging and suddenly there's rage inside me, fury, and that makes sense too. Jose's a murderer, after all, he kills the woman he loves.

That's how our session goes. We zig and we zag, trying one thing after another. Yet, the weird thing is we're always together, always in synch. Despite the change-ups, he's incredibly easy to follow. With him, a downbeat's a downbeat, a genuine full-fledged one, not a two, or a three, or a seventy-five, like with Egon, that nutcase conductor in Calgary. Come to think of it, ST's his total opposite. All he wants is for his singers to thrive. In no time at all, I feel he knows my voice better than anyone who ever worked with me, including Rigby and old Maestro B. In fact, he knows it even better than I do.

When we come to the final scene, where Don Jose murders Carmen, I finally understand the opera's a terrible human tragedy. ST shapes the scene so it builds to an unbearable climax. By Jose's last desperate line, when he calls for the police to arrest him, I'm ready for the slammer myself. And, man, does it ever feel good.

At last Francesca breaks the spell, "*Scusi, caro,* it's almost seven thirty. Concert begin at eight." That means we've been going at it for an hour and a half. It felt like maybe five or ten minutes.

"Richie," ST says, "come over here, please." I make my way to him and he puts his hands on my shoulders and looks me straight in the eye, which feels kinda weird, since that's exactly what I do with my boys when I'm laying down the law. "Look, I'll make certain Herr Klauzer auditions you tomorrow. I can't promise how he'll react, he's off in his own strange world. But I will do everything to help your cause. I'll fight for you tooth and mouth."

"Tooth and *nail*."

"Sorry?"

"We always say tooth and nail, Maestro."

He gives a slight smile, which is a first. "My name is Sami Tomi."

"You mean, I don't have to do that Maestro thing?"

"No, not at all. My parents called me Sami Tomi. So can you."

"It sounds like I'm talking to two guys at once."

"Yes, we Finns can be pretty odd."

"But in a really good way." Then, in a crazy impulse, I lunge forward and give him this giant hug. A big mistake. He freezes up, goes stiff all over. He gently but firmly frees himself, takes a step or two back and I go, "Gee, sorry, it's just that—"

"*Caro, scusi.* I remind you conduct tonight a concert."

ST asks if I'd like to hear it and of course I would. He calls someone to make arrangements and Francesca takes me out to the box office. As she goes over to pick up my ticket, I notice the crowd's pretty fancy. There's furs on the ladies, silk scarves and dark suits for the men. They really dress up for their music in Geneva, Switzerland, and Richie Verdun has dressed down, way down. Francesca gives me my ticket and tells me not to worry, nobody really cares what I'm wearing. I'm not so sure, I have the feeling people everywhere are giving me the hairy eyeball. When we get inside the hall, we split up, her seat's down front, mine's way in back. I duck into the men's room to tuck my shirt in, it's the very least I can do. As I unzip and start tucking, a doddering geezer in a fraying tuxedo stares at me like I'm a homeless person. I think, *stare all you want, asshole, you'll pay top dollar to hear me one day.*

ST strides out to the podium and looks twenty years younger than anyone else on stage. Twice as attractive, too – like a swimming or diving champ off to the senior prom. Once he lifts his baton, though, everything changes. He's inside the music, way inside, like no one else I know.

The first piece on the program is *A Survivor from Warsaw* by Arnold Schoenberg. I know it's not cool, but I gotta confess I never heard of the guy before. The Met wasn't doing any of his operas, so how could I? Anyway, his piece is a short one about the horrific suffering of the Jews at the hands of the Nazis. There's no melody, just crashes and bashes in the orchestra. As it clatters on and on, I'm thinking *this sure as hell isn't for me, it's way too raw and ugly, and it's probably not music anyway, just noise and sound effects.* Then the chorus stands up and starts singing this passionate melody, not a tune you can hum, maybe, but it's obviously a prayer, obviously deeply felt, the *Shema Yisrael*, a famous old text. Somehow, hearing heartfelt religious music in the midst of all this ugliness really gets to me, which is amazing, since the music's totally modern, you know, the broken-dishes school, a lot of clatter and batter, but the prayer takes it somewhere else and gets me totally hooked. The music keeps building and building till it reaches an unbearable climax and then it just snaps off, like the end of a monstrous nightmare.

I'm stunned and so is the crowd. Even if you don't really like or understand it, even if you're not sure it's music, the piece makes a giant impression, and that's genius, you know, absolutely fantastic.

Now, something even more amazing happens. The music just cut off, right? There's silence in the hall. Guess what ST does. Nothing. He holds the silence, nurses it, molds it, expands it, till we're all on edge, wondering what comes next. I mean, how long can a thousand people keep absolutely still waiting for something, anything to happen? ST doesn't waver. We're totally in his grip, while the silence grows and grows and builds and builds.

At the very last moment, when we feel we can't endure a single second more of this emptiness, there's a deep low humming in the strings. It comes from out of nowhere, like a dream, a distant vision. After a while, we begin to make out a tune, a sketch of a tune, very faint and stretched out. I realize it must be the beginning of Beethoven's *Ninth Symphony*, a piece I'm sorry to say I never heard live until that evening. The effect is completely amazing. Beethoven's music comes from another world, a kinder, gentler one than Schoenberg's, but somehow the cruelty of *A Survivor* doesn't completely vanish, it lingers, like a dark echo in the hall. It's there even at the very end, a grim shadow, in the midst of Beethoven's hymn to joy, when ST basically whips the orchestra and chorus into an insane, go-for-broke ecstasy.

Once the Beethoven ends, and ST ends it just like he did the Schoenberg, he snaps it right off, cuts it dead in its tracks, there's silence again, a long gap between the music and the public's reaction. Did it work? Will they go for it? Finally, someone squawks out a tiny bravo from way up in the peanut gallery. Then the crowd goes wild. Okay, not wild like I've seen in Chicago or London. I mean, it's still Switzerland, the place is one big bank. Even so, the audience cheers like crazy. My man scores a giant success.

Like with any really good performance, it's taking a lot of time to clear the auditorium. It's as if the public wants to hang on to the magic as long as possible. With the aisles and exits clogged, it takes forever until Francesca and I can meet up and make our way backstage to congratulate the maestro. Once we're in the green room, we don't stand a chance. He's completely surrounded by a mob of musicians and well-wishers. There's not much we can do but hang back and observe the spectacle.

"Wow," I tell her, "you really struck it rich with that guy."

"Yes, he is very talented." We look over at ST and his admirers. It's like everyone who heard the concert needs to make physical contact with him, like there's something golden about him, something magic, and everyone wants a piece of it.

"You don't mind all those folks pawing at him, do you?"

"No, of course not. He not like much, but what can he do? People have crazy ideas, like conductor is magician, make something from nothing."

"Well, doesn't he?"

"No. The *composer* is magician. He take blank paper and make out of it *La Traviata*, the Beethoven *Ninth*."

"Yeah, I guess. But we sure as hell need conductors too."

"Maybe, I don't know..." It's like she's hardly paying attention to me, she's a thousand miles away.

"Hey, is anything wrong?"

"No, no. He very happy he hear you. He do for you all he can."

"Well, I really appreciate it... Francesca," I go, "don't mind me, but I just can't help asking. Are you sure everything's all right?"

"Why you ask? Everything completely fine." But she looks as if her heart is breaking.

In a few minutes, it all comes tumbling out. Sami Tomi has told her that they won't be taking their vacation at Lake Como this summer. "They just call him last minute for Tanglewood. Four weeks he conduct new music and two concerts with Boston Symphony."

"Wow, that's really a great gig. Tanglewood's extremely prestigious."

"What I care for prestige? Just want nice vacation together, for once." She's as startled by her outburst as I am. "Sorry, we only just now hear. It come like very big surprise. Sami completely excited, of course, but very bad for me."

I suddenly think of Kit, thousands of miles away. We try to keep in touch and phone whenever we can. But it isn't easy with me zooming around Europe and her dealing with her job, especially in different time zones. The truth is, I'm pretty much on autopilot over here, doing it all on my own. Which is fine in one way. It's my voice, after all, my dream. But still, it's hard not to be able to share things on a day-to-day basis with the woman I love, not to have her calm quiet support, her delightful humor, her gentle kicks in the butt. I suddenly feel sad, but what can I do?

"I never see him," Francesca goes on. "He always rehearse or study. And now no vacation, only *musica, musica, niente per me.*"

"Sorry, I didn't get that last."

"Is not important. He comes now this way. Please don't say nothing."

"About what?" She gives me a weak smile and pats my arm gratefully.

Sami Tomi walks over to us and says, "Come on, we'll drive you home."

"But you've still got lots of visitors."

"I've done my duty. It's time for you to go home."

"It's okay. I'll get there on my own."

"Not at this hour. The trains stop running." He spins on his heels and starts towards the exit. The crowd sees that he's on his way out and clusters by the door. He works through them in record time, shakes the hands of the last two musicians, gives a slap on the back to the actor who narrated the Schoenberg and before you know it, he's off to the parking lot with Francesca and me huffing and puffing after him.

Francesca gets in the car, as ST leads me a few steps away, so she can't overhear. "I need to tell you something, Richie, and I really hope it won't sound too condescending, but ... I think you're much more talented than you give yourself credit for." I give him an *aw, shucks,* sort of shrug because his words make me strangely uncomfortable. "I mean it, Richie. Don't sell yourself short. Fight hard for your art. You've got something."

"You think so?"

"Why else would I say it?"

"Sorry," I go, "I just never worked that way before. I had no idea I could sing like that."

"You obviously can."

"Yeah, well, it really felt fantastic."

As we walk back towards the car, he says, almost as an afterthought, "You know, music is much more than notes on a page. It's who and what you are. That's the music behind the music. And that's what really counts."

It's not long before we're cruising in that gorgeous Mercedes of his, heading towards Lausanne with me folded up in back and ST and Francesca in front, staring straight ahead, not saying a word. Even though the vibe from them is tense, I'm feeling pretty great. The ride's smooth and beautiful, calm and quiet. I'm alone with my thoughts as we whiz through deserted streets onto a broad empty highway. I look out at the shadowy hills and black open fields and realize there's thousands of pinprick stars blinking away like fireflies in the distant nighttime sky. It's like the whole universe is throbbing with all this mysterious energy, this trapped lightning.

CHAPTER EIGHT

Sami Tomi

The Hotel des Alpes Excelsior, where Reinbert was staying, is a bloated nineteenth-century pile masquerading as a seventeenth-century French palace, a monument to bourgeois opulence. Like most of the luxury hotels in town it faces Lac Léman. How else could it charge such exorbitant rates?

As I walked into the lobby, Reinbert greeted me with an ironic smile. "My spies tell me you had a great success last night."

"Yes, it went rather well." I wasn't about to tell him how important the evening had been for me. He'd only accuse me of being sentimental, a slave to the whims of the public. But why make music if not to engage them? Why not sweep them away in a torrent of sound?

"It seems that Signor Marchesi, the *sovrintendente* in Genoa, is a great admirer."

"He was there last night?"

"Yes, acting as my spy. He wants to bring our new *Walkuere* to Genoa."

"Does he realize what he's getting into? That's Red Rebecca's production."

It was as if I'd slapped him. "That's not her proper name."

"It should be. She's drags Marxist theory into every opera she stages."

"Now listen here, Frau Richartz is a brave and bold theatrical explorer."

Until that moment, I hadn't really been aware how deeply Reinbert believed in her. I thought he had hired her more as a political gesture, a well-meaning nod to East-West reconciliation. Obviously, I had it wrong. "Look, I actually like her work, admire it even, but sometimes it's way off the mark."

"Of the conventional, the old fashioned, the moribund."

He seemed alarmingly resolute. I worried he might keep it up all day. "All right, Reinbert, you win. You always do."

"And so should I. I'm your *Intendant.*"

"Yes, you most certainly are."

"Then be so kind as not to forget it." I had to smile. Reinbert's pomposity never failed to amuse me. "My dear boy, we're still colleagues. I'll always take you and your opinions most seriously."

It was just the opening I was hoping for. "Then you'll be pleased to know I've found the solution to our *Carmen* problem."

"What *Carmen* problem?"

"We need a new Don Jose."

"There's always Herr Kuehn."

"I've got a far better idea. He's waiting in my car. I'll be right back..." Without giving him a chance to contradict or question me, I rushed outside, where Francesca and Richie were waiting. "All right," I said, "time for our little show."

As soon as Reinbert saw us, he stiffened with displeasure. "Uh, oh," said Richie, "I don't think your boss is very happy."

"I guess we'll have to cheer him up." Francesca squeezed my hand in sympathy. "It's nothing, *carina,* I'll handle it. In the meantime, take Richie to the bar and get ready." I kissed her and quickly sent them off.

When he saw Richie wasn't with me any more, Reinbert visibly relaxed. He leaned back against the cushions and grinned. "So, it's Signorina Simioni now. How intriguing. Tell me, what language does she use, Italian or German?" He pitched his voice like a woman's. "*Dio mio, più forte, più forte! Mein Gott, mein Gott, weiter!*"

I didn't find it amusing. "Reinbert, it's none of your business."

"It most certainly is. You're members of the company, you're under my protection, as it were, my supervision. Actually, I always assumed it was that Fernandez girl, the little mezzo. I've often seen the two of you off in a corner somewhere, fumbling around."

"That was months ago."

"Only a few. And now you've found La Simioni. How fickle, how very Don Juan."

"Reinbert, I'm not here to discuss my sex life."

He sprang up from the sofa, seriously annoyed. "And I'm not here to listen to that buffoon."

"He's no buffoon. He's a serious artist, a first-rate singer. He sang Don Jose for me yesterday, the entire role from beginning to end. He's exceptional."

"I'll hear him at auditions in June."

"He can't be here then."

"How tragic."

"It's a simple audition, a matter of fifteen minutes."

He stared at me with cold hard eyes. "How quickly they forget, how swiftly they shift and trample you in the dust."

"What on earth are you talking about?"

"You, Herr Pekkonen, you. Despite the advice of my associates, the warnings of the press, the outrage of my colleagues, I chose a skinny young unknown Finn to be music director of the Frankfurt Opera—"

"And I had tremendous success."

"Not with *Ballo.* Not with *Così Fan Tutte.* Herr Walter wouldn't work with you. Frau Giannini resigned in a huff."

"In every case there's a perfectly good reason why they... Look, why are you digging up this old garbage?"

"You've gotten too fancy, *mon cher*, you forget who's in charge. I'm the *Intendant*, I do the casting. It's my prerogative, not yours. I will not be ordered around."

"I'm General Music Director, remember? You've got to hear this singer. He's a first-rate talent."

This irritated him even more. "How would you know? You're a conductor. The orchestra's your toy. Stay in the pit and play with it."

It wasn't just his words. It was the condescension, the arrogance, that really got to me. "This is mad. You know perfectly well I have a say in casting."

"When I want your advice, I'll ask for it."

I stifled my rage as best I could, even though by this point, I was tempted to rip off his silk scarf and throttle him with it. "The man deserves to be heard. Just give him a proper chance."

"I told you we're using Herr Kuehn."

"Why? He's busy enough with *Walkuere.*"

"He's a distinguished artist, one of the very best."

"Not any more." Reinbert seemed shocked. "Sorry, but it's true. He's been having a great deal of vocal trouble lately. There's the start of a serious wobble." In my zeal for truth-telling I had forgotten that Herr Kuehn was one of the very few company members Reinbert deigned to socialize with.

There was a long deadly pause. "Don't get ahead of yourself, young man. Herr Kuehn has a great following. I will not have you insult him."

"I only want the best for Frankfurt Opera. The simple fact is my man's much better."

"Nonsense. You only want the best for the great Sami Tomi Pekkonen."

Normally I'm cool and reserved, always a bit cautious in my interactions with others. I only lose myself when making music or having sex. But at this moment, I was on the verge of physically attacking Reinbert, hitting him, pulverizing him. Outlandish, I know, almost operatic in its appalling excess, but still, opera has its own truth which, in the end, I respect and believe in. And so, I exploded.

"Will you shut the fuck up and listen!"

My outraged reaction had its effect. Reinbert climbed down off his very high horse, either because he finally realized he had gone too far, or because he feared for his physical safety. Either way it didn't matter to me.

He didn't apologize. He was still Reinbert Klauzer, he hadn't transformed into Saint Francis of Assisi. But he agreed to follow me into the hotel's empty bar where Richie and Francesca stood waiting alongside the long sleek Boesendorfer. Richard sang not two, but four arias in his strong fresh tenor and Reinbert offered him a provisional one-year contract as *jugendlicher Heldentenor*, including Don Jose in our new production of *Carmen*, on opening night, no less. Whether he did this out of genuine conviction or a desire to appease me, I'll never really know and I certainly don't care. I'd had my fill of manipulative martinets.

CHAPTER NINE

Richie

By the time I get to the Frankfurt Opera I've learned that you dress the part in Operaland, you don't do the Graystone slouch, which means no baseball caps or lumberjack shirts or crumpled chino pants. Everything's fancy and upscale. A colleague told me that when I appeared at the first rehearsal of the Calgary *Butterfly* the leading lady thought I was the janitor. Those days are gone forever.

Shortly before heading to Frankfurt, I asked my pal Rigby, who's always been a sharp dresser, to give me a hand assembling a new opera-friendly wardrobe. He took me to his favorite shop in Greenwich Village and we spent an hour or two going through all their selections. To tell the truth, I never spent more than ten minutes shopping for clothes before, but Rigby made me try on so many different items I worried we'd never get out of there. My favorite purchase was a high-end Harris brown tweed sports coat. Rigby said Franco Corelli often wore something like it, so I had to have one for myself. I also picked up a nice pair of dark wool slacks and two white button-down dress shirts. We even went to a nearby tie shop to complete the outfit. I had Rigby pick out the ties, since I never know which color goes with which. (My beloved Kit thinks I'm terminally color blind.) By the time Rigby and I were done, I'd spent way more than I wanted, but at least I wouldn't look like a janitor.

Standing at the door of a large rehearsal room at the Frankfurt Opera, I feel like it's the first day of school and I'm the new kid. Summer vacation has just ended and the decibel level's high. There's maybe twenty or thirty people here and everyone knows everyone else. Company members circle around, shaking hands and laughing and chitchatting, while I hug the doorway, getting up the courage to enter the fray. As I'm about to wade into the group and start introducing myself, I notice that I'm the only one wearing jacket and tie. I start wondering whether Rigby and I got it right.

As I go up to people to shake hands and give them my standard greeting, their bodies stiffen and they switch to English. Even those who don't speak it well give it their best shot. They say the right things, like *how nice to meet you, welcome to Frankfurt,* but their eyes are saying *who the hell are you? can you actually even sing?*

In the midst of this meeting and greeting, a skinny beanpole of a guy waltzes into the room. He's got this hungry *artiste* look, with a bright red beret slanted low over his forehead. He's followed by a swarm of guys even younger than he is, with notebooks at the ready. I never saw anybody with so many assistants, or groupies, or boyfriends, or whatever the hell they are. In any case, I put two and two together and realize he's the director, the man I need to know.

I make my way up to him, stick out my hand and go, "Hiya, Mr. Wolverton, I'm your Don Jose. Verdun's the name, singing's my game."

He takes my hand, pumps it once, then lasers me with his eyes. "Ah, yes, Mr. Verdun." Holy cow, an Englishman, just like that guy in Calgary. Are Brits the only people they allow to stage operas? "Singing isn't too much of a game for you, I hope. We all need to dig in from time to time."

"I'll dig as much as you want. I even brought my own shovel." This doesn't get a laugh, just a quizzical look. "Don't worry, whatever you want, I'll deliver," I bumble on. "And then some."

"That would be lovely. Thank you…" He's giving me this intense stare, like he's pondering one of the world's great mysteries. "Mr. Verdun, is it really true that this is only your second operatic production?"

"Yes, it sure is. I guess I'm one for the record books, huh?"

"Yes, you probably are… Ah well, I'm always up for a challenge."

"So am I." I give a little smile to show I really mean it, but he's doing more staring, more pondering. It goes on so long it's a relief when this slim young man, very elegant, very fine featured, slips up alongside us and says, "Sorry to interrupt, Herr Wolverton, but I think it's time to begin."

Wolverton sighs and says, "Ah, yes, duty calls."

As he slithers off, the young guy introduces himself as Toni Koenig, Wolverton's assistant, a sleek, slender twenty-something who reminds me of my older son Timmy, except Timmy's got way more muscle and way less fashion sense. This Toni dresses like a hipster Cary Grant.

"*Guten Tag,*" I go, eager to showcase the little German I have. It's a big mistake. Toni starts chattering away so rapidly I'm forced to stop him and admit the sorry truth.

"This should be no problem. I stay close to you in rehearsals and keep you always in the ropes."

"Nice try," I go, laughing. "It's actually *I'll keep you in the loop.*"

"*Ach,* I knew it was not right."

"But you came damn close. What is it with you guys? You speak so many languages."

"We hear them all the time, especially in the opera."

"Yeah, well, I guess it's no secret that I'm new to the game, so any help you can give me, especially in the language department, will be greatly appreciated."

"Absolutely. At your service. By the way," he continues, "I like very much your jacket. Is it Savile Row?"

"What's Savile Row?" I ask, a little distracted, and start looking around the room. "By the way, how come the Carmen isn't here?"

Toni arches an eyebrow. "Ah, yes, the great Frau Romanescu. She is protected property."

"What's that supposed to mean?"

He's about to answer when Wolverton claps his hands. "Okay. *Komm, Kinder, wir fangen an.*" We pick up chairs and arrange ourselves in a semicircle around the long table where Wolverton and his many assistants are sitting. Once we've settled down, our fearless leader bounces up off his chair and plops down alongside a model of the stage and begins his presentation. In German.

I've been in Germany for quite a while now and people pretty much always speak English. I never have problems getting around or making myself understood. But here in rehearsal, I'm totally at sea, as Wolverton, who's not even German, delivers this long lecture about the most important show of my life in a language that's just a wash of sound to me, a blur of meaningless syllables and guttural gurgling.

That's when it hits, it really and truly comes home, that there's this giant barrier between me and everyone else, a thick wall of foreign language that prevents me from joining the party and playing the game. I start longing for Kit and the kids and all the friendly, familiar things I left back home.

I'm still back in Graystone, when I start hearing *Verdun* this, and *Don Jose* that. I force myself back towards reality and discover that Wolverton and everyone else is staring at me. He's obviously been asking me a question, in German, of course, so I gotta come clean. "Sorry, Mr. Wolverton, could you repeat that in English?"

He says drily, "*Logisch. Er ist erster Tenor bei der Oper und spricht kein Wort deutsch.*" This amuses some of my colleagues, though I'm happy to say others seem more sympathetic. "Sorry, everyone, I'm afraid I must repeat much of what I just said in English for Mr. Verdun's benefit. I'll try my best not to bore you."

So now I'm on the receiving end of a public lecture in a very clipped British accent about who Don Jose is and what he wants and why it all matters. I get the distinct impression that Wolverton's talking down to me, like a high school teacher trying to save the class dunce from flunking out.

Fortunately, his comments don't go on long. As people start filing out, Wolverton makes his way over to me. *Uh, oh,* I think, *more trouble.*

"My dear Mr. Verdun," he says, like I'm not his dear anything, "you're an American, correct?"

"Absolutely."

"So I can assume you've got some jeans?"

"Yes, sir, I do," I say, wondering where this is heading.

"Please be certain to wear them for all staging rehearsals. Don Jose spends a great deal of time writhing around on the floor. There's no need for fancy clothing. Oh, and one other thing--a minor fashion tip, if I may? The next time you put on your brown hacking jacket, it might be best not to wear that purple tie."

CHAPTER TEN

Frau Rebecca Richartz

We had no warning. Richard Verdun appeared as a total surprise from somewhere or other in America and made his debut as Don Jose at the Frankfurt Opera in a new production- on opening night, no less. We were all *total perplex.* Who is this man? Why is he here? The artist I saw that night – well, artist is not quite the word, journeyman, no, raw beginner – was stiff, almost amateur. However, as the opera wore on, and in this particular production it wore on very slowly, Verdun gradually fought himself free of the misery surrounding him and became a rather interesting stage figure, almost frightening, which was quite remarkable, considering his dismal surroundings.

It was difficult being Herr Klauzer's guest that evening. Obviously, the production displeased me but, even worse, the Romanian lady who sang the title role, with hands on hips and much wiggling of the rear end, was the *Intendant's* current girlfriend, though what any man, especially a man of Herr Klauzer's intelligence and refinement, could see in her was and is totally beyond me. Although I am extremely fond of saying what I think – I beat around no bushes, even when perhaps I should – this time, I couldn't indulge myself. I was in the process of creating a new *Ring* for his company, a giant undertaking, both for him and for me. It was no time to exercise my right of free speech.

When the curtain fell to considerable applause (audiences aren't always the best judges of artistic quality), the *Intendant* sighed and shook his head wearily. "It wasn't much good, was it?"

"*Na ja*, Herr Klauzer, they do the best they can."

This seemed to reassure him. "I won't ask about Madame, I know you're no admirer, but our new tenor, that Verdun fellow, what do you make of him?"

"Not very much."

"Well, prepare yourself. He's your understudy for Siegmund." The news didn't thrill me. "There's no need to worry. Herr Kuehn is a veritable rock. He'll sing every performance and give you what you want."

"I most certainly hope so."

"You won't be disappointed, I assure you… Oh, by the way, I very much wanted to be at your meeting tomorrow to introduce you to the cast, but, alas, I have a crucial meeting in Munich. My assistant Frau Kasel will do the honors." I just stared at him. "Believe me, it pains me even more than it pains you, but we're in the midst of some important negotiations."

"More important than a new *Ring*?"

"I truly regret I can't be there, but nearly everyone else will."

"*Nearly* everyone? I asked for the full company and music staff."

"Even Herr Pekkonen?"

"Of course, he's the conductor."

"Well, it pains me to say it, but he's got some concerts in Oslo."

I couldn't believe what I was hearing. "He's essential to the success of the show. He's got to be there."

Herr Klauzer, usually so suave and self-assured, seemed unsettled, even a bit embarrassed. "Alas, the fact of the matter is he's got the contractual right to—"

"To make an extra fee and insult your company."

"For heaven's sake, the full cast is coming, even Frau Neville, who's flying in from Paris. We've got all the understudies and most of the music staff."

"But not the great Herr Pekkonen. He's off making money, a typical capitalist."

"That's unfair. The Oslo Philharmonic had an emergency."

"And offered him a generous fee, which he eagerly accepted."

"That's not the point."

"The point is, there's only one way to work in an opera house, as a collective. Everyone together, everyone engaged, everyone sailing the same ship to the same destination. I intended this *Ring* to be the highlight of my career, my masterwork, but that can only happen with a like-minded conductor, who feels as I do, thinks as I do, sees as I do. All Herr Pekkonen sees is Deutschmarks."

Herr Klauzer was so worn down by this, so startled and shocked by my tirade that he just stood there, dumbfounded. I spun on my heels and marched out through the lobby, dragging my coat behind me à la Tosca. When I reached the street door, I glanced back and saw he still hadn't taken a step. Good. It serves him right for trying to sabotage my work.

On the other hand, to be absolutely honest, I had laid it on a bit thick. The actual harm Herr Pekkonen might cause by missing that one meeting would be slight. As for the young man himself, I rather liked him. But that wasn't the point. It was the principle of the thing, the basic gesture. Many of my colleagues have the unfortunate habit of wanting to be liked by the people who hire them. That's a mistake. Opera is not a popularity contest. You must make it clear to one and all that you *know* and *care* and *will fight to the death for your vision.* If not, if people somehow got the notion that you'll "listen to reason" and make "minor adjustments," they'll chip away at your work, softening it, eviscerating it, until the magical construction you spent years and years inventing crumbles into dust.

I arrived at the theater early the next day to prepare for the cast meeting. Normally, I lead such things with my full staff beside me, designers, staging assistants, movement team and so on. Not this time. I wanted to forge a special bond with the performers, make them understand how personally I took this assignment, how intensely and passionately I needed their reality as singing actors.

I had tried to reserve the main stage for the gathering. It's a vast space, one of the largest in Europe and a perfect emblem of the opera itself. Its icy immensity echoes the grim world Wagner's characters contend with; they have nothing to fall back on but their own flawed selves. Unfortunately, Herr Klauzer's staff claimed the stage had already been reserved for another project and shunted us to a nondescript coaching room with muddy light and stuffy air, barely big enough to hold the participants.

The staff had set up a chair and small desk for me at the far end of the room. As I took my seat and faced the rows of empty bentwood chairs, I was suddenly hit by the *trac*. Was my concept as bold and audacious as the *Ring* itself? Would the cast understand the intensity I was seeking, the forcefulness, the profundity? Would they, could they make it come alive for the public? They were my emissaries, after all, my troops sent out to battle on the front lines of art.

To calm my nerves, I opened a small volume of Brecht and reread *An die Nachgeborenen*, a masterful poem written just before the calamity of the Second World War. It perfectly expressed the underlying idea of my staging. Every attempt to improve the miserable lot of humankind creates its own new miseries. That's the tragic heart and soul of Wagner's *Ring*.

As I was reading, a balding rotund man stopped at the doorway and peered into the room. "Guess we're both kinda early, huh?" I looked up from my book and nodded. "I figure I'll settle down here in back. I'm just an understudy." As the man eased his broad frame into one of the chairs, I recognized Klauzer's Don Jose, Richard Verdun. He seemed totally transformed from the night before. Not only had a wig hidden his bald spot and framed his face in flattering curls, but the makeup department had sculpted and shaded his features so cunningly that he seemed like a relatively young man, when in fact he was middle aged.

"In case you're out of the loop, I was the Jose last night in that new production. Were you there? Did you see it?" I had, of course, but I shook my head no. The last thing I wanted was to offer comments to a needy performer. I do it all the time in rehearsals, of course, but then it's part of my job. I'll tell a cast member anything if it can help the performance. "Well," Verdun went on, "you missed a big one. The show went really well. Even Herr K seemed to like it, though with him you never know." He adopted a grotesque German accent. "Ze mysterious Reinbert Klauzer... Anyway, after the party, I was so damn excited I stayed up until four A.M...."

Thank heavens this bore was just an understudy. My assistants would have to deal with him, not me. I put my finger to my lips and pointed to my book, hoping he would understand. "Okay, okay, sorry... I've actually got my own reading, the *FAZ*. That's the local newspaper, you know... Hey, are you following this? Do you even speak English? *Sprechen Sie englisch*?" I'm rather proud that I do, so I nodded. A bad decision, it only encouraged him.

"Ever since I got here, I've been trying to learn some German, but it's really rough going. I mean, what is it with that *die, der, das* stuff? And then, the routine of the opera house. You rehearse all day but you still gotta sing at night. And vice versa. I sang my heart out yesterday evening, Don Jose, no less, a giant leading role, but I still gotta come to this meeting. At eleven o'clock in the morning. How crazy is that?" I was eager to tell him it wasn't crazy at all, but restrained myself. It would only prompt more chatter.

"Last night was something else. I had to pace myself like a race horse and not give too much at the start, so I'd finish in a blaze of glory. And I did, all modesty aside..." Here he gave a truly endearing smile. There was a certain insouciance to him, an effortless boyish charm, but it was all a bit much. I picked up my Brecht and gave him a definitive shush. He seemed genuinely surprised. "I'm not disturbing you, am I?"

"What do you think?"

"Gosh, sorry, I didn't mean to. I'm just trying to find my name in this review. By the way, I'm Richie Verdun, the new kid on the block." We shook hands. His grip was strong, his shake alarmingly vigorous. "Verdun's the name, singing's my game."

"It's not a game. It's art."

He looked at me sharply. "You think I don't know that?" I tried to return to my book but the chatterbox wouldn't stop. "So, which role are you singing?"

"I'm not a singer."

"Really? Then what are you doing here?"

It was a bit insulting that he failed to recognize me. My picture was in every program book, on every brochure. "Don't you read the *New York Times*?" A few months before they had done a big interview with me, more about politics than aesthetics, I'm afraid, but the piece made clear how important my new *Ring* would be, not just for Frankfurt, but all of Europe.

"I live in Frankfurt now. Why would I read a New York paper?"

"Why indeed."

"Look, my name's gotta be in this review somewhere. Could you do me a big favor and find it? It's Verdun, v e r d u n."

I quickly scanned the piece. It was one of those typical *nicht sagende* critiques that Hermann Rademacher, the chief music reporter for the *FAZ*, came up with from time to time. He obviously disliked the evening, but he was in Herr Klauzer's pocket and wasn't about to say anything too incendiary. His mention of Verdun was indeed hard to find. I finally unearthed it in the second to last paragraph. "This critic, Herr Rademacher, is not the last word on singers, you know. It's just one man's opinion."

He braced himself for the worst. "Okay, fire away."

"'As Don Jose, the provincial psychopath who tumbles into Carmen's lap, Richard Verdun, an American making his debut here, displayed a rather weak voice and used it unmusically.'"

He turned white as a sheet and snatched the paper away from me. It felt a bit cruel to trick the man, but if he's making a career here, why doesn't he at least know the language? After struggling with the text for a while, Verdun looked up and said, "*Stark* means strong, doesn't it?" I tried to suppress a smile. "Hey, you're messing with me."

"Sorry, I couldn't resist."

"Why? Because I'm a dumb American sucker who doesn't know his ass from his elbow?"

"You said it, Herr Verdun, not I." I felt twinges of embarrassment about toying with him. Under his thick coating of Yankee exuberance he seemed to harbor a curious vulnerability. I read it again: "'Richard Verdun, an American making his debut here, displayed a strong, almost heroic voice, though he often used it unmusically.'"

"I'm not unmusical. It's the damn conductor. He took those crazy tempos."

"Now, now, mustn't blame him."

"Why not? I'm sensitive. I feel things. And who are you to lecture me, anyway?"

"As a matter of fact, lecturing singers is one of my major occupations."

He thought it over for a moment, then gaped at me in astonishment. "Oh, my god, how could I miss it? You're the director." He faced me with a strange, rather naive fascination. "So, I finally get to meet the famous Red Rebecca."

"Frau Richartz to you, Herr Verdun."

He gave me his smile again, his glowing smile; charm does atone for a multitude of sins. "By the way," he went on, "I just saw the dress of your *Butterfly*."

"Yes, they make another revival."

"They want me to do some Pinkertons next spring."

"They do?" My heart sank. How on earth could this bumpkin portray the suave cruel lover in *Madame Butterfly*?

"Yeah, well, they know I did the role in Canada and I'm here already, so why not?"

"Why not indeed."

"I gotta say your production sure makes a big impact, especially at the start with all that rubble everywhere."

"Yes, they dropped the atomic bomb on Nagasaki."

"Can I ask you a question? That moment at the end, when the kid takes the sword his mom just used to kill herself and waves it over his head, what was that all about?"

"The sword is the power of the old ways, the ridiculous Japanese honor ritual, their love of blood and death. It is also the boy's father."

"His father?"

"Symbolically. Poetically. The sword is the penis which creates the child that drives Butterfly to her death. The horrible cruelty of imperialism, the blindness of Pinkerton's racism."

"But doesn't Pinkerton feel bad about what happens? In his aria he says he behaved terribly."

"He does not really mean it. He got his geisha with child, so he comes back with his white wife, his proper wife, to steal this boy from the real mother, the Japanese mother who has done everything for him, and bring the child back to America, which will treat this child of two races like garbage. But he does not see this and he does not care. He is only interested in himself."

"Wow," he said, "that's a hundred and eighty degrees different from how we did it in Canada."

"I certainly hope so."

"Can I ask another question? How come your English is so terrific?"

"I went to university in England many years ago to study Shakespeare."

"Wait, don't you live in East Germany? How come they let you out?"

"Who are you, the CIA?"

"No, but it doesn't make sense. People are desperate to get out of there and you just fly to England to..."

"You spend too much time believing the propaganda of your President Reagan and know nothing of our life there, nothing!"

"Hey, don't get upset, I was trying—"

"Of course I'm upset! People constantly insult my country even though they are completely ignorant."

He seemed stupefied by my reaction. "God, I'm really sorry, I didn't know."

"Americans never know. They are always the good guys, always the innocents and it makes the whole world crazy." I spun on my heels and went back to my table, determined to call Herr Klauzer and demand a more suitable Pinkerton. Just as I was thinking this, my *trac* returned. Verdun had succeeded in knocking me off my stride.

By this point, company members were filing into the cramped rehearsal room, greeting one another and chattering away brightly, no doubt about last night's opening. The biggest chatterbox was Verdun. From the corner of my eye I could see him holding forth at the back of the room to a cluster of young women, Valkyries, no doubt, who seemed highly amused by his antics. No doubt they'd soon regret it.

Frau Kasel, Herr Klauzer's little assistant, arrived out of breath and rushed over to greet me. "You are five minutes late," I said. "Kindly begin at once."

Didn't she realize how important this project was? As for Herr Klauzer, how could he fob me off with his secretary? A new production of the *Ring* is a major event. It is not something you assign to underlings.

Frau Kasel clapped her hands and called the meeting to order. After some formulaic words of greeting penned by the absent Herr Klauzer, Frau Kasel introduced me. She pointed out that my first production for the company, *Madame Butterfly,* now three years old, had just completed its sixtieth performance, which made it the most successful and most visited Puccini production in the company's entire hundred-year history. She quite elegantly neglected to mention that this staging, like so many of mine, had a bumpy start. I had set the action in Nagasaki, 1946, at the start of the American occupation. The curtain rose on an atomic wasteland of shattered brick buildings and makeshift cardboard huts. There were no picture-postcard geisha girls, just demoralized victims struggling with their lives, their time-honored traditions blasted away by the bomb. I showed the American conquerors for what they were, brutish racist exploiters of a desperate defenseless land. How they booed on opening night, how they howled in protest, shrieked! While most of the press was outraged and dismissive, Hermann Rademacher, writing for *Die Welt*, called my work revelatory and published not one, but two articles, showing how I had freed the opera from embarrassing sentimentality. It wasn't long before others followed his lead. My work may have been challenging, even harsh, but it certainly was not to be missed. It remains in the *Spielplan* to this day and still shocks grandmothers and delights their grandsons, proving you must make art for the sake of art and not worry about pleasing the public.

As Frau Kasel ended her little talk, there was a brief round of applause. I shook her hand and thanked her. She left to return to her office and I faced my cast for the first time. There was tension in the air, both on their part and mine. I worried whether they could do what I wanted. They worried I might push them too far.

Almost as soon as I started, I realized I wasn't myself. My *trac* was still there, the words refused to flow. I did get through it, that much I know, but at the end when I asked for questions, there was only silence. Never in over twenty years of theater-making had I failed to get a strong response to one of my presentations. This was a disturbing first.

Finally, breaking the almost stifling quiet of the room, Herr Kuehn, our Siegmund, spoke, a paunchy but well-dressed company regular. "Frau Richartz, first and foremost, let me thank you. You certainly have many daring and inventive new ideas. I do have one question, though. You said you wanted this *Walkuere* to be a wake-up call for our audience. Could you please elaborate? From what, exactly, are we waking them up?"

"Their complacency, their acceptance of the status quo. I see Frankfurt as Brecht's *Mahagonny*, *Bankfurt* am Main. It's only about money. Like Wotan lusting for the ring, financiers chase Deutschmarks here without the slightest regard for anything meaningful, anything human."

"Surely, some of them must love their children. Or rescue dogs from the pound."

There were a few titters, but Frau Neville, the lady who was singing Bruennhilde, was distinctly unamused. "This isn't a joke, Herr Kuehn. Frau Richartz is speaking quite seriously."

"So am I. In fact, I wonder why she chose to make her first *Ring* in Frankfurt, since she so obviously dislikes our city. Why not stage it on the other side of the wall, in the *workers' paradise*?"

I was outraged. He knew bloody well that the party never allowed me to work at home, I was far too radical. Fortunately, Frau Neville kept defending me. "Their loss is our gain. We are happy to have her. She's a distinguished and respected colleague." A few scattered voices said *hear, hear*, but the floor was still controlled by Herr Kuehn. He cast a bizarre spell over his colleagues.

"But does Frau Richartz respect us? Why should we offer our faithful public a critique of modern-day Frankfurt? It's like slapping them in the face."

"I'm not slapping anyone. I'm making an artistic statement."

"Which has very much to do with Rebecca Richartz and very little with Richard Wagner. You've discarded all his marvelous fantasy, his giants and dragons and walls of magic fire." The cast stirred uneasily.

"Those things are passé," I snapped, "outmoded relics of nineteenth-century Romanticism. We live in a different universe."

"Really? I rather suspect our public would enjoy that sort of thing."

"Let them go to the movies. They can find such nonsense there."

"It's hardly nonsense. Wagner wrote an old-style Teutonic myth about gods and goddesses, which makes no mention of banks or factories or machine guns, all of which you're putting on stage."

"That's her right. It's her point of view," said Frau Neville, my steadfast defender.

"Yes, but is it Wagner's? Is it even yours, Frau Neville, or yours, Herr Knef?" He acknowledged the giant young bass who was singing Hunding. "Frau Richartz may not like it, she's from the other side, but we've got democracy here. We're free to speak our minds."

"And so is Frau Richartz." I was rapidly falling in love with the brave and clear-sighted Frau Neville.

"That doesn't answer the question. Why take Wagner's masterwork, which everyone knows is steeped in German mythology, and transpose it to modern-day Frankfurt, or *Bankfurt*, as Frau Richartz insists on calling it?"

"We need to reach our public," I replied, "and engage with how it lives."

"We're not a social service agency, we're an opera company."

"That lives in the here and now, and connects with its community."

"We connect with it very well when we present conventional productions."

"The time for nostalgia is past. The public must have something new."

"Even if they don't like it, or want it?"

"Especially then. Theater must be a challenge, not a soporific. And, yes, I do call this city *Bankfurt.* How can I not? It's dominated by banks, ruled and bullied by them."

"Yet those very same banks pay enormous taxes, which underwrite the generous subsidies our humble opera house uses to pay your fee."

"Sorry, but I do not work for free."

"No one expects you to. Still, the *FAZ* reports that your fee for this *Ring* is the highest in the company's history."

This was truly beyond the pale. "How dare you!"

"I must inform you that we have a free press here. And most of my colleagues read the same article."

I looked around the room and saw that they had. They clearly wanted an explanation. "First and foremost, my fee, like that of anyone else, is a private matter. No one's business but my own. However, since the press has chosen to dredge it up, let me give you the actual facts. The East German Concert Agency takes most of my fee in taxes and commissions. I routinely earn less than my West German colleagues."

"Ah, the blessings of the socialist state."

"I do not object. It is for the public good. Some people actually care about their fellow man, Herr Kuehn. As for your claim that I am distorting Wagner's *Ring*, that's ridiculous. All I do is release the drama contained in the score."

"And that's why Siegmund is a crackhead?"

"Of course, Wagner was fascinated by drugs. He often used them."

"The *Ring* is myth, not autobiography. You say Siegmund should sniff up some cocaine before he even sings. The audience will die laughing."

"Not if you do it properly."

"How can I? It's nonsensical."

"Siegmund's exhausted, he's on the run. He needs drugs to give him courage."

"No, he stands on his own two feet. He's a brave and valiant warrior. He's the father of Siegfried, the greatest of German heroes."

"Don't talk to me about Siegfried. He's a bumbling bruiser who doesn't even know what a woman is."

That proved decisive. Herr Kuehn turned on his colleagues and bellowed, "This woman is a lunatic! The whole show is a farce!" He stormed out, leaving the room shocked and silent.

I let the silence sit for a while, then spoke, "*Meine Damen und Herren,* just now, a colleague stood up and derided everything I proposed. No matter how insulting, or excessive, or inartistic his comments were, he kept on ranting and no one said anything, except, of course, Frau Neville, and I thank her very much. The rest of you offered no opposition. Why? Do you agree with him? Do you simply want me to resign?" There was widespread protestation, *no, no, of course not, you're the director.* "Then why did no one speak up?"

Another deep silence, another embarrassed pause until Herr Knef raised his beefy hand. He was a well-built sturdy fellow, exceptionally tall, a basketball player who sings. "Excuse me, Frau Richartz, Herr *Kammersaenger* Kuehn has been in this company for twenty-five years. We respect and admire him. What else could we possibly do?"

"You know, you remind me of my father when I confronted him after the war, *but, daughter, what else could we possibly do?*" There was a gasp, an enormous collective intake of air, as if I'd slapped the whole lot of them. And I had. They deserved it. "That is the problem with this country, its perennial tragedy, the true *Deutches Miserere.* No one takes responsibility. No one has any guts. The only person in this room who faced the bully down and stood up for artistic freedom was Frau Neville. And she's Australian."

"Sorry, I'm actually Canadian."

Everyone laughed. "This isn't funny!" I yelled. "This isn't a joke! Meeting dismissed!"

I grabbed my book and rushed out the door before people could offer fraudulent expressions of support. I raced through the dark crisscrossing hallways in the front part of the complex that led to the *Intendant's* elegant hideaway. I wanted to get there before my antagonist did.

When I arrived, Frau Kasel rose and greeted me with an almost courtly formality. It was clear that I was too late. "My dear Frau Richartz, I know, I heard. I'm extremely sorry."

"I need to talk to Herr Klauzer."

"I'm afraid he's still in Munich. He'll be back in a few days."

"That's too late. We have an urgent problem."

"I know, but you've got to realize that Herr Kuehn has given twenty-five years of his life to this opera house, twenty-five marvelous years. We've never had any trouble from him. Why, just last year the city council appointed him *Kammersaenger*, a rare and exceptional honor. He wanted me to assure you that he's eager to appear in your production. The only sticking point is this matter of Siegmund taking drugs. You see, he had a teenage son and this poor boy got into terrible trouble with—"

"I do not care about his addict son! *Schluss! Punkt! Ende!*" With that, I marched out and slammed the door. I will not let anyone corrupt my artistic vision.

Still shaking with rage, I headed for Tante Olga, which offered a refuge from gossipy colleagues, especially at lunch time. I chose a seat far from the public eye and ordered a *Gulaschsuppe* to calm my private furies. I had taken maybe three spoonfuls, when, like a dread vision, Richard Verdun materialized, hat in hand, his face curled in a childish smile.

"Surprised to see me?"

"Herr Verdun, perhaps you notice I'm having lunch."

"I sure do. *Guten appetit.* This will only take a moment."

"That I very much doubt."

"I couldn't really follow all the ins and outs of the meeting, my German's pretty elementary. But Sally Neville gave me the whole story. Actually, she's the one who told me where to find you."

"I do not care. Just let me eat my lunch."

"Of course, no problem, I'll make it short and sweet. Sweets for the sweet." He flashed what he supposed was an endearing smile.

"Don't overdo it, Verdun. Don't push too far."

"I'll keep it short." He sat down, folded his hands on the table and asked me point blank. "So, what's the plan? Are you gonna fire him?"

"That's got nothing to do with you."

"Yes, it does. I'm the understudy. If he gets sick, I go on."

"He's not sick."

"But he's on his way out. I mean, come on, who does he think he is, mouthing off to you like that? You're the director."

"Yes, I most certainly am." I looked at him sternly. "Don't get your hopes up, Verdun. You won't sing Siegmund here, it's just not possible. I was at *Carmen* last night. I saw your Don Jose."

His face fell. "You told me you weren't there."

"Based on what I saw, I cannot possibly allow you to be my Siegmund." For a blissful moment, he seemed ready to go, but then he steeled himself and stayed right where he was.

"Look, I'm not a complainer, but that *Carmen* was a nightmare. The director hated me from the get-go." At this point, he switched to a rather tasteless parody of an effeminate Englishman. "*My dear boy* – the guy's ten years younger than me – *my dear boy, mustn't be vulgar, mustn't be a klutz.* Sorry, but Don Jose *is* a klutz. He's a goody-goody mama's boy until he meets Carmen. Then he turns into a sex-crazed maniac. That's the character, right?"

I had to smile, he wasn't really wrong.

"Look, I may seem dumb or naïve or too pig-headed American but inside, man, I'm burning. When I was struggling with *Carmen*, I didn't complain, I didn't despair, I gave it my absolute all. That Wolverton guy may be a pal of yours, but, sorry, in my book, he's a dick. He kept flirting with the ballet boys and totally ignored me. Anything you saw on that stage was something I figured out, not the moves, of course, but the feeling, the intensity. And you gotta admit I was pretty damn intense."

"Do I?"

"I'll be a great Siegmund, I really will. He's my kinda guy. He charges straight ahead, he never ever gives up."

"That's all well and good, but there's really no chance."

"Oh, yes, there is." With this he leapt onto a nearby chair and began singing Siegmund with a force, a contained violence I never imagined he might command.

Waelse...

He held the G flat a considerable, almost unconscionable length of time. It couldn't be ignored, you had to notice. I did, and so did all the others in the restaurant.

Waelse...

The high G lasted even longer, not as long as Melchior, perhaps, but long enough to sear your eardrums. Bit by bit, a group of diners and waiters clustered around us, drawn by the spectacle of a man singing his fool head off in a crowded restaurant at lunchtime.

"Thank you, Herr Verdun, that's quite enough."

"It's never enough when you've really got it." He jumped off the chair, picked up a butter knife from the table, then jumped back onto the chair and waved the thing high in the air, like the great sword Siegmund rips from the tree at the end of act one. He launched into the final sequence like a man possessed. He gave off the glow and glare of pure theater.

At the end, there was scattered applause, but he didn't acknowledge it. Even a few snide remarks from some less charitable listeners passed unnoticed. Richard Verdun had sung his heart out and I had heard him.

Schluss. Punkt. Ende.

CHAPTER ELEVEN

Richie

Right after I sing for Red Rebecca at *Tante* Olga, I've got a coaching with old man Greissle in his tiny apartment right by the Theater am Turm.

"Why must you act the fool?" he asks.

"To get the part, obviously."

"You think Herr Klauzer lets you sing Siegmund because you make a public spectacle?"

"It was the only way I could get her to hear me. She's the director. She calls the shots."

"She calls however she likes, but Herr Klauzer signs the contract. Sorry, *mein Lieber*, they get a name singer for Siegmund."

"But how? Those guys are booked years in advance."

"*Ach,* they pay enough and they find one."

"But I can sing Siegmund just as well as any of them."

"You know this. I know this. Maybe now even Frau Richartz knows this. But you are still the little understudy." He gives me one of his wise-guy looks. "Maybe not so little. But they do not want the understudy, they want the name."

I wish I could say Otto was wrong--I mean, Siegmunds don't grow on trees--but the rumor mill keeps churning out singers who aren't me. I eventually get so crazed and hyper-anxious that when Herr Klauzer visits a *Carmen* rehearsal, I ask him flat out if he's got some good news for me.

"About what?"

"Siegmund."

"I assume you are well aware that you are the understudy."

"Yeah, but I'd really like to know if I'll be singing it."

"Are you *able* to sing it?"

"Yes, absolutely. I'm even taking extra coaching with Herr Greissle and paying for it myself."

"You do not expect *us* to pay, do you?"

"No, no, of course not, I'm just saying I got the role in tip-top shape and Herr Greissle thinks so too."

"You pay him. Of course, he thinks that," he says and turns to go. Then he adds, over his shoulder, "You are the understudy, Herr Verdun, ready to step in at a moment's notice, exactly as in your contract. And that's that."

Another few days go by, and they still haven't found a Siegmund. That morning, I don't have any rehearsals, so I'm sleeping in when the phone jangles me awake.

"Herr Verdun, good morning. I hope I do not disturb. It's Frau Kasel, Herr Klauzer's assistant." I mumble something or other and she goes, "I am calling to inform you that we have to cancel your release next month."

"You mean, at the end of November?"

"Yes, exactly."

"But that's when I'm going back home. It's Thanksgiving, a big family holiday."

"I'm sorry, Frau Richartz absolutely insists that you be present for all the rehearsals of *Die Walkuere.* After all, you are the understudy for Siegmund."

"But I need to go home to my family."

"The end of November is the final week of stage rehearsals. Frau Richartz has to have her Siegmund."

That does it. Everything finally clicks. "Fantastic," I go, "I actually got the part!"

"No, no, not at all. I do not say this. All I say is we cancel your release--force majeure, we call it. We try to make it up to you next spring."

"But I'll be singing all the shows, right?"

"Sorry, it is not my place to say."

"Then let me speak to Herr Klauzer."

"Unfortunately, he is in Paris."

"Then give me the number of his hotel."

"You know he never allows this."

"Honey, sorry, but does Herr Klauzer really think I'm about to give up a chance to see my family at Thanksgiving while he plays his silly games? I'm calling my agent. I refuse to be treated like shit." I slam down the phone, too riled up to go back to bed, and start pacing. I got a lot of time to kill before I can call Erich in New York.

The phone rings again. I dash back to answer it.

"Herr Verdun, Reinbert Klauzer here. I trust it's not too early."

"What the hell is going on," I say. "Am I singing Siegmund or not?"

"Patience, patience, my friend—"

"No! Now! I've waited long enough."

"I know, and I do apologize. You have to appreciate that I am sometimes under extreme pressure to do things I really do not want to do and in this case, alas, it has also affected you."

"It sure as hell has."

"You see, once Herr Kuehn had eliminated himself from the cast, Frau Richartz told me she very much wanted to work with a certain singer, whose name we all know and whose name I shall not utter. As you probably realize by now, *la* Richartz can be very insistent, very obstinate. She forced me to embark on a complex and difficult negotiation with this dreadful man and his impossible agent, which prevented me from doing what I had wanted to do in the first place, which was, of course, to ask you to sing all six performances of *Die Walkuere.*"

This is, of course, a gigantic deal, the fulfillment of my wildest dreams, but I know Herr Eel well enough to keep the cheering to myself. "So," I ask warily, "I'll be doing the entire run?"

"Yes. Unfortunately, this also means that you need to be in Frankfurt throughout November. How can we rehearse a new production without its leading man?"

"My family's gonna take it real hard. Thanksgiving's a major deal for us."

"I know. I'll try to make it up to you as soon as possible."

"Okay. Fair enough."

"One other thing. You may not know that we are required to make an additional payment each time a company understudy steps in to perform. It's a modest fee, five hundred Deutschmarks, but in this case, since it's such an important role, I'm raising it to a thousand. That means you'll have six thousand extra Deutschmarks before the end of the year. You can be extremely generous with your Christmas presents."

The moment he says it, I realize I could also use the money to bring the whole family over to Frankfurt. What a great way to celebrate Thanksgiving.

"In any case, Herr Verdun, I feel extremely fortunate to have such an exceptional artist in my house and thank you from the bottom of my heart."

It's another four or five hours before I can get Erich Hirschmann on the horn. When I finally reach him, his reaction is completely bizarre.

"Of course, you do not accept his offer."

"I have to. I'm the understudy."

"With a one-year contract. They pay you a few extra marks and kick you out the door."

"Actually, they're paying me a whole lot of extra marks, a thousand for every performance."

"Do you know how much they pay any Siegmund, even the most insignificant? 10,000 Deutschmarks per performance. 10,000. And that does not include the air fare and the hotel and the per diem. Herr Klauzer has found for himself a bargain."

"Yes, and I get a terrific opportunity."

"And make no career!" Crazy, no? I get a giant break and my agent's yelling at me. "You think I let them keep you on this ridiculous one-year contract when you save for them the *Ring*? *Nein, niemals*! They go all over the world looking for a Siegmund. They even have the nerve to call me to see if Brent Cavendish can do it."

"But he's a baritone."

"And never has any free time. I tell Herr Klauzer he has already Verdun in his house, the perfect Siegmund, and he says, 'I easily find someone much better.'"

"He actually said that?"

"Of course. He takes you completely for granted. For him you are the understudy, the nobody."

"Okay, but I don't want to lose my big chance."

"Herr Verdun, let me do my job. I know very well how to make this Klauzer thank god he has in his company the remarkable Richard Verdun."

"Do it carefully, okay?"

This gets him even angrier. "You tell me what to do when you very nearly ruin everything, when you say *yes,* instead of *sorry, please call my agent, he makes for me all decisions.* Now I have to come in and say *wait, wait, my client is not your slave, you must pay him the proper amount and make the proper contract.*"

"But I'm the understudy."

"You are the star! You save the show! Either they treat you properly or they have no performance."

"Sounds like a plan to me."

CHAPTER TWELVE

TJ

Dad had been over there only a few weeks, when out of the blue he called me from Frankfurt and said he'd buy me the ticket if I could visit him around Columbus Day. Carol was too busy at work and Billy had just started senior year high school and actually had to study and Mom has this thing about flying, so I was the lucky one and, frankly, I was thrilled. I mean, how cool is that? I'd never been to Europe, none of my friends back in Graystone had either, but I knew from travel shows that it was pretty amazing, so of course I said yes, I'd take off in the middle of fall semester, but then Dad got all Dad and said maybe it wasn't such a good idea, I'd get behind in my studies, and I said the term's just getting started and my course load's pretty light and I can easily cut my Thursday ethics class so I'd have four full days there- which really was pretty crazy since I never dreamed I'd ever do something so wild and adventurous.

Long story short, I organized everything and flew over to Frankfurt the second week of October and there was Dad waiting for me at the airport, looking just like Dad, except he was wearing a brand-new long (and I mean way long, like flopping-round-his-ankles long) black leather coat, which he bought because all the guys at the opera house told him it keeps out rain and cold better than fleece or wool and that's pretty important over there, because if you think the weather's bad in Graystone, it's way worse in Frankfurt. I gotta admit that, even though Dad was real proud of his new purchase, he looked pretty ridiculous in it.

If you're gonna ask me what Frankfurt's like, I'm sorry to say I really can't tell you because just about the only thing I ever got to see was Dad's tiny apartment a few blocks from the theater and the opera house itself. I mean, the weather totally sucked. It rained every day, usually pretty hard, and that made sightseeing kinda unpleasant – okay, *very* unpleasant – and then when I did take a few walks around the town center, all I saw were these weird old buildings that looked totally new, which made the whole place seem like a German Disneyland and then I learned from Dad that they were brand-new reproductions of very old buildings which were bombed out during World War Two, which still seems to be going on there in some weird way, even though no one ever mentions it, like, *duh, what war*? Anyhow, when I strolled down the main drag of Frankfurt, it sure seemed boring, nothing much was going on. I don't speak German, so I couldn't strike up conversations with people on the street and that was unfortunate, since some of the ladies striding around looked pretty hot in a leather kind of way. I still regret I never got up the courage to speak to any of them, though in the end it's probably just as well, since Dad would have gone ballistic if he knew I'd been propositioning ladies out on the street. He was always very cool and easy about most guy things, like sports and cars. But when it came to women, he got totally uptight, "Respect your woman, boys, no sex before marriage." Yeah, Dad, as if.

Not speaking German was kind of a drag, but lots of people at the theater spoke English, which really helped, though I gotta say it wasn't the English I'm used to, kinda flat and British, with lots of mispronunciations, but, hey, who am I to talk? I still can't say three words of Spanish without my buddy Luis cracking up. Anyway, on the language front, Dad's got his own problems; he barely speaks

German and he's working in this German opera house, where they expect him to speak the language, so he's studying like crazy, not that it does much good. We'd bump into some buddy of his on the street and the guy would be talking at him a mile a minute and Dad would be nodding and smiling, and after the guy left, I'd ask what the man had said and he'd go, "Beats the hell outta me."

Anyhow, my visit rolled along in a low-key way until the last day, when Dad was gonna perform. I'd never been with him on a day when he had to sing. I didn't know he turned into an entirely different being. He basically slept the whole time and wouldn't say a word because he was saving his voice for the show. I mean, come on, he wouldn't even tell me where he kept the coffee, he just pointed. As luck would have it, it poured all day long, so I was stuck inside Dad's grim little apartment while he went mute and all I could get on his tiny black and white TV were programs in German about parrots and recycling and other exciting shit. I got so desperate I decided to start on my ethics paper, which meant I had to wade through Plato's *Republic*, which pretty much finished me off. As the day dragged on, I felt pretty stupid for having asked Dad to spring all that cash to fly me over to Germany. Some glamorous European getaway, him snoozing on the couch, me stuck with my Plato, while the rain slammed down outside.

Finally, after what felt like twenty years, Dad had to go off to the theater. He gave me my ticket, sketched a little map to get me there and left. Great, now what? I tried killing time by dressing for the opera very slowly, piece by piece, till I looked neat and tidy, not my usual sloppy Joe, because Dad said they dress for the opera. I brushed my hair over and over till it stood up just right and buffed and rebuffed my shoes and tied and retied my necktie until the dimple of the knot was exactly in the middle, right where it belongs, then I borrowed one of Dad's umbrellas and went outside into the rain, which hit me like a machine gun, and ran down the empty streets till I reached a crowd of wet unhappy Germans standing outside this big boxy building where the opera was.

I tried to go to my seat but they wouldn't let me in till I checked my coat and umbrella, so I went downstairs to this giant coatroom and left my soaking stuff with a lady who looked like my first-grade teacher Miss Masterson, only angrier. Then I went back upstairs and took a program and the lady held out her hand for money. I guess they charge over there for programs and not just ten cents. I decided not to buy one, since it wasn't even in English. Then I entered this tall gray cement room filled with old men wearing dark suits and women with harsh makeup and tight-fitting dresses, too tight for the shape they were in. Everything felt gloomy and businesslike– nothing like what we had back home, nothing open, lively or fun, everything serious, severe and solemn. Even the way they talked sounded different. No laughs or giggles, no highs or lows, just a steady even hum, like the dull sound of a low flying plane or a car in first gear. Finally, the house lights dimmed and I heard the short, sharp slaps of a thousand people clapping together almost in unison, very tight, very rigid, then it cut off sharply and the opera began.

It was the first I'd ever seen, so of course I was very curious. This was what my Dad had dreamed of for so many years, this was what he wanted to do. The audience seemed totally into it, really concentrating. The atmosphere was more like a church than a theater. The guy next to me would glare or shush me every time I shifted even a little in my seat, until I got so uptight and paranoid I felt I could barely breathe.

I almost didn't recognize Dad when he finally came out on stage. His costume and makeup made him look and feel so different, so new and unfamiliar, he just couldn't be the man I knew. And then he started to sing. Obviously, I'm no judge, but Dad was mighty impressive. He sounded really powerful, like he could rip us out of our seats. He did the action pretty well too, though I got kind of squirmy at some of the make-out sessions. I mean, there was my Dad all over the lady who sang Carmen, feeling her up and pumping it into her and I'm thinking *come on, man, this is gross.*

Anyway, after a while, Dad had a big solo and really laid into it. He socked it and rocked it and the public gave him a good hand. I did too, of course, though I didn't do much of anything at first, since I found it so freaking odd to see the guy who's been part of my life since forever up there on stage with this giant audience staring at him, judging him. But he didn't care, he batted the music out to us full force and it couldn't have been easy, hell, it probably isn't even natural for any human being to make so much sound, and yet he did and it was really something, almost heroic, to see him make that gigantic effort. Good for you, Dad. Way to go.

By the end, everyone seemed totally lost in the opera, in this incredibly mean and depressing story, and when Carmen suddenly spit at her jerky lover boy just before the end, everyone gasped, me included. I mean, come on, lady, that's my Dad you're spitting at. Finally, Dad got his own back and did Carmen in and I felt this insane release of tension, like I'd been trapped in a cage and suddenly set free. Then came the applause, strong and steady, and while I gotta admit the lady doing Carmen got most of it, Dad did pretty well too. Some people even shouted bravo, so I did likewise, which caused the guy sitting next to me to glare once again. I didn't care. He was my Dad and he was great and now the show was over and we could finally go out and get some food like normal folk, because, frankly, I was starving. My metabolism's pretty intense and for me to hold off dinner until after 10 P.M. is really tough, if not downright excruciating, so I sprinted backstage and went past room after room filled with singers taking off wigs and costumes, until I finally got to a closed door with this sign Herr Verdun. I entered and found my Dad stripped down to his shorts, which wasn't a pretty sight. I'm sorry to say he'd gained twenty or thirty pounds since last summer, too much potatoes and wurst, I figure. Anyway, there he was dripping with sweat, toweling off, talking to this elegant slim guy in dark jeans and a black turtleneck who was reading from a tiny notebook.

Dad beamed when I came in. "Toni, this is my son Timmy." We shook hands. "Toni's the assistant director. He's the guy who keeps me in line."

"Sounds like a tough job."

"My son's a kidder, just like his dad."

"I see. Then I watch myself very carefully." Toni smiled at me in a tense kind of way. Everything about him was immaculate, like he'd been dressed by some kind of super chic robot. "What happened with the blood tonight?"

"You missed the best part, son. After I knife her, there's usually a bloodbath on stage. Takes me half an hour to shower the stuff off."

"We need this stuff, we want this."

"I know. Germans love the sight of blood."

Toni got all excited. "*Nein,* we do not. We are a pacifist country."

"Easy man, lighten up." Dad seemed pretty amused that Toni lost his cool.

"You do not make it for me very easy."

"I know, I'm just a big, bad, vulgar American. Please forgive me." Dad was looking my way again. "I keep trying to kid him, but he doesn't go for it."

"We are here to work, Richard, not play."

"In my opinion, all work and no play sucks."

"I was asking what happens with the blood."

"The bag wouldn't pop. I punched it as hard as I could."

"I speak to the *Requisitenmeister.* It's very important."

"I know and I swear I gave it my all. The bag just wouldn't break."

"Okay, we take care of this. One other thing, the act three move to the stairs comes after you hit her, not before. It makes no sense for you to run all the way up the stairs, then in two bars you run down again like a crazy man and hit her."

"So that's why it felt odd."

"Of course, it looks ridiculous." Toni couldn't have been much older than I was and he was reaming out my Dad. Amazing. "Richard, you must promise me you do not forget this."

"Any chance I can shower now? I'm starting to stink up the dressing room."

Toni checked through his notes. "*Ja,* okay, that is all. This was a good show, Richard, much improved."

"God knows I keep trying."

"Maybe you try even harder, especially in the third act."

"*Jawohl.* As you command. Any other words of wisdom?"

"Just be sure to wash under the armpits."

"Want to come and help?"

"Thanks. I think I keep this time dry." Toni smiled as Dad passed by him.

"Be with you in five, son." Dad snapped his towel at me and ran down the hall to the shower.

I turned back to Toni. "That scene at the end where Carmen spits at Jose is pretty intense."

"Yes, your father has a very surprising talent for violence."

After a pretty long, pretty awkward silence, he spoke again. "You know, when your father signed his contract here, the people were very suspicious. They wonder how someone can come to opera so late and still be good. But I think he now wins them over."

"Yeah, it seemed like everyone was pleased tonight. Except for you, of course."

"This is my job. I must always be correcting the artists."

"It's pretty weird for me to think of Dad as an artist, whatever the hell that means."

"No one knows, but everyone has an opinion."

"There wasn't much culture around where I grew up. I was more focused on sports and friends. I didn't see my first play until junior year in high school."

"Which play was that?"

"*Our Town.*" Toni gave a blank stare. "It's a kind of corny love story. Small town guy marries small town girl and then she dies."

"It sounds like a bad opera."

"Nah, it's just a play. It's done all the time back home." Toni had a kind of pitying look on his face, like he really felt sorry for someone as deprived as I was.

"You know, I enjoy very much to work with your father. He keeps me in my toes."

I couldn't help laughing. "We say *on* our toes, *on.* Like ballet dancers, you know?"

"*Ach*, forgive me. My English gets bad since I come back from New York."

"You used to live in New York?"

"*Ja*, for three months. I did not want to leave. I love that city, always new, always different. It is not boring like Frankfurt."

"Yeah, Frankfurt sure seems dull."

"The only good thing we have here is opera, theater and clubs."

"Clubs like we got in the States?"

"Of course, why not?"

"I figured they wouldn't want them here. Everyone's so serious."

"Only at the opera. Across the river we have Sachsenhausen. It is much livelier. You should go there."

"Unfortunately, I'm leaving tomorrow."

"What about tonight?"

"I'm eating dinner with my Dad."

"And then what?"

"I don't know, getting some sleep."

"Why sleep when you can go out and dance? Hausenheim is a very good club, very young."

"They got hot babes there?"

"Everyone is hot, even me. I take you."

"I don't think so. It's the last time I'll be seeing my Dad until Thanksgiving."

"He can survive this – he'll be too tired after dinner, anyway. The club is very good. Only hot young people. No one from the opera is allowed."

"Toni, you're from the opera."

"I am so hot they make in my case an exception." A funny guy, this Toni. I really was starting to enjoy him. "So, we meet here at the stage entrance in two hours. First you have dinner with your father and then Timmy and Toni have fun."

"Call me TJ, okay? Timmy makes me feel about five years old. Only my parents call me that."

"*Ach,* parents..."

At that point Dad bounced back into the room, all pink and refreshed from his shower. "What's that about parents?" Neither of us said anything. "Come on, I can take it."

"Well, Dad, just so you know, Toni wants to take me to this club after dinner."

"What kind of club?"

"The kind you are too old for," Toni said.

"I'm not too old for anything. Am I, son?"

"In this case you probably are."

"So, what kind of club is it?"

"Very clean, very safe. Nothing to worry."

"The only father who doesn't worry is a dead father. You sure you really want to do this, son? You got a full week of classes facing you."

"I can sleep going back on the plane."

"Can you?"

"Of course, I can sleep anywhere."

Dad looked unconvinced and Toni looked eager to leave. "I leave you two to continue this great discussion. TJ, I see you here at half before midnight. Okay?" And Toni was gone.

Dad was still wearing his parent look. "Son, you know what side of the bed Toni's on, right?"

"Of course."

"Maybe there's only guys at that club."

"I can handle it. Toni's a total pushover."

"What about his friends?"

"First of all, I'm sure it's just a regular club with lots of girls. Second, Toni works at the opera. He sees you all the time. He won't do anything foolish."

"What about you?"

"Dad, I said I can take care of myself, okay?" Dad always trusted me, always gave me my head of steam. Growing up we had this low-key, easy relationship, pretty much I keep out of your hair, you keep out of mine. He made me laugh, he always cheered me on. Yeah, things could get weird when we were roughhousing or shooting hoops because Dad was so competitive (and not very athletic) but early on I decided it was far better to let the old man win once in a while than deal with a sore loser. Basically, though, I figured I was pretty lucky in the dad department.

I sat and watched as he got dressed. He had just bought this shiny gray suit and was very proud of it. He claimed it was the latest fashion by this famous Italian designer and he really needed to look sharp since he was the new leading tenor at the opera house. As he struggled to put the thing on (it was cut way too tight), I remembered all those plaid shirts and baggy chinos he used to wear back home. They were sloppy, I guess, and kind of faded, but they covered up his belly and gave off this warm and cozy vibe. The new suit made him look awkward and uncomfortable, but I kept my mouth shut.

We made our way through the rain (yeah, it was still pouring) to this big fancy restaurant not far from the opera house. We entered a high-ceilinged room filled with diners, most of whom reeked of old age and money. Once we took off our coats and hats and shook off the rain, some of the people realized that Dad had just arrived and started applauding. There even was a bravo or two. He gave the crowd a bow and then turned back to me with this giant shit-eating grin. "I guess your Dad's really catching on here," he said and turned back to bow once again, but he wasn't fast enough, everyone had gone back to eating, so Dad looked kind of disappointed and shrugged his shoulders as if to say *go figure* and we followed the waiter in silence to our table.

Once we were seated, there was a commotion at the other end of the dining room. "You gotta see this, son. Frau Olga's making her grand entrance."

He pointed to this very old woman, all hunched over, who had just come out of the kitchen followed by two young waiters carrying a small bronze sculpture of a naked lady, a real babe. Dad explained this was a sculpture of the old lady made by a famous artist who was her lover at the time. She usually didn't show the piece because it was so valuable, but when she did, she made a giant deal of it, with two waiters serving as a kind of bizarre honor guard. There even was a bouquet of red roses at its base, which made it seem like a religious icon, an extremely weird one.

What a contrast between that sexy girl in bronze and the actual woman herself. I mean, this Frau Olga was really, really old, more like a crone than a living, breathing human, so frail and skinny you thought she might go at any minute. That didn't stop her from fixing herself up like a hooker with firehouse red lipstick and gobs of bright rouge. She was real generous with the perfume too. I could smell it halfway across the room.

From the way she lurched and swayed from table to table she had to be hurting with every step. Yet she seemed to be having a ball. She worked the crowd like a pro, kissing the men, hugging the women, chatting and giggling and flirting. She was incredibly proud of the sculpture. She kept stroking and patting it, as if to prove how gorgeous and sexy and irresistible she'd been. I gotta confess the sculpture was pretty hot. The girl was sprawled back on some kind of sofa, her breasts tight and high, her slinky legs pretty much wide open to the world.

Dad was completely awestruck. When Frau Olga finally reached our table, he rose to his feet, took her bony hand in both of his and kissed it, like he was an old-world diplomat in one of those black and white movies.

"*Ach*, Herr Verdun, they tell me you sing magnificent tonight."

"We do the best we can, ma'am. This here's Frau Olga, son. She was a famous actress after the war, and now she runs this place." He reached over and tried to hug her but she squirmed away, flashing a little come-on smile, not a pretty sight on a lady her age. Dad leaned in to take a closer look at the bronze. "Olga, you were one gorgeous creature."

"*Ja.* This work is now very valuable. The museums all the time ask for it, but Oskar made it for me and so I keep it."

"Who's Oskar?" Dad asked.

"Kokoschka. I show you his pieces upstairs, remember?" Dad gave her his *I'm just from Graystone* look and she shook her head. "*Ach,* Herr Verdun ... Oskar made this during the month we spent in Vienna together. I was only a child but I made him very happy."

Dad gave Olga's scarecrow body the once-over. "You could make me happy too."

She roared with laughter. "*Ach, mein Gott,* you have a wife."

"She's back in Michigan. Right, son?"

The old lady, who had only focused on Dad during the whole of their conversation, suddenly looked at me like I was this giant surprise. "*Nein, nicht moeglich.* This beautiful young man is your son?"

"That's Timmy, Olga, the oldest of my two boys."

"Two boys? *Nein,* you are much too young to have such a grown man as your son."

"Oh, he isn't all that grown up. I still have to pick up his socks."

"But the women like him very much, I think," said Olga, staring hungrily at me.

"Maybe. Can't understand why."

"So, when do they come over?"

"Who?"

"Your wife, your family."

"Not anytime soon."

"But how do you do this? You sing here, they live there?"

"For the moment. The wife's got a good job at the high school. Timmy's younger brother Billy is still a student there and my daughter, well, she's been out on her own for some time now."

"Impossible. You must marry when you are fifteen."

"Actually, Kit and I were twenty."

"Babies shouldn't marry."

"Maybe not, but we did."

"You think she not give you sex otherwise?"

Dad didn't seem too pleased with the direction their chat was taking, so he went, "Gimme a break, Olga. I just moved to Frankfurt a few months ago. Kit and I need some time to work things out."

Frau Olga wasn't letting him off the hook. "Herr Carson, he sings here at the opera for the last ten years. He has everyone with him, the wife, the children. They go to German schools. They speak perfect German. The family lives the life here together."

"I know, I know. We're working on it."

I had so much stuff going on, with college and all, that I hadn't ever really thought about it, but, I mean, Mom and Dad were living separate lives. For years and years Mom had been stuck at home while we were growing up. Now at last she had a great job, a job that really delighted her, and she wasn't like me, she couldn't just hop on a plane and fly over whenever she liked. She was terribly afraid of flying. So what was going to happen? How were they going to work it out?

"You need the wife here, Herr Verdun, a healthy man like you."

"That I do, Olga, that I do." Then he went into jokester mode and said, "If she doesn't make it, can you and me set up house together?"

Olga found this completely hilarious, but I found Dad's flirting pretty pathetic.

"*Herr Intendant!*" Olga suddenly shouted and made her wobbly way towards the door, followed by the waiters and her portable sculpture. A tall, thin man had just entered, escorting a lady I immediately recognized as the woman who had just sung Carmen. Dad explained that the man was Herr Klauzer, his boss at the opera, the guy who made all the decisions. "Herr Klauzer and the Carmen are real good friends, if you catch my drift, so if you could butter the lady up a bit, I'd appreciate it."

"Gotcha," I said.

By this time, Frau Olga was greeting this Klauzer guy like a long-lost relative, with kisses on both cheeks. She didn't seem nearly as interested in the Carmen. She just shook her hand, smiled politely, and pointed in our direction. Dad jumped to his feet and waved. Carmen didn't seem to notice, which was kind of odd, since Dad's a hard one to miss, but his boss acknowledged us and set out for our table, leading his girlfriend by the hand. She wasn't in any big hurry to follow. The diners had finally realized who was in their midst and were cheering enthusiastically – much more enthusiastically than they had for Dad.

Boy, did that Carmen lady milk the applause. First, she gave this *who, me?* modest look, followed by an awestruck, touched-to-the-depths-of-my soul humble routine, ending up with a hand-on-the-heart, undying-gratitude act that nearly made me puke. Herr Klauzer had a hard time tearing her away from her adoring public, but after a while she realized enough was enough and they headed over to our table. Klauzer was a pretty impressive type, a real take-charge guy, tall, straight as a board, stern and scary smart-looking, with wire rim glasses and a broad clean-shaven head, like a German Mr. Clean.

"Sit down, sit down please, Herr Verdun. You need your rest. You worked hard tonight."

"Nah, I'm rough, I'm tough. I could do it all over again right this minute."

"Ah yes, that relentless American energy. My advice to you is spare yourself, guard your resources. You'll need them very much for Siegmund." He presented the Carmen to us. "You know this woman, I believe?

"Yes, indeedy. How are you doing, hon? Hope I didn't beat you up too much in that death scene."

"I think I somehow survive," she said. Dad pecked her on the cheek. It didn't improve her mood, so Dad turned back to his boss. "Reinbert, this here's my son Timmy."

Herr Klauzer shook my hand and formally introduced me to Frau Romanescu, the Carmen, a big sexy lady, who clearly didn't enjoy socializing with low life like Dad and me. Remembering that Dad wanted me to make nice, I gave her my baby-blue-eyes look, the one all the girls go for, and trotted out the biggest compliments I could think of, *you sounded fantastic, I really loved it*, etcetera, etcetera, but it didn't seem to impress her. She heard me out patiently, said she was hungry, then went off to order her supper.

Once she was out of the way, Herr Klauzer gave Dad his full attention, discussing the performance in great detail and amazingly good English. If I hadn't known he was German, I'd have thought he was a British lawyer or something. He hit a lot of the same points as Toni, only he was even pickier. At the end of his long laundry list of mistakes and mess ups, he suddenly changed gears and said, "You know, Richard, I make all these criticisms only because you have such promise. Each performance improves on the last."

"I'm trying my best, Reinbert, I really am."

"I know and I very much appreciate it, just as I very much appreciate that you jump in for the new *Walkuere*. I know it involves personal sacrifice but you can be certain we will make it up to you."

"I'd very much appreciate it," said Dad. With that, Herr Klauzer stood, shook Dad's hand, nodded briskly to me and left. "Typical Reinbert – he does his business and he's off."

"What was that he was saying about 'personal sacrifice'?"

"I'm doing them a big favor. The lead tenor for this new production of *Walkuere* suddenly got sacked, so I'm jumping in to save the show. Rehearsals start next week."

"That's good news, right?"

"I'll say. It's the major event of the season. Of course, it's a lot of extra work. I've been studying the part like crazy."

"You'll do great, Dad."

"I'd better. It's my first Wagner. If it goes right, it'll put me in a whole new bracket." He hesitated for a moment, then said, "This is a tough one, son. Mom was gonna tell you once you got back, but I guess there's no time like the present. I'm not making it home for Thanksgiving this year. *Walkuere* opens the end of November. The final dress falls smack on the big day itself. I've got to stay here in Frankfurt." I didn't say anything, I couldn't. I was shocked. "When I signed my contract, I made sure they gave me a release so I could be home for the holidays, but they can drop it in case of an emergency."

"What the hell's an operatic emergency?"

"In this case, a giant stroke of luck."

"Not for us. It ruins Thanksgiving."

"That's bullwacky and you know it. The people in Frankfurt are so desperate for me to save their ass on *Walkuere,* my agent got them to make me a permanent company member, no more of this provisional bullshit. I get lots of benefits, much more money and plenty of time off. It's terrific news. Even for you."

"But Dad, I was going to bring a girl home for Thanksgiving this year. Her name's Consuela. She's pretty great..." After that, I couldn't get any more words out.

"Look, I figured you guys and Mom would fly over here instead. We'd all have Thanksgiving in Frankfurt. You'd see the new show. We'd have our turkey. But you know Mom and flying." He looked away. His shoulders slumped.

"Couldn't they find anyone else to sing?"

"Son, it's a giant opportunity. If I really hit it big, every opera house on earth will want me."

"Lucky you."

Dad picked up the menu. "So, what are you in the mood for?"

"Turkey." It shot out of me before I could even think. Dad glared at me, then sat there smoldering quietly. After a while, he called the waiter and ordered steak for both of us, while I fell into one of my moods. Consuela calls it cave time, when I get bad thoughts and sulk.

"Look, I thought it would be so cool to have Thanksgiving over here this year."

"But Mom can't fly."

"Of course, she can. She just won't deal with it."

"Dad, it's a phobia."

He threw his napkin down on the table. "It's a pain in the ass, a royal pain in the ass. I don't know how many times I've asked your mother to take one of those fear of flying courses. They've got an incredible success rate. It could fix her right up, but, oh no, she won't do it, claims it's a waste of money." I didn't reply but remembered that awful day in the airport when she was trembling so bad I thought she was going to die. "All your mother has to do is take that course."

"Whatever you say, Herr Verdun."

"Look, I'm here because everyone in my family, and I mean everyone, even you, thought it would be terrific for me to quit my job and follow my dreams and I followed those dreams further than anyone ever expected. All I ask from you is a little patience and understanding while I fight my way to the top and I can get there, son, I really can, as long as I have your support, as long as you're all on my side." Dad reached for my arm. I pulled away.

We pretty much stopped talking until the food arrived, two perfect rectangles of beef with neat crisscross grill marks and a silver tray of ivory-white boiled potatoes, incredibly smooth and clean looking, like pieces of polished stone. As I started in on the steak, the bad feelings drained away. I felt human again. After a nice, calm period of eating, Dad asked, "Still pissed off, or can I ask you a little favor?"

"What is it?"

"When you get back home, could you be sure to tell Mom how nice Frankfurt is?"

"Dad, the whole city sucks."

"You didn't see it. You were stuck indoors. Frankfurt's really an attractive, fun place, one of Europe's great cities. Mom would love it."

"How's she even gonna get here?"

"If you and your sister asked, she'd take one of those fear of flying courses and that would solve everything. Besides, there's lots of great things to do in Frankfurt, plenty of English speakers too, even English language schools. Mom could probably get a job in one of those."

"You mean you want her to move here?"

"Why not? She'd have a wonderful time."

"I thought you were in Frankfurt for a year or two. Are you saying it's gonna be forever?"

"I'm saying I need to be with my wife, and you kids can make that happen. And it would be great if Mom could hear from you in particular, seeing as how you've actually been here and seen the apartment."

"It's a tiny white box, like for witness relocation."

"It's convenient, it's affordable."

"Mom will hate it."

"She'll fix it up in no time. Come on, son, where's that old Verdun spirit?" He scrunched up his face and put on a fake British accent. "I am absolutely convinced that if you would make use of your considerable powers of persuasion, you and your sister would be able to convince your dear mother to fly to Germany and experience the thrilling life one can have in Frankfurt."

"Especially when it rains."

"And your Dad has to sing a performance." We both cracked up. It was hard to stay mad at Dad for long. "Deal? Give it a try?"

"Well, okay, if that's what you really want."

"I do, son. Thanks." He patted me on the back and went off to the bathroom. After he left, I started feeling really strange, like something was way out of kilter. I tried to shake it off, tried to concentrate on Toni and the club and the evening ahead, but it didn't do any good. My dad was really going to be living here for a good long while, maybe even forever.

When he came back, I asked, "Isn't there something you need to tell me?"

"About what?"

"You and Mom."

He laughed. "Everything's fine, son. Don't worry."

"I'm grown up. I can handle it."

"Sit back. Relax. Take a load off. How about dessert? They've got this amazing apple strudel." I crossed my arms tight across my chest and waited. "Look, I'll be home at Christmas. We'll sort it out then. In the meantime, let's have a good time, okay? Dessert?"

"I don't want any."

"What's the matter? Worried about making weight?

"No."

"What's going on with wrestling anyway? You haven't said anything about it since you've been here. Had any matches yet?

"No."

"Hasn't the season started?"

"It started."

"Is something wrong?"

"I'm trying to have a nice time here. Let's change the subject, okay?"

"Look, I know you had a tough season last year. But that's how it goes. You just fight your way back to the top."

"Dad, I'm not wrestling any more. I quit."

"You quit?" Dad was stunned. "What about that scholarship?"

"Typical. All you think about is money." The moment I said it, I knew I shouldn't have. Dad's whole face turned red, even his bald spot. It was pretty scary. "Sorry... They said I could keep it. My grades are good enough."

"Well, that's something."

"Yeah, great, I'm not a total fuckup."

Dad wasn't real happy with that either, but all he said was, "So, why did you quit?"

"Dad, come on, there's no point."

"Of course, there's a point."

"Not if I'm just a sub. Not if I'm sitting on the bench."

"You didn't make the cut?"

"There's a new guy in my weight class, a freshman. He's really tough. I can't beat him."

"Never say never."

"Dad, I won't ever beat him. No way. Even coach can't pin him."

"So what? That gives you a goal. Go for it."

"Dad, don't you get it? I'm just not good enough."

"Son, all you have to do is work, make it a long-term project and—"

I cut him off. "Dad, it's fine. I quit. Everything's back to normal."

"It's not normal for my Timmy guy to get beat by some freshman and just quit. No sir, that's sad. That's sick. You gotta fight. You gotta stand up like a man."

"I am a man. Just not a very good wrestler."

"Don't you talk like that. Don't you put yourself down."

"It's the truth."

Dad was furious. He grabbed me by the shoulders and shoved his face real close to mine. "You always do this. The moment things get tough you throw in the towel. You did it with calculus. You did it with hockey. And now you're doing it with wrestling. I paid for fancy conditioning machines and after-school coaching and expensive training camps year after year, cost me a goddamn fortune, but I didn't object. Why? You were good at it. You worked hard. You had success. Along comes some smart-ass freshman, throws you a little curve ball and you give up. What the hell's that? What sort of guy are you? Be a man."

"*I am one!*"

"Bullshit! Everyone thought I was nuts, a car salesman going out and singing opera at age forty-two. Impossible. Unheard of. Never gonna happen. I had no technique. I couldn't act. I wasn't musical. I didn't know languages. Every single thing an opera singer needs I didn't have, except a voice. And guts. That's what really counts. Guts. Determination. Balls. I didn't crack. I didn't run. And now I'm first tenor at the Frankfurt Opera."

"So fucking what?" I pushed Dad away and ran out of Tante Olga's and dashed through the rain to the opera house where Toni was waiting.

In the taxi to Hausenheim, he started making a play for me. Before he could really get anywhere, I popped a sleeper on him, which put an end to it fast. (I mean, no one gets fresh with TJ Verdun, *no one!*) When he finally came to, he looked so ashamed and frightened, I decided to laugh it off and let the whole thing slide. We left the cab and, drenched to the bone–yeah, the rain never once let up–we made our way to this amazing club with television monitors everywhere and jagged neon lights and fabulous pounding music and hundreds of kids dancing and drinking and hooting and hollering like a pack of demented robots.

It wasn't long before I met up with this incredibly hot girl, Monika, who really turned me on and for the first and last time in my life I got aroused so fast that I dragged her off to the men's room where we fucked like bunnies in a tight little stall. We weren't the only ones doing it there, of course, and that made it even more exciting. I knew Consuela wouldn't like it, but that night in Frankfurt it was something I had to do and it helped, it really did. It got me free, worked out all my simmering fury. And the next day, things were fine with Dad, no lectures, no drama. We even cracked some lousy jokes. It was just like old times, like nothing had ever happened, except, of course, it had.

CHAPTER THIRTEEN

Richie

Once Timmy leaves Frankfurt I figure I'll miss the family more than ever, especially our big Thanksgiving feast, but the Frankfurt Opera shovels so much work at me so fast, gives me so many coachings and stagings and orchestra readings and tech rehearsals and costume fittings and interviews and publicity shots, rinse, wash and repeat, that I'm totally lost in Operaland and only break free when it's Christmas vacation and I'm finally back with the family in Graystone.

Things have changed. Kit drives over to her office every day now, ordering books and materials and meeting with architects and donors and trustees and teachers and plumbers and janitors- you name it, she's got it- which leaves me plenty of free time to take out my score and trusty Walkman and wrap my head around *Butterfly auf deutsch,* which is my next assignment at the opera. It's quite a trip, the German makes it sound like some grim World War Two drama. I'm not even Pinkerton any more, I'm Linkerton, since *pinken* means *pee* in German. I haven't sung the part in nearly a year, so there's lots of catching up to do.

Just as I'm making some headway, Timmy shows up with this sultry Puerto Rican chick, Consuela, with gleaming black curls and shiny white teeth and eyes only for him. We put her up in the attic in the maid's room while Timmy stays down below in his. That was the deal, no sleeping in the same bedroom. He's only nineteen and she's just a freshman, which means she's probably underage and I don't run that kinda place. I know my colleagues in Frankfurt would laugh if I told them – they think nothing of their little Max or Liesl getting it on at age fifteen. Sorry, folks, I'm American. Sex is only for grownups. Now, it could be that young Timmy is scampering up to the attic every night without my knowing, but if he is, at least I'm making him hustle.

On Christmas Eve, Carol comes by early with Hal, her fiancé. Yeah, that's what she calls him and that's what I hope he is. I found out about him last summer and wasn't too thrilled when Kit told me they were living together in a tiny apartment out by the mall. She assured me he was a standup guy and madly in love with our daughter. She also pointed out that it's 1983, they're both over twenty-one, so I can put away my shotgun and join the twentieth century.

I barely know this Hal, we met only once or twice last summer, and I'm trying my very best to like him. While Carol goes off to the kitchen to help her mother, I chat up my very earnest and very wary possible future son-in-law, but all the time we're talking I'm going over *Butterfly* in my head. They changed *addio, fiorito asil* to *lebwohl, mein Bluetenreich*, talk about losing something in translation, and I keep wondering if it's *Bluetenreich* or *Blumenreich*. *Blumen*, I know, is flowers, but what the hell's *Blueten*? So, while Hal's doing his best to keep our conversation going, I'm hearing him with only half an ear. Every now and then, Carol rushes in to give him a taste of something she's whipped up in the kitchen and only offers it to me when I remind her of my existence. Of course, it tastes great, because just like Kit, Carol's a champ in the kitchen, as opposed to me, who, like both my sons, is a total dud at cooking. In all my time in Frankfurt, I never cooked myself a meal. (Thank god they got takeout over there.)

Kit finally calls us to the table and even Billy, who's a full-fledged teenager by now, honors us with his appearance. We sit down and gorge ourselves on one of Kit's standout feasts with prime ribs of beef as the centerpiece. At the end, after we demolish coconut angel food cake and chocolate pecan pie, I stagger to my feet and clink my glass to get everyone's attention and, believe me, it takes time. Timmy's sniping at Billy as usual, or is it vice versa, his new girlfriend is trying to referee, good luck with that, while Carol and her current squeeze seem totally lost in la la land. In fact, the only person at the table who really seems interested is Kit and I've told her most of it already. I keep clinking away until Kit claps her hands and says, "Okay, everyone, enough chitter chatter, Dad wants to make a speech."

"Not exactly a speech, but even though we must have chalked up hundreds of dollars' worth of phone calls, you guys still don't know much about what's going on with me over in Frankfurt – even you, Timmy, despite your recent visit." He gives me his wise-ass look, but I pay him no heed. "Anyway, now that we're all together, I'd like to tell you a few things and brag a bit too, since I just had another big success. But, first off, let me say, thanks, Kit and Carol, this was stupendous." The kids clap and shout *hear, hear*! and clink their glasses. "Second, I'm happy to say it's official now. I just signed my new three-year contract as permanent company member with full benefits, health insurance, pension, a lifetime German work permit, a salary twice the old one and four weeks free the first two years, six during the last, which really matters, since guest engagements pay way better than my standard company fee."

I pause, expecting a little reaction, not wild cheers maybe, but a fair amount of respect and appreciation, since it's a very big deal. "I promise you it's a really great development. I'm getting a reputation as a real Heldentenor and Heldentenors are the best paid singers on the planet."

Even after this, the family's pretty quiet. "Any chance I could get a little support here, a little enthusiasm?" I clap my hands together lightly to start them off and Kit, bless her heart, joins in quickly. The others eventually get the idea, though they seem unsure why or for what they're applauding. "Thank you, thank you," I say, shooting off a few bows. "I bet you guys are curious about what it's like to work in a big opera house."

Timmy interrupts. "I'll tell you. Dad sits around all day in his boxy little apartment, it's about the size of our laundry closet."

"Come on, it's way bigger than that."

"Not! Anyway, all Dad does is stare at scores and, get this, on the day of a performance, he goes mute. He doesn't talk at all, not one single word."

"But Dad's the biggest talker on the planet," goes Billy.

"Not any more. He's given it up."

"Only on days when I sing." I wait for the laughter to stop, then go, "As soon as you're done ragging me, maybe I can get on with my story?"

"You're actually telling one?" says Kit and everyone laughs again.

"So, okay, you gotta understand that over there, the stage director is king. They can ask us to do all kinds of stuff and no matter how hard it may be, or whether or not we like it, we basically have to do it. Maybe a few big stars can get away with *thanks, but no thanks,* like the gal who sang Carmen, Frau Romanescu. Remember her, Timmy?"

"Yeah, she was a creep."

"She most certainly was. And is. Well, she can do whatever she wants because she's sleeping with the boss. Yours truly doesn't have that option."

"I should hope not," says Kit.

"Anyway, a month or so ago, we're staging the end of the first act of *Walkuere,* where Siegmund, my character, runs off with Sieglinde, his newfound love. She's also his sister, which makes it a bit icky, but the music's so fabulous you just go with it. Anyway, the audience is supposed to understand that after the curtain goes down, Siegmund and Sieglinde have sex somewhere out in the woods, because in the next act she shows up pregnant with her brother's kid."

"Ew, he's gotta turn out a moron," says Billy, who was very into biology at the time.

"That's not the point, Billy. The point is, the director is Rebecca Richartz, who's famous for her wild and crazy productions. We call her Red Rebecca, because she's from East Germany and keeps trying to convince us how great things are over there, when everyone knows it's a shithole."

"Richard, perhaps you could tone down the cursing?"

"Sorry, hon, you're right. In light of what Mom just said, I want to be sure that everyone's okay with full frontal nudity, because that's what my story's about."

Everyone looks kinda startled. There's a little pause, then Kit says with a knowing smile, "I'm sure everyone here is mature enough to handle it."

"Not Billy," goes Timmy.

"Can't you ever give it a rest?" the little guy shoots back.

"Not till you grow up."

"I am grown up."

They go back and forth until Kit yells, "Guys, that's quite enough!" She's fed up with both of them by now and so am I.

"You know, I traveled four thousand miles to be here with you and it's just awful to see you still fighting like five-year-olds."

The boys gradually simmer down and I continue my little story. "So, we're working on the end of the first act and it soon becomes clear the director doesn't want it to end with us running off into the woods like we're supposed to. No, she wants me to strip buck naked and hammer away at the soprano as the curtain falls."

"*Hammer away*? What kind of talk is that?"

"Sorry, Kit, I was trying to keep it G rated."

Carol and Consuela look shocked. The boys do too, but they're also intrigued, like *they really pay you to do shit like that*?

"In any case, here's my dilemma. There's no way in hell I'll do it, but I have to by law. The guy they originally scheduled for my part refused to snort cocaine at the beginning of act one. Oh yeah, that's something else I gotta do, snort cocaine. Unfortunately, it's not the real stuff."

"Richard!"

"Sorry, hon. Anyway, the guy wouldn't do the cocaine and they fired him on the spot, even though he'd been with the company twenty-five years, which is how I got my big break. Anyone care to guess how your brilliant father handled the situation?"

"You said you'd get pneumonia if you were naked on stage?"

"Very clever, Kit. But there's plenty of nudity in the new *Manon* and that crazy Gregor Nordlinger goes full nature boy at the end of *Wozzeck.*"

"They seem to like their singers undressed over there," goes Kit.

"And how. So, here's my solution. The minute I hear what the director wants, no pause, no hesitation – bam! – I take off all my clothes."

"You do?" goes Kit.

"Yeah, I had to show I was totally with the program. So there I am in my altogether, shivering and quivering in the center of the not very well-heated rehearsal room, and I say to Frau Richartz, 'As you can see, I'm perfectly happy taking off my clothes, even if I am a bit chilly. My only question is, does the public really want to see this?' Red Rebecca takes it totally in stride. She walks around me very slowly, like I'm a slab of raw beef being checked out by the health inspector."

"Ew, Dad," says Billy, "gross."

"I second that," goes Kit.

"Me too," says Carol.

"Anyway, the *Frau Regisseur* takes her own sweet time checking out my merchandise, then says, 'I thought you Americans were puritans.' 'Not this one,' I go. She laughs and that's the tip off, everyone in the room heaves a sigh of relief. 'All right, Verdun, you win. I find another ending. Please dress.'"

"That really happened?" asked Kit.

"It sure as hell did. I beat the lady at her own game."

"What are those people doing to you over there? The whole thing sounds mortifying."

"Actually, it was kinda fun."

"Fun?" She's astonished. So is everyone else. I assumed they'd take it as a cute little backstage story, but, no, my family finds the whole thing bizarre, even distasteful.

I take a deep breath. The next thing I need to say is way more difficult. "I just got a call from the rehearsal department.".

"Today? On Christmas Eve?" asks Billy.

"Yeah, I know, it's very unusual. They've got a big emergency over there. They have to put in a new Sieglinde for *Walkuere* and we have to rehearse on January 2."

"But that's when you were supposed to leave," says Kit.

"I know, I just moved my flight up to New Year's Eve."

Kit turns white as the tablecloth. "Without even telling me?"

"They put me on the spot. I had to act fast."

There's this long grim silence. Finally, Kit says, "I'm sure you realize how upset we all are."

"I do, I do. It really breaks my heart."

Timmy mutters, "Bullshit."

"I heard that, Timothy," goes Kit.

"Come on, Ma, it's all a giant act."

"IT IS NOT!" I shout.

Kit tries to calm us down. "Of course, it's upsetting that Dad won't be here New Year's Eve, but he's got an obligation to his employers."

"It's called force majeure," I say lamely. "They put it into my contract."

"It's really a shame," goes Kit. "I made a special point of inviting Doc and Marcia Williams to come to our New Year's Eve party this year. They believe in you so much, they've done so much to support you."

"I know and I'm truly grateful, but what can I do? I've got to get back to the theater."

The whole table is sunk in gloom. Finally, in a thin, shaky voice, Billy pipes up, "Don't we count at all?"

"You guys mean the world to me, Billy, you know that. Anyway, you'll have a great time without me, flirting with all the girls, guzzling down champagne."

"I don't want champagne. I want a family."

"You got one."

"Not any more!" He gets up and runs towards the stairs.

"Billy, come back!"

Kit turns to me and says, "I told you he's taking it badly."

Billy has always treated his room like a sacred hideaway. There's a big KEEP OUT sign on the door, a hasp for a padlock on the side, though as far as I know, he never actually locked it, which is just as well, because Kit or I would have cut the thing off in two seconds flat.

I knock on his door. No answer. I enter. There's no sign of him anywhere.

"Billy, where are you, guy?" His room is smaller than Timmy's and far neater, lots of books, of course, but no posters, no magazines piled up to the ceiling, no trophies, no dirty laundry lying around either, thank god. It's like he's keeping everything under wraps and below the radar, which makes me apprehensive, especially at this moment.

I open the closet door. There he is, sitting cross legged on a pile of shoes and sneakers. "Want to come out and talk about it?" He shakes his head no. "Are you sure? You certainly don't look very comfortable." I reach in to help him up, he pulls away like he's been torched. "Come on, this is ridiculous, you're acting like a two-year-old." I squat down to face him through the open door. "Look, there's nothing I can do about leaving early. It's in my contract. I'll make it up to everyone as soon as I can, promise."

"How can you promise anything?"

"Billy, I'm your Dad."

"But you live in Germany."

"I have to. It's where I work."

"Then go back!" he shouts and slams the door in my face.

Rather than ripping it off its hinges, I count to approximately 3,000, then say as mildly and pleasantly as I can, "Here's an idea. Let's surprise ourselves and have a grown-up conversation."

"That's bullshit."

"Starting with appropriate language."

"Fuck you."

I lunge at the door, then reconsider and wait till I stop seething. Once I'm relatively sane, I go, "I expect an apology, son. Right now."

"Sorry..." His voice is muffled by the closet door.

"That's more like it. Any chance I can see your smiling face?"

It's a quite a while before the door swings open.

"Guy, believe me, I didn't get into opera just to rile up my family."

"No?"

"Of course not. It's really important to me. It's changing my life."

"Lucky you."

"Damn right I'm lucky. I'm just about the luckiest guy on earth. And I want the same for you."

"You do?"

"Of course. Not that you have to sing or anything like that, god, no. I just hope that some day you'll find work that gives your life meaning. It can be helping the poor or teaching kids or being a doctor or even going into business and making yourself a damn fortune. I just hope and pray that whatever you do, you'll love it like I love singing. It's a blessing, man. Every day's a miracle. And all I want for you is lots and lots of days like that... Look, I know it's icky, but how's about giving your father a good old-fashioned hug?"

I open my arms to him. He stares at them a while, then slowly, gravely closes himself back in the closet.

Kit's waiting for me in our bedroom. I plonk myself on the bed, loosen my tie, take off my sport coat, flip off my loafers and go, "Well, that was fun."

"Yes, Billy's very sensitive these days, very febrile." She sits down next to me, still dressed in her holiday finery. She looks like the queen of Graystone, beautiful, but very much on guard.

"Richard, sorry, but I think you have to face the fact that he doesn't want to move to Frankfurt. He graduates next year. He wants to be with his friends."

"He can see them in the summer."

"He wants to see them all the time. He's a teenager."

"He'll make friends over there."

"How? He doesn't speak a word of German."

"They pretty much all speak English, so he won't even have to learn the language if he doesn't want to. Though he really should, it'll help him a lot with college."

"His whole life is here, Richie, don't you understand? He'll be miserable."

"Only if he wants to be. Listen, Kit, Frankfurt's cool, he'll love it."

She shakes her head. "All right, be blind. Pretend that everything's fine... Anyway, it's not only Billy who's having a hard time."

Alarm bells go off. "I thought we settled this weeks ago. You and Billy are coming over at Easter to get the lay of the land, then you'll make the move next summer."

"Frankly, Richard, I'm not sure either of us is going anywhere."

"What?"

"It's great that you've been asking about work for me over there, I'm touched, but the fact of the matter is I've got a splendid job here. I've opened two high school libraries, I'm developing two more. Every day I have the pleasure of seeing kids turn into readers and explorers."

"But they got libraries at the Army base in Frankfurt."

"I'm not interested in a bunch of bored Army wives. I want to work with kids."

"No problem. Those wives have lots of kids."

"Richard, honestly, were the past months so terrible? Couldn't we carry on as we do now? You come back whenever you can and we do our best to make the most of it."

"The most isn't enough. It's way too little."

"Nonsense. You've opened up your life and so have I. That's good news, Richard, it's really wonderful."

"It doesn't feel so wonderful to me."

"It should..."

We don't speak for a while, just mull things over.

"Kit, I really need you. I'll do this great show and get lots of applause and be totally charged up, but then I remove my makeup and make my way home and walk into this empty box and the pleasure and delight I take in singing vanishes, because you're not there to share it. My life's been hollowed out."

"If you're feeling down, you always can call me, you know that."

"Most times you're not even home. Or you'll be sleeping. Anyway, one phone call more or less isn't really the point. I need contact, physical closeness. There's loads of people out there on stage and hundreds more in the audience, but you're the one I'm singing to. You're the person who counts. And when I say counts, I mean really and truly matters, really and truly sparks and excites me and makes my life worth living." By this point, I'm directly behind her, hugging her close, my body pushing hard against hers.

"Not now, please, Richard. The kids will be coming up."

"Who cares?"

"I do. Sorry, but I really and truly do..."

"Kit, singing's the miracle of my life. All I want is to share it with you."

"We share it already."

"Not enough. Come on, you're a giant part of the picture, a central part of my life. Remember how hard you worked to make it happen? You kept urging me on through all the hoo-hah and horseshit. You always kept me focused on the goal."

"Well," she goes, "I guess no good deed goes unpunished..."

"My career's a punishment for you? A *punishment*?"

We sit in silence, on opposite sides of the bed, miles apart, until Billy pounds on the door and tells us it's time to lay out the Christmas presents.

CHAPTER FOURTEEN

Toni

It is the fall of 1984, the year Orwell always warned us about, yet somehow we seem to survive. Richard Verdun now begins his second season with the opera and I have to admit I stay far away from him, not because I do not like him, in fact, I very much do, but because I still am uneasy and rather embarrassed about that stupid episode last year, when like a total idiot I try to seduce his gorgeous young son. However, I do see him perform from time to time and in that department I am very surprised. His singing is much stronger than last year, but, even more amazing, almost a miracle beyond human comprehension, his acting also improves. In fact, he stands out in our new *Walkuere*, a Rebecca Richartz production with much anti-capitalism and very little sense. Every one of her productions is a commentary on modern-day politics, what horrible things our parents did, what horrible things our grandparents did and also, because she is DDR and very far left, what horrible things the Americans always do, especially their idiot President Reagan. This creates work so completely insane and so far from the music and text that I want to beat my head bloody on the sidewalk.

Amazingly enough, Richard Verdun survives her ridiculous new production of *Die Walkuere.* At the very beginning she gives the poor Siegmund an impossible entrance. As soon as he rushes on stage he must reach into the pocket of his black leather pants (yes, he is dressed in black leather like an aging hippie from Schwabing) and start sniffing up a bag of cocaine- to get courage, I suppose, or maybe just to shock the public, and that it most certainly does. It is all the newspapers talk about. The papers on the left find it profound, those on the right are *perplex.* When the production had its premiere last season, Richard did this snorting so *direkt* and awkward the audience collapses in laughter. I see the revival last month and to my amazement, he makes the moment work.

I am so deeply surprised that anyone can create something theatrical out of this completely stupid idea that I ask him how he does it. "I just listen to the score, my friend. Sami Tomi whips up this giant racket in the prelude and I go where the music leads me." Of course, this does not really explain anything, but for a tenor you must always make allowances.

I have to make many more when we bring back *Carmen.* We start the first rehearsal completely normal, completely okay, shake hands all the way around, lie about how nice it is to be working together again. Richard makes his usual jokes, which Frau Romanescu, as usual, does not like. She is always all business and Richard all play. This makes for not the best working relationship, but they somehow find the modus vivendi. After a few minutes I realize Richard has forgotten his music for the final duet, which is not very long or very hard, but in the last six months he has learned two new roles and sung very many performances. I instruct Frau Spinngold, our ancient rehearsal pianist, to give him a quick coaching. Maybe it helps him remember that the tenor in the end kills Carmen.

We take a half-hour pause and I stay behind to work on a list of furniture for the show. I am busy with counting chairs and tables and benches when suddenly there is perfume in the air, very good perfume, Joy perhaps or Guerlain, and a hand on the back of my neck, warm, slightly damp, caressing, a hint even of fur. Frau Romanescu always comes to rehearsals wrapped in her thick sable stole, suggesting hot nights, satin sheets and many orgasms in the hotel room.

"So sorry to interrupt, but we must talk now, Maestro, very urgent." Frau Romanescu studied mainly in Milan, which means she calls everyone on the staff Maestro, even me, who is twenty years younger than she is, though she, of course, would say we were born the same day. "I have a little favor to ask you, very little, very simple and not for me, no, no, but for Richard, he much too gentleman to ask for himself. At the very end, you know, just after he sing *eh bien, damnée*, Carmen spits at Don Jose."

"Yes, it's the best moment in the entire show." Such a smile she gives me, a caressing pitying look.

"Maestro, the public no like. I hear all the time they get terrible shock from this."

"I most certainly hope so."

"*Caro Maestro*, easy, eh? Nothing here to disagree and nothing to do with me. It's just not nice for Richard. I spit and try not to hit him, but sometimes I do, eh? Sometimes, even though I not want, I spit on *povero* Riccardo and this not fair to the dear sweet man." This is the first time she has ever described Richard as dear or sweet, so, of course, I am now quite suspicious.

"Frau Romanescu, I must say Richard has never complained to me."

"He nice gentleman, eh? Too polite to make big fuss."

We are discussing the high point of the production. The audience is shocked every time, shocked in the best possible way. They immediately understand why Don Jose must kill Carmen. It is magnificent theater. I defend it to the last. But gently, carefully. Madame is the diva; I am the little assistant. I put on my diplomat's hat and say, "You can be certain I will speak to Richard so he understands you spit only because the director requires it. It is nothing personal."

"But it's not nice. This spit is very cruel."

"Carmen *is* cruel."

"But they not like me then and Carmen is good, the spirit of life, love, freedom."

"At this point in the story Carmen is cruel and hard and totally fed up with this idiot Don Jose."

She looks at me with almost maternal concern, also a bit of menace, as if I am getting dangerously near the sacred precincts of her art. "How old you are, Maestro?"

"Twenty-six."

"Still very young, not yet understand central, most important fact. They must like you on stage. They must love you or they not ever care about anything you do."

"Frau Romanescu, the Frankfurt public adores you." Strangely enough, she really does have a strong following here.

"Well, *non lo fa.* Excuse me, I not spit. Richard not like. I not like. We not do."

"Frau Romanescu, unfortunately this is not allowed in Germany. All singers are obliged by contract to do the production exactly as staged by the director."

"But you are director now, not Wolverton."

"My obligation is to reproduce his production." And a good one it is. Aside from a bit too many fans and lace mantillas, too much come-visit-scenic-Spain, it is serious and completely okay.

"You good boy, very sensitive, understand very well what artist needs." And with this she leans forward and pats my fresh young cheek.

"I am very sorry, but I cannot allow this. They take away my job."

"Oh, no, they like you, *I* like you."

"I like you too and respect you very much, but I am required to keep this production in its original form."

"This not ego, eh? Not being difficult, only artistic question. I give you plenty other choices, anything you like. I can make fun of Jose, mock terrible with very big laugh. Listen." Here she gives a giant shriek, followed by an ear-splitting cackle. I immediately see the entire audience falling to the floor with laughter. "Also can do big slap that not hurt colleague. I show you." She is about to demonstrate when I cut her off.

"I'm sure it's quite brilliant, but you have to understand it's just not possible for me to..." At this moment Richard and Frau Spinngold return, offering at least temporary salvation. It seems that Richard is now ready to rehearse. I hurry to put them in their starting places because we have already lost nearly an hour and also because I very much want to distract Frau Romanescu from her obsession with the spit. Speaking fast and using the liveliest images possible, I quickly remind them of the basic shape of the scene and the atmosphere beneath it. Frau Romanescu, eyes half closed, listens like the grand czarina while her majordomo reads out the schedule of another boring day. Finally, completely ignoring everything I just so carefully and exactly explained, she turns to Richard and says, "*Senti*, I know you worry about the spit, but nothing to fear. I discuss already with Maestro. We take care of it."

I must act before we get even more problems. "Frau Romanescu, sorry, but as I just told you, I cannot allow you to make changes to the production. This is protected work and I have to make sure—"

"Last year you nice clever boy, hundred percent all right. What come into you?" Here her face darkens, as if the whole world has ended, as if the tenor gets more applause than she does. "*Potere.* This make you change. Give you little bit power, make you in charge and what happen? Go completely crazy, turn upside down, act with disrespect against artist."

"Forgive me, I completely respect you, I hope you understand that, but my job is to make sure the production is done exactly the way the director wanted."

"Look, speak open, friend to friend. If Carmen spit at Jose, people hate me, destroy my chance for success."

"Frau Romanescu, you had an immense success last fall in CARMEN and I'm sure you'll have it again."

"What you know, eh? What you understand? Only *piccolo assistente.*"

This makes me so furious that I'm truly unable to speak.

"Now you angry, Maestro. *Perche?*" The answer to this question is of course so obvious that I am tempted to give up the subtle approach and right away rip her limb from limb. Instead, I freeze my face in neutral and hope she eventually remembers she is at the Frankfurt Opera, where people try to make theatrically convincing productions. Of course, her ego has swollen so big by now, you can fit all of Sicily inside it, and maybe you should, since that way the Mafia could take care of her.

She suspects none of these dark thoughts and keeps talking as if everything is perfectly fine. "Nothing to worry, *caro, niente paura.* Work it all out myself." With this, she grabs a very startled Richard and says, "Come, we show what we do instead of nasty spit. Carmen give big slap to Don Jose. It work completely perfect." To my shock and amazement, she proceeds to set up the old fake slap routine, the one I used to do with my friends when we were seven or eight, and it never fooled anyone. With her back to me, Frau Romanescu places poor puzzled Richard directly in front of her and gives instructions. "When I say slap, make big slap with hands but not so public can see. Then hold face like I hit you very hard. It work completely perfect."

Richard, more sleepwalker than living performer, nods. I doubt he understands what she is getting after. This little exercise is an old *commedia dell'arte* trick and, like most of their gags, very hard to do. It takes timing, it takes control, it takes rehearsal, but this seems not to trouble Madame. In her bizarre, unlikely English she instructs Richard, who seems completely bewildered. This does not stop Madame or slow her down even for one second. No, she charges ahead and tries in five minutes to make up for the years of training she and Richard never had. Finally, she turns proudly to face me. "Okay, ready."

Madame takes a big swing while Richard ducks and claps his hands. He claps a bit late, so the noise comes after the action, like a movie where the sound is *defekt.* I look over to the piano and see Frau Spinngold bobbing over the keyboard, holding back her laughter. I am the exact opposite, ice cold, furious even. This isn't kindergarten. This is an opera house, a palace of art. The way they perform the climax of a world masterwork is disgraceful. But how to tell her and take back the rehearsal?

"Riccardo, clap come too late, must be sooner."

"Okay, hon," he says, ever the willing student.

"Because must be real, eh? Must make public believe."

"Lord knows I'm trying. I just find the whole thing tricky."

"No trick at all, use *concentrazione.*"

The master director and her star pupil get ready to make another try. When the big moment comes, Richard makes the slap before Carmen even swings. Once again Frau Spinngold is a broken marionette folded up over the piano, which is not for her so easy, since she is nearing retirement and has a difficult back.

Madame is not amused. Her artistic vision is at risk. "Riccardo, what you do?"

"Sorry, I'm just not getting it." Richard now turns to me, clearly frustrated. "Toni, does any of this actually look okay?"

Madame answers before I can get a word out. "Of course not okay. This why we have rehearsal."

"Look," says Richard, "I really apologize, but I think we need to regroup."

She eyes him suspiciously. "What means this regroup?"

"Brainstorm, get a better idea so the scene can actually work. Tell you what, how's about you and me go off for a bit, leave these good folks alone and come up with a genius solution?" Richard gives Frau Romanescu his most charming, party-boy look, and to my complete amazement, she seems to soften.

"Well, I do it for you, Riccardo. We have little private conference but *presto, prestissimo,* eh?" Richard winks as they go off, like he wants to reassure me, but I am far from reassured.

Once the singers leave, I throw myself down on the piano bench next to Frau Spinngold. As my rear hits the hard wood of the seat, I let out a groan of despair worse than the dragon Fafner when Siegfried sinks in his sword. Moments later, I feel the gentle tap, tap, tap of Frau Spinngold's wrinkled hand on mine. I see she is smiling.

"I thought you did well."

"Yes, really well. She steals the whole rehearsal from me."

"Don't worry, she'll soon see the light."

"If anyone was ever blind it is that lady. God, I hate this Italian tradition, sing, sing, sing and never act."

"Callas was part of it too."

"Frau Romanescu is not Maria Callas."

"You need to remember that sometimes an artist brings to a production things a director can't even imagine."

"Like a nervous breakdown."

"Poor Toni, so young and so pessimistic."

At this moment, a strange sight, a total contrast from what happened just minutes before, the singers walk back into the room smiling, laughing together. I ask what they have to report. Richard points to Frau Romanescu, who looks at him now with fondness. She never before respects this man, never even likes him. What is going on?

"My buddy here realizes I'm never gonna get the hang of that slap, so we're back to doing it the old way."

"You mean, Carmen will spit?"

Frau Romanescu nods and says in a mild voice, totally unlike the one she used just minutes before, "*Maestro, non oggi*, okay? Let save until tomorrow." Terrified she might somehow change her mind again and drive us back into chaos, I accept her suggestion and discover that Madame is now living in Opposite Land. Before, she was irritated and impossible, now she is helpful and quick. *Mamma mia*, is this woman quick. In no time, we get through all the Carmen and Don Jose duets. What did Richard say to her in the hallway? What sort of a miracle worker is he?

At the end of the day I take him aside and ask how he managed such an amazing transformation. "Simple as pie. I told her we're in Germany. Rules are rules. We gotta do it like we did before or Toni's up shit creek without a paddle. Of course, I puffed it up with a lot of comments about how her slap idea was fantastic, how sorry I was to be so slow, how I'd love to try it some other time, because it's really a great idea..." He gives me now his comedy look. "...if we want to look like fools!"

"For this I owe you a dinner, my friend."

"Look out, I'll eat you under the table and into the poor house."

"Do not worry. The poor house I am in already."

Everyone who is summoned to the office of *Herr Intendant* Klauzer must follow a solemn and most specific ritual. First, you must be properly dressed. Herr Eel, as everyone calls him, is an aging peacock and expects no less from his visitors. This makes for me no problem. I often see him studying my clothes in rehearsal, looking for what comes next and then, a few weeks later, he copies it in a much more expensive version with colors a bit less bold. Today I choose hip bohemian chic- my beloved black cashmere Byblos sweater, brand new Levi's from my last trip to New York that I wear only on major occasions, which this certainly is, finished off with black Italian loafers shiny like mirrors, and red and white check socks to prove I am not dead yet.

Second and more difficult comes the ritual of the wait. You present yourself in the outer office ruled by his assistant Frau Kasel, who gestures to the black leather sofa where you sit while she calls the *Herr Intendant.* If you are a major artist or, even better, a representative of the Ministry of Culture, no problem. Very soon the big door opens and the great man presents himself in all his splendor, posing right next to a life-sized photograph of Gustav Mahler when he was director of the Vienna Court Opera, so you can make for yourself the connection, even though there is none. For those of us in the lower orders our wait can be quite long and he does not come out to us. We enter and present ourselves to him, while he studies us from behind his fortress desk.

Today I am required to wait only ten minutes, an encouraging sign. I go in and find my boss sitting very much erect, Prussian army style, in his seat of power, a harsh modernist black leather armchair that looks like it survives from the last dark days of the Berlin Bauhaus. He wears a tweed hacking jacket in rich autumn colors cut close to his body by Savile Row tailors, which I instantly desire, even though I can never afford it, and a collarless shirt, heavily starched, which he wears buttoned up right to the top without necktie, a look of the moment but for him a bit young. It does, however, make him seem very in control, very much the *Herr Intendant.* Do not misunderstand. Peacock he may be, old he may be, this man runs the best opera house in Germany, possibly even in Europe, and for this I greatly respect him.

He gestures broadly in my direction, the great Maestro acknowledging, not very enthusiastically, his band. The only place to sit in his office is a white leather sofa directly across from his desk whose seat is almost ten centimeters lower than his, the better to illustrate what is what. I have to confess I am always a bit uneasy in his presence. Like everyone else, I never really know where I stand with him, I never can pin him down. That's why we call him Herr Eel.

"So tell me, Toni. You don't mind if I call you Toni, do you?" I mind greatly, of course, but all possibilities spring from his fortress desk. "How did rehearsals go yesterday? I heard things were rather fraught."

"Only at first. We actually got a lot accomplished."

"Not according to Frau Romanescu. You seem to have made her quite unhappy."

"Not at all. We ended rehearsal on a very positive note."

"Madame was being polite, her Romanian upbringing. She didn't want to embarrass you in front of colleagues. You do realize, of course, what I'm referring to."

"Yes, *Herr Intendant*, but there is little I can do. I am specifically required to reproduce the production exactly as Herr Wolverton first staged it."

"*If* conditions permit. In this case they do not."

"Nonetheless, the production is protected under German performance..."

"I know the law far better than you. It's never enforced for one simple reason. It can't be. Times change. People change. Productions change."

"But, sir, the moment when Carmen spits at Don Jose is the most brilliant and shocking part of the entire production."

"Not according to Frau Romanescu and she's our Carmen. More than that, she's a major artist. She does us a special favor to come here and rehearse, even though she's very busy in Paris." And very busy in Herr Klauzer's bed. "If she expresses concern about something, you'd be well advised to take heed."

"Of course, but just last week Herr Wolverton explicitly ordered me to make sure the effect was done. It's a total shock and incredibly effective. "

"No doubt, but I sit at this desk and run this opera house day after day, year after year. I have to be practical. Both feet on the ground. Things as they actually are."

"I completely understand. It's just that Herr Wolverton insisted I keep this particular moment."

"You are paid by the Frankfurt Opera, are you not? As far as I know, you haven't received one pfennig from Herr Wolverton. Now listen, Toni, I appreciate your zeal, your dedication. Like most sensitive young people, you're obsessed by art and aesthetics. You make a grand fuss about it night after night, but art, if it is art at all, is mysterious, unclassifiable. Only critics think they know what it is and they're wrong, every last one of them. They wouldn't know art if it kicked them in the balls. Now, art may kick, but it never ever spits. Understand?"

"Yes, sir."

"It does, however, occasionally slap." He smiles like the cruel and cunning fox he is.

"I understand, sir, but to be honest, her idea didn't work very well."

"Really? How strange. Maybe you should try a bit harder."

I want more than anything to tell him that there is no point, this phony slap is a complete and total disaster, but he has sex with her night and day. Instead, I meekly ask, "What if Herr Wolverton finds out?"

"He's busy in Glyndebourne, a thousand kilometers away. The only way he could possibly know is if you told him and that would never happen, correct?"

"Yes, sir." My voice is so small, so feeble I barely can hear it myself.

Herr Klauzer rises from his desk. He seems amazingly tall. "Well then, you've got your work cut out for you." He goes over to the door and opens it. "You're very privileged to be working here, you know. You have a rare chance to collaborate with outstanding professionals. Listen to them, learn from them, grow." He shoots his hand out. Fool that I am, coward that I am, I take the steel hand of power and shake it. He folds himself back into his slick leather seat, well satisfied with his destruction of art.

"By the way, I like very much the sweater. Who makes it?"

I start the day's rehearsal by swallowing the poison pill Herr Eel had given me. "Good morning, everyone. I have just come from a meeting with the *Intendant.* He has asked me to be sure we keep rehearsing the slap."

"It doesn't work," says Richard.

"Of course, it work. Just need more time to rehearse," replies Madame, clearly relishing her triumph.

"But we agreed to stay with the spit..."

Frau Romanescu abandons all pretense of friendliness and collegiality. "No. Only say yesterday *consider* spit, *think* about spit. Spend whole night terrible worried, terrible upset. Then realize it *assolutamente impossibile.*"

Richard now turns to me. "You're not really gonna allow it, are you? It wasn't in the original show."

"It is now, according to the *Intendant.*"

Dangerous patches of red pop up on Richard's plump cheeks. "Come on, are you fucking shitting me?"

"Herr Verdun," says Frau Spinngold, "even I have enough English to know those words are not correct for the opera house."

"Sorry, Frau Spinngold, we got a serious problem here." He takes a threatening step towards me. "Why didn't you fight him on this? You hated that slap, too."

"If the *Intendant* insists, there's nothing I can do."

"You could show some courage for a change, show some fucking balls."

I am furious, of course, but Frau Spinngold gets there before me. "Herr Verdun," she says, raising her tiny frame from the piano bench and wagging her finger at him like a schoolteacher, "I wash now your mouth out with soap."

"Riccardo, why you worry? Is nothing difficult. Signor Annigoni learn in two minutes."

"Who the hell is he?"

"Very nice tenor, very quick, very young. We do *Carmen* together in Bari."

"Then go back there and sing it with him."

"If only could be so fortunate, but Herr Klauzer engage me here."

"We're very happy that he brought you to Frankfurt, Frau Romanescu," I say, bending the truth so much it breaks in a thousand pieces. "All we want is to create a magnificent *Carmen.*" And never see you again.

"But Riccardo make such problem about slap," says Madame, as relentless as the Romanian state railway, and far more reliable. "Why you not like?"

"The stupid thing doesn't work."

"No, no, not stupid! Work every time. Only not with you. *E perche?* Come to opera without proper training. Never learn how to move."

"Don't give me that!" he shouts.

"Richard, please," I say, "we are all colleagues here."

"That's what you think. She's been after me from the get-go."

"Why you say such terrible thing? Never do nothing to nobody."

"Bullshit. I know you asked Herr Klauzer to fire me."

"No, never! Just tell him you make difficulties with slap," says Madame, all open-eyed innocence. "And that completely true."

"You said a helluva lot more than that. You told him I wasn't an artist, you said I looked like a joke."

"*No, no, giammai*!"

"Well, let me tell you, babe, there's only one joke in this opera house and it sure as hell isn't me." Before I can stop him, Richard grabs his score and rushes out – amazing how fast the man can move when he really wants to – and slams the door for maximum operatic effect.

Frau Romanescu gives her best impersonation of bewildered injury. "Why he act like that, Maestro?"

"I haven't the slightest idea," I say, even though I know perfectly well, as does everyone else in the opera house, except, of course, the *Intendant*, who is too busy fucking her to care.

I dash out and race through the hallways till I catch up with Richard as he goes down the stairs to the stage door. "Wait, where are you going?"

"Home. Everyone loved the spit. Why are we giving it up?"

"Ask Madame. Ask Herr Klauzer."

"Don't pass the fucking buck."

"Sorry, I have Herr Klauzer's direct order. I cannot go against it."

"You at least could fucking try."

"I did! I did!"

By now, Richard has made me beyond crazy and in this craziness of mine, there suddenly flashes before me a blazing new vision that will end this madness once and for all. "Richard, I think we can work our way out of this. What would you say if the lady actually hit you?"

"You mean, slapped me for real?"

"Yes, of course. No faking, no old-fashioned theater tricks."

"And I won't have to do the fake stuff any more?"

"Well, I've also got to convince Madame, but first and foremost, I need your agreement. Would you allow her to actually hit you?"

"Sure, why not?"

"I must warn you that Madame is highly unpredictable. It might prove quite painful."

"So what? I kill her in the end, don't I?"

"Yes," I say, "and about time, too." We share a little laugh. "One other thing. I think you have to offer Frau Romanescu an apology."

"Are you kidding? For what?"

"Saying she always hated you."

"But she does. She's complained about me to Klauzer not once, but many times."

"Such is the world. We must kiss the hand we hate, even at the Frankfurt Opera." Remembering my recent meeting with the *Intendant*, I add, "*Especially* at the Frankfurt Opera."

When we return to the rehearsal room, the lady in question greets us with another stellar performance. "Riccardo, Riccardo, why you say such terrible things? Never want hurt no one."

"I know. I'm sorry. I completely lost it."

"La Romanescu only want best for you, for Maestro, *il teatro*."

"Of course. Everyone knows that. The fact is I got some bad news from home and I'm feeling pretty upset."

"Very important separate home and theater, eh?"

"Yeah, I know. I blew it. You've been amazingly patient. I don't know how you put up with me." I find myself marveling at Richard's performance, it's almost as excessive as Madame's.

She looks up at him and flutters her false eyelashes. "*Mio caro* Riccardo, you such good person to sing with."

"So are you, babe. Those *Carmens* last year were a blast."

They were actually one long argument but, fortunately, Madame forgets all that and rejoices in happy memories of something that never was or could be.

"I try, eh? Do very best. You try also now. Together we make perfect slap."

This is my cue to intervene and propose the alternative. I try to soften the blow by telling Madame how inspired we all are by her brilliant idea but, unfortunately, we must acknowledge that the fake slap wasn't as easy to do as we had thought, not her fault, of course, or that of anyone else, it just didn't work, as happens all too often in the theater, despite the brilliance of the original conception, and the exceptional artist who created it.

"You mean, hit right on face?"

"Of course. Richard's quite willing to let you do it."

"But what if hit too hard? He get me in serious trouble. Sing Marina last season in Hamburg. Director say push the *tenore*, so I push. Next thing I know, he take me before *sindicato* and say I do on purpose. But only follow the director!"

"Look," says Richard, bravely taking his life in his hands, "I promise I won't bring you up on charges, no matter what. Did you hear that, Frau S?"

"Yes, indeed, I did," says Frau Spinngold from the piano.

"And you too, Maestro?"

"Yes, absolutely."

"These two are witnesses. I said I won't complain and I won't. Agreed?"

"Agreed," we chorus.

Frau Spinngold plays the sequence and when we come to the fateful moment, Madame hits Richard so gently it's like a blessing from his fairy godmother.

"That was a love tap, hon. You gotta do better than that."

"But maybe hurt you."

"So what? Just go for it."

"Okay, if you want..." Suddenly, without warning or preparation, she slaps him with enough energy to send him flying all the way to Donaueschingen.

The left side of his face is in flames, and not just the cheek, also the ear, the forehead, everything.

I am about to step forward and give the standard speech about respecting the safety of our fellow artists when Richard says, "Great, hon, thanks. Okay, Toni, let's do it with music."

I'm impressed by his stoicism. Amazed, actually. And so we continue.

At first, it is a normal opera rehearsal. I am watching people I know well go through what is required of them– Richard, rather stiff and awkward, Madame, more polished, but still too grand for a street girl like Carmen. They use half voice and make their moves efficiently without getting completely lost in the stage action. This makes good sense, since if there is a mistake, I will ask them to repeat and voices tire quickly. A singer's voice is a precious commodity. Even as ruthless and insistent a director as Frau Richartz realizes that singers need to spare their instruments from time to time. Our rehearsal progresses smoothly in an everyday sort of way. I have no need to stop and make adjustments.

Then, most unexpectedly, Richard stops marking and switches to full voice at the moment when Don Jose, the blindest of all blind fools in opera and, believe me, there are many, finally realizes that he has lost Carmen. Richard's sudden intensity makes the moment come alive and Frau Romanescu, to my amazement, rises to his challenge and also gives full voice. This changes everything. They no longer rehearse the scene, they perform it and feed off one another like never before. When we get to the famous slap, Madame hits Richard so hard he falls over. I immediately worry that he is hurt, we have to stop, but no, the singers keep going. She studies him lying there on the ground with bitter amusement, as if she wonders how she could ever make love with such a ridiculous mama's boy. Richard, his face still red from the slap, is outraged by her mockery and rises from the floor, a fury now, an avenging angel. I never have seen him like this, never felt the rage and power that so clearly live inside him. He races after Carmen, grabs her with an almost absurd brutality and stabs her from behind again and again like a crazed automaton. It is horrifying, this violence, shocking. Frau Romanescu, clearly astonished, looks at him with a strange new respect as she crumples to the ground. Once she has fallen, Richard sinks to his knees and faces us, no longer a savage, but a lost soul, a boy almost, who has killed the woman he loves.

Believe me, I am not easy to impress. When I give my notes after a performance, the colleagues always say, "All right, Toni, what did you hate this time?" In this case, I promise you, I have nothing but praise.

I finally break the spell. I do not wish to, but I must observe the rehearsal protocol and ask if the singers would like to run through anything just for the sake of security. They look at each other with a curious intimacy.

Richard speaks first. "Nah, I think it's all pretty clear. How about you, Ileana?"

She shakes her head. "No need."

"I didn't hurt you on the stab, did I?"

"No, very comfortable. But slap little bit hard, eh?"

"Hell, no, I loved it. It got me right into the scene."

With this, the rehearsal ends. I say goodbye to Madame, who gleefully rushes off to her suite at the Frankfurter Hof. I escort Frau Spinngold to the door and thank her for her support. As always, she plays the schoolteacher and reminds me that I must learn to be patient. No doubt she has a point.

I go back to gather up my things and notice to my surprise that our tenor is still on his knees in the middle of the rehearsal room. "Richard, are you all right?"

"I guess so."

"That was a remarkable little rehearsal."

He seems to ignore my comment, which is strange for a man so hungry for praise. "Actually, Toni, you got a spare hour or two?"

"Right now?"

"Yeah, I got a few questions I'd like to ask you."

"Shall we go to the canteen?"

"Nah, too many people there. Let's go to my place. I've got some nice beer in the fridge."

We walk back to his apartment maybe ten minutes away from the theater on a tree-shaded street. It is a six-story building from the 1960s, which means thin plaster walls, big windows and no charm. His apartment shocks me. It is almost as small as mine and much plainer. The living room has no pictures, no bookcases, just a sofa with a coffee table in front of it facing a small television. A dining table with four wooden chairs, all identical, stands in the far corner next to a sort of pseudo kitchen with a tiny refrigerator, a two-burner stove, a pair of narrow cabinets. How can someone as open and outgoing as Richard live in a place so empty and faceless?

He goes to the refrigerator and returns a minute later with three cans of Becks, a bland, totally ordinary German label I never would order myself. He gives me one, the others are clearly for him.

We open our drinks and take a few calming swallows. "I suppose you wonder why I asked you over. I just wanted to ask you this one question."

"I have already the answer. Yes, you are the world's greatest living Heldentenor."

He laughs. "Come on, I'm not really that pathetic, am I?"

"Do you really want an answer?"

"Okay, okay, I get it. Listen, no kidding around, please, here's the real question. Am I any good? Am I actually getting somewhere?"

"You ask me after the rehearsal we just have?"

"Yeah, it did kinda work, didn't it?"

"Kind of? It's the best you've ever done, and by far. Even Madame was impressed. You made her get off her ass and do something."

"Yeah, we really clicked."

"It was something I thought I'd never see. And *you* made it happen. *You.*" He seems genuinely surprised. "Now, now, don't play Mister Modest. Surely, you felt it too."

"I don't know, maybe."

"Of course, you did. You had to."

"You still didn't answer my question. Do you think I should give it all up?"

This is the last thing I ever expect. "Give it up? You're first tenor at the Frankfurt Opera. People would kill for such a position."

"I'm not people. I'm just me, Richie Verdun... The thing is, my family's pretty impatient for me to come back home."

"You told me they were moving here."

"So I thought."

"That must make it very hard."

"Well, it sure as hell ain't easy..." He reflects on this as he drinks more beer. "You know, my wife said she'd come over last Easter to check out Frankfurt and help me buy a home. She never made it. She's got this fear of flying. We worked it out last summer that she'd go see this famous psychologist and then visit for Thanksgiving. That's two weeks from now. Today she tells me she can't do it. She's still too scared to fly. Great news, huh?" He finishes his beer and immediately opens the other can. "So nice they played it twice. Cheers!"

"Prosit," I say, raising my can, which is still almost completely full.

"Frankly, my friend, I'm not sure she even saw that psychologist."

"Really? Why?"

"Man, you tell me... And the crazy thing is I did all this with her blessing and now it's like she's mad it all worked out."

"You really think she doesn't want you to have success?"

He makes a face. "She doesn't flat out say it, of course, but the message is pretty clear. You know, set your sights lower, move back home and be with the family. There's plenty of work in the States."

This is a terrible suggestion. While they do, of course, have opera companies in America, I know very well it is nothing like what we have here. "You have a major position in a major house. Does your wife not understand this?"

"Beats me, friend."

"And are you really prepared to give it up? Does your work mean so little to you?"

"Of course, it means something. But I don't know that it means *everything*..." At this point, he drinks so long and hard, it is as if he never before tastes anything as wonderful as this lousy Becks. Once the second can is empty, he gets up, goes over to the fridge in his dwarf kitchen, tosses both cans in the garbage and takes out another. "Want a rematch?"

"Heavens, no. I still have plenty."

"Now, don't get me wrong. Kit's the world to me."

"Even when she does not understand what you do here, what you achieve? Do you really want to put all that at risk, just because she has trouble with airplanes?"

"It's more than that, man. And it's not just problems *she* has." He opens the new can and greedily starts gulping it down. I begin to wonder how long it will be before I have to pick him up off the floor. "You know, the women around here, they're great and amazingly free and, well..."

He suddenly gets red in the face like a bashful teenager, he, a grown man with grown children. I have to laugh. "Wait, let me guess, you now are thinking of sex. You get it on the brain just like I do."

"Hell, my thoughts turn that way all the time." Before my eyes the shy schoolboy transforms into Don Giovanni's twin brother. "Remember yesterday, when I went off with Ileana to rehearse her stupid slap routine? Well, she may be a pain in the ass, but she's one hot-blooded woman..."

"She's also the property of *Herr Intendant* Klauzer."

He gives me a wicked little smile. "That's what *he* thinks." How this pudgy middle-aged man can be a sex object for the women of this company remains one of the world's great mysteries. "Sure you won't have some more beer?"

"No, thanks, I learn in New York you can never be too rich or too thin and since riches I never get, I protect my boyish figure."

We share a little laugh, then he goes on. "And if Kit's not coming over, *really* not, what the hell do I do? My boys are pissed at me too. They just don't get it."

"Well, no one ever said that this is easy work."

"You're telling me. Sure, you give me a hand from time to time, and I'm really grateful, and there's Frau Olga, of course, and Sally Neville, and one or two others. But, basically, it's just me on my lonesome, doing my damnedest to get folks to take me seriously, and, okay, I'll say it – why the hell not? I'm not young like you, I'm in my forties, it really wears me out." He stands by the refrigerator and drinks and drinks until the third can is finished also. He tosses the can in the garbage and, to my considerable surprise, he opens the refrigerator door and takes out another one.

"Richard, haven't you had enough?"

I say it in all innocence but it sets him off. "I've had enough bullshit, I've had enough problems!"

"My friend, come, this is ridiculous. The beer makes you say these terrible things."

"Life does, Toni. *Life*." Even though he is by now walking rather unsteadily, he makes his way safely back to the sofa and collapses. He opens his beer, can number four, in case you lose count, and starts drinking even faster. "Oh, man, sorry to be such a downer, but what I'm going through, I wouldn't wish on my worst enemy."

"Not even Frau Romanescu?"

"She solved it long ago. No husband, no kids, just opera. And plenty of sex with the boss. Nice work if you can get it..." He takes a few more swallows of beer, then crushes the empty can with his big bratwurst fingers. "Fuck opera. Who needs it?"

"You do. I do."

"Oh yeah? Why?"

Even though I hear in his voice a kind of mockery, I decide I must save him from his crazy self. And fast. "Richard, what I next tell you we keep *unter vier Augen*, okay?"

"Four eyes?"

"We keep very private. I don't want Herr Klauzer to know I go with men."

"I think pretty much everyone knows."

"Still, just in case, *unter vier Augen.*"

"Of course, whatever you say..."

"A few weeks ago, I hear from this fellow Maurizio. We go together for maybe three or four months, very occasional, until I break it off. Anyway, he is now on the phone, drunk, of course, hysterical. He always liked too much his schnapps. He's sobbing and screaming how I destroy his life and shame him to the world and make everything he cares about broken. At first, I am just angry that this idiot disturbs me with these ridiculous accusations, but, after a while, it becomes a real problem. I have duty tonight at the theater, *Così Fan Tutte.* Did you see it?"

"No, not yet."

"The production is almost ten years old but very good, it really stays alive. This night, I have a new baritone coming in. I must leave for the opera, no questions, no exceptions, so I very firmly tell Maurizio I have to go and, somehow or other, he quiets down and I finally can hang up. At the theater, once the overture begins, in one minute, truly, one single minute, I am completely transformed, saved. Even though I was trembling with frustration because of all the crazy hurtful things my ex said to me, Mozart's music pulled me out of my ridiculous problems into a world of tenderness and delight. By the end of act one, I realize there is more to life than this idiot Maurizio, there is *Così Fan Tutte.* There's the miracle of art."

Richard is giving me a very strange look. Is it fascination, amusement, mockery? "Wow, you're really into this, aren't you?"

"Why else would I do it? The opera does not make me rich. It won't even make me famous, except to a handful of people who don't have much power in the so-called real world. But who cares? Opera makes these little miracles."

"I don't know, pal, maybe..."

"*I* know, Richard. I firmly believe it."

"It's nice to be so certain."

"How can you not be? How can you sing one bar of *Winterstuerme* and not know that it absolutely must be sung, that the whole world needs to hear it?"

"Yeah, I guess... You know, a few days ago we had another *Walkuere.*"

"I heard it went well."

"So they say... Anyway, the day of the show my agent Erich calls me from the states. He's got terrible news. Right away I worry this means I won't get that audition for Bayreuth."

"You're singing for Wolfgang Wagner?"

"Yeah, early next month. Red Rebecca set it up. She's doing a *Dutchman* there in three years' time and wants me for Erik. She doesn't see him as a young buck. She wants him the same age as Senta's father, or even older, a kinda capitalist moneybag chasing this hot young girl."

"Typical Richartz, always the anti-capitalist, even with no capitalists in the opera."

"So, I ask my agent what the bad news is. He says he really doesn't know how to break it to me, it seems completely impossible, but Rigby Converse just died. I'm totally shocked. This guy, Rigby, wasn't even thirty. It turns out he got this horrible infection. They tried to stop it, he was in the hospital for weeks, but nothing worked. I'm basically so stunned that a young guy can die like that so fast from a fucking infection, especially this particular guy, I can't wrap my head around it. I mean, he was the fella who taught me basically everything I know about opera. The whole time I was studying in New York he was my biggest fan, my best pal. After I get the grim news, I stumble around the apartment like a zombie till it's time to go to the theater. I'm sitting in the makeup room waiting for Herr Kindl to work his magic, when it hits me that Rigby, who worked so hard to train me, who put so much of himself into me becoming a professional singer, would never get a chance to hear me on stage, never see what his patience and big heart had made out of me, hammered out of me..."

He turns away to hide his face. When he speaks again, his voice is soft and low. "Poor guy, he was all alone in the big city while I was here in Frankfurt, singing my head off. Anyway, I'm still thinking about him as we head into the second act, which for me is just the *Todesverkuendigung*, when Bruennhilde tells Siegmund he has to die. Suddenly, we're out on stage, starting up the scene, when it just smashes into me, the unfairness of death, the outrage, especially for my man Rigby, a kid in his twenties, poor and struggling, with no family, no lovers, nothing, just a passion for music and a kind and generous soul. That such a kid could be eliminated, bam, just like that, stamped out, stomped out, it's savage, man, brutal...

"Sami Tomi is in the pit, he's a wizard, of course, and it's like he senses something in the air. He keeps pushing me to really lay into Bruennhilde, Sally Neville, at her very best. Somehow or other, we're all in great voice that night, maybe it's the full moon. Anyway, while we're singing, I get so outraged by Rigby's fate, and Siegmund's too, so infuriated by the total unfairness of it all, I nearly throw poor Sally halfway across the stage. Trooper that she is, she just puts it in the show and uses it to fuel her lines, so we're cooking like never before, all three of us, ST, Sally and me, and then Klaus Gruendahl, the Wotan, comes storming out and he senses it too, this fury in the air, and he goes after Bruennhilde like a hell hound, he burns up the stage. It's like everyone in the show is protesting Rigby's death, even though I'm the only one who actually knew him. Somehow, every one of us is yelling and screaming about the unfairness of it all and, man, it's wild, it's fantastic. When the orchestra finishes its final riff, the audience goes nuts. They shout and scream and hoot and holler and Sami Tomi rushes backstage and hugs us, which for him is an absolute first, he's such a standoffish type. He tells us this is what it's about, this is what opera can do. That's real nice, of course, but I keep thinking about poor young Rigby..." Richard, usually such a vivid presence, starts drifting away again.

I let the silence hold a bit, then I speak, I really have to. "Richard, my friend, listen, this you get only in the opera house. This you get only through art. You need it, Richard, everyone does. Live for it. Fight for it. Stay..."

CHAPTER FIFTEEN

Richie

Frau Kasel is pretty surprised when I drop by unannounced and ask if the royal eel can spare a few minutes of his precious time. I guess it's my lucky day because she tells me he'll be with me shortly. There's a sudden buzz and click, which means the door's unlocked, my appointment with destiny begins. His royal highness doesn't look up. He's studying a calendar so big it covers the entire surface of his desk and flops over on both sides to the floor. It's the year's *Spielplan*, a master schedule of all the performances and major rehearsals of one season at the opera.

"Herr Verdun," he goes, still without giving me a glance, "an unexpected pleasure. I hear the *Carmen* rehearsal went well yesterday. Frau Romanescu said it showed marked improvement, especially from you."

"What can I say, Reinbert? I always give it my best."

"And so you should."

"Of course, Ileana's pretty fantastic too. We had a great time together."

He looks up sharply from the *Spielplan*.

"I mean, we just really enjoy doing that final duet."

"Yes, it's always an immense pleasure to murder someone." And that's it for chitchat. He switches off the charm and slaps on his *I'm the boss* hat. "But surely this isn't why you wanted to see me."

"No, sir. I've come to ask for a release."

"Why? Is Richard Verdun the new international sensation?"

"I sure as hell hope so."

"Who is it this time? La Scala, the Metropolitan Opera, Covent Garden?" The way he spits out their names it's like only lunatics would want to sing there.

"Actually, it's not a theater, sir. It's a family matter."

"Oh, dear, not too serious, I hope."

"Very. I really need to go back to the States to see my wife."

"Is she ill?"

"No, not at all."

"Then wait till Christmas vacation. It's just another month."

"I can't, sir. It has to happen now."

"Why?"

"I'd rather not say. It's a private matter."

"Nothing's private in the opera house. You know that very well."

"Herr Klauzer, I wouldn't be asking for this unless it was terribly important."

"All right then, what are the dates?

"Just November 23 and 24."

"But that's two weeks from today."

"The problem just came up."

"You do know we require far more lead time."

"Sure, but I only heard about it yesterday. It can't be solved on the phone."

"Why not? Surely, you can give me a little idea of what the difficulty might be."

"I'd like to, but it's just not possible." He's annoyed, of course, but my private life is none of his fucking business.

"So, give me those dates again."

"November 23 and 24."

He consults his giant calendar. "You've got a *Carmen* here on the 25th. Do you really intend to fly to and from the States on two consecutive days and then sing Don Jose the night of your return? That's virtually impossible."

"I'm rough. I'm tough. I can do it. Last season I did Siegmund and Pinkerton one night right after the other, not once, but twice."

"Yes, so you did..." He smiles and leans back in his chair. "For argument's sake, let's say I were to go against my better instincts and let you do all this flying just before an important Don Jose. If I were mad enough to allow such a thing, surely you'd expect to pay a small price."

"Of course, Herr Klauzer."

"I take it you've heard that we're reviving *Magic Flute* next season. In it, there's a very significant supporting role, a charming cameo. It's very brief, which means it's easy to learn, even for someone like you." The guy just can't resist. "The part in question should be done by a dramatic tenor, though it rarely is. It was sung in Covent Garden by none other than Jon Vickers."

"Really? Which part?"

"The first armored man." This draws a total blank. "He appears in just one scene in the second act, but it's highly significant. There's only one man in my company who can give this role its proper depth and weight, and that man is Richard Verdun. The question is, will he do it?"

"How many performances are we talking here?"

"Six, spread through the winter months."

"Do I get extra pay?"

He gives me one of his *are you out of your frigging mind?* looks. It's meant to intimidate and in this case, it really does. "Herr Verdun, I must be very frank with you. Either you give us these performances out of the goodness of your heart or mine turns cold indeed."

"Okay, sir, you're the boss."

"Yes, I most certainly am."

I know, I know, I just threw six extra performances into my *Intendant's* lap with nary a Deutschmark to show for it. So what? Now I can go back to Graystone and sort things out with Kit.

The next day, when I tell Erich Hirschmann what I've done, he chews my head off. "But I needed the release," I go.

"I need a Jaguar. That doesn't mean I actually get it."

"That's not the same thing."

"You are first tenor at the opera, not third. This role is far beneath you."

"Herr Klauzer said even Jon Vickers sang it."

"When he was still a schoolboy and could not find work."

"At least it's only six performances."

"That's six too many. And the man doesn't have the decency to pay you. I must check with your union to see if they even allow such a thing."

"Fine, but not right away. I don't want to lose the release."

"It means so much to you?"

"Erich, believe me, it's everything." Since Kit is too scared to fly to Frankfurt, I'll go home and give her a personal escort.

Two weeks after the royal eel gives me my release I fly back home. I arrive at JFK with just a carry-on bag, so I get through customs fast and show up at my Detroit flight way early. I decide to kill some time by getting myself a snack, since what they served on the plane was foam rubber wrapped in plastic dusted with Ajax. I'm in a crowded coffee shop eating a cheeseburger, when I hear this burst of Italian from a nearby table. I turn around and see a gorgeous older lady, very elegantly dressed. (Actually, she's overdressed for something as unglamorous as plane travel.) She gets up and heads towards the ladies' room, leaving behind a handsome older guy in a gray wool overcoat that looks so sharp and slick you know it cost a fortune. Even though the dye job on his hair can't hide how thin and scraggly it's become, even though his neck has got some turkey folds, it gradually dawns on me who this aging prince is.

I drop my half-eaten cheeseburger, wipe off my greasy fingers, and march right over to him. I'm so thrilled to meet this incredible man that I blunder into the side of his table. "Oops, sorry, sir, really sorry, I'll get it fixed right away." I put the salt and pepper shakers back in their stand and sweep the stray grains from the table top while the great man stares at me and wonders which rock I crawled out from.

"Look, I don't want to ruin your moment of peace and quiet, I'm sure a famous man like you doesn't have all that many, but I had to tell you how much you mean to me. You helped me change my life."

He doesn't seem particularly interested, so one part of me is thinking, *okay, give it a rest, let the poor guy alone*, while the other's going, *don't be a jerk, it's a once-in-a-lifetime opportunity.* Guess which side wins. "If you've got a spare moment, there is one question I'd like to ask. I promise it won't take long." To my amazement, he gestures for me to join him. I'm actually sitting down with Franco Corelli!

As I get settled, he unleashes a whirlwind of Italian and the only word I hang onto is *moglie* which means *wife*, probably the lady who just left the table. "Sorry, I'm afraid my Italian's pretty primitive. I mean, I get *ciao* and *tenore*, easy things like that, but I'm no great linguist, which is pretty unfortunate, seeing as how I'm an opera singer."

"*Un cantante? Lei?*"

"Yeah, I know, it always comes as a surprise. I'm actually first tenor at the Frankfurt Opera. Richard Verdun, sir, an honor to meet you, a very great honor indeed."

"*Un tenore?*"

"Yes, just like you, though not in your league, of course. I'm only starting out. It's my second year in the profession."

"And how old?"

"Nearly forty-five."

"*Incredibile!*"

"You bet. I'm pretty amazed myself."

"And sing in Frankfurt Opera?"

"Absolutely. Last season I did Don Jose, Siegmund and Pinkerton. This year I add Eisenstein in *Fledermaus.*"

"So, when you want study? My wife come back soon, tell you about studio in New York, have for you all the information."

"Actually, sir, I wanted to ask about your own plans. When will you give your next concert?"

"*Senti,* I sing for public enough."

"But what about your fans?"

"*Mamma mia,* the fans. Every time I go on stage, they expect *il grande tenore, l'incredibile* Franco Corelli, like they hear on record, like they see on TV. I must always give them more- bigger fortissimo, longer diminuendo, louder high C. And I try and try, and give and give. *É una crocifissione,* you understand?"

"Crucifixion? But you always sound so incredible."

He gives a bitter little laugh. "Is difficult to sing, incredible difficult."

"Sure, I won't deny it, but somehow or other I always forget that part, I just go out there and sing. I may get a bit tingly but I'm never really scared. I guess you could say I got the benefit of low expectations. For me it's just a big adventure, a wild and crazy ride. If it doesn't go well, I work my butt off and correct my mistakes and hope they like me next time."

"And they like?"

"Usually. I mean, the roles keep coming in. They just renewed my contract."

"*Sei molto fortunato.*"

"Amen to that, and then some."

"*Senti, tenore,* we love to sing, we love *la bella musica,* but not understand how difficult it is, how cruel, especially inside yourself, here, here..." He thumps his chest so hard it sounds like a muffled drum. "In your heart it go so deep, this desire to make beauty, this desire to give to others, but it make you pay the price."

"But there's big rewards, too, especially for someone like you, those amazing nights with the crowd on its feet, screaming like crazy for more."

"*Scusi, ma no,* you sing one night only, one sacred *momento.* They clap, they cheer, and then it vanish. All you got left is some little memory, some distant *vibrazione – piano, pianissimo.*"

"But your fans remember, Maestro. They never, ever forget... My colleagues told me that last concert of yours was fantastic. When are you gonna give another?"

"*No, tenore.* Is finish. *La commedia è finita.*"

I don't know what gets into me, but I just can't bear the thought of Franco Corelli giving up singing. "Sorry, Maestro," I go, "with all due respect, and, believe me, I'm the last person on earth who'd ever want to contradict you, but the first time I heard you, on a record, of course, not live, it transformed my life. That's no exaggeration, you really and truly are the reason I became a singer. I know I'm out of line and I know it isn't my place, but for you, the great Franco Corelli, to give up singing when you're still belting it out so fantastically, well, it's a tragedy, sir, a terrible, horrible waste, a..."

"*Tenore,*" he finally goes, "you know best day of my life?"

"Your debut at La Scala? *Turandot* with Nilsson at the Met?"

"No, the day I no more sing. The day I say no to *terrore,* no to *agonia.* The day, *finalmente,* craziness end."

That's when his wife comes storming back. She goes after him in rapid fire Italian - she's obviously bawling him out for speaking to the great unwashed without her being there to protect him. Then she turns to me, very businesslike, very prim and proper, and says, "You understand my husband only gives lessons in New York City. You come to our studio, we give you good care."

"Thanks, but I'm actually living full time in Germany."

"Germany? Then you need our help even more. They kill the voice over there, completely ruin it."

"Oh, I don't know, Hermann Prey sounds pretty great, so does Christa Ludwig."

She's obviously not buying it. She rummages around in her pocketbook until she finds a battered business card and slaps it in my hand. "Don't you worry, *tenore.* We take care of all problems, make you good as new."

"Kit, Billy, I'm home." There's no answer. The lights in the entryway are off. I see a soft light near the kitchen and walk carefully through the darkened living room, dodging a few chairs along the way. "So, what's with all the darkness?" In the dining room, the overhead lights are also off but the silver candelabra we use for big holidays is set out on the table with its candles lit, bathing the room in flickering fluttering light.

"Hey, Kit, where are you?"

"Richie!" she calls from the kitchen. "You finally made it."

"Yeah, I'm still pretty much in one piece."

"I'll be right out. I'm just finishing up in the kitchen."

"Well, make it snappy. I'm about to get a major dose of jet lag."

"I can imagine..."

While waiting for her to come out, I notice that only my place is set. She and Billy must have eaten already. "So, where's the little terror?"

"Billy? I sent him to Carol's for the night. I thought we needed some alone time."

"Good thinking."

On the sideboard I see a can of Becks, my favorite beer. I didn't even know they sold it in the States. "You're a miracle worker," I go. "How did you find the beer?"

"I have my ways."

The woman herself finally appears in person, wearing a plain cream-colored house coat that glows in the candlelight. I'm amazed that a garment so simple could look so beautiful. She brings a steaming dish over to me, mac and cheese, her own special recipe, my all-time favorite. As she sets it down before me, I'm suddenly so excited to be near her again that I grab her hand and give it a giant smooch. She pulls away gently and glides over to her place at the other end of the table.

"Why so far away?"

"I don't know. I'm nervous, I guess. Just like you..."

I turn to the mac and cheese and dig in. It's warm and creamy and beyond delicious with a faint hint of nutmeg that drives me round the bend. For a long time, the only sound in the room is me gobbling down her fabulous dish.

I can barely hear her when she speaks again. "I'm very sorry to have to say this, Richie, but I can't fly to Frankfurt with you tomorrow."

"But you promised! I'm dying of loneliness over there. I need you."

"I know. I need you too."

"Then take the damn plane!"

"Sometimes we've got to make sacrifices." She gives a faint smile. "Sometimes even someone like you has to postpone pleasure a bit."

"A bit? It's been three months since we last saw each other, three long months."

"Yes, I suppose it is."

"You *suppose*? Kit, don't you miss me?"

"Yes, of course, very much."

"Then why can't you do this one thing?"

"You know perfectly well. Besides, I'm dealing with this impossible architect on the Gaylord project. He's got this absurd notion that—"

"But what about me? What about us? What are we going to do?"

"Wait. Be patient."

"I'VE WAITED LONG ENOUGH! Sorry, I didn't mean to shout."

"Didn't you?"

"Okay, okay, I apologize."

"I also have to point out that I'm very annoyed that you called Harvey Rosenstone."

I'm really thrown. Kit's boss promised he'd keep our chat confidential. "Sorry, but I had to be sure he'd let you fly to Germany."

"That's not the point. I can't have my husband going behind my back like that."

"Come on, I had to make certain he'd give you some time off."

"You should have discussed it with me, not him."

"Okay, okay, I'm sorry if I crossed some red line. The simple fact is I love you. I need you by my side."

"But I'm busy here. I'm about to open two more libraries. And while I'd like to see you conquer Frankfurt, I can't be both places at once."

"You could try."

"I did! I just couldn't go through with it."

"You still can't take a plane, even after seeing that guy in Ann Arbor?"

She seems to fold in on herself, she deflates.

"Actually… I never was able to arrange it."

"*What?*"

"I wanted to, I really did, but I was incredibly busy. I was opening a new library, Billy was acting out, Timothy was unhappy at college. I never could find any time."

"We agreed on this, Kit. You gave me your solemn word."

"You've been busy too. You even forgot our anniversary last month."

I slam my fist on the table. My plate clatters. Silverware jangles. "That's not the same thing, and you know it!"

"I thought I'd be able to do it on my own, but I just can't..."

"You break my heart, Kit. Snap it in two."

"I promise I'll make it up to you. Maybe that man can see me next year."

"No, Kit, now! Look, I don't want to say this, it's too terrible even to imagine, but if you dig in your heels and refuse to fly with me to Frankfurt tomorrow, I don't know what's gonna come of us. There's been so much waiting and delaying and avoiding - on your part, Kit, not mine - I just can't take it any more. I want us to stay together and try new things, do new things, but together, not four thousand miles apart, not divided by the fucking ocean. I know it's tough talk, but it's where I am, it's what I want. And I hope and pray you'll want it also... I realize it's been hard for you. You held down the fort and worked like hell to keep the kids on the straight and narrow. But we're living a different chapter now. We've got to move on..."

She slowly sinks into her chair at the other end of the table, like my words have somehow shoved her back into it. She starts sobbing softly. I want to rush over and hold her tight in my arms, but it's not the moment.

"Why can't we two just wait?" Her voice is faint, a tiny sliver of sound.

"You know, truthfully, flying's no big deal. I spoke to the company doctor. He may not be a world-class expert like that guy in Ann Arbor, but lots of singers get scared of flying, so he's very familiar with it. He told me one of the best quick fixes is a good stiff drink before takeoff. That's good news, right? You're a cheap date when it comes to alcohol, which means it really should work. But if it doesn't, he also gave me a new type of sleeping pill. I tried one coming over and it's amazing. You wake up totally refreshed. It's like a miracle."

"It will take more than a miracle to get me on that plane."

"I'll be right beside you, your guard of honor. I promise I'll get you through it."

"Richard, don't you understand that my life is entirely here."

"But once you get to Frankfurt, you'll see you can do so much over there, learn so much, grow so much. I mean, everyone needs to go outside their comfort zone once in a while. I did, and it's been amazing, I'm living a life I never could have imagined."

"Am I supposed to applaud, break out in cheers?"

"Kit, come on, I'm just asking you to broaden your horizon."

"Thanks, it's broad enough already."

"You gotta realize there's a whole new world waiting for you over there, a great new adventure crammed with fantastic possibilities, amazing experiences. I'd love to tell you about it. May I? Please?" She gives a tentative little nod.

"One day, not long ago, I was on break from rehearsal and somehow or other stumbled on the Charles Dickens English Language Bookshop. I never realized there was anything like it in Frankfurt. I mean, it's Germany, *wir sprechen deutsch*. I walked inside and discovered it was stuffed floor to ceiling with books, we're talking an incredible number of volumes, American, British, Canadian, even Australian, you name it, they got it, as long as it's in English. I went from room to room, past thousands and thousands of titles, till I came to a little office with a lowered ceiling and a wooden table piled high with flyers and folders and bills and mail, kinda like Erich's office in New York, only messier, if you can believe it, and in Germany they don't do messy.

"Anyway, a round-faced gentleman with puffy red cheeks sat at the desk reading a letter, looking the way I always imagined Colonel Mustard must look. He seemed very retired professor, very *no sex, please, we're British*. He was smoking a pipe, just like you'd expect, and when he saw me, he asked if I needed some help, in this clipped English accent, which explains why his place is so messy – he's not German, he's a Brit. Anyway, when I tell him I'm killing time before my next rehearsal at the opera, he staggers back, like he just had this giant revelation and goes, 'Oh, my heavens, Mr. Verdun, I didn't recognize you. Welcome, welcome to the Dickens Bookshop.' It turns out the guy's an opera nut and a giant fan. He starts giving me this spiel about how great my work in

Carmen and *Walkuere* was, how lucky Frankfurt is to have me, how much he's looking forward to my Eisenstein, and I'm lapping it up. I mean, what's not to like? He's got terrific taste in tenors. Then it hits me he owns a big English language bookshop and you're coming over, maybe he could offer you a job, so I start pitching you to him as the highly literate wonder woman you are. Of course, it's not long before the guy's saying he'd love to meet you, maybe he can work something out, and if he can't, he knows the head of the Frankfurt American High School, which the army set up for the kids of servicemen in the area in the exact same format as the schools we got back home. Everyone says it's a great place with very high standards. Maybe they need a librarian or teacher of American literature, and, even if they don't, there's a big expat community with lots of wealthy army types and bankers and businessmen. There's gotta be lots of interesting positions for a smart English speaker like you, and you'll have no problem with work permits. I'm a state employee with permanent residency, which entitles you to employment as well, and let me tell you, that's a giant deal in Germany.

"So, anyway, while I'm talking to him, I get another inspiration. I ask if he maybe has some Jane Austen novels, and, wouldn't you know it? she's his favorite novelist. Long story short, I bought the complete Jane Austen for you in paperback, which means that when I'm working at the theater and you're not in the mood to sightsee, you'll have your beloved Jane to keep you company. That's a bribe, hon, an out-and-out, shameless, sorry-ass bribe."

"I assumed as much." She seems to be smiling, though I can't be sure. Some candles have gone out, everything's harder to see.

I go on with my pitch, explaining that, while Frankfurt itself isn't all that great to live in, there are these beautiful little villages not far from the city, magical places with old-fashioned farm houses newly fixed up to satisfy us modern types. There's even one with cobbled streets and gas lamps that's got a brick oven bread bakery right in the center of town, where they make bread the way they've made it for centuries and it tastes great, fresh and chewy and tangy, and the building's surrounded by all these small two-story houses with red tile roofs and large gardens in back and big front windows, so they're bursting with light inside, and you don't even need a car to get into Frankfurt, there's excellent regional trains every twenty minutes or so, and these cool little houses really don't cost much, at least not by American standards, and the amazing thing is you can walk out the door, and in ten, fifteen minutes, you're strolling through the wild rolling countryside of the beautiful Taunus mountains with nothing but trees and meadows and streams surrounding you, and it's so calm there, so lovely...

I look over and realize she's sobbing again. I guess I've been so lost in my storytelling, so eager to describe all the fabulous things I've got waiting for her, I wasn't really paying attention. "Don't cry, sweets, everything's okay. We'll have the time of our lives… Remember last summer when I came back from Frankfurt for summer vacation and the whole family rented a cabin out at the lake? We had six weeks together, six glorious weeks. What fun we had, how close we felt. What could be more important than that? What could be better?"

Her tears keep coming. I haven't seen her weep like that since her mom's funeral, when she was this frightened teenager, facing a cruel new reality. Suddenly, out of nowhere, the *Duidu* starts flooding through me. I've got an Eisenstein in *Die Fledermaus* coming up pretty soon. There's a great romance in the second act, where all the guests at this fancy masked ball turn to their neighbors and sing *duidu*, which is basically a nonsense word, but not entirely, since *Du* is sort of like *thou* in English, only much more direct and sexy. I'm suddenly so caught up in my feelings for my woman, so moved, so emotional, that this beautiful tune just blossoms out of me and I sing it full out in my operatic voice. I keep on until the melody's almost a physical presence in the room. It threads between us, twists around us. "*Duidu, duidu, la, la, la...*" This big sound, this amazing force surges through every part of me out into the room and slowly, like some miracle, her sobs fade away. She faces me across the table in the shimmering candlelight while I keep singing opera to her, only opera, as if my life depends on it.

And it does.

CHAPTER SIXTEEN

Kit

I can't fully explain it, can't even justify it, but I couldn't go to Germany with Richard, I simply couldn't. I knew he'd be terribly disappointed. I worked hard to soften the blow. I gave him all sorts of more or less credible explanations and excuses – the libraries I was opening, my continuing concerns about our sons, especially young Billy who still was mired in teenage angst – but the intensity of Richard's visit, its startling urgency, threw me off balance. I wasn't really myself, I couldn't be cogent or calm and in the end I failed miserably. I'll never forget the look of pain and disappointment on his face when I dropped my bombshell. But I had to do it, I just had to. I had felt so pressured by him, so *forced*, that there was no space left for me at all. It seemed as if his was the only reality. What about mine?

Our grim minuet of parting haunted me all day. I fell into a deep funk. I called the office to explain my situation. (My boss, Harvey Rosenstone, seemed puzzled I wasn't flying to Frankfurt but, decent man that he was, didn't probe or pry.) I took the day off and slumped around the house. Not even my beloved Jane Austen could dispel my emotional smog.

I was getting ready for an early bedtime when the doorbell rang. It was Carol. Usually she was calm, almost placid. Tonight she was clearly distraught.

"Come in, dear, come in. Is anything wrong?"

"Is Billy here?"

"No, he's over at a friend's."

"Good. He won't barge in and distract us. We need to have a talk."

"About what?" She didn't answer but went straight into the living room where she installed herself on a side chair like an imperious CEO.

"How could you do it, Mom? How could you let it happen?"

"Let what happen?"

"Daddy called me at work this afternoon. He sounded incredibly upset... Mom, why didn't you go with him?"

I was disconcerted. My hands traced vague circles in the air.

"How could you disappoint him like that? He was crushed."

"That wasn't my intention."

"Wasn't it?" Her voice was ice cold, rock hard. I had never experienced such hostility from her. "He was so sure you'd go back with him. He felt blindsided."

"Look, this is disturbing for all of us and I'm perfectly willing to discuss it. Only not right now. It's too fresh, too raw. I need some time to reflect."

"You're breaking up the family, Mom, smashing it to pieces." Carol had always been the calm one, a welcome contrast to her volatile brothers. Not any more, apparently.

"Carol, I'm sorry you're taking this so hard, but you're overreacting. Please calm down."

She shook her head in annoyance. "You told him over and over you'd visit Frankfurt. It made perfect sense. You're a couple. You need to be together."

"We were together the whole summer."

"It's obviously not enough. At least, not for him..." Her voice turned plaintive. "Don't you want to spend time with Daddy? Don't you miss him?"

"Of course, I do."

"Then go over there."

"It's not the right time."

"It never is!" Another first. Carol had never raised her voice at me, not even in the grim years of her teenage rebellion. "Sorry... Mom, aren't you curious? I mean, you went to that little concert he and Doc Williams gave in Graystone a few years back, but that's it. You never saw him on stage. You never heard him sing opera. For me, going to Calgary for Dad's performance was the biggest thrill of my life. He won't disappoint you, I promise."

"Carol, I just told you now's not the moment. I'm terribly busy with my work."

"He sounded so desperate on the phone. He really and truly scared me."

"Your father's quite resilient. His depressions never last long. He's called me once or twice from Frankfurt in utter despair, ready to throw in the towel and come back home. I'd calm him down as best I could and after a while, an amazingly short while, he'd say he felt better and hang up. And he *was* better. His depression had completely vanished."

"It's different this time."

"Nonsense. I'm sure he's perfectly fine."

"But he needs you!"

"I assure you he'll feel better in the morning. He's got a *Carmen* coming up. It's bound to revive him..."

"Mom, are you happy?"

"Why do you ask?"

"You've been so sad lately."

"Have I?"

"Yes, you look sad now."

"Well, it's clear you and your father are disappointed in me. I've somehow let you down. That disturbs me, of course. How could it not?"

"You didn't really answer my question."

"I thought I did."

"Remember how great it was last summer when Dad had the whole summer off and we rented that cabin on Lake Killian?"

"Yes, that was a lovely time."

"The whole family was there. You and Dad were reunited. You seemed so happy then, so lighthearted."

"Only because I was."

"It was like an endless party. We did crazy things. Dad even got you to jump off the high diving board."

"It was utter madness. I don't know how he convinced me to go up there."

"By making you laugh. By making you happy... You'll be happy again when you visit him."

I had to smile. "You're very persistent, aren't you?"

"Of course. I'm a Verdun. Which is actually a pretty good lead-in to the proposition Hal and I want to make."

"An offer I can't refuse?"

"Exactly... Okay, you hate flying. It makes you nervous. We understand and totally respect that. It's a common problem. Thousands, maybe millions, of people have it and most of them conquer it. Why not you? If you go from Detroit to Frankfurt, it's a long day of flying in two separate airplanes. Hal did some research and discovered that you can fly direct from Toronto, so there's only one plane and much less stress."

"Carol, Toronto's hundreds of miles from here."

"It's just five hours by car."

"But you can't seriously expect me to drive all that distance and then take my very first flight."

"No, of course not. Hal will drive you there."

This left me nearly speechless. "He will? Really?"

"And guess what, I'll fly with you. Yes, why not? We've got some money saved. It's really no big deal. I'll sit beside you and cheer you on and hold your hand and give you pep talks and make sure you get to Frankfurt safe and sound."

I was amazed. I was touched. It was such a bold and selfless gesture. "But what about your boss? He's lost in the office without you."

"I talked to him already. He wasn't enthusiastic, but I got him to agree."

"My, you've been one busy bee."

"It's for a good cause... So, what do you think of our proposition?"

"It's certainly well thought out."

"Yeah, we've been discussing it nonstop since we got home from work." She grabbed my hands and held them tight, as if to infuse me with her youthful enthusiasm. "What do you say, Mom? Can I book our trip to Germany?"

"Ah, if it were only that simple."

"But it is! Just take the plunge and cross the mighty Atlantic." She grinned and imitated her father. "Come on, babe, you're rough, you're tough, you can do it."

"I'm afraid that only works when Richard says it."

"Nah, it works for everyone. It's the V effect. V for Verdun. V for victory..."

She was looking at me with such hopefulness, such tenderness, I was very nearly won over. "Carol, dear, everything you've said, everything you've done is very touching, very considerate. As I said, you've been one busy bee. You make me extremely proud. But and this is a big *but*, I'm afraid, it's all premature. Dad's coming home for Christmas. That's less than a month away. Let's deal with it when he returns."

She was shocked. She obviously couldn't believe what I had just said. It was some time before she spoke again. "TJ was right."

"About what?"

"About *you.* He told me you'd never go over there. And you won't. You'll always find a way to postpone it."

"Carol, that's not fair."

"It most certainly is. You're not ever going to Frankfurt and Dad will get tired of waiting."

"Carol, no, that's ridiculous."

"Is it? Mom, I'm scared. Everything's falling apart..."

CHAPTER SEVENTEEN

Richie

I didn't sleep much on the plane back to Frankfurt, I was too upset and angry, so when I finally get to my apartment, a weary wrung-out wreck, I plop on my bed for one last try and somehow or other succeed. I'm cutting some serious *zzzs* when the phone rings and jangles me awake.

I hear Carol's quavering wavering voice. "Daddy, it's me. Did you make it back okay? Are you all right?'

"I picked up the phone, didn't I?"

"No, seriously."

"I am serious. The phone's pretty far from my bed."

"No, honestly, how are you doing? Are things a little easier?"

"Honestly?" I take a deep breath and go for it. "I'm still in hell. I need to be with my wife."

"I know. I'm so sorry."

"I thought I won her over, I thought she really would try."

"I tried also."

"You did?"

"Yeah. I went to see her last night. She wasn't very receptive."

"Well, that's a big surprise."

"If it's any consolation, all us kids are behind you. Even Billy. It's just Mom who's the problem."

"Thanks for reminding me."

"I'll keep working on it, Daddy. I swear I won't give up."

"Forgive me if I'm not optimistic."

"Come on, who can resist the famous V effect?"

"Your Mom."

"Daddy, don't talk like that."

"Sorry, but it's how I feel... Hon, it's getting late. I need to go to the theater. Thanks for calling." I'm about to hang up, when it suddenly hits me. "Carol, you still there?"

"Yes?"

"You're the greatest, kid, my rock of Gibraltar. Thanks for giving it your all."

A little while later I'm at the opera house and bump into Toni, the only guy in the company who knows the full story with Kit. He's shocked when I tell him my news. Good guy that he is, he tries to cheer me up and says she'll come around. I pretend to agree and quickly change the subject.

As for the *Carmen* that night, it goes okay. Which is really odd. I'm at my absolute worst. I'm singing one of the most demanding roles in the repertoire while dealing with extreme jet lag and extreme heartache. Who knows? Maybe all that negative energy is good for me. I get through the show just fine. Toni has very few notes for me.

Afterwards, I hustle back to my apartment and decide to call Kit. Maybe she'll finally see reason. When my call goes through and I plead my case, she jumps on my ass for getting Carol involved and making it a major thing. "But it *is* a major thing," I go. This gets her even crazier. She's like, *how can I drag the kids into it, it's so unfair to them and her and everyone else on the planet.* I'm so startled by this, so white-hot angry–after all, she's the one who canceled, she's the one who's wrong– that I slam down the phone. A minute or two later, though, I'm more or less back to my normal self. I'm not furious with Kit any more. I know she's not the devil and neither, of course, am I. It's just business as usual, a normal everyday tragedy.

The next morning, bright and early, I'm flying again, this time to Venice. *Wow, Venice,* you say, *how great, how glamorous, the most magical place on earth.* Yeah, maybe. But I'm not a tourist. I'm working. And working goddamn hard. I'd been engaged to sing one Pinkerton at La Fenice, sort of a paid audition. If things go well, they'll hire me for something big. So, there I am, sitting in the plane with my Walkman plugged in, trying to relearn the Italian, I just sang it *auf deutsch* in Frankfurt, but the text goes blurry, the music fades in and out. All I can think about is Kit.

Once in Venice I go straight to the opera house for rehearsal. It's just me, a pianist and this staging assistant, Toni's local equivalent, except this guy is middle-aged and pudgy and not especially friendly. When I tell him I don't speak their lingo, he pulls a face and speed-talks me through the show in a godawful hash of Italian and English. He zips me through the moves so fast, *wham, bam, thank you, ma'am,* I end up more confused than ever. The whole experience is so demoralizing I limp across the plaza to my fancy hotel room with its thick velvet curtains and old-fashioned furniture and plunge back in my black lagoon. I don't even go out to the real one and hire a gondola, something I had really looked forward to. Of course, that was when I assumed Kit would be with me. She always had talked about visiting Venice. For her it was a lifelong dream. Not any more, I guess, not any more.

As far as the show goes, I actually do get the Italian right, I don't even screw up the staging. When I go out at the end for my solo bow, I'm thinking, *well, okay, the aria was pretty lame, but I held my own in the love duet and didn't trip on the scenery.* I face the public, relieved that I somehow survived, when a bunch of boos explodes in my ears like cherry bombs. It doesn't last long, but I distinctly hear a bunch of people flat out booing me. Now, this is a first for me, a horrible shocking first. I mean, sure, it wasn't my best, but I gave my all, tried as hard as I could. To be attacked like that, as if I've got no right to be singing there at all, well, let me tell you, it's a miserable experience, it makes me feel like shit. I race off stage as fast as I can, headed straight for my dressing room, when my cute little Butterfly, this sweetheart of a gal, cuts me off at the pass and goes, "*Eh,* Riccardo, don't take serious. They just angry with company management." Kind words, thoughtful words, I'm extremely grateful. But I know I really screwed up.

Just as I have no real idea why things went so wrong in Venice, my next *Carmen* in Frankfurt a few days later makes no sense either. I mean, first off, I arrive back in town really pulverized by the experience of that *Butterfly.* My confidence is down the toilet. Of course, I'm no idiot. I don't tell anyone about the booing, not even Toni and certainly not my agent in New York, but I show up at rehearsals and coachings like the zombie of the opera. If anyone asks about the Venice *Butterfly,* I say it went great and I'm really glad to be home. In my head, though, I'm shaken up big time. Maybe I'm out of my league. Maybe my success is pig-ass luck.

As the curtain goes up on the last *Carmen* of the season, I'm really feeling the strain. I'm completely disoriented. I've no idea where I am or who I am or why. I know I'm singing Don Jose, of course. That far gone I'm not. But somehow, this feeling of not knowing, not even caring translates pretty fast into this *let it all hang out* involvement with the show. I get so into it, so completely bizarrely *engaged,* I'm not sure where Don Jose begins and Richie Verdun leaves off. In that cruel scene in the second act where Carmen tells Jose he doesn't love her, I get so beet-red furious with her, so outraged and upset, I damn near kill her two acts early. Of course, ST picks up on this and conducts with a crazed intensity that inspires me to sing full throttle all night long. By the time I finish Carmen off, I'm drained and exhausted. I totally and completely collapse. And I mean that literally. I faint on the stage of the opera house. Now, I've passed out lots of times, especially as a kid, but this is different, it's like a dive in the black beyond.

Next thing I know, Toni's grabbing me by the shoulders and slapping me awake. "Richie, come on, enough." As I come to, I'm thinking, *wow, that nearly did me in.* I try to get up but feel so winded, that panic washes over me. Maybe it's really serious, maybe I just had a stroke. I take some deep breaths, wiggle my toes and feet, flex my arms and legs and realize that everything works, everything's back to normal, or what passes for normal in Operaland. "Hurry up, Richie. The public's waiting." He hauls me to my feet and half drags, half pushes me over to Frau Romanescu, who's standing right by the curtain. She reaches over to me, grabs my hand and leads me out to face the public and...

I've never heard anything like it, a solid wall of shouts and screams, like everyone's gone gaga, everyone's completely nuts. I'm thrilled, of course, but also completely astonished. Even with all her experience Ileana is too. There's a beat where the two of us just stand there, dumbfounded, gawking and gaping at the crowd. Finally, she beams at me, I beam right back at her and we're suddenly this mutual admiration society. Sure, she can be a pain, sure, she can drive men mad, but she's a stupendous artist, she gives the public her all. It's an honor for me to sing with her. As we float off stage, ST comes charging up from the pit, clapping like crazy. He grabs us both in a big team hug and goes, "This was truly *Carmen.* This we must never forget." We gather up the other colleagues and go out for another bow, and another. All told, we must have taken nine or ten bows, surely a record for me, and pretty rare at the Frankfurt Opera.

Once the cheering dies down, I stumble back to the dressing room and crumple into my chair. They finally got the gag for the murder working right, so I'm soaked in fake blood from head to toe. As the makeup guy Florian scrubs it away, he raves about what a great night it was, *ein grosser Abend.* It doesn't really sink in. I'm suffering from what I call the Corelli effect, you know, when the excitement of the performance dribbles away and you wind up completely depleted. After Florian leaves, I'm still stuck to my chair, staring dumbly into space, like *duh, what the fuck just happened?*

I'm not alone for long. Frau Olga busts in, takes one look at me and stops dead in her tracks. I must be quite a sight – butt naked, except for my jock strap, with bright streaks of blood that Florian didn't get.

"What a strange one you are. You have tremendous success and look like the world just exploded."

"I got my reasons, believe me."

She gives me her laser-like stare, the one that pries loose all secrets. "It is the wife, *nicht wahr*?" She's a witch, that lady, a total mind reader. "*Ach, mein Armer, was fuer eine Tragoedie.*"

"Goddamn right it's a tragedy. It tears my guts out."

She pats my cheek gently. I get a big dose of her lilac perfume. "*All song comes from suffering*, an old German saying. Surely you know this."

"Actually, I never heard it before."

"It is very useful and also very true. How else to explain La Callas? She sings like a goddess and lives her whole life unhappy."

"And that's somehow good?"

"She creates beauty from her sadness. She makes of it great art."

"She probably just wanted to be happy."

"It was too late. She was infected." She gives me her crooked smile. "Just like you."

"Me? Come on, Olga, give me a break."

"You make already the leap. You are an artist."

The news doesn't exactly thrill me.

"We need your sorrow," she insists. "We need your song. We learn from it, we grow. And so do you."

"Who says I want to?"

"You have no choice. You open already the door. And the public loves it. You give a magnificent show."

"Yeah, I guess it was pretty good."

"It was better than that, much better. Even the *Herr Intendant* says so."

"He was there?"

"For the last two acts."

"Why didn't he come back to see me?"

"You know Herr Klauzer. He slips away like the eel."

"Yeah, he can be a real dick sometimes."

"But he makes for us great opera."

"We do the making, babe, not him."

"Yes, maybe you do, especially when you sing like tonight... Come, my friend, no more sad face. Smile. We have now Happy End."

"Speak for yourself, Frau Olga."

"How can you not be happy after such an evening?" She answers her own question. "*Ach, Quatsch.* So what if she does not come? You easily find someone else."

That does it. I take her by the elbow, thank her for dropping by and show her to the door.

Only a minute or two later, I'm gathering up my stuff to go to the shower, when Toni bounces in, all smiles and giggles. "Wonderful show, Richie. Your very best by far. It makes for you many new fans."

"So what?" That's how miserable I am, that's how grim.

"Do not dismiss them. An artist needs his fans."

"Not this one."

"Oh yes, even you, I bring them back so you can meet."

"Not now, man, I'm not in the mood."

"They insist I let them in."

"Later, after I've showered."

"Sorry, they cannot wait."

"But I'm basically naked."

"They get over it." He marches to the door and opens it. The Richard Verdun Fan Club troops in, all two members.

I'm floored.

I'm thrilled.

I'm astounded.

I rush over to Kit and embrace her so tight her inside's on my outside and vice-versa. Our daughter Carol's right behind us, looking incredibly pleased with herself. It's nice, of course, that she's such a terrific psychologist, I'm grateful, but all that really matters, all that really counts is that Kit is in my arms again, Kit, the amazing Kit.

"Toni, Kit and I need a little privacy. Maybe you and Carol could wait in the canteen."

"Of course," he goes, "I show her where we have the big orgy."

Carol's a little startled. "Orgy?"

"He's just kidding, hon. You'll be okay."

Carol comes over and gives me a peck on the cheek. She turns to her mother and says, "You be good to him, okay?"

"Don't worry," I go. "I can handle it..."

They leave. The two of us are alone now, it's just me and her.

"Do you finally get it? Do you see why I have to be here?"

"How could I not?"

"It's everything to me, Kit, everything. Except for you and the kids."

"I know..."

The room grows very quiet. I set her down in my chair while I hop up on the edge of the makeup table facing her. God, it's scary how much I love this woman, how much I need her.

"You know, from that first day in choir I sensed you were much more complex and interesting than everyone thought. And I was right. Every year you've shown me and the children more and more who you really are. But tonight, that Don Jose you gave us... This will sound idiotic but, why not? That I've taken so long to come over to Frankfurt is idiocy enough."

"You had your reasons, sweets. I understand."

"What you did tonight on that stage was so generous, so brave and truthful, that, not to go overboard, but to go overboard, it's like a miracle."

"*You're* the miracle."

She smiles and shakes her head. "No, sorry, I beg to disagree."

"And I disagree right back."

It's not especially funny but she laughs and so do I. We're a pair of giggly school kids.

"Okay, Kit, here's the plan. I've got the whole day off tomorrow so we can rent a car and explore the countryside. We can even go to that village I told you about, the one with the old brick bakery. Maybe we could get a realtor to show us some properties there."

The cozy mood shatters. "Richie, now's not the time for house hunting."

"Just to look, just to check things out. I'd never buy anything unless you liked it."

"That's not the point. My moving over here is a totally different conversation and now is not the time for it."

"Okay, okay..."

In the distance I hear my colleagues trooping down the hall, eager to leave the theater, eager to get home to their families. Finally, Kit goes, "Sorry, I've had an exhausting day."

"I can imagine."

"We'll have plenty of time to talk later on. Carol and I won't be leaving until the end of the week."

"So soon?"

She snaps at me again. "I'd have thought a five day visit was better than none at all."

"Of course, of course, sorry... It was a stupid thing to say."

She reaches forward and rests her hand on mine. "Look, I've just been catapulted into a new city, a new culture and it's daunting. I hardly know what

I think or feel. All I know for certain is that you're an explorer, a very brave one. I hope I can be one also."

That's all she says but it's enough. I sweep her up in my arms and swing her around till the room's a fuzzy blur. I get wobbly pretty fast, so I cut the gymnastics and set her down easy and hold her tight in my arms. We sway together lightly as the dizziness slowly fades.

It's not long before I realize I'm a filthy stinky mess and run off to take a shower.